A GAME W[...]

John Kirkland's wife has been kidnapped. To track her down, and stop the madman who has taken her, he must first uncover the clues that have been carefully set in place. . . .

—the Silver Star that mysteriously appears in his trophy case, a hint to a time long forgotten . . .
—the old blind man with the deck of fifty-four cards, who wonders what secrets the six of diamonds and the five of hearts hold . . .
—the taped message in the motel room, where his wife's haunting voice urges him on into the night . . .

GAME
RUNNING

Praise for Bruce Jones

"Credit the author with a vivid imagination and a taste for the macabre."
—*The New York Times Book Review*

"Jones does an exceptional job of luring the reader on with starting clues . . . Enthralling to the last."
—*Associated Press*

"Intriguing . . . with [a] particularly nice twist at the end."
—*Publishers Weekly*

GAME RUNNING

Bruce Jones

A SIGNET BOOK

SIGNET
Published by the Penguin Group
Penguin Books USA Inc., 375 Hudson Street,
New York, New York 10014, U.S.A.
Penguin Books Ltd, 27 Wrights Lane,
London W8 5TZ, England
Penguin Books Australia Ltd, Ringwood,
Victoria, Australia
Penguin Books Canada Ltd, 10 Alcorn Avenue,
Toronto, Ontario, Canada M4V 3B2
Penguin Books (N.Z.) Ltd, 182–190 Wairau Road,
Auckland 10, New Zealand

Penguin Books Ltd, Registered Offices:
Harmondsworth, Middlesex, England

First published by Signet, an imprint of Dutton Signet,
a division of Penguin Books USA Inc.

First Printing, May, 1995
10 9 8 7 6 5 4 3 2 1

PUBLISHER'S NOTE
This is a work of fiction. Names, characters, places, and incidents either are the
product of the author's imagination or are used fictitiously, and any resemblance
to actual persons, living or dead, events, or locales is entirely coincidental.

Prologue

The kid he was chasing to his death wasn't much older than twelve or thirteen.

It could have been him, John Kirkland, thirty or so years ago—same height and build, really. What would have distinguished them, aside from the kid's obvious poverty background and the fact that he was black, were the darker needle marks on the boy's dark forearm. And the dopey, dilated eyes. And the Saturday night special clutched in his fist.

And the willingness to die for so little.

"Don't go in there!"

It had been a stupid thing to yell.

But Kirk knew the building was condemned, having passed it countless times on his old beat so long ago, and he was as fearful for the boy with the gun and the needle marks as he was fearful for himself: old floors give way, rotted stairs crumble. He'd seen it before. Twenty years and then some had taught him that.

As for the warning, well, sometimes kids still listened to the sound of adult authority. Less than they used to ten years ago, but sometimes.

This one didn't. He fired wildly again over his shoulder and clattered into the black cavity of the front door. John Kirkland—whom his friends and many of his enemies called Kirk—hesitated only an instant and plunged after.

He hid behind a piling while his pupils dilated in the gloom and tried to get a location fix on the echoing footfalls of the kid's slapping Reeboks. The sounds, somewhere ahead in mote-filled dimness, were flat and solid for maybe twenty strides, then hard and ringing. The kid had found a stairwell.

Ducking and weaving and holding the piece before him, Kirk pursued, prepared anxiously for his feet to slip in the thick film of dust, legs to tangle in a hidden pile of debris, the kid's next bullet to slam into his skull—things that existed as a bubble of dire possibility enveloping his headlong flight, things felt rather than thought about. The bubble had been with him for years, ever present in the face of trouble, almost an old friend. Sometimes a firm pressure, sometimes a barely felt presence, but always, reliably, there.

But nothing of dread consequence occurred by the time he'd finally reached the base of the stairwell, breathless and gasping; the cop gods were permitting him a few moments more of life. Somewhere back deep in his mind, he thanked them.

.He paused to get his breath and bearings, a sense of his surroundings: deep shadows and the deeper smell of must mixed with something else.

The vague, hulking shapes of some kind of machinery. The sense of an endless ceiling.

As he took the metal stairs with grunting leaps, he recognized the something else as the smell of oil: they were in some kind of abandoned machine shop, for lathing tools or something. For reasons not immediately apparent, this made him uneasy. Already the urge to turn back, let this one go, was plucking at him. Since this was as groundless as his uneasiness, he elected to ignore it.

The second level was a row of abandoned office cubicles and peeling paint and more dust. Progress in decay. Someone's abandoned dream. Tracking the kid was a cinch, the waffle tread of the Reeboks almost purposely clean and directional. They led across a narrow corridor, past a rusted water cooler and up a second flight of metal stairs. Kirk paused, trying to slow his breathing enough to hear, squinting upward into a canyon of indefinite shapes: maze of exposed ductwork, tiers of silent pipes, cathedral ceiling of filmed-over, gaping windows. No sound of footfalls; the kid was either out or waiting for him. He hesitated. Then took the second flight of stairs.

The Reebok prints turned right, tracked perfectly for ten yards past more grime-caked glass office fronts, halted mysteriously beside a blue metal railing. In a moment Kirk saw the yard-wide catwalk extending beyond the railing and his heart hitched painfully.

The kid was huddled at the shadowed end of it, gun thrust forward in both hands, eyes haunted: a trapped animal.

Kirk waited in shadow, trying to decide if the kid had seen him yet.

Feeling reasonably safe half concealed behind a steel beam, he said: "It's over, let's go."

The answering gunfire, like a cherry bomb in a well, shattered his ears, made him wait some more.

He was about to say something about there being no other exit when a grinding metallic sound began and a shuddering sensation tingled up through his soles. His heart went icy, his brain recriminatory: *I told you not to come into this place!*

Then he saw it was not the metal floor beneath him that was shaking so violently, but the extention of catwalk on which the kid crouched. It was sagging downward under diseased rivets, the kid with it. In another second . . .

He was moving now, the kid, running, wide-eyed and slack-jawed, eyes like pale eggs floating toward Kirk, toward the safety of the solid metal floor. It would be a race.

Which the kid lost by instants.

The catwalk plummeted with a shriek, then a heart-knocking silence, then an explosion of echoes as it crescendoed and collided with other metal far below.

When Kirk gazed past the railing, he found the terrified eyes still gaping up at him, clawed fingers clinging to a length of sagging pipe two yards beneath the metal floor. The kid dangled in black space, an astronaut against starless night.

"I'm—!" the boy said.

Kirk waved him silent, holstered his piece, and looked around for something to extend, a rope or pipe or board—something, but there was none. He could dash downstairs, look for something there—he could sprint to the nearest pay phone, get the firemen . . . and the kid would have dropped by then.

Kirk's own strong arms, that was the lifeline.

But he'd have to climb down some to do it.

And he didn't know if he could do that. Not at his age, not in the dark.

He licked dry lips and looked at the terrified face below him and thought that yes, he guessed he could.

He threw a leg over the gritted rail, held his breath, gripped tight, looked down . . .

. . . and thought no, he guessed maybe he couldn't.

But you have to try.

Otherwise, how will you live with yourself?

He had never been wild about heights.

He clung undecided, every muscle frozen.

I can't.

Do it anyway.

It gave him the edge, the strength to kick the other leg over, reach down, straining. But not far enough. He'd have to lose his grip on the railing to reach the kid, and it was the best purchase he had.

He looked back over his shoulder to find something. Anything. Quickly.

A dubiously thin rung caught his eye, jutting from the underbelly of the metal floor, swathed in cobwebs. He took it gingerly, testing gradually until the full weight of his body hung there in the moist

darkness like a drunken spider. He looked back at
the kid.

Looked right into his eyes. Reached out—
and froze.

A face. Another face superimposed over the
kid's. A stranger's . . . and not a stranger's . . .

Another face, eyes wide with terror—

And then the kid was gone. Falling into night.
Swallowed in shadow.

A second later he heard him: a single terrible
scream in the blackness that made his heart jump
into his throat and every inch of surface tissue slick
with sweat. A second after that he heard the kid
again, his adolescent life smashed to pulp against
the dark canyons of machinery below.

Kirk hung and stared and refused to believe.

He'd been so close.

Waited too long.

Too long.

Maybe he'd waited too long for something else
too. If you can't do your job right, you shouldn't do
it at all. It wasn't the first time he'd thought it.
Hardly the first.

He hung there in the indifferent shell of the
abandoned factory and smelled its factory smells
and listened to the kid screaming. Still screaming,
on and on as though his own mind had become a
dark, hollow tunnel through which the hideous
sound echoed repeatedly, reverberating over and
over and into forever. Until he could stand it no
longer and his fingers grew numb and his mind cal-
cified and he must surely let go now and fall . . .
fall after the kid, into the bottomless black maw

and the awful endless screaming that would not stop, would not stop, would not.

He closed his eyes and waited.

When he opened them again he was on the street, squinting into sunlight, listening to horns honk and people shouting, and other people hurrying, and a dog yapping somewhere. And David, his brother, leading him away. Past the staring people.

Leading him home to the tight, worried face of his wife.

Leading him to the hospital and the two-week vacation that would stretch into four weeks, then ten, then a forced early retirement. His working days were finally, after months, even years of gradually perceived deterioration, at an end.

The real fun was just beginning. . . .

One

walking up the tenement stoop
  gaudy red and blue lights . . . Chinese lanterns . . .
someone must be having a party
  an old tenement . . . rundown . . . concrete porch
crumbling . . . ready for the wrecking ball
  David's waiting in the car . . . he'll back you up if
there's trouble . . . don't worry . . . won't be trouble
. . . routine . . . done it a million times
  moving past the foyer with its stinking urine smell,
discarded butts . . . past the elevator that doesn't work
anymore
  up the stairs, the creaking, piss-smelling wooden
stairs, roaches eyeing him from the broken handrail
  down the hall . . . an awful hall . . . dark . . . smell
of must and mildew and beer . . . gaping plaster holes
. . . doorways of flaking wood
  some of the doorways open . . . black cavities with
white, floating eyes . . . little animals in dark caves
  and now the seven
  the door with the seven
  the room with the voices

". . . yes . . . do it . . . do it, Johnny . . ."
drawing the gun
". . . I like it that way, Johnny . . ."
bracing himself
". . . you like it too . . ."
kicking in the door
the startled faces
the white flame of thunder . . . the blood . . . the blood . . . the blood
the awful screaming

He awoke with sun in his eyes. A blinding stripe of it across his rumpled pillow, his rumpled face.

He hadn't had the dream in years. Why was he having it now? Why the splitting head, the thick tongue? Drinking last night? A party at someone's house? Was Meg there? Was he still married to Meg? They'd talked of divorce. But he was pretty sure he was still married to her.

Waking up now.

The sun in his eyes.

It must be spring.

In winter the sun was smaller, slanting long and buttery over the suburban lawns.

—and the suburban roofs and suburban Glad Bags stacked neatly before suburban driveways on the morning of Monday, suburban trash day—the winter sun didn't quite stretch to the Levelor blinds on his suburban bedroom window and thus find its way into his eyes. And the dirty gray sparrows outside didn't shrill and quarrel as loudly in the dogwoods between his house and the Foleys' next door. And he didn't hear the squeal of the paperboy's bike in the winter because he wasn't awake to hear it. So it must be spring.

This day, like the million days before this day, he rolled to his right shoulder and squinted glue-filled eyes at the clock radio to see if he still had a few precious minutes' snoozing before the six-thirty alarm jangled the quiet house. He didn't. It went off in his face a second before he could clamp a hand over the button. . . .

"—ohnny Ace with 'Pledging My Love' here on the Big K-90! Great song, great man, sad story: shot himself in the head backstage before a big performance. Some say it was Russian roulette. Don't play with guns, kids. Hey! six-thirty on the button on a bee-u-tee-ful Monday morning in Chicago land! And we've got the hits all this a.m. right here on the Lance Sterling Sh—"

. . . pushing back dreams, pulling him toward his robe, the toilet, the smells of coffee and bacon and Meg's morning face and the sluggish momentum that would end with David picking him up in the company car and then start all over again with another kind of momentum at the office.

He actually underwent the ritual act of reviewing the day's paperwork in his mind, ordering sluggish synapses to supply dates, cases, first priorities—

—before he woke up enough to know that there hadn't been any David coming by or any office to go to or any dates, cases, or priorities in months, that he had all the time in the world now.

Retired.

The word—fraught with too many simultaneous emotions to deal with when awake, much less on a sleepy morning—let him sink back to the sun-striped pillow and close weary eyes against the glare. The glare of being alive. The glare of what was left of his life, his marriage.

He sighed deeply, trying to think.

Why had the radio gone off? He hadn't heard the Lance Sterling Show in months.

Who cares?

He was vaguely chilly, but not chilly enough to fumble for the sheet Meg had doubtless kicked and wadded against the foot of the bed. He was used to sleeping naked.

He had a mild erection. Not from dream-tossed sexual fantasies but from simple urine retention. He had to go. Piss like a racehorse. Like a big Indian. What was it David used to say at the office: Squeeze my sponge. S'cuse me, fellas, gotta go squeeze my sponge. He smiled away some morning puffiness remembering. He missed them, he missed them all. Even the shit work. He missed being a cop, even if he had only been a cop for hire. David called all the operatives "protectors." Polite word for it. They were really just P.I.'s, bodyguards with a badge, but one thing Kirk knew, still knew after all these years. He was the best.

And now he was gone.

He rolled over, eyes closed, and banged softly into Meg, face in her curls, morning erection nudging her buttocks, resting confortably in the crack. The poking stirred her momentarily before she drifted back to her own dreams. He could smell the oil in her hair, hear the gentle rustle of her breath. He missed Meg too. Missed having sex with his wife. Missed her touch, her urgency, her eyes when she came. You miss a lot these days, he told himself and answered, shut up, and let his own dreams reach out to envelop him again. Dream life was better than real life, that's what it had come to. Even the dark dream about the tenement. He hadn't had that dream in years. Why had he had it this morning? Would he have it again now?

In a moment he smiled.

He was with David again, in the car.

When the company was new, David still breaking him in. They had pulled before that insurance agency one balmy evening to meet with the two agents about how to handle a job, David swishing to the curb, flashing his famous smile, saying *hop in* to the two curvy agents like it was a dinner date instead of business.

It was business, all right, just not the kind they'd banked on: turned out the real agents were late, he and David had just picked up a couple of hookers. David just kept grinning his ass off as the realization sank in, winking and making the most of it with the one in the front, a stacked black girl. Charm the pants off anyone, his brother could: "Your friend there looks a little underage, Selma."

"Ain't no frien' a mine."

The white girl with the innocent face suddenly popped two ample globes from the top of her sparkly dress, held them up like ripe fruit. "These look underage to you, sugar?"

David looked over at his kid brother and split a gut laughing. "Ain't life grand, Kirkie?"

Kirk had laughed too. And thought: Bet your ass.

The dream shifted nonsensically, as dreams do. Somehow he had gotten in the backseat with Selma. Or maybe it was some other girl. Or maybe it wasn't the backseat at all but some other place. He could hear birds chirping, maybe it was the park. She had her back to him, wide, generous buttocks pressed against his throbbing organ. She had reached around and gotten hold of him, squeezing and pulling and engorging him with blood. She was purring like a cat. "I'm a married man," he was giggling. "That's okay," she was whispering back, "me too." He was thinking he was going to come before he got it in when he woke up.

It was Meg's hand squeezing him that had awakened him. That and her purring.

He fought for comprehension, still swimming up from sleep. Meg . . . ? Now?

She was actually asking for—? Meg?

Was she still asleep? They hadn't . . . not for months. Not since—

She was whispering something. ". . . please . . . baby, please . . ."

He shoved closer on the mattress to cooperate, head whirling with lethargy and questions, the urge to urinate fading into another kind of urge now.

Was this fair, when she wasn't fully awake? Was she dreaming of someone else? Was she thinking about her phantom lover, the one she had admitted to last year but would never identify? They rocked together lazily on the bed without entry, building old, familiar rhythms that weren't, somehow, quite familiar.

His hand curled around, touched her waist tentatively, slid up her flat stomach to her breasts. Which were heavy with a fullness he hadn't remembered. Was she gaining weight? Meg?

Wait a minute here.

He opened his eyes wide, blinking back matter.

Blond hair spilled across the adjoining pillow.

Meg's was dark red.

"What the hell—?"

She turned to him with a smile. That went wide-eyed with shock and a scream that caught and gurgled and choked in a long, pale throat that belonged to someone else.

And then she was across the bed and almost onto the floor, knocking Meg's nightstand lamp to the rug, and he could see very clearly that not only were the throat and the breasts and the hair not Meg's, but most assuredly neither was the face.

"Jesus Christ—!"

Or the voice.

She scrabbled to gather claws full of pillows, his and hers, clutching them to the ample bosom, shoving them between her legs. That's when he noticed the sheets and blankets were missing. "Where—? Who—?" She looked about his bedroom like a cornered animal, pulling a clump of blond curls from blinking eyes still traced with yesterday's mascara. Eyes that finally settled on him with a vengeance of remembering. The next words were launched with little flecks of spittle: "You bastards! Did Riff put you up to this?"

Riff?

He couldn't rememb—

He didn't—

And now it was all coming back . . .

Late last night. They'd had company. This woman and her—husband? boyfriend? Riff. And her name was—what? A common name . . . Janice? Judy? They'd shown up unexpectedly out of the blue, rapping at the door. He'd just been thinking about going to bed, saying good night to Meg and the flickering screen and going up. When the rapping came. Who could that be?

Before he could think about it, Meg was opening the door.

Kirk had stood there on the staircase watching it with a growing heat: this guy, this Riff guy, claimed to know him from his army days, only Kirk couldn't remember the face at all—started down the stairs when Meg stepped back—*don't let them in, goddammit!*—but she was turning now, giving him that level look, letting them in anyway, getting even, always getting even, the way she had countless other times . . . since the affair.

They were inside now, Meg shutting the door with a hospital smile. Someone to see you, Kirk.

Hiya, pal! The crooked smile, thin lips, bright teeth, narrow, almost skull-like face in the deathly glow of the porch light. The marine haircut.

Don't you remember me, Kirk?

Meg's voice behind him, sarcastic: Kirk, who is it?

Who indeed . . .

And now that he was awake, so was the head-ache. Hammering.

The man had invited himself in, brandishing a bottle and a sheepish grin. Riff Walker! Don't ya re-

member, Kirkie? They'd drunk. Not so much, really,
but something unfamiliar, something Riff had
found. Oriental beer? Riff had laughed a lot, loudly,
he remembered that. And . . . and danced with
Meg? And the blond girl—Janice? Judy?—had
smiled at him and Riff's stories and squeezed Kirk's
leg once with a warm hand. And they'd played music, Kirk's old Motown albums, remember how he
and Riff had loved the Temptations in the army?
And the Doors? Play "Light My Fire" again, Kirk,
Jesus, listen to that lead guitar! And he—Kirk—had
danced too, with the blonde? Maybe. It got late. It
was already late. But this guy Riff was funny, really
funny, did movie star impressions. Good. Could
have been an actor. Funny. Why couldn't he place
this guy? 442nd Combat Engineers, third batallion.
Mekong Delta. Riff had that part down, all right.
Gunnery Sergeant Caulfield, old leather face. Had
that right too. And Ken Goldman, Kirk's buddy,
blown to shit by a slope mine. Riff helped pick up
the pieces. Riff had chow with him that night. Riff
patted his shoulder there in the mud and rain and
told him to hang in there. But goddamned if he
could remember who Riff was . . .

Kirk winced, squeezed his temples between
thumb and forefinger. Jesus, this headache . . .

The blonde was still glaring at him. "You and Riff
thought this would be a real cute idea, I suppose!
Did he give you permission to screw me too? How
long have I been sleeping with you? Where are my
clothes?"

He looked up from the headache and tried to remember more. He got as far as her right name and no further: Jill.

"I don't remember, Jill. I don't remember much past the dancing, do you?"

She turned away in disgust. Her eyes fell on the gold framed photo of Meg on the bureau across the room. "I might have known it'd be a swap party, I might have know he'd be up to this!" She stared silently at the photo for a moment. ". . . might have known." Whispered, nodding distractedly. She shook her head slowly, mind gone off somewhere else.

Then, abruptly, she was back, eyes piercing him. "Well?" she demanded.

He was conscious instantly of his nakedness. But she'd comandeered both pillows. There was nothing for it but to cross in front of her in his birthday suit and grab his robe from the closet. He did so, glancing askance to see if she was modest enough to turn away. She wasn't. She stared directly at his crotch, getting her revenge.

Exposed, humilated, feeling more than a little foolish, Kirk ripped open the closet door to get his robe and find Riff and Meg and get to the bottom of this.

The closet was empty. Entirely.

He stood, pale buttocks facing her, and stared stupidly at the rows of empty hangers. "—the hell?"

He turned to her, covering himself with his hands. "Your husband's a real clown."

She pulled up her knees, clutching the pillows tightly. She seemed somewhat calmer now, as if used to this kind of thing. "I'm prostrate with laughter. Now why don't you go kill the son of a bitch? And it's ex-husband, if you don't mind."

He slammed shut the closet door and stomped into the bathroom to grab a towel, flicking the wall switch. White tile and chrome bounced back at him. And nothing more. All the towels and washcloths were gone. Even the little green throw rug.

He nodded at his silly reflection in the medicine chest mirror. "I get it: I'm supposed to feel vulnerable and stupid."

It would have been genuinely funny, a pretty good joke. But blond Jill wasn't amused and something else felt off kilter. He sensed a distant panic.

That grew as he stalked naked down the hall to the guest bedroom. It was empty. The bed had been stripped bare. All the curtains had been removed. The closet door was shut, but he knew that was empty too. No, it wasn't funny at all, it was infuriating. And maybe something worse.

"Meg!"

He'd known she wasn't there to answer, known probably before he'd left the master bedroom that they were no longer in the house. He caught another glimpse of his nakedness in the bureau mirror and felt the blood rising. He was supposed to feel stripped and impotent, supposed to look that way in front of the other guy's wife. Why?

He suddenly had a hunch about something and padded quickly back down the hall to the bedroom.

Jill watched him patiently if petulantly. A looker even without makeup, even in puffy early morning light. I'm noticing this, he comprehended absently, even at the verge of panic: the male mind blunders heedlessly on.

He strode to the bureau and pulled open the bottom drawer. All the shirts were gone as he'd suspected, but the drawer was not empty. He reached in and pulled out the neatly folded shoulder holster and the .38 Colt nestled dark and oily within. He unwound the straps, broke the piece with a snap of his wrist, held it to the window light: full chamber. Locked and loaded, as they used to say in the army. He stared at the familiar firearm silently, another part of his mind enjoying the familiar heft. Stripped him bare, took his wife, but left him his loaded weapon.

That was perhaps the most terrifying thing of all.

Two

Meg awoke to Mahler, swelling strains moving dark and ominous over her, around her, through her.

Mahler and orange light.

An all-pervading tangerine glow that stretched to the farthest boundaries of her blinking, sleep-heavy eyes, pressing down warm and insistent and mono-chromatic on her wondering brain. Bringing with it a distant musty odor. I have been swallowed by the sun.

Mahler and orange and now, with an abrupt jolt, movement.

Rocking, like a boat . . . a boat moving toward the orange, omnipresent sun.

Rocking, lulling movement that teased her back toward sleep, toward that place where troubles were never real . . . But she had troubles. Even in her half-conscious state she sensed danger lurking just beyond the veil of true understanding. Danger and a need to worry she could not yet place. The boat is sinking . . . get off!

Then followed muted honking, overhead birds,

swish of other vehicles, and the recognition of the soft firmness beneath her for what it was: the backseat of their car. Or *a* car.

And the endless orange sky was their old beach blanket. And they were traveling somewhere but not, she thought surely, to the beach. To where? A hospital! There had been an accident! That's why she felt partially paralyzed, why a wedge of pain lanced the small of her back. Why her arms were bent back behind her, like her wrists were

tied.

Wrists and ankles. Tied.

And Kirk didn't listen to Mahler. He listened to rock'n'roll.

There hadn't been an accident.

Not yet.

She looked down at her chest, doubling her chin: she wore panties and bra, her new pink ones.

Another few moments of confused mental organizing, the dread concession that this was somehow not right, that the link in the normal chain of events that was her life had been broken and the need to be afraid was a real need. That her troubled dreams were nothing, a more real nightmare just beginning.

Finally, and finally, the memories.

The evening before. The couple that had come out of the night to their pale porch light. The thin-faced, smiling man with the short hair cut who knew Kirk. Or claimed to know Kirk. The pretty blonde who was his, what?—wife, girlfriend? The joking and drinking. The laughing at too much that wasn't truly funny.

And . . . dancing? Had there been dancing? And . . . and . . .

And just darkness after that.

Meg's head pressed sharply into the vinyl paneling beneath the side window as the car made a sharp turn. After another few moments of gentle rocking she noticed something new, or rather something missing: the sounds of traffic. All that remained now were the bird sounds, which were louder and more frequent. The vehicle jolted occasionally as if from rural roads.

She had read a story once where a person being kidnapped, bound, and blindfolded had later led the police back to his abductors by memorizing the turns in the roads and the surrounding sounds. The notion seemed about as plausible now as a television episode.

It wasn't Kirk driving, she knew that with a gut-tightening intuition. It might be the man from last night or it might be someone else, but it wasn't Kirk.

So where was Kirk?

Kirk was the best cop—ex-cop—in the whole world. If Kirk wasn't here, then Kirk must be d—

She didn't allow the thought to complete itself. Not simply because it was emotionally intolerable, but because it didn't hold any real sense of validity. She would know when he was dead, and she did not know that now. She was neither a blissfully naive wife nor a protectively fatalistic one, but strained as their marriage had been, she never once truly believed he would die that way. Fixing the roof maybe, or something equally prosaic. But not the other way. He was simply too good at his job. Everybody knew it. Kirk most of all.

Or maybe it was something even bigger than that. David had said it once that summer evening over barbecue and drinks: "Kirk has that glow about him. It stops bullets. Some men have it." And David didn't have to say it just to make her feel better; she'd learned it along the way. Kirk wouldn't die by violence.

But she might.

She twisted in the narrow confines, her own trapped breath suddenly suffocating beneath the musty orange blanket. She had stored the blanket in the garage beside the winter clothes; how had he found it?

She found by twisting her head back and forth she was able to move the smothering material a few inches. It didn't appear to be tied down or wrapped beneath her, just carelessly thrown over her body. Perhaps if she twisted long enough she could slip it off, breathe more freely. It was growing warm under here, she could feel trickles of sweat starting down her back like little insects.

Then she sensed they were no longer moving. And a moment later—heart in her mouth—she heard the engine die.

A car door opened, a rocking motion as a weight left the vehicle. Another door opening, followed by a cooling swath across the blanket. Something seized her ankles and she was being pulled across the seat cushions.

Still beneath the orange canopy, Meg felt herself being hoisted into strong arms, the metallic thud of the door closing again. More jostled movement now as she was carried along, the sounds of heavy footfalls with an occasional snap or twig or kicked stone. The air was fresh and strong with pine. Bracing. Bird calls were clear, loud, and plentiful.

The jogging movement lasted for over a minute at her best guess of mental counting, but the figure that bore her neither broke stride nor altered his even, regular breathing. She sensed easy power in the enfolding arms, hard-packed muscles in the stomach she bobbed against, a quiet determination that was palpably disquieting.

Now she was being lowered and set down upon hard earth.

And now the blanket was being removed.

It took a moment, squinting in the blue brightness, to be sure, and his back was to her as he faced a wide, placid lake: but it was him, the man from last night. Roger? No, Riff. Riff was it.

He wore sun-bleached jeans, beltless, tight-fitting, and tucked into scuffed engineer boots. Above that was a tucked-in T-shirt with a jean vest over that. Above that was a thin but muscular neck and blondish, closed-cropped hair. He stood with arms akimbo, regarding the lake. The arms were tanned and muscular but not histrionically pumped. He was somewhat shorter than Kirk's six feet.

He turned to her and she saw her own white, open-mouthed face in mirrored, wire-rimmed lenses.

He came toward her, lean-faced and thin-lipped, neither smiling nor scowling. She had remembered him as being borderline handsome. His walk was so casual it might have been friendly. He stopped a few feet before her.

She could not look straight up without tearing; he had placed himself in front of the morning sun, probably, she thought, intentionally.

He stared at her.

She could not remember his last name. "Riff—?" It came out a croak, her throat dry, her neck straining off the ground. This is a joke, right? she had meant to say.

She had to lower her eyes away from the glaring sun. Doing so, she caught the movement at his zipper. He burrowed inside the tight jeans and brought out his penis, long and pale and hanging above her in a drooping half U.

She closed her eyes. Oh, God. It *was* to be this, then.

She yelped at the first arc of hot urine. Eyes bulging in surprise and anger, she opened her mouth to shout her indignation—closed it quickly as he played the stream across her face and neck, breasts and clenched stomach, the latter reverberating with a sound like rain on canvas. Meg kicked out, screamed, tried to worm away from the sun-glistened thread. He urinated calmly in great languid loops, moving a few feet down the length of her until her legs and feet were hit. Then he stopped.

Meg whimpered, curled fetally, as he moved around behind her with crunching boots. He placed one leather sole between her shoulder blades and rolled her, carefully, onto her stomach. She started as another gout of burning liquid splashed her thighs and soaked her buttocks, matting the thin material to her like a second skin. He trailed up her narrow back and finished, dripping, in her hair.

She lay with her mouth against a stone, shuddering involuntarily, hearing the sound of him zipping up like a needle across a record, then the crunch of boots again. She opened her eyes and saw him bent among the weeds some distance away, gathering stones with one hand, cupping them into the other. Pissed on and stoned, she thought deliriously. Why? What had Kirk done to this man?

He returned and began placing the stones at regular intervals around her reeking form. When he'd completed a rude circle, he began undressing. Before he threw the jeans aside he withdrew a small metallic cylinder from the front pocket and inscribed his chest with a simple, livid design. A snake. Then he began his dance.

He danced around her seven times, muscular legs kicking up gouts of dust, a big penis flopping in rhythm, corded throat uttering a guttural chant. It might have been American Indian.

Meg lay in the dust and stench, swallowing back the rising urge to vomit, waiting for whatever was next.

Three

He stood naked there in his bedroom looking down at the revolver in his hand. He was thinking of Time.

The blonde on the bed, pillow clutched to her bosom, waited patiently. "What are you doing?" Then, looking away: "Please put something *on!*"

Kirk turned to her almost casually, the gun at chest level and pointed away from her, no longer concerned with his nakedness, seeming to stare straight through her. Her anger was born of fear. "There aren't any clothes, Jill. He took them. And anything else we could wrap around us. He took Meg too. Would you have any idea where?"

He could see her fighting to push down the panic. Blond and built, but eyes of cool gray intelligence.

She sighed heavily in a moment, bowed head to hand as if from a headache, golden curls spilling. "Probably as far from me as he could get." She cast her eyes ceiling-ward, biting her lip. "He owed me

money. Alimony. Lots." And as a whispered adden-
dum: "Bastard."

Kirk watched her. "Was your husband—ex-husband
prone to practical jokes?" It sounded ludicrous but
needed to be said. He felt he was slipping off the
edge of something; it angered and frightened him.

She shrugged ivory shoulders, head thumping defeat against the headboard. "I don't know . . . I don't
know . . . it's been so long since I've been with him.
He was always a little . . . strange. Practical jokes?
Not exactly, no." She swiveled her head to him
wearily. "Look, I don't know him that well anymore.
If I ever did. If anyone ever did."

It had been an empty question anyway: even if
Riff Walker was prone to jokes, Meg wasn't.

Kirk holstered the piece, placed it atop the bureau. He looked up and found himself staring at
Meg's framed photo across the room. She smiled
back. He chewed his lip, mind racing.

He could not place a man named Riff Walker in
his memory.

"Give me one of those pillows." He reached a
hand to her.

She gripped it, covering her modesty. "W-wait a
second!"

He snapped his fingers. "Gimme a goddamn pillow!"

She twitched at his tone, drew her legs up tight,
and tossed him the bottom one. He pulled out the
fluffy, striped innards, took the casing in both
hands and ripped it lengthwise with a grunt. He
wrapped the torn piece about his middle and

stalked from the room. "Where are you going?" she called, voice thin with returning fear. He ignored her and padded into the garage. He got the light on, sidled around the cool hulk of the Nova, and grabbed the aluminum ladder standing next to the barbecue grill. He positioned it below the row of box-laden planks stretching across the wooden ceiling above his head. He climbed up, hefted a large suitcase from between boxes of Christmas ornaments, and snapped it open. Even before he threw back the lid he knew it was empty: it had come free too easily. So. He had taken their winter clothes too. . . .

How had the guy known where their winter clothes were stored?

By asking Meg. Had he threatened her? Kirk shook away the thought. Don't. Don't be a husband just now, be a cop. Just get the s.o.b. Then worry.

He climbed down and moved back through the house to the kitchen. There in the little wicker basket atop the connecting bar, he found his wallet, sunglasses, change. The wallet was unrifled. His car keys were beneath it. Another chill snaked through him. He was supposed to follow. It was to be a chase, a planned one.

Why?

He fingered the keys absently a moment, then turned quickly to the wall phone above the sink. He lifted the receiver, placed it to his ear: dead.

He hung up, not surprised, and padded back to the bedroom.

Jill was busy trying to wrap the other pillow case around her loins. When she saw him, she dropped the material to cover her crotch, cursed, picked up the material to cover her breasts, cursed again, sank back on the bed in a huddled ball, arms wrapped around her legs. The absurdity of it all almost tickled him.

Kirk checked the bedroom phone just to be sure, already knowing. He dropped the receiver in the cradle and turned to her. "I'm going next door."

She pointed. "Like that?"

"It's early, it'll be all right. Stay here." Then realized what he'd said: of course she'd stay here, where else would she go?

He started down the hall, her calling after him frantically again. "Hey, wait a minute! You can't just leave me like this! What are you going to do? Kirk?"

He went out the back way, leaving the kitchen door ajar. The June air was cooler than he'd thought it'd be, the concrete stoop chilly under bare feet. The grass, a moment later, was slick with cold dew, a not unpleasant sensation. It reminded him of something in his boyhood he didn't have time to recall completely.

He pushed through the hedges bordering his house and Foleys', snagging the pillow case on a branch, almost losing it, came around the back through the Foleys' gate, hoping their two-year-old cocker would sleep through this. Then he saw the empty dog house and remembered: Harold and Jean were on vacation. Disney World or something.

But that was maybe better anyway. He strode across their back patio amid deck chairs and little girl paraphernalia: plastic scooters, naked Barbie, a dew-flecked jump rope. Kimberly would be seven this summer. Seven years older than the little girl he and Meg never had. Stop it. Not now, for chrissake!

Bordering the south end of the patio next to the back door were seven earthen pots bearing brightly colored flowers he couldn't name. He lifted the seventh pot from the left facing the house and slid out the aluminum spare key. It had been Foley's idea; Kirk thanked him silently for it now.

He twisted the key, pushed the door inward; a vacuumed sigh and he was inside a kitchen of week-old stale air. He went straight for the phone, dialed the precinct.

"Forty-seventh Precinct, Sergeant Mallory speaking."

"Let me speak to Ken Brenan."

"Just a moment."

He rested his weight on one leg and watched a garage door going up across the way. A steel blue Thunderbird inched out in a fanfare of billowing exhaust. Bill Salsbury off to make big advertising deals. The neighborhood was waking up.

He looked around at Jean Foley's familiar but still unfamiliar kitchen: bright yellow, clean, neat, faint odor of chlorine. A place for everything and everything in its place. Exactly what Meg's kitchen was not. Meg's kitchen was dark and messy and pungent with food odors. An embarrassment. He could never find anything in it. After a time he'd quit looking. Not unlike their marriage . . .

"Sorry, Detective Brenan's not here just now. Can I take a message?"

Kirk cursed mentally. "All right. Let me speak to Lieutenant Fairfield, then."

"Just a moment."

Kirk shifted his weight in the thin pillow case and looked down at his bare feet again on the spotless linoleum. If it was Meg's linoleum, his feet would be sticking to it. He shook his head slowly.

There was a movement at the kitchen window, and his head snapped up painfully. A robin was watching him from a cottonwood branch just outside.

I'm standing in the Foleys' kitchen wearing a pillow case watching a robin stare at me while my wife is being kidnapped somewhere. And I'm not at all uncalm. He held up a strong, tanned hand. It was rock steady. Cop instincts. Once you have them—

"Lieutenant Fairfield here . . ."

Kirk hung up.

It surprised even him.

But all of a sudden he didn't want to talk to Lieutenant Fairfield, or didn't think he should. The act, or the thought, or both, set his heart pounding suddenly. He was convinced he'd nearly put Meg in great danger.

He stood indecisively a moment, hand hovering over the receiver again. Then he blew out a calming breath and headed for the Foleys' bedroom.

Harold Foley was a shorter man than he, but Kirk found a pair of slacks that didn't make him look like a complete bumpkin and a sports shirt that was blousy enough to hide the tight armpits. He rummaged in Jean's closet and found too fancy dresses and flimsy things he wasn't sure about. He settled on a pair of summer shorts and a yellow halter top.

He got socks from the drawers and two pairs of adjustable sandals; the men's pair pinched his over-sized feet spitefully, but he didn't have time to be particular. He dressed quickly, trod back through the house, leather slapping his heels, locked the kitchen door behind him, replaced the key, and headed back. He made it through his own kitchen door just as Mrs. Turnbull was emerging across the street to walk her basset.

Jill was sitting passively against the headboard, arms knotted in front of her. It was hard to read her mood. Drained? She looked up as he entered the bedroom. "May I be allowed to know what is going on?"

Kirk tossed her Jean Foley's clothing. "You can wear these. I'll be in the kitchen when you're dressed."

She was about to say something as he exited again, but let it go.

Kirk started back toward the kitchen, intent on throwing down some breakfast cereal and a glass of orange juice. It was going to be a long day, and he didn't want something like hunger slowing him down once he got rolling. He'd try Ken again in a few minutes. What he needed to begin with was a readout on Riff Walker, and a back file if one ex-isted. He had ample suspicion that one did. Brenan, his partner from the old days, would get it for him ASAP.

He faltered going past the den. Slowed, turned,

and walked back to the doorway. He glanced inside at his orderly sanctum: polished burl wood writing desk, rack of pipes and Mixture 79-stuffed humidor, neatly stacked papers, red leather couch, Columbia University diploma on the wall behind the swivel chair, pictures of Meg, framed citations, framed awards, glass-fronted trophy case . . .

He stepped inside. Everything looked in place as usual, and God knows he kept it all in place. He knew the room by rote. This is where he smoked and dreamed. This is where the famous book of his memoirs never got written. He stopped and stared at the trophy case.

"What are we doing?"

He turned as Jill came in behind him, paused at the door, eyes going to the impressive array of gold and silver statuettes, bowls and oak-backed citations: three shelves of them, four by six feet. Jean Foley's halter and shorts were too snug for her zaftig figure, which she didn't seem overly concerned with under the circumstances. When you're built like that, Kirk reasoned, you're probably used to being stared at.

"I'm working on it," he told her, to have something to say.

"We can't very well just stand around—" she began.

He made a distracted face. "I'm *working* on it, Jill. I have some calls on the line!" Easy. Stay loose. Think of it as a job and you'll win. "I think we need to play this cautiously," he added less curtly.

She started to say something, nodded lightly instead. Regard for his position shone in her eyes, his position being far worse than her own. "I'm sorry. I know you're upset about . . . Meg, is it?"

"Meg, yes."

"I don't think he'd hurt her, if that's any consolation. He's a bit . . . *extreme* at times, but I don't think—it's obviously some sort of joke." When Kirk made no reply she said: "You still don't remember him? From the army?"

"No."

She considered. "Strange . . ."

"Yes, it is."

Neither of them spoke for a time.

Jill nodded at the trophy case. "What's the tall silver one for?"

"It's a citation from the department. The precinct."

"What for?"

"Outstanding achievement."

"What did you do?"

Kirk looked at his watch: just after eight. "Saved some lives."

Jill approached the case, buttocks tight and round in the other woman's shorts. "And the gold one here?" Was she genuinely interested or just stalling off reality, trying to make an awful morning mundane again? He felt himself wanting to join her in the fantasy.

"Marksmanship medal."

She nodded approvingly. "Army?"

He nodded.

She tapped the top of the case with a red lacquered nail. "This gold one with the points?"

Kirk took a step forward. "That's a Silver Star."

She turned, impressed. "Really."

He stared at the case.

She looked back at the gold-embossed metal, the smaller silver star surrounded by the gilded wreath within a larger gold star. "That's wonderful. What did you do to receive it?"

"Nothing."

She looked up again as he came next to her. He bent and opened the glass doors, plucked the star-shaped medal from the shelf; it's what had caught his eye from the hall. He held it up appraisingly. "It isn't mine."

She cocked her head, looking from the medal to his eyes and back again. "No? Whose?"

Kirk weighed the gold object in his hand distractedly, eyes roaming the den, mind elsewhere. "Your ex's, I imagine. No one else has been in here since last night." That cold snake of fear again.

Jill frowned. "You think Riff put it in your trophy case? Why?"

He stared at the far wall, still juggling the medal in his hand. At last his eyes found hers. "Well . . . I'd say it could be intended as an extreme form of respect, giving something of that obvious importance away. An acknowledgment of admiration from one medal winner to another." He looked down at it. "Or it could be viewed as an insult, a jab: you won a lot of medals, but not this one, not the big one."

His eyes flicked to her. "Did he ever mention it to you?"

She shook her blond curls. "He was pretty private about the war. Besides, we weren't married very long, and we didn't do a lot of talking when we were."

Kirk started to ask exactly what they did do, but, unable to avoid staring at the porcelain cleavage spilling from her top, he realized it was a stupid question. He slid the medal in his pocket and turned. "There's breakfast food in the kitchen, better grab something while you can. I have to make a phone call."

He left her there in the den and marched back over to the kitchen phone at the Foleys'. He dialed the precinct, hung up again before anyone could answer, thought about it, dialed his brother's office instead, waited for David to get on the line.

David was not in either. Kirk cursed softly and hung up. As he returned, Jill was coming into the kitchen pulling at the too-small yellow halter top, pale bosom swelling over. "Any luck?"

She seemed calmer now, more in control. Nicer. When the blond face wasn't twisted in fear or effrontery it was not unattractive.

"No," Kirk told her.

She nodded, leaning against the door jamb. "What do we do now?"

He wasn't sure, frankly.

Something kept telling him not to contact anyone he couldn't unequivocally trust, which—outside of his brother David—was no one he could think of at the moment. He clung to the distant hope that Riff might not be a true psychopath, but so far the signs weren't good. The idea of involving the police at this point, having an all-points issued for the man, sent a bolt of cautionary fear through Kirk's vitals: he kept seeing Meg's blood spattered against a windshield somewhere. Something needed to get done immediately while the trail was still warm, yet he sensed the cause for real panic was being held in abeyance for the moment—time was not the enemy, except for what it was doing to Meg's psyche. Urgency, yes, but there was time. Riff was giving him all of that he needed. What there might not be enough of was something else. He searched in confusion for the word, standing there in front of Jill, and came up with it when he remembered the silver medal: skill.

This was a challenge, an invitation. Meg wasn't really at stake. Something else was.

And even though he suspected he was playing right into Riff's hands, Kirk knew that he must pursue it alone. That those were the unspoken rules.

"I go after them," he answered her.

Something about his tone took her aback. "By yourself?"

"That's right."

She gave him a look that might have held momentary admiration. "Look . . . Kirk . . . maybe it really is a big joke; maybe they'll be back from the grocery store in a minute."

He wanted to think that with all his heart, but he said: "Neither of us believes that anymore, Jill."

She made a wry face. Then: "At least see what the police have to say."

"No. I have to do this my way."

He started to turn, but she grabbed his arm. "Follow them? Which way?"

The sixty-four-dollar question.

Never before had he needed the department so much; never before had he been so reticent about using it. He had friends there, good friends, but it didn't sit right. He allowed himself a patient sigh for the first time since it started, and immediately regretted the brief lapse—it made him realize just how frightened he was. "I don't know yet. I'll have to think about that."

He sensed impatience and fear outweighing her empathy; she was withdrawing into herself again. "Maybe it would be best if I called a cab and got back to my crummy little private businees in Wyoming. I was never much of a foil for Riff. Probably stupid to track him down in the first place."

"What about your alimony?"

She shrugged. "He'd find a way around it. He always does."

Kirk looked levelly at her. "You're afraid of him."

She studied him a moment. Looked away. "I'm tired of him."

He was looking right at her but seeing something else. The two of them on the road together.

It made sense. She might claim not to know her ex very well, but that was still better than Kirk knew him. He needed to learn as much about the enemy as possible, even the slightest nuances. Unwilling or not, she was coming.

She read it in his face. And swallowed. "No. I can't."

She started away, but he took her arm. "Please."

She tugged, then harder, face flushing. "Let me go. Please!"

"I need your help."

"He'll *kill* you!"

There it was at last.

And no sound of threat to her tone, more of promise. It was chilling.

Kirk nodded, going for bravado, his gut telling him she was probably right. "Maybe. But not before I get my wife away from him."

Still gripping her wrist tightly, he guided her to a wicker kitchen chair and sat her down. He folded his arms, towering over her. Principal to schoolgirl. "Tell me everything you remember about him."

She stared at the floor, somewhere between anger and fear.

"Tell me, Jill."

She stared at the linoleum. "I have to use the bathroom."

"Come on."

"I mean it. Please."

He took her wrist again, guided her up.

"What are you doing!"

"Taking you to the bathroom."

"I can pee by myself, thanks!"

"You can climb out the bathroom window by yourself too."

He pulled her down the hall, through the door of the guest bath, flipped up the toilet lid, and pushed her down. "There. Pee."

She was livid. "I can't with you watching!"

He turned his back.

His eyes fell on the medicine chest mirror.

There was a rustle of clothing behind him, but he scarcely heard it. He was staring open-mouthed at the slash of blood-red numerals angled across the silver-backed glass:

10/31/53

Heart in his throat, Kirk reached out quickly and touched the scarlet numbers. His finger came away with a waxy residue: lipstick.

Meg's lipstick.

But not her handwriting.

He stood staring numbly, the porcelain ringing of Jill's urine in his ears. A thump of toilet paper, a quick flush, and she was beside him, staring over his shoulder. "What does it mean?"

"It's a birth date," he said hollowly. A thin line of perspiration had appeared across his upper lip.

"Whose?"

He cleared his throat, stared hypnotically. "A woman named Susan Hathaway."

Jill looked past the crimson slashings at his stony reflection. "Do you know her?" she almost whispered.

Kirk nodded. "She's a friend."

Friend. Yes.

And lover.

Four

Meg was staring at the large, shiny object in his hand, realizing with sudden swooping horror as he turned into the sun that it was a hunting knife.

She had never seen anything like its size. It looked like something Jim Bowie would have used. Nor had she seen where it came from; it just seemed to appear in his hand, to be suddenly a part of his hand. That was the way he held it: as though it were a natural outgrowth of his fingers.

The man named Riff had finished his dance, addressed the lake again for a few moments, naked and lean, head thrown back, then started toward her again when the knife materialized. The gleaming length of it hypnotized her. She found herself mentally measuring it, her conservative guess, nine inches at least. It could gut a horse.

A brilliant point of miniature sun reflected from its serrated edge as he bent and shoved the point into her back.

But no, not into her back, as she'd imagined, but into the cords at her wrist, snapping them, and then, likewise, those at her ankles. Meg spilled free in a grateful tangle of bloodless limbs, breath rushing from her in an unbidden groan.

She hadn't realized until this moment of being cut loose how badly her circulation had been impaired. Her legs, the least affected, felt the warm rush of returning blood, her arms dangled uselessly numb for a time. She hoped he wouldn't ask her to stand by herself, she wasn't sure she could yet. She lay in the dirt, feeling her racing heart, smelling his urine.

She heard a kicking sound behind her and realized after a second that he was scattering the carefully laid stones with his boots. In a moment he was behind her again, lifting her into his strong arms. Meg let herself be carried, without struggling, to the lake. Bide your time. This is not the moment. He would suffer for pissing on her, the bastard, but this was not the moment. God grant her a respite, a return of strength. Her fury would supply the courage.

He set her down on the muddy shore and went away.

She guessed he knew she could not run.

She sat on the soft, cool bank, arms hanging at her sides, and looked past the screen of reeds and water grass to the placid, sparkling surface and the piney shore less than a mile away. The sky was cloudlessly pristine. She had never been here, but she guessed from the maps she'd seen that this was either Big Piney or Great Bear, somewhere north of Chicago, about two hours out of Mount Prospect, where she and Kirk lived. They had talked about camping here but had never gone, Kirk wasn't the camping type. Not since the army. He liked his bed.

The cool air was giving way to the warming rays of the rising sun; she was grateful for the June warmth, and let it soak into her tingling limbs, aiding circulation. Her watch was at home on the bureau, but from the sun she reckoned the time at about seven or eight. If this was indeed one of the two lakes she'd surmised and her guess about the sun was correct, they must have left the house sometime around five. The fact that she had not awakened until already bound and placed in the car pointed up the probability Riff had drugged them, simultaneously explaining why Kirk had not followed immediately. Though this did not explain about Riff's wife—ex-wife?—unless he drugged her too. Why would he do that? But then, why would he do any of this? Why don't you ask him?

She knew the answer even as he returned. The man with the big knife and the boots and the lipstick on his chest was not the man of last night. That had been an act, a sham. And a well-played one too. This man who had abducted her and urinated on her and danced around her like a savage was not open to questions or even idle chatter; you could see it in the relaxed but expressionless face, the calm but compassionless gray eyes. She had an overpowering sense that he would either ignore her proddings or, worse, find some coldly efficient way to quiet her. In his brief absence she had felt like a normal human being; in his presence she was merely a burden, packing material to be got from one spot to another. If she became difficult or re-calcitrant . . .

When she'd felt the first burning splash of urine, she'd been compelled to curse him, and later, when the opportunity came, to spit viciously at him. First a flood of outraged invectives, followed by a barrage of incriminating questions. Maybe it would shock him back to sanity. But something in his detached demeanor warned against this, prompted—even in her outrage—restraint in her. His indifference was chilling. She knew instinctively she was lucky to be alive, to have gotten this far. Push past a very short point and she'd pay for it. Killing was not beyond him. Any respite would be wasted in feeble retaliation. She must use it to run from him. Quickly.

Despite this, she did not sense, deep down, he was much interested in her death. Or even her. This was not about her. This was about Kirk. Something about Kirk.

She felt his presence behind her again, then his rough fingers on her back. He was unsnapping her bra. He did it quickly and efficiently and without the least fumbling, exactly the way he did everything else. He jerked down her panties the same way, as though he were peeling fruit. He gathered her in his arms then, against his own nakedness, and walked into the water. It was hissingly cold, but he walked, as always, without faltering or slipping until the water reached their waists.

Cradling her in one arm, he began to soap her. It was what he'd gone back to the car for.

He did it quickly but gently, expertly but very thoroughly. He didn't linger on her chest, but he didn't skimp there either. Between the cold water and his caressing hands her breasts stood up hard and taut in a way they hadn't in a long while. Meg's surprising gratefulness at this in his presence both appalled and fascinated her.

He scrubbed her stomach and legs, back and buttocks, including the cleft.

He ran slippery fingers over her crotch, working lather into the pubic hair, even soaping her labia carefully. It was neither the sensuous touch of a lover nor the clinical ministrations of a doctor, but something she could not put a name to, something at once gentle, efficient, and distant. And strangely relaxing. Meg stood calmly under his busy fingers staring listlessly at the opposite shore, half waiting for one finger to probe inside, half surprised when one did not. She recognized the possibility that she might be in shock, yet she couldn't shake the belief that his intent was more than merely to clean her.

When he took her shoulders and forced her under, she stiffened with flaring fear, grasping his wrist. But he was only wetting her hair, then attacking it with the soap and the same adept determination. He dunked her again to rinse away suds, ran the soapy bar across the lipstick design on his own chest, threw the bar over his shoulder, and lifted her in his arms again.

He carried her to shore and deposited her on a clean towel waiting there. He picked up another towel and began to dry her hair first, wrapping the material around her head like a tent and scrubbing roughly but not inconsiderately. He removed the towel, snapped it once in the warm air, and bent to dry her back. He might have been her hairdresser.

He ran the terry cloth material over her ankles and legs, up her thighs; bent at the waist, cock and heavy testicles looming over her, his penis brushed her cheek mindlessly as he stooped. If this aroused him, or if he even acknowledged it, it never showed.

Gazing down the thickening shaft of him, into the whorl of dark pubic hair, Meg wondered listlessly at how absurdly lovely men are made, at how her life—a thing that had seemingly rambled on directionlessly—could find itself plummeting down this single, inconceivable path. At how in the face of all this, the sky could remain so breathlessly blue.

The tanned body bent farther, toweling her buttocks, forcing her into the camel musk of his crotch. She closed her eyes, tried to envision a childhood birthday party, telling herself that the vague stirrings down inside her were from thinking of Kirk. When in fact she could scarcely remember the last time with Kirk . . .

Riff finished, snapped the towel at the air again, threw something into her lap: clean panties and bra she recognized as her own, and one of her favorite summer dresses. No shoes.

She slipped them on quickly while he toweled himself and dressed in his jeans and T-shirt.

He stood waiting, hands on hips, and Meg found that she could stand now with ease. That was partly what the vigorous bath and toweling had been for: her circulation. She knew from the way he stared at her, he was not going to tie her up again, and she knew also exactly what he expected from her for that privilege. Exactly what would happen if she abused it.

She turned without comment and walked up the short bank to the car waiting among the trees, an unpretentious green Volvo sedan she noticed for the first time. Perhaps twenty minutes had passed since their arrival at the lake. It must be close to nine or so. If Kirk had awakened at approximately the same time as she, he might have started after her by now.

If only he knew where to start.

Riff opened the passenger door for her and she slid in. Immediately he bent and slipped a pair of shiny handcuffs over both ankles, clicking them into place. He tested quickly to make sure they weren't too tight. Something in the offhand gesture supplied the answer to all the symbolism of before: she was someone's, and then he took her and pissed on her and defiled her, and she was no one's. Then he cleansed her, every inch of her, remade her, essentially, and she was his. Not as a woman but as a prize. Intellectually it meant nothing; like the stone dance, it was a metaphor for something else.

Yes, this was about Kirk, not her.

Riff came around the front, slid into the driver's seat, and started the engine with a grumbling roar that belied the vehicle's innocuous exterior; the car was equipped for speed.

The gleam of mirrored steel caught her eye as he placed the big hunting knife on the seat between them. He put the car in gear and started unhurriedly away. He wore a simple, inexpensive watch, but she had never yet seen him glance at it.

She looked askance at the serrated blade as they pulled onto a country road. She could reach down and grab it as easily as he. Just you try it, the gesture seemed to say. Despite the fact that his eyes never left the road or mirror, she felt not the least inclination. Even sitting still, his body bespoke lightning motion, unimaginable speed. He was coiled, and the longer he sat, the tighter he became. She just knew it.

And he knew she knew it. It was the axis of their relationship: unspoken acknowledgments.

A commodity, she couldn't help thinking ruefully as they swept away into dust, she had never shared with Kirk.

Five

Once he'd seen the lipsticked message on the mirror—Susan's birthdate—everything changed.

Not only did he have a decisive reason for action now, not only was there a tangible locale, a place to start, but even the most tenuous hopes that this was all a silly joke perpetrated by Meg and Riff were erased.

And something else changed too. Something in him.

He could feel it in his newly acquired gait, in the subtle, eager shift of muscles as he dialed his lover's number (no answer), rechecked the revolver, hunted down the spare box of shells, dialed the office again for David (still not in) and, finally, made sure the Nova in the garage hadn't been tampered with, was running properly. He could feel it somewhere deep inside himself as well: an ancient stirring, the sudden clarity his surroundings took on, the quick but officious calculations his mind made, the paced but unhurried decisions—pondered, discarded or acted upon—each in their proper order.

The familiar professional aura surrounding him like an invisible haze—half forgotten but instinctively called up.

It was nearly Pavlovian: he was acting like a cop again.

He was vaguely shocked at how much this pleased him.

It pleased him a great deal. More than he would have imagined, maybe even more than he liked.

He'd simply hadn't the vaguest concept, not until this moment, of just how terribly he'd missed it, how terribly he needed it, how much it was a necessary part of all that he was and had been. How much of a somnambulant shell he'd been without it.

Meg, though. Meg had known for some time.

Yes . . .

He guided Jill into the passenger's side of the Nova, slid into the driver's seat himself, turned over the engine. Something about its familiar roar chilled him suddenly. . . .

Again he felt the sensation that his actions were being directed, puppeteer-like, by someone else. Someone like Riff. He was racing off to his doom. . . .

His fingers lingered over the gearshift long enough to allow the growing doubt to form a wedge.

He swallowed back fear, embracing control again. The time to think with absolute steely calm and clarity was now: the initial step in retrieving Meg was through his ex-lover, the only lead he had now. It might be a trap, going to Susan's house, it might be a ruse, it might be nothing more than the humilation that now Meg knew about him and Susan. Or it might be something far worse, like the end of Susan's life. It might be many things, but it was some things for sure: it was clever. And insidious. Even uncanny in its forethought, planning, and imagination. Even, yes, admirable. And it was exactly what it was supposed to be: nerve-wracking. Someone had gone to almost supernatural lengths to know everything and anything about the forty-two-year history of John Philip Kirkland, and all those about him—a someone Kirk could not recall.

He looked at his hands resting on the wheel, still amazingly steady. Whatever this seizured brain had conceived, it was more elaborate than merely a chase, more than merely a war. Something, perhaps, more akin to chess. Of that he was more and more convinced.

The gameboard was out *there* somewhere, the highway, maybe the whole country.

The pawns . . . the pawns were he and Meg.

The rules appeared simple: there were none.

And, as is inevitable in all games of sport, the best man would win. Which was what the game was really all about.

Kirk put the car in gear and hurled from the garage. It was his move. . . .

Susan's house, a simple shrub-flanked, clapboard, two-story stencil of other clapboard two-stories on Chicago's South Side, looked wrong when they pulled up across the street.

No one else would have noticed it: the lawn was

cut, the papers collected, the curtains sensibly open to let in summer sun. The "wrongness" came from looking beyond the exterior, more a feeling than a visual fact. It took years of practice, and then wasn't always accurate.

He was wondering if maybe the back way might be better, wondering what exactly it was he was going to say to Susan when he saw her, wondering if, once out of the car, Jill would try to escape, when she turned to him in the front seat. "Who is she?"

He stared at the house, eyes flickering to all the windows, mind racing. "I told you: a friend."

Jill's gaze shifted curiously to the house. "Does Riff know her?"

Kirk turned to look at her eyes. "Why don't you tell me?"

She shrugged innocently. "As I said, I really haven't seen him in ages. We didn't talk all that much when we *were* together." She paused to study him a moment, but his face was a mask. "Why do you think he would write her birth date on your bathroom mirror? Is she a friend of your wife's?"

Kirk turned away and pushed out of the car, not prepared for this yet, angry and frustrated because of it, trying not to let it get him. Meg was in danger somewhere, and he felt like he was moving lethargically through heavy oil. He slammed the door, moved around to Jill's side, and let her out. He laced his right hand into her left and turned to her. "Stay close to me. Don't say anything unless I ask you. Don't try to run away or I'll break your fingers. Do you understand?"

She gave me a reproachful look. "I understand.

And it really isn't necessary to talk to me like that—"

He moved off before she could finish, pulling her close. He stepped quickly across the street and right up the front walk without breaking stride, eyes not leaving the window nearest the front door.

He tested the door, found it locked.

He knocked. Waited as long as he could endure waiting.

He produced a credit card and opened the door, conscious of the effect the effort had on Jill.

They stepped carefully through the threshold.

The living room was in perfect order, silent, empty, familiar, dust motes dancing to the big throw rug from the south window.

Kirk pulled Jill along, eyes constantly moving, ears pricked for the slightest sound. There were none.

The kitchen was closest, so he checked that first. It too looked familiar and empty and wrong because Susan wasn't in it and he had never seen it without Susan in it. His eyes lingered a second too long on the new kitchen table and chairs. He had been with her the weekend she'd bought it while her husband was out of town. He'd come by and they'd set it up together and she'd brushed against him and he'd said he was sorry, sorry because he'd brushed her breasts and she'd said are you, are you sorry, and he'd looked at her and she at him and he'd started to say no, not sorry at all, but her arms were already around him and then his around her and her tongue and the couch against their knees and then against her back and it happening so fast and frenziedly she'd lost a button or was it two? All this in the middle of a lazy Saturday afternoon while Bill Clinton got inaugurated and jet planes flew overhead and his wife planted roses in their garden across town and thought he was at the Bears game with David. Afterward he and Susan had coffee and cheesecake, both of them wanting him to go but this weird mutual decorum hanging in the air.

On the way home he'd thought he'd feel great guilt. What he'd felt was a great vacuum.

He'd also thought that was the end of it.

But business brought them together two weeks later. This time over lunch. Afterward he'd followed her car at a discreet distance, hoping she would, hoping she wouldn't: three blocks later Susan had turned into the motel.

On the cheap bed they were high school kids. Or pretending to be. She coming like cannon fire, screaming things she'd never screamed to her husband; Kirk knowing it, screaming them back, unafraid, unabashed, reveling in it; how sweet the forbidden fruit, how electric the touch of strangers. In the shower as well, her throaty cries ringing off the broken tile, ringing forever in his mind: *yes! fuck! Kirk!* Her great pleasure, great skill was in blowing him. She was his whore, gladly. Playing, discovering, letting it all go in a comet's rush, knowing it was doomed, ephemeral as a spring rose. *I'll just hold it this time—I want to watch as I hold it.* Twice more at the motel then, and one final time at her house. Then their business ended and took the too-brief affair with it. He was secretly so glad.

Because he knew, in his heart of hearts, that it never would have happened at all if he hadn't found out about Meg. . . .

Upstairs now, he turned down the hall, pulling Jill after him, heading across the carpet to the polished wood banister. It was an old house and an old banister: going up it reminded him of the scene in *Psycho* where the detective is going up to the crazy old woman's room and she comes out of the upstairs hall and stabs him. He wondered if someone would come out of the hall now.

He turned right at the top, Jill in tow, heading past the master bath toward the bedroom. As he passed, he looked quickly inside, got a thrill of adrenaline from his own reflection without breaking stride.

He looked in on the master bedroom and got the same empty-without-Susan feeling. He made himself not linger on the bed.

He came out of the bedroom and heard Jill's gasp and saw someone coming at them down the hall, a man.

Kirk's hand was half inside his coat before he made the face, half swathed in a snowy beard of shaving cream: Susan's husband. He held an old-fashioned tortoise-shell straight razor in one hand. "Who the hell are you?"

Kirk stepped forward calmly and authoritatively, letting loose of Jill's hand, risking it. "It's all right, Mr. Hathaway, I'm a detective. I'm sorry if we startled you, nobody answered and the door was open."

Hathaway eyed them carefully in the dim hall, holding the razor at waist level. He seemed to want to believe. "I was in the shower. May I see your badges, please?"

He was a big man, shorter than Kirk but compact, even beefy in his Italian undershirt. Kirk ignored the request and turned toward the stairs; the hall was narrow, and he'd need room to maneuver in case things got out of hand with the razor, not that it looked that way yet.

"I need very much to talk to your wife, Mr. Hathaway," he went on officiously, moving downstairs ahead of Jill, letting the sentence trail off, hoping to divert Hathaway away from the badge. At the bottom of the stairs, he stood with his hands on his hips, gazing about the living room with professional elan, trying to exude a commanding presence he didn't feel. He turned to Hathaway's ruddy, suspicious face, a face he'd seen before only in the silver framed photo in the hall. "Is she at home, Mr. Hathaway?"

"Is my wife in some kind of trouble?"

"We hope not. Do you know when she'll be back?"

Hathaway started to answer, turned to peer at Jill. "I'd like to see your badges, please." Polite but firm. There would be no bullying him, not without a tussle.

Kirk glanced at his watch. "Mr. Hathaway, I think you can surmise from the way we're dressed that we're plainclothesmen; this particular case excludes the luxury of carry police ID." It was gobbledegook, but it might work, if Jill went along.

"Well . . . what do you want to see my wife about?"

"Kirk—?"

They all turned to see Susan standing in the doorway to the kitchen, arms laden with groceries. Maybe it was her surprised state, or the harsh lighting, or just the general ambience, but something about the way she stood there gaping and shocked was oddly repellent. She's gotten older, Kirk was struck. Still lovely but older. Which means I have too. Of course I have. Isn't this a senseless thing to be thinking at the moment?

"I need to see you, Mrs. Hathaway."

But the old man wasn't buying. "You know this guy?"

Susan made a mouth like a fish on land.

"Just some technical questioning, Mrs. Hathaway." Kirk headed it off, giving Jill a warning shot and moving to Susan to help with the groceries. He turned offhandedly to Mr. Hathaway. "This might be best, for security reasons, if it was private," urging Susan's stupefied form toward the kitchen. "We won't be a moment."

Confused, unconvinced, Hathaway looked to Jill, who, thank God, was smiling reassuringly and pointing her bosom at him. "You have a lovely home, Mr. Hathaway. Reminds me of my mother's house." Wandering into the living room in Jean Foley's tight shorts, snug crack inviting him to follow.

"Your wife has terrific taste!" She nodded at the heavy curtains, hating them. She touched an end table with forced admiration. "This is early American, isn't it?"

Hathaway was looking after Kirk and Susan. "Yeah, I guess. You'd have to ask my wife."

Jill scanned the oak shelves above the mantel. "Lots of books on fishing. Are you a sportsman, Mr. Hathaway?"

"I fish some."

Her eyes caught, hesitated, hand flinching upward, brows knitting. She brightened. "Oh, is this the family album?"

Hathaway managed a patient nod, wandering into the living room after her. "Yeah," craning toward the kitchen one last time, finally letting Jill's long legs take his eyes. She already had the album in her long-fingered hands.

Perched prettily on the sofa edge, she bent deeper than necessary at the waist, offering ample proportions of cleavage. "Do you mind? I love family pictures!"

Hathaway allowed his eyes to carry him around the coffee table, never wavering from her untanned globes, sitting down across from her, jockeying for a good angle.

Jill made a great show. "Is this you? No, this can't be you! This handsome thing must be your son!"

Hathaway fell into it, a clumsy bear. "Naw, that's me. Younger days, still had the hair."

Jill clucked her tongue. "You certainly were a looker!"

Hathaway grinned modestly at the halter top.

In the kitchen, up against the formica counter, Susan's eyes were saucers. "Kirk, what—?"

He made an impatient gesture. What to tell her? No time. Tell her all. "Meg's been taken."

She opened a questioning mouth, but he gestured it closed again. "Some guy claims he used to know me, came by last night, stayed late, we drank. This morning they were gone, he and Meg. I don't know where, don't remember the guy at all."

Susan glanced toward the living room.

"His ex. She doesn't know anything either, or claims she doesn't."

"He *kidnapped* Meg?"

"Looks like it."

Disbelief, followed by eyes clouded with questions. "Why?"

He nodded. "Yes, why."

She shook her head. "It's a joke!"

He shook his head. "No. The ex doesn't think so. Neither do I. He wrote your birth date on the bathroom mirror."

Her expression was one of shocked outrage, as though she'd been defiled. *"What!"*

"He's clever, knows a lot, how much I'm not sure. But about us it seems. I think he's dangerous. Have you seen—has anybody been around, anyone suspicious?"

She shook her head, face more and more aghast.

He was grasping at straws, a man drowning, the impact of it burning through his bladder. "Have you noticed anything, anything out of place, anything out of the ordinary in the past few days?"

"Like what?"

Like what. "I don't know, things missing, notes, messages, I don't know."

"What about the police?"

He sighed impatiently. "I'm waiting to talk with

my brother. I can't go blundering to the cops, Susan! The guy's a looney! He might start shooting! Do you understand?"

"Did he threaten to kill Meg?"

"He didn't need to!" He was close to the edge.

She came to him gently then, held up a trembling hand, voice conciliatory-fearful. "I'm sorry. What do you want me to do?"

He took the hand, a self-reproachful gesture, felt its icy fear, let it go. It seemed alien. She seemed alien. He seemed alien. Shit. "I need to search the house," he said quietly. "Something's here, I'm sure of it, some sign or message or clue indicating which way to go next."

" 'Which way'?"

"It's a game he's playing. I'm suppose to follow his little treasure hunt. He's out to prove something. If I just ignore him, call in the cops . . ."

"But no one could get in here, Frank's been home all week."

"I don't think that would stop this guy. Look, let's start with the mirrors, then with anything that looks out of place, moved from one spot to another." His eyes darted to the doorway again. "I'm sorry about—I didn't know any other way, there isn't time—"

"I know. I shouldn't have blurted your name. I wasn't thinking."

"You couldn't know." He needed to reassure her, and he needed to be far away from her at the same time. This helpless impotency engulfing him, he knew, was exactly what Riff had intended. As was his sudden, nerve-frayed desire to strike out at something, anything tangible. He had never been out of control in his life—sorry, regretful, used up, but not out of control. He didn't adjust well to the feeling now. "Is there any way—can you distract Frank, even get him out of here?"

"What the *fuck!* Christ!" The bellowing came from the front room, followed by Jill's breathy gasp.

Kirk spun, hurried to the door, Susan at his shoulder, saw the open photo album lying on the carpet, black-and-white prints strewn across the coffee table. Hathaway, beet red, was glaring daggers at him.

Kirk had time to say, "Wait a second!" before he realized Hathaway was attacking him, charging like a bull, head down, balding crown gleaming. In shock, Kirk sidestepped into Susan clumsily, losing his balance, crashing backward under the bigger man's weight, to Susan's musical screams. *wait a minute! wait a minute!*

Locked like pit bulls, they slammed into the oak cupboard below the sink, the air driven from Kirk's chest, a metallic note of rattled pans behind his head. He managed to get his hands up to ward off the worst of the blows raining at his face, but until he could get his breath again, there was little else he could do but lie under the crushing pressure and listen to the mindlessness of Susan's shrieking. "Stop it! stop it! *stop it!*"

Why is this man doing this?

And at the same time he felt the royal fool for letting Hathaway get the best of him this way in front of his ex-lover. It shocked Kirk how out of shape he was, how quickly his legs had buckled under when the heavier man came in. He told himself he'd muffed it because Susan was in the way, but he only half believed it. He should never have stopped the push-ups, the curls. It took more than fashionable jogging and looking trim to be truly fit, the way he'd been in the old days when he was winning citations. When he was younger. The acknowledgment started another dredge of fear in him that was not from Hathaway, really, but from what was surely to come later on the road.

Hathaway, meanwhile, was a determined foe but no street fighter; the ill-placed facial blows were having little effect and he wasn't smart enough to realize it, change his tack. Kirk waited until he could draw in a shaky, solid lungful, then reached under and grabbed Hathaway's nuts, squeezing harder than absolutely necessary. You won't be pumping little Susan this week, schmucko. Hathaway bellowed, reared up off Kirk in a motion that was almost endearingly vulnerable, and left himself wide open for an easy uppercut with which Kirk was happy to oblige him.

The beefy man flopped over with a smack of back and buttocks, and Kirk pushed up, sure that it was over.

It wasn't, quite. Hathaway, one hand cupped over his genitals, got hold of Kirk's ankle with the other and wouldn't let go. Kirk kicked out but to no avail. The other man held bulldog tight and now his other hand joined the first. Kirk began to do a little half hitch dance around the linoleum floor, kicking and swearing and pinwheeling his arms to retain balance. Hathaway held on.

Kirk gripped the counter edge with one hand, the refrigerator door with the other, placed the sole of his free shoe against the man's neck, and pushed. Hathaway held on. Susan, still spitting and fuming obscenities, ran up with a spatula and began striking her husband across his shiny dome. "Frank, *stop it!*" Hathaway held.

Kirk fell back against the counter, supported on both arms, breathing hard. This was fucking ridiculous! He stared down almost lazily at his trapped ankle, at the top of Susan's head as she drubbed her husband with the kitchen utensil. He could see a single strand of gray nestled with the darker browns just next to her part. Something about the little gray hair made the whole scene tragically funny. He had mentally prophesized the moment of their unmasking a hundred times, of Frank or someone walking in while they embraced: it had never played like this.

After a moment he straightened, took the .38 from his holster, and placed the barrel against Hathaway's left eye. Not letting himself look at Susan, he said, levelly, "Please let go of my ankle, Mr. Hathaway." Hathaway let go.

Kirk tucked in his flopping shirttail, still avoiding Susan's eyes, and limped into the living room, where Jill was gathering the fallen photographs from the floor. He picked up the nearest one. It was a black-and-white, hand-processed, grainy but clear enough. It showed a naked, muscular man bent over Susan Hathaway, entering her from behind. A muscular man that was Kirk.

He had the silliest damn notion he'd seen the picture somewhere before.

He smoothed back the hair dangling across his forehead and picked up another picture. It was exactly the same as the first. And the next and the next, the entire pile.

He tossed the photos onto a stack of a dozen or more, shuffled the stack even, and put them in his inner coat pocket. He caught Jill's eye as he turned. "Close friends," she murmured, poker-faced.

Kirk ignored her and picked up the album. He flipped through it rapidly, looking for anything familiar, dimly aware of a flaring pain in his back. Behind him in the kitchen, Hathaway was groaning softly and Susan was saying something undecipherable to him. A small drop of crimson exploded across the album, and Kirk sniffed back automatically, cupping his hand beneath the nose bleed. He looked up and saw Jill proffering a Kleenex. He took it, pressed it beneath his nose, and flipped pages. He stopped when he found what he was looking for, tore it out, closed the book, and tossed it on the table.

He went to stand over Susan, who was cradling her husband's head in her lap. "I found it," he said. "What I was looking for."

She looked up, and there was something new in her green-flecked eyes. Or something missing? "Good," she replied hollowly. "You'd better go, then."

He hesitated, but not long, knowing it was no use. He withdrew the deck of black-and-white photos and held one up for her. "I found these too."

She stared a moment, then closed her eyes. Then lowered her chin to her chest. Hathaway groaned beneath her. She smoothed the hairs on his balding head, looking, to Kirk, like a little girl huddled on the kitchen floor who has just been punished for stealing cookies.

"Susan . . ."

But there was nothing to be said, nothing that could be said, and no point in looking up at him, so she didn't. It wasn't just the photos; it all held a new kind of reality now.

He left her there on the linoleum.

On the way back to the car, hardly conscious of Jill struggling to keep up, all he could think was that no matter what he might have considered before, what he wanted most now was to kill Riff Walker.

Of course, some part of his mind told him as he opened the door and entered the steamy interior, that's exactly what he intended you to want.

He started the engine and pulled quickly away, leaving Susan, the house, and all of it behind him.

In a moment Jill turned to him, watching. He looked over unflinchingly. All right, she was my lover.

Was she smiling in sarcasm? "She takes a lovely picture. Nice ass."

He made a sour face. "Yeah. Your ex is just full of surprises."

She nodded aloofly. "Aren't we all." Then regarded the side window solemnly. Sighed. "No one's who he appears to be anymore . . ."

Kirk groaned mentally. Great. The philosophic

blonde with the big knockers. "Fine. I'm a cheat and a prick. Humanity sucks. Can we get past it now?"

"Well, I can get past it, certainly."

"But not Susan, right? I'm not exactly the innocent victim anymore, that it? Well, I'm sure that's what Riff intended."

"I'm not here to judge. I don't want to be here at all, remember?"

He looked at her. "What on earth got you two perusing the family album, sheer luck?"

She gave him a labored look. "Luck had nothing to do with it. You went there to look for clues, right? Well, while you we're pussy-footing in the kitchen with your lover, I was entertaining the old man with my halter top and checking out the decor. Happened to notice a vaguely familiar lipstick smudge on the lower spine of one of their book shelf albums."

"Familiar?"

"Shaped sort of like a Silver Star, if you catch my drift. It wasn't your girlfriend's shade."

He nodded. "Very good. Does this mean you're helping me?"

She looked away. "Look, I was there, I noticed, that's all. Anyone who'd seen the mirror message could have put it together. Hardly the work of genius."

"You underrate yourself."

"Anyway, even if I hadn't spotted it, I'm sure one of the Hathaways would have paid you a little call. Sooner or later you'd have ended up looking in that album."

Kirk grunted. "Better sooner. At least you spared us the possibility of the police getting involved. Anyway, thanks. And thanks for not blowing the whistle on me."

"I was afraid you'd break my fingers."

He had to smile.

He appraised her a moment. "You did it well. Where'd you get such sharp little eyes?"

She settled back in the seat, shrugged. Proud of herself?

"Watching you."

Six

They stopped at a McDonald's on Route 4 about two hours from the lake, west, as far as she could tell.

Meg had estimated the distance by watching the mileage counter below the speedometer, and if the man named Riff had objected to this—surely he had seen it—he didn't show it. He bought them cheeseburgers, fries, and Cokes at the drive-thru window and they had eaten driving. They had not spoken once. She was pressing back the building urge to urinate but decided not to mention it until it became critical. It wasn't a fear of being hit— though she did fear him—but a feeling in the air. Talk, and explanations if there were any, would come later, or they would not come at all. It seemed best to bide her time at this point, try to keep things cool through complaisance, let events unravel of their own accord and not let her mind stray beyond the now. Hope linked itself with escape and rescue, silent sentinels at the periphery of thought. Not private thoughts, though, she knew. Whatever schemes or strategies she might entertain in the hours ahead, he had doubtless foreseen weeks or months in advance. Every breath he took was a consciously scrutinized one; his intelligence was no more to be questioned than his determination.

When she had finished her burger and fries and still had enough Coke, he gave her a small yellow capsule and indicated her mouth. She took it, toying for a fleeting moment with the idea of hiding it under her tongue, but when the sugary liquid spilled into her mouth she swallowed it all with resignation, some distant part of her mind half hoping it was deadly, some other part knowing it was not. In a few minutes she felt the guessed-at sleep welling up and gave into it peaceably, concerned only that it would not cause her to wet herself.

She awoke—seemingly scant minutes later—to late afternoon stillness and the gentle shaking of his hand. The window was rolled down and she could smell newly mowed grass, or maybe hay, a clean, almost heady early evening smell that cleared the cobwebs quickly and made her think of lemonade and sleeping over. The whole world seemed to be lingering reverently on the edge of twilight, holding its breath for the sure, swift fall of cooling dark and nighttime sounds.

He was out of the car before she knew it and opening the door for her. To her surprise, the manacles at her ankles had already been removed. He reached in and gave her a supporting hand.

She stood with cramped wobbliness, facing the wonderful smells, the burning need in her bladder amplifying as her heels struck the hard gravel earth. Red neon bathed her dress and the dust-coated sheen of the car from the half-lit sign flanking the road: LUCKY 6 MOTEL—VACANCY.

A row of white-trimmed cabins stood before them, country neat but inexpensive. From the lack of traffic sounds, the musky air, she guessed they were far from anywhere, distant farm country. A dog barked clearly somewhere, a sound that might be coming from miles away. He guided her up a short wooden step to the front door, which stood slightly ajar. She noticed the big number 7 before she was inside.

It was dark and close in the cabin, but he got the shades drawn and the lights on quickly, and after the two squeaky wooden windows were up, the cross ventilation cooled it rapidly. Under other circumstances it might have been romantic. Her eyes went immediately to the bathroom; he acknowledged the look and nodded. She stepped to it quickly, hesitated, then shut the door discreetly, flicking the light switch.

There was a lock, which her fingers lingered over, but she sat down without using it. There were no windows in the tiny bathroom, and he would just break the door down anyway. She could try shouting now, her first time alone since it had begun, but he'd probably arranged them far from other guests and she had seen no other cars out front; this place was on its last legs, victim of newer, better highways. Besides, she had built a kind of silent trust up to this point she deemed unwise to erode. It was granting her polite favors, however small.

She flushed the rusty stool and looked at herself in the clouded mirror beyond a light tracery of spiderwebbed glass. The weariness showed and the fear too. Even so, she felt the instinctual tug for lipstick and blush. Vanity endures. Purseless, combless, she gave an open-palmed swipe at her hair, still frizzed from the lake, shook it once, drank from a paper-wrapped glass, and opened the door. The brief respite in the bathroom offered neither real sanctuary nor a diminution of his presence as she'd imagined it might; he'd been right there beside her on the toilet. She would not be truly alone again until free of him.

The outer room was small too: one twin-sized bed, worn hooked rug, simple nightstand with single lamp, another small wooden table fifties style with a water glass stain, tiny closet, no TV, no air conditioner. Riff was sitting on the edge of the bed with one boot off, removing something within it.

She moved sedately to the little table and leaned against it. He put the boot back on and looked at her, patting the bed beside him in a gesture that said *sit here*. After a cautious moment she came and sat near him, heart in her throat, body straining away, rump as close to the foot of the mattress as would support her.

He turned and placed a hand over hers, firm but with light pressure, eyes impassive, tone level but not challenging.

"It's this simple: you can live through this, but it must be my way. That can be comfortably or otherwise. I have no sadistic interest in you, though it may be necessary to use you in some ways. It's your husband I want. Stay close and without a fuss, and I'll meet him fairly, openly. Try once to escape and I'll dispose of you. He'll still come then, but in a blind rage, which will give me an edge. I'd prefer the former way, and I think you want to live. Even in the unlikely event you escape, contact the authorities, I'll elude them and come for both of you later. You won't know when. Your situation is desperate but not hopeless played by my rules. Played by yours, it's doomed. The choice is yours. Do you understand?"

Meg nodded.

"Answer that you understand."

"I understand."

He managed a tight smile. "Fine." That vanished again.

He turned casually and took a brown paper grocery bag from the closet, dumping the contents on the bed: her purse, a newly purchased bottle of shampoo, a comb, brush, even a bottle of conditioner. He must have put it in the cabin while she was still sleeping in the car. "There's a dress in the closet too, one of yours. You'll want a proper bath, I imagine."

"Yes."

"Go ahead, then."

"May I ask why you're doing this?"

"There's time for that."

She nodded compliantly and picked up the purse, heading toward the bathroom again.

Inside, she once more closed the door without

locking it, ran hot, rusty water, and undressed, thinking of his words, some phrases playing back.

may be necessary to use you in some ways
you won't know when
dispose of you

She stepped into the steamy water, lay back, waiting for it to calm her, ease her shrieking calf muscles. It did only marginally. The bottle of shampoo on the lip of the tub appeared oddly forbidding. The discrepancy between normal life and her current incarceration was only amplified by familiar things like warm baths and toilet articles. It made things more comfortable, but strangely harder. He must be aware of this too, and she wondered vaguely, in the steamy clouds, if it had something to do with his plan.

Was this new attentiveness a trick to put her off guard, a ploy in case they were caught—*he treated me well, officer*—or merely an oil-scented preparation to rape? She opened her eyes with this last, found herself staring at a daddy longlegs crouched demurely in a ceiling corner above the tub. She found herself wondering how long the spider had been there, and then how long spiders lived, period. She wondered if enough flies or bugs got into this little motel bathroom to make a place worthy of the spider's web. And now that she looked she didn't see any web. Maybe it hadn't spun its web yet. Or did daddy longlegs spin webs at all? And now that she thought about that she realized it mattered not at all, that her mind was desperately seeking refuge in the inane, the commonplace, that it was a mind no longer completely hers, and that perhaps she was further gone than she'd imagined. For one desperate moment she thought she would swoon, drown. She sat up, added a rush of cold water, took deep breaths. The room had been listing lazily. Hang on. Kirk will find you. Kirk will beat him. No one is better than Kirk. . . . There, that's better now. . . .

She lay back again, head resting against the tub side, chin touching the suds. She was like this when the door opened and he came in.

Her only reaction was inward, a painful thrill in her stomach; she deliberately lay still, not looking up, staring down at the bubbles just covering her nipples. He came and stood by the tub. Staring? After a moment she had to look up because not to do so felt absurd. She was greeted by his long penis again, this time aimed at the opened stool. She looked away but could not avoid the sound he made, which was loud and forceful and seemed to go on forever. Kirk never peed in front of her, he liked his privacy. She had resented this without once telling him so; she had wanted to know everything about Kirk in the beginning, even how he made water, but he had never let it get that close, that everyday intimate. This man had already done it twice in twelve hours.

"What do you like to eat?"

His voice made her jump, and the bath water rolled aft. She folded her arms casually across her chest. "Excuse me?"

"For dinner. What's your dish?"

Her mind was on hold, all memory banks shut down. "I don't know . . ."

He shrugged. "Must have a favorite."

She stole a glance as he was finishing, milking the last drops in rubbery masturbation. "Anything's fine." Her gaze lifted and he was looking down at her with that tight little grin again. Holding his penis in a motel bathroom and smiling at her. " 'No matter how many times you shake the peg, the last few drops run down your leg.' " He sniffed a laugh.

She grinned nervously. He wasn't flirting and he wasn't humilating her. He just was completely immodest. She might have been his sister. Or wife was more like it. There was something tension-settling about it, a privacy shared. And a way of putting her at ease. That's why he'd come in here, to apologize for christening her at the lake. See, it's just urine. Silly.

He tucked himself away. "What about lobster?"

It took her a moment. "That's fine."

"Lobster it is."

He started for the door.

"Is—" She broke off.

He turned, holding the knob.

"Is there a place like that—I mean, way out here?" she asked.

He turned to the mirror, ran a hand over his face as if checking the length of his stubble. "We're not spending the night here, we're just registered to."

Anticipating her reaction to this, he added: "It's part of the itinerary."

He left, shutting the door with a draft across her exposed skin that dried it like a tightening carapace.

Seven

Kirk left Susan Hathaway's house and drove straight to his bank.

The silence on the way was probably uncomfortable, but he hardly noticed it; his foot kept wanting to jam the pedal to the floor. He could feel the blood tight against his temples. It wasn't entirely that he'd just been made a fool of. He knew now that Meg was in the hands of a complete maniac. Worse than that, a skilled one. Kirk felt beyond helpless, as though everything were rushing away from him at once.

After a time, Jill turned to him in the seat and said, "Longtime affair?"

If there was sarcasm to her tone he couldn't detect it. He was tired already—his powers of detection worn thin (not a good thing so early on)—and the last thing he needed to concern himself with was this woman's sarcasm or lack of it. Maybe she was just naturally acerbic, like a lot of too-bright people. He decided to give her the benefit. He said: "Long enough."

She nodded. "I guess that sort of put it on ice, huh?" nodding back toward the Hathaways'.

He shifted lanes, avoiding a green panel truck. "It was already over. Are you going to ask me about the gory details now?"

"I don't know. Would you like to talk about them?"

"Not at the moment."

She watched the road, probably contending with her own problems. He hoped she would drop this now, was glad when she read his mind and did. It gave him the opportunity to see his relief and be surprised by it. In some unfathomably masochistic way he was glad Hathaway knew. Now it was really over, could never happen again. Not that he'd thought it would, but this made it all cleaner somehow—in a messy sort of way. Certainly final. He had always thought Susan and he should be punished, that that kind of hedonist euphoria must surely have a price. Or himself punished, at least. Maybe deep down inside he'd wanted all along to get caught. Why was that?

So Meg would know?

So Meg would know how much *her* affair had hurt him?

Nearly killed him? Had he done the whole thing for Meg somehow?

And what of poor Susan now?

Why did he feel deep down that Hathaway wouldn't leave her? That the big bear might even— after the initial shock—come to regard it with curiosity, even linger on it, channel it into their limp marriage. Something perversely agreeable in knowing another man lusts after your wife. Even that he's been there. The invariable midnight questions: was he good? was he big? what did you do with him? Show me.

Or was he just bullshitting himself, salving a guilty conscience? Kirk sensed a chapter closing. Susan or Meg or both? He felt a mild buzzing in the back of his skull, pushed his mind elsewhere.

He pulled into the First Illinois Federal and braked in the sun-drenched lot behind the low brick building. It was already hot out and not even noon. There were no shadows to park under, and the car would quickly become unbearable with the windows rolled up, and there was no way to lock her in anyway. He could plead with her that he needed her for this, but that would do no good if her mind was intent on escape. One thing for certain, he couldn't keep dragging her around by the wrist.

He gathered air and weariness into his lungs and turned to her. "Look, I can't very well chain you to the car."

She watched him calmly. "No."

"And I have to sleep eventually. So, if you want to go back to Maine or wherever, I'll drop you at the bus station. I can give you some money, not much. I mostly want you with me because I don't want the police alerted yet, but I also think there might be some small things you can tell me about Riff that will help. I'll make things as comfortable as possible, but I have limited funds and time and I think you know it's going to get dangerous eventually. I'll try to let you out before it does. If you do

go, I'd like your promise not to contact the authorities for forty-eight hours. But I'd prefer you
stayed."

She regarded him with a vague, almost hidden
smile and eyes that might have held pity or curiosity or both. "You haven't told me where we're going."

He produced the photo he'd torn from the album
and handed it to her. It showed a tiny tin-roofed
house with a debris-strewn yard, broken toys, a
rusted Ford engine, snaggle-toothed length of
picket fence.

"Riff planted this in the album?"

"Yes."

She studied the shabby dwelling. "Who lives
here?"

"Guy I knew. About two hours west of here. I'll
tell you about it." He consulted his watch again and
looked at the sun-baked facade of the bank building. "I have to know now," he said, his urgency
hanging in the car, saddening even him.

She leaned back. "I'll give you my answer when
you come back."

He nodded, that was fair. He pushed at the door
and stepped out into the heat.

It was cool and antiseptic in the bank, artificial
with manufactured plants and piped-in music. The
air of reserved order and business-as-usual decorum
pressing in at him gratingly. So many oblivious
faces. So many people running about like chickens,
leading their dismally dull lives with no more
thought than the next meal, the next paycheck. In

a moment he realized his irritation was born of envy.

He had to wait for ten minutes in line, and he took this time to curse himself for not applying for an ATM card. He wasn't comfortable with banking procedure; it came under one of the household chores Meg always attended to.

When it was at last his turn, he found that the hands reaching for the checkbook in his coat were trembling now. Yes, he was weary of it already, physically anyway. You can't survive on adrenaline forever. He hoped the pinched-faced lady teller didn't notice. She wore unflattering glasses with rhinestones in the rims; hairstyle: severe; attitude: librarian patient. Someone's aunt, he thought and tore off a withdrawal slip. He scratched across the dotted line: eleven thousand dollars and forty-eight cents, and announced quietly to her, "I'm closing my account," because it seemed like the right thing to say.

The pinched woman took the slip courteously, studied it a moment, and looked up at him. "Are you dissatisfied with the bank's service?"

He hadn't been ready for it. "No, it isn't that. I just . . . need it."

"If you're transferring to an out-of-town bank we can transfer directly from here, it's safer."

"No, it's not for another bank."

That stopped her, provoked an uncomfortable pause. "I assume you've checked with our lending officer about emergency loans, Mr. Kirkland?" She was trying to be helpful, but it was also a lot of money and it didn't look right. He'd thought of traveler's checks, but there wasn't time for that. Besides, he had a premonition he'd need hard cash, though what it might buy he wasn't sure.

"Yes, I've checked; the eleven thousand is more than enough. Thanks."

She hesitated, slip in hand. "If you're happy with our bank and wish to remain on file, it might be wise to leave a few dollars in your account. It saves the red tape and the waiting period of opening another account. I really advise it. Five dollars will do."

He nodded quickly. "All right, let's do that."

She smiled with satisfaction and stamped the slip. "I'll be right with you, Mr. Kirkland." She turned and disappeared into teller land, having won her victory.

He lost her for moment behind a white pillar and a bank of filing drawers, then caught her bent over a desk, talking with a bespectacled man in a light tan suit. The man was frowning and nodding. He looked up once at Kirk, and Kirk looked away.

After a minute the pinched teller was back. "Thank you for waiting." She opened a drawer and counted his money out to him. She smiled. "There you are, and good luck!"

"Thank you."

When he came back out into the lot, the car was empty.

He didn't even give a cursory glance around.

He jumped in and headed for a Mobil station on Tenth he knew of; he could use his credit card there—save the cash—and they had an outside phone booth. He pulled into the full-service island, had the boy fill the tank and check the oil while he himself phoned the office. This time David came on the line.

"David Kirkland here."

"Where the hell have you been? It's Kirk."

"Hey! Missy had her braces today, Anna's at her mother's. How's our boy?"

Again the grudging sensation of envy: to David the world was a normal, even prosaic place, comfortable with tomorrow's redundancies. For an instant it seemed unfair to burden his brother with something this close to home. But where else to turn? "We're in trouble, Meg's been taken."

"Taken?"

"Kidnapped, David."

There. He'd said the word.

He could almost see the scene on the other end: David's abrupt, sobering expression, his snatching out for pad and pencil, phone cradled between ear and shoulder. "Shoot."

"Guy named Riff Walker. Says we were army buddies. I don't remember him, did I ever mention him to you?"

There was a slight pause at the other end of the line. "Nope, don't recall the name."

"That's what I thought. Listen, before we go further, I don't want this in the office."

"Huh?"

"He's a psycho, planting little clues I'm supposed to follow. This isn't about Meg, at least I don't think so, but I also don't think he'd hesitate to . . . get rid of her. He wants me to follow alone, and that's how I'm going to play it for now, understand? David?"

Hesitant: "I understand. That's Walker, W-A-L-K-E-R. What else?"

A tractor trailer rumbled by, making it hard to hear. "He has an ex, Jill . . . shit, I forgot to ask her last name. Blond, a looker, yellow halter, built. I just left her at the Illinois Federal on Seventeenth and Grand. She's probably heading for the bus station. She might blab. If there's anything you can do . . ."

"We'll detain her."

"I don't want—"

"I won't use our boys. I've got friends, remember, in the Bureau and elsewhere. Experts. They owe me. We'll keep her quiet, keep the lid on, and we'll nail this s.o.b."

"No!" His voice was hoarse with fear. "I don't want anyone contacting him but me! I told you, he's psycho."

"Kirk, you can't do this alone."

"For now I have to. Charge in, David, and he'll kill her! I'll give the signal if and when I need assist. I don't want a lot of sirens-in-the-night shit, understand?"

"Calm down, you're high as a kite. Understandably. But you know better than anyone this vigilante shit won't play. Now we can—"

"I'm hanging up."

"Goddammit, let me help!"

"Have you been listening to any fucking thing I've said?"

"Kirk, for chrissake! I love her too! I love you both! Now, listen to an objective voice—"

"Forget it, I should have known."

"Don't hang up! Shit! Wait a second!"

Kirk felt tears behind his eyes. Poor David.

"Are you there?"

"I'm here."

"All right. Okay. We'll do it your way for now, but do me one little favor and keep in touch, huh?"

"Right."

"Now, where's this guy headed?"

"West."

"Come on."

"That's all you get for now. I'll call tonight and brief you. Believe me, when it's time for the big artillery you'll be the first to know."

"What's he want, is he saying yet?"

"Depends on your interpretation. Stay near a phone, huh?"

"Here or at home, I promise. Don't let it get cold, Kirk."

"I don't think that's the problem." He hung up.

David hung up too. He stared at the phone. Tapped the pencil eraser on the pad. Chewed his lip.

He snatched up the receiver and dialed a number. While it rang he looked askance at the idle office movement of a slow Monday. A voice came on the line.

"Talk."

"It's David Kirkland. I need some muscle."

* * *

Kirk drove back down Grand to get on the highway, 35 West.

He was passing the bank again, not really looking, when he saw Jill standing in the lot in the warm sun holding something. She had one hand on her hip, eyes flicking in all directions.

He eased over, braking at the curb as she turned and spotted him. She came to the passenger's side with a frown. "Where'd you go?"

He squinted up at her. "Where'd *you* go?"

She held up the plastic cup of Coke. "I'm sorry, the car was an oven, I was parching. You were in there forever!"

He nearly smiled. In that ridiculous outfit she was all but bringing traffic to a halt.

"What's the decision?" he wanted to know.

She studied the straw, and he could sense her mind racing. Finally she dumped the cup in a green curbside barrel, turned, and got in.

She slammed the door, chewing her lip, staring straight ahead through the windshield as though she were ad-libbing her next thought: "All right. Okay. I'll stay. For now."

"Good." He put the car in gear.

"With a drop-out clause whenever it suits me."

"Agreed."

There seemed nothing else to say, so he pulled away from the curb and into the flow of traffic.

He glanced at his watch: just past eleven. Riff had a big head start now. It didn't matter, he could sense time wasn't important at all. Bigger things mattered. Time was just a state, an invisible something to push through, neither passive nor aggressive. It was what was on the other side, what was coming, that counted. It lurked at the periphery of his thoughts, a formless, black ambiguity.

He became aware that he was grinding his teeth, leaning forward unconsciously in the seat, speeding. He forced control, and it was like racing into whipped cream, but the last thing he wanted was the Highway Patrol.

He was assailed with the sudden, vivid sensation of dreaming, that this was a nightmare and the waking up would come sometime later in a world of sensible perspectives and rational continuities, not these fragmented, fractured sections. Perhaps if he closed his eyes . . .

He recognized the interstate sign and took the ramp, easing on dreamily, merging effortlessly and shifting into high, feeling the real game catching him up, propelling him outward. Weightless.

He glanced at Jill as he changed lanes: blond hair whipping from the open window, a fine line of sweat seeking the ample cleavage: day witch.

"Will we stop for lunch?" she inquired politely.

He hadn't thought about it. "Of course."

Good idea. He needed coffee.

Black. At least two cups.

He was bordering on mild hallucination.

Eight

He had picked, from her closet back in Chicago, one of her few formal evening dresses. She hadn't worn it in years, but she wore it now and found herself pleased that it looked neither too tight nor noticeably unstylish. He had selected a pair of dark shoes to go with the dress and an appropriately shaded bra and panties.

Something remarkable about his doing that, at once admirable and repellent. A passive violation.

Meg stood before the rusty little motel mirror and looked at herself, cocked her head, cocked it again.

What am I doing? Here I am in my best dress, or one of my best dresses, looking shockingly great for a woman of thirty-eight that has been abducted and peed on and brazenly bathed by a stranger, and probably drugged and dumped in this dump, and all I can think about is how I would look better still if I could get a permanent and have my nails done. Am I that godawful vain? Why the hell am I bothering to put on makeup at all? Whom do I think I'm looking pretty for? Why doesn't Kirk come rescue me? Where the goddamn hell is Kirk anyway?

She stared at her reflection.

And threw, almost without knowing it, the brush in her hand in one violent, unbidden movement. It hit the mirror a glancing blow, thankfully did not shatter it, and clattered to the sink.

There was an immediate light knocking. "Everything okay in there?"

She snatched up the brush and flicked savagely at her hair. "Yes, fine. I dropped my brush."

"We have a long drive till supper."

"All right, I'm coming."

She gave herself a final look.

He could have picked the other dress, the one that didn't go so well with my eyes, but he picked this one. He picked this one.

It was almost instinctive with him, that sort of thing. Like so many other things about him. Instinctive.

She threw the brush in her purse. It was irritating, his instinctiveness.

She paused, clutching the purse to her stomach, staring at the tips of her new black shoes. And it was something else too.

She came out of the bathroom and found him staring at the window. He had changed too: a dark blue dress suit, tie, evening shoes. He looked thinner, somewhat less imposing. More human?

Then she saw that the blinds were pulled on the window he was staring at, which meant he was staring at nothing, and the familiar unease returned to her stomach.

He turned, smiling cordially, as she came into the room. "Ready?"

"Yes."

"Got your things? We won't be back."

"I've got them."

"Hungry?"

She was, now that she thought about it. "Yes."

He stared at her a moment quietly. Then he said: "Are you all right, Mrs. Kirkland?"

She hesitated, curious. "Yes."

"You're sure? No broken bones, no abrasions?" He smiled as if this was all academic.

"I'm all right."

"You're sure, I mean, you'd tell me if you were hurt in any way?"

She folded her arms, waiting for the joke. "I'm perfectly all right, thank you."

He nodded with seeming satisfaction. He opened the door, bowed low, swept his arm out ostentatiously.

She walked through the door, stepped down the short step to the cement slab of porch. It was a lovely night, soft, balmy. She couldn't get over the stars. On any other occasion . . .

. . . it might have been nice, but why are you thinking about that now?

She moved to the edge of the porch, waiting for him to close the door, bring up the rear. For the briefest moment she enjoyed the silly fantasy of rushing to his car, starting the motor, and tearing away. But, of course, he had the key. She turned to see where he was and found only the open cabin door, no Riff.

Get out of here! Move!

But which way? And how far could she get on foot?

Go to the motel office, get help!

Too late, here he was coming through the door, smiling pleasantly, shutting it behind him. "Had to leave the room key."

You might have made it if you hadn't been mooning over the stars!

He joined her on the porch and gestured gallantly at the car. "Shall we eat?"

But it was hours before they did eat. He drove and drove, in utter silence, eyes flicking occasionally to the mirror, passing every roadside diner and restaurant in sight. Not that this was surprising, he doubtless had a prearranged location in mind, part of the "itinerary." She wouldn't have been surprised if they had reservations.

Which, it turned out, they did.

The place was called Chez Gloria. It was on the outskirts of a little town called Mountclef, about four hours west of the little motel. It was large and elegant and surprisingly chic for a seafood restaurant near a small town in the Midwest she'd never heard of. There were few guests—though the place seemed to be thriving—and no menus. The waiter, immaculately tailored and mannered, explained this evening's cuisine with rehearsed enunciation and took the order without referring to pad and pencil. The line and tableware were bone white, simple, and expensive. The music was piped in but unique and tasteful. The lighting was perfect: soft and glowing, gentle but romantic. She found herself ravenous.

Riff ordered for both of them without asking her. When the waiter left he turned to Meg graciously. "Forgive me: I know you weren't expecting the shark's fin soup in addition to the lobster thermador, but I think you'll like it. The preparation is excellent here."

She nodded, chin resting on her folded hands, still adjusting emotionally to this sudden contrast, in him, in her surroundings. It felt weird. Almost like a date. "That's fine."

She looked around the room at the softly talking couples, the silently moving waiters. She waved her hand at the air. "Isn't this all a bit—conspicuous?"

"Don't you like it?"

"Yes, it looks like a nice place to be discovered."

He laughed softly. "Kirk won't tell the police. Not yet. He'll come for you alone."

"Will he?"

"Trust me."

"Oh, *can* I?" she exclaimed with mock relief.

He grinned at the sarcasm. "It's an old game, but Kirk knows it. He may be a bit rusty, but he knows the rules. Just relax, if you can, and enjoy yourself for now. Anyway, you've been wanting to go to a place like this for some time." He grinned a private grin, waited for a response.

Her eyes narrowed. "Have I, now?"

He unfolded his napkin carefully, placed it on his lap with practiced ease as their appetizers arrived. His demeanor was nearly coy now, a shocking contrast to his earlier Marine Corps efficiency. He'd softened an inch, though she did not trust this to last or even to be genuine. It might have been part of the game. A game he very much coveted. He held great truths within, he seemed to be saying; if she was good he might confide them. "I mean, you and Kirk don't exactly have the same taste when it comes to dining out, do you?" To the waiter: "Thank you." To Meg: "To the extent you dine out at all, that is."

She picked up her own napkin. "Is that so?"

Her heart was beating rapidly again, not entirely, she suspected, from fear. It annoyed her.

He nodded, lathering yellow sauce onto her side plate. "You adore sea food, he tolerates it. Ergo, you get it rarely and, usually, poorly. Try the mustard sauce, it's extraordinary."

She stared at the food. Something about his confident manner made her want to dash the sauce in his face. And something else about him made her want to obey. She took a crisp golden shell from the warming basket and nibbled it daintily. "You seem to know all about us."

He smiled. A charming smile. He was, let's face it, charming just now, in a smug kind of way. A new evening, a new man. He could overplay it a fraction and blow it all. But he hadn't yet. And he was, after all, nothing if not instinctive. It occurred to her that he might be doing all this to put her at ease, further apologize for the lake, the whole abduction; soften his earlier abrasiveness. Clearly she was a necessary evil in his scheme, a bait probably. But an innocent. Maybe he recognized this and regretted what he thought of as unfortunate necessity. She watched his face.

Or maybe not. He didn't look like he'd ever regretted anything in his life.

"Well," he said, answering her, "I'm afraid I know a bit more about Kirk than you." He smiled his charming smile. "Not that I'm the least content with that status. I should like to know a great deal more about you, if you'll grant me the pleasure, of course."

The fritter was indeed delicious; she found herself unconsciously devouring it. "You like to get to know all the girls you pee on, that it?"

His laugh was explosive and unbidden; he barely had time to cover his mouth with the napkin. "Oh, God," he chuckled, wiping crumbs from his lips, "you're really going to have to forgive me that if we're going to go on together."

She studied the ruddy cheeks, the little handsome crinkles at the edge of his eyes. His mirth had sounded genuine. She found herself strangely pleased she'd been able to cause it. He wasn't the only one who could be charming. That was interesting: it didn't really make her any less vulnerable, but she was enjoying the illusion it did.

"So why did you do it?"

He examined a delicate silver dessert fork with strong but surprisingly slender fingers. "The peeing or the abducting?"

"Let's start with the former."

He smiled. "I think you must know it's a kind of ritual. Certainly not something I go about performing on women as a daily rule." He looked up at her. "Particularly beautiful women."

She could halt neither the flush nor the anger it brought nor the thrill in her stomach that followed the anger. Nor his eyes on her, acknowledging all.

Her cheeks burned. "I'm *real* flattered."

He laughed again. "It won't happen again." He held up a hand. "Scout's honor." He extended the hand, closed it over hers, dwarfing it. He lowered his head endearingly, looked up with little-boy apprehension. "Friends?"

"What about the kidnapping?" she asked impassively.

He toyed with the fork. "Ah, now that gets somewhat more convoluted. Do you really want to get into that"—his eyes swept the restaurant—"now?"

She looked away, shrugged. "It's your abduction."

He grinned. "Regrettably, yes."

She munched the last bite of fritter.

"Though I wish you wouldn't look upon it entirely in that light," he added.

"What should I look upon this as, prom night?"

He sighed, face suddenly inert. Even wistful? "I'd just like to make this as comfortable for you as possible, that's all. I know we can never truly be friends, but I'd like you to know that despite what you might think, feel, despite the scene at the lake, I have a great deal of respect for you. Perhaps, if you allow this to progress that far, you may begin to feel somewhat the same about me."

She watched him carefully, chewing slowly. Even insanity can be dealt with to a point, she was telling herself, even psychosis has its roots in reality. Just take this one step at a time, feel your way along. "How can I respect a man who threatens to murder me . . . *promises* to murder my husband? How can I do that?"

He put down the fork. Sighed again. He might actually have been sad. "Well," he said, and he said it to the tablecloth in a soft, nearly inaudible tone, "we all have to die."

That stopped her chewing for a moment.

Their wine arrived.

Riff looked up, smiled at the steward.

Meg didn't know wines, but the label Riff had ordered sounded expensive and the bottle looked dark and European and promising. The steward uncorked it expertly and handed the stopper to Riff, who whiffed it once and nodded. The steward moved to Meg's side, poured, bowed a fraction when she said, "Thank you." He poured for Riff, wished them a pleasant evening, and left.

Riff was watching her quietly.

Meg gazed at the bubbling liquid in the long-stemmed crystal.

"I'm sincere in my respect for you," Riff said softly, "but it pales in comparison to my respect for your husband."

She looked up. "Did you really know him in the war?"

His expression was unfathomable, blank. Then, abruptly, ebullient. "Ah, yes . . . the war, the war." He stared down at his wine. "Your husband was quite without equal, you know . . . quite without equal . . ." He sounded almost mesmerized, eyes on the tiny, bursting bubbles.

Meg watched him. "I'm afraid I don't know. Kirk never talked much about Vietnam."

Riff nodded. "He didn't know much about Vietnam."

She watched him, fingering the slender stem of her glass. "What do you mean?"

He stared downward, as if contemplating diving in there among all the giddy little bubbles. . . .

Then his head snapped up, eyes alight, as if he were coming back from somewhere far away. "We none of us knew much about what was going on—they kept it that way, the brass. Kirk, though . . . Kirk was remarkable . . . just really remarkable. A thorough soldier. Magnificent warrior."

She nodded. "I'm not surprised, his record with the company is pretty formidable. Did you know that he received more—"

"—awards in one year than any other man in private security, more civic awards in eight years than any other man in the business. I know. I'm his biggest fan."

Meg studied him. "Then why are you doing this?"

Again the almost saddened look. "To see if he'll come after me."

"Why?"

"Because he was the best."

"And for that you'll try to kill him?"

His face grew abruptly hard.

It was as if a wedge of solid ice had been driven between them.

Which he immediately attempted to melt with his quixotic smile.

"You'll notice, you said, 'try to kill him.' I didn't

say I could. He's the best, you know, among his peers. Maybe the best in the whole world. Certainly better than he knows. Maybe even better than me. We'll see. We'll see about that."

Some small part of her still refused to believe in any of this. But at least he was talking now. "You still haven't given me a reason."

He sat back, looked away a moment, pursed his lips as if searching for just the right phrasing. Then looked back at her. "To find out who's the best. So we'll both know."

She sagged. "That's absolutely childish."

He regarded her almost pathetically. "Oh, no . . . it's absolutely necessary."

She shook her head as if to clear it, let her eyes wander over the other tables for a moment. Then she said, "There's always going to be someone bigger, someone better. What's the point?"

He absently rubbed his chin, eyeing her wryly. "You mean you don't believe we're in charge of our own destinies?"

She thought a moment, shrugged. "Well, I don't believe we're in complete control of them, no."

His eyes crinkled warmly again. He shook his head at her admiringly. "You're a beautiful, perceptive woman, Meg Kirkland, and you're probably right. But"—and the sadness edged back quietly again—"some of us have to try."

Yes, she thought with sudden, complete conviction, he's quite mad. And I've got to do everything I can to get away from him and save Kirk. I've got to start thinking. She picked up the wineglass, strong with sudden resolve, and brought it to her lips.

And yelped as he slapped it from her mouth.

It hit the bone tablecloth and shattered musically, liquid gouting outward like a bright wound.

She trembled so abruptly, so violently, she could do nothing but stare at him impotently, saucer-eyed, and plead with her heart to stop slamming at her. Dear Christ, he's read my mind!

But he wasn't staring back, or even looking at her. He was signaling the waiter, snapping his fingers.

When the waiter hurried over, Riff set the broken glass upright perfunctorily, smiling. "We've had a little accident."

The waiter smiled graciously and began plucking up glass shards immediately. "Nothing to it, sir."

"And the wine," Riff added, shoving the bottle at him. "I'm afraid it won't do."

The waiter hesitated in his pluckings, looking personally affronted. "Another vintage, sir? I'll summon the steward . . ."

"No, we'll just stick with the water. Right, dear?"

Meg jumped as if she'd forgotten her turn. "What? Yes, that's fine."

"Very good, sir. *Bon appetit.*"

The waiter bowed with his hand full of shards and left.

They ate the rest of their dinner in silence.

Nine

"Tell me everything you know about Riff Walker."

They munched cold sandwiches in the car, not very good sandwiches, though Kirk hardly noticed this. He could tell from Jill's expression that she had wanted to stop and get out for a while, stretch her legs, ease her aching rump. His own posterior attested to this. She'd used the facilities in the little roadside diner they paused at, but the moment she was through, he'd hustled them back into the Nova with the white bag of sandwiches and black coffee and hit the road again. Even though his gut told him his wife was in no immediate danger, he couldn't allow himself the luxury of slowing down until it was absolutely necessary. Besides, he wanted to reach Dieter's little rundown shack before sundown.

"I wish there was something to tell," she offered, blowing out a weary breath, patting a moisture-soaked napkin against the back of her neck, making him wish he'd opted for the Nova with air conditioning. "Believe it or not, it's entirely possible to be married to someone and still not know him, really know him."

Kirk thought about Meg, let it go. "How did you meet?"

She sighed, mopping cleavage. "Not romantically, I assure you."

"How?"

"At a restaurant bar. The Cat and Fiddle on Sunset."

"Hollywood?"

"I was a film school brat fresh out of UCLA."

"Brat?"

"Well, semi-brat. You know, too young to run with the Spielberg crowd but jealous as hell. My senior thesis was a critical essay on the decline of the art of American cinema in our time, a rather obvious oxymoron when you think about it. 'Twentieth-Century Pox' I had the nerve to call it. Verbose with sophomoric platitudes about how Lucas and Carpenter and that whole baby mogul pack had led Hollywood to ruin under the misguided banner of Coppola. All they did—according to my theories—was take the best parts of Hitchcock, Ford, and Capra, stir them up, light everything for deep shadow, bake for twenty minutes, and come up with a recipe for pleasing postilliterate audiences weaned on sixties sitcoms. That kind of crap."

"Was it crap?"

"My essay? Oh sure, for the most part. I wrapped myself in the mantle of film noir and pretended to be above it all. I was just pissed because I'd missed the seventies wave of filmmakers and mostly because I was a woman. Women don't direct, in case you're wondering."

"Is that what you wanted to do?"

Jill considered, watching the rushing country: rows of wheat and barley, ruddy sun sinking westward, tingeing the sky pink. "I wanted to be in control of something. Myself, I guess. I certainly wasn't. Which was when I met Riff."

"In the bar."

"I was doing the rebellion routine with my parents, out of the house at nineteen, off to make it on my own as soon as I dreamed up a good cause. I had this English lit friend from school, Laurel Murdock. She called up one day out of the blue with the insane notion it would be mutually beneficial if we moved in together. She had one of those prewar bungalows off Melrose before Melrose became trendy and you could still find a steal. The place was a wreck, a flophouse for misplaced ambition. But I needed a vacation and I had to get out of the house. So."

"So?"

"Well, it didn't work out great. She had this alcoholic boyfriend who kept wanting us to sleep together while he watched. And this army of cats. Surrogate children or something, she couldn't have kids. Anyway, we had absolutely nothing to say to each other after the third day. My Jacques Tourneur crusade clashing head-on with her Jim Thompson crusade. She had this temple built to Thompson, all these original Lion edition paperbacks hermetically sealed in plastic that no one was allowed to touch. She'd lock herself in the bathroom with him for hours. I didn't ask. Have you ever read Thompson?"

"The Killer Inside Me."

"That's the best one. Anyway, we got on each other's nerves pretty fast. I finally gave in and fucked the boyfriend just to keep him off my back. He thought telling Laurel would be a brilliant idea, lead to a threesome. Laurel didn't see it that way. When it got bad, I borrowed her car and took a drive one night, ended up in the bar. I only stopped off to have a quick one, settle my nerves. Riff came over to my table and poured on the charm. I was in no mood, but you could see in a wink the guy had a terrific mind, knew about everything, just everything. It was all Truffaut's fault, he said, him and that bullshit auteur theory, ripping off postwar Alan Ladd movies and sucking Hitchcock's dick. Needless to say, I ate this up with a spoon. We were in bed together before the sun had set. He was even a better lover than he was an intellect. God, was I stupid. Young and built and stupid. I thought, now here's a man who sees beyond the tits to the woman that lies beneath. Right. Problem was there wasn't all that much beneath, not in those days."

Kirk looked over at her; she was dabbing her bosom with the napkin again. "Anyway, it went on that way for a while. I had no place to go and I couldn't bear the idea of Laurel's cats anymore. And I thought, what the hell, maybe this is love. We used to make love in the car up in the Hollywood hills, watch the sun come up. He was sweet. Self-absorbed, but so was everyone back then. And he could just bury me with that IQ. We dated before we were married for just under two months. Then on a whim we eloped to Las Vegas. In all that time I never asked him what he did for a living."

Kirk turned to her. "You're joking."

"Not in so many words. Something about government work. Covert stuff. I didn't even know what covert meant. I was so out of it, half stoned every night. Sex, drugs, and rock 'n' roll, that was my relationship with Riff. Then one day there wasn't any relationship . . ."

"He left you?"

"We were living in Wyoming by then. Riff was going to start a dude ranch. Maybe if I could have kept my hand off his crotch long enough, he would have." She heaved a great sigh, shook her head. "Anyway, once Riff was gone I woke up one day and realized that nobody in the real world wanted an ex-film school student whose sole area of expertise lay in a working knowledge of dead Japanese directors and vintage Warner Brothers cartoons. I put all that was left into the dude ranch idea and actually made it pay. Every time I had enough saved for a vacation, I went looking for Riff. This time I found him. In Chicago. I have absolutely no idea what on God's earth he was doing there." She turned to him. "Unless it was to study you."

Kirk made a noncommittal sound. "What did he say when you found him?"

She stared ahead solemnly for a moment, then smiled. "He said, 'Hiya, Jill honey! How about dinner?' "

"What did you say?"

"I said go to hell and where's my alimony?"

"And what did he say?"

"He said, swap you for an incredible fuck instead."

Kirk watched her. "And—?"

Jill sighed, shrugged. "I fucked him, of course. Then asked again about the alimony. I figured my chances for the latter were slim, but I might as well get something for all my trouble. Riff could make one evening in bed pay for a lifetime of alimony, or almost. Bastard."

Kirk shook his head at a passing cow. "What a man."

Jill snorted. "He just knows the buttons. There aren't that many."

"How'd you end up at my place?"

"After two or three days in bed at the best hotel in Chicago, he began to talk about you. Incessantly. He'd become very animated. His eyes would light up, he'd get this faraway look. I said, he sounds like a great guy, why don't you marry him? He said, let's go see him, he lives right here in town! I suggested we call, he said that would spoil the surprise. You know the rest."

Kirk studied the road.

"He mentioned our war experience together?"

Jill nodded. "Some. Mostly you were just the greatest guy in the world. I believed him, he spoke with genuine affection, or genuine respect, anyway." She turned to him in the seat. "Were you really a war hero?"

Kirk shrugged. "I guess."

"What did you do?"

He shouldered sweat from his brow. "It's a long story."

Jill picked up the black-and-white photo of Dieter's tattered house. "How long 'til we get here?"

"Another hour."

"We've got time, then. Tell me."

Kirk adjusted his itching backside in the seat. "You know much about the war in 'Nam?"

"I know nobody liked it."

His smile was mirthless, wry. "Some liked it well enough. Anyway, you're right it wasn't generally popular, no more there among the grunts than here in polite society."

"What's a 'grunt'?"

"Anyone with less than three stripes on his arm. Which was everybody in my platoon but the captain, and he had the brains of a grunt. Or worse." He shook his head incredulously, remembering. "Captain Ethan Ross, 442nd Combat Engineers, Third Battallion. What an asshole."

He took another swig of coffee from his styrofoam cup.

"I got into it just after the '68 Tet offensive. Charlie was clobbering the shit out of everyone, but he was really clobbering anyone on the ground trying to build bridges and float tanks, which is what we were doing. The monsoons and the jungle made it bad enough, but with slopes running all over the place in black pajamas, popping you off from behind trees or hiding dung-smeared pungi stakes for you to step on, it was just about impossible. I saw a guy step on one of those things once that went through his arch right up to the swimmer's tendon;

he walked ten yards without even knowing it until the guy behind him saw the blood. Christ, your feet were so eaten up by jungle rot and mosquitoes, you didn't feel your own fuckin' toes half the time."

Jill watched him, marveling at his subconscious slip in vocabulary as he relived a time that must have been akin to a life on another planet.

"Anyway, we were trying to construct these bridges like I said and getting the shit kicked out of us. Charlie was a tough little nut, and he knew the lay of the land. He could go all day on an hour of sleep and a handful of rice, and if you actually did drop him, six more black pajamas took his place." He shook his head again. "Goddamn tire feet."

"Tire feet?"

"They used to make their thongs from pieces of treads from our blown-up half-tracks. They were making fools of us. And Captain Ross was a ninety-day wonder straight out of college ROTC, didn't know his ass from his elbow, had us doing maneuvers on open roads, for chrissake, cannon fodder for the gooks. I mean the Cong. After the first half-dozen casualties or so, the men got real edgy about open roads. Some of them refused to march altogether. Ross always put them up front. Asshole. There wasn't a goddamn thing you could do about it, not in the daytime."

A sardonic smile crept over Kirk's face, his eyes looked very far away. "But at night things cooled down a little. At night we were on our own. We took shifts while the others slept, the others including Captain Ross. One night I was awakened by a rustling sound—I was always a light sleeper. It was

Jackson's turn at guard. I looked up and saw him moving slowly into the jungle, his weapon at port. It was against the rules, leaving the others open like that. I should have reported it, but I got curious, slipped on my boots, and followed. Jackson was a good soldier, I knew he must be up to something. I followed at a distance I knew he wouldn't hear me from. All I had was my field knife. After about five minutes, it started getting interesting: the hunter became the hunted, Charlie was stalking Jackson. I hung back until I was sure it was only one Cong, probably on reconnaissance or something, then I crept up behind him and cut the bugger's throat. Jackson turns around with eyes like saucers. 'What the fuck are you doin' out here?' I asks him. He says he thought he heard something. We both looked down at the dead Cong. We went back to camp and never said another word about it, but I could see the admiration in Jackson's eyes. The next night he nudged me awake with the toe of his boot. He didn't say a word, just nodded at the jungle. I grabbed my knife and we went out together, silent as panthers. Jackson left his rifle behind this time too. It was crazy, reckless, probably stupid. We got two of them that night. When we got back to camp, Ernie Little was waiting for us. He'd come that close to waking the captain, but since he hated the bastard as much as everyone else, he decided to wait a few minutes and see what we were up to. He grinned all over when he found out. It was great: we were beating the fuckin' enemy at his own game.

"The next day we weren't bothered so much by

raiding Cong. The captain attributed it to the rain. We kept our mouths shut. That night we got three more of them: me, Jackson, and Little. We got good at it. Then very good. Little had studied a lot of American Indian folklore. He claimed to be part Sioux, said his real name was Little Feather. He taught us about moving, about walking in the jungle without making noise. About how to wear our clothing—which was just about no clothing at all—so we could feel the breeze on our skin, sense heat. He taught us how to smell, how to recognize the odor of enemy campfires by what they ate, what wood they used. And he mostly taught us how to listen. We learned fast, and I guess I learned fastest of all. Little said I was a natural. We began to keep score, to compete. But the funny thing was, the more bodies we racked up, the less reckless we became. In order to learn to kill efficiently with only a knife, you have to become more careful, not less. You have to learn to move like the wind, silently, and hear like a hawk. And you have to learn patience. And . . . and you have to learn to like it. We loved it. Not because of bloodlust or any of that crap, but because somebody was finally making a monkey out of Charlie. And Charlie, believe me, knew it. And he was scared. He was terrified. He was on the fuckin' run. Oh, we'd find an occasional retaliation, sure. We found a guy from C Company one day hanging from the trees, dick and balls cut off, stuffed in his mouth, that kind of shit. It shook the others bad, but the three of us just grinned tightly and poured it on all the more the next night. It was weird: America had its war with Vietnam and we had ours. Funny thing, we were winning. If Westmoreland had had more like us, we'd have mopped up that little country. I'm not bragging, Jill, we were that good. Hell, if he'd have been in the territory, we could have sneaked in and stolen Ho Chi Minh himself out of bed.

"Anyway, it got around camp pretty fast. The men all knew who we were, what we were doing, and they kept tight about it, though you could see the look in their eyes, the admiration, the envy . . . the gratitude. We were like a private club there for a while, with a strict and rigorous membership. For a time I think there may have been more than six of us. Some got killed. Some transferred. But we cut a swath there for a while . . . we cut a hell of a swath.

"Then one day this jeep pulls into camp loaded down with brass, and the next thing I know me and Jackson and Little and two other guys are being hauled off for Saigon. We spent six months in the stockade, three more months of R and R in an army hospital for 'battle fatigue,' and then it was stateside and for us the war was over."

Jill was riveted. "What happened?"

Kirk shrugged. "Who knows? Maybe someone squealed or maybe our fame just spread that far by then. Whatever the case, they shut us down. I think they thought we were a bunch of iconoclast psychos, maladjusted hippies or something. Hell, maybe by that time we were. You should never have to kill, but you should definitely never have to kill *that* much. It inures you to it. And that sort of defeats the point, right?"

Jill shook her head slowly, watching him. "Jesus," she whispered.

He looked over at her. "That was a long time ago, Jill."

She looked back at the road. "Maybe not for Riff."

Kirk shook his head. "Riff wasn't there."

"It sounds like he was."

"No, I'd remember. I knew every one of those faces. We were like brothers. We'd have died for each other. We did die for each other. Riff wasn't a Crawler, he wasn't even in my platoon."

"Is that what you called yourselves?"

"Yeah, the Nightcrawlers." Shaking his head. "Crazy . . ."

"Maybe Riff was in a neighboring platoon. Maybe he heard about you guys and wanted to be one of the group but didn't have the guts."

Kirk looked at her. "And he's trying to make up for it now, by stealing my wife?"

She shrugged. "You said yourself you guys were good enough to steal Ho Chi Minh right out of bed. And maybe your image stuck with him, a kind of symbol, the hero he always wanted to be but could never measure up to."

Kirk considered. "Don't people usually revere their heroes?"

"Normal people. I wouldn't say Riff is behaving exactly normally, would you? Haven't you ever heard that phrase, man always kills the thing he loves? John Lennon had a fan like that, remember?"

Kirk nodded slowly. Maybe, maybe. It might fit. Kirk had seen guys like that in the army, even later on at the police academy. Guys always on the periphery of the action, dogfaces with pimples and glasses and sunken chests, watching and admiring and secretly hating. The skinny, owl-faced types that always fucked up on the rifle range and always marched out of step and always ended up on K.P. or cleaning the latrine.

Riff might have been like that. A kid who was picked on all his life, laughed at, made fun of, got zilch attention from the opposite sex. A kid like that would have been discharged like everyone else, would have grown up, gotten a job, even gotten married, all the while boiling and building and raging inside. Until one day it comes to a head, one day his boss yells at him, his kid screams at him, a perfect stranger says just the wrong thing at just the right time, and all the years of derision and failure finally find a focus, finally burst forth in one great white-hot image of hatred: John Kirkland, Vietnam hero.

Yes, it was possible.

Except for one thing.

"Riff Walker's not exactly the high school nerd type."

"I didn't say he was anemic. Just passive. Besides, even boys with slight builds can grow up with muscles if they work at it."

Kirk conceded that. "Maybe."

Maybe it did fit.

Maybe that's all Riff Walker wanted, to best Kirk in a fight. But how? Fists? Knives? Pistols at twenty paces?

He shrugged away another band of sweat.

Something was missing. You don't abduct a man's wife, then send that man chasing all over the place if all you want to do is prove you can lick him.

There had to be more to it than that.

They sat across the street from the little tin-roofed house with the broken picket fence.

It was nearly dusk, but there was still enough light to see the other broken-down little houses and the potholes in the broken-down street and the broken-down dogs rummaging in overturned garbage cans and the broken-down people shuffling along the weed-choked sidewalks with their brown bags of whiskey and their tattered clothing and their broken-down dreams.

Jill shook her head solemnly, eyes roving the debris-strewn yards and shoeless, dirt-smudged children. She made a sucking sound with her mouth. "Jesus, kids have to live in this."

Kirk rechecked the chamber of the .38, snapping it closed again with a twist of his wrist. "All over the world, sweetie. Here, I want you to hang on to this. It's a rough neighborhood and it's getting dark. Try to fire a warning shot into the air first—I'll hear it."

Jill took the gun gingerly, holding it like an alien utensil. "It's heavy."

"You ever fired a gun before?"

She looked briefly offended. "Why don't I just go with you? Is Dieter that dangerous?"

He shook his head. "Dieter's blind. It's his son I'm concerned about. He'd be about nineteen by now. Put that in your purse."

She did as she was told. "You never did tell me what it was you did to him."

He paused, hand on the door handle. He settled back a moment. "It wasn't . . . him, exactly."

She waited. "Oh?"

He took the hand away from the door, looked back toward the little decayng house. The sky was bloody behind it now. "I killed his other son. Or at least that's what some people think."

Her voice softened. "In the line of duty, you mean."

He didn't answer for a moment. "It was about four years ago, downtown Chicago. He was a runaway, a dope dealer. I was working private security at a pharmaceutical company nights when he tried to break in. I chased him into an abandoned factory. He was packing, got off a few shots before we entered the building."

She leaned forward. "Go on."

"It was dark in there. I had to keep hidden most of the time to avoid a slug through the head. I chased him up to the third floor of this place, dust and cobwebs and . . . darkness . . ."

Jill watched his eyes, those faraway, mesmeric eyes she'd seen before: eyes dark and unfocused. Or focused on things not of their current surroundings.

"He was sitting on this narrow catwalk . . . sitting there watching me on this rickety old catwalk suspended high above the floor of the building. It was . . . it was like a pit down there, a vast, black pit with no bottom. Like an elevator shaft falling away to China. This kid, he was just so scared . . . if you could have seen his face, his eyes . . . like saucers."

Jill licked lips gone suddenly dry. "And then what happened?"

"The catwalk gave way."

"Oh, God."

"He'd got a running start, managed to grab onto the lip of the floor I was standing on. Only . . . he was below me, dangling there below me, looking up. I couldn't reach him, I couldn't reach the little shit!"

"Easy."

He ran a hand across his face. "I climbed over the railing, tried to get a handhold of some kind, tried to reach down there in the dark and grab him. And then, all at once, he wasn't there anymore."

"He fell?"

"A lot of the local people didn't think so. They thought the pig cop didn't do his job to full capacity. His brother was even convinced I'd pushed him."

"That's ridiculous."

"Tell him that. Anyway, things got pretty fuzzy after the kid dropped. I don't even remember coming down out of the building; the next thing I knew I was standing out on the street in the bright sun next to Dave. He's my brother, he owns the security firm I work for—used to work for. . . . Higgins and Murphy did the mop-up. Dave sent me home. Home became retirement. End of story, and career."

"Your own brother got rid of you?"

He looked back at the little house, deep in

shadow now from the sinking sun. "Oh, it's not that he didn't believe me, more that I was having trouble reconstructing the pieces. That I got dizzy every time I tried. It didn't make a terrific report, I can tell you. Which may have had something to do with the fact that I was asked politely to fade away."

He saw the look on her face. "It was okay, I was ready anyway, tired of getting my ass shot off. Pretty much fucked up my marriage, though."

"The incident or the retirement?"

His eyes were unfocused again. "I went to see the kid's old man out here in the boonies. He just sat there in his rocking chair and stared at me with his blind eyes and didn't say anything after I told him who I was. His fifteen-year-old boy didn't say anything either, but he wasn't blind and there was murder in his eyes. Dieter offered me a drink and I was so grateful I took it, and we sat there in that smelly little house with the tin roof listening to the rats and getting drunk and talking about how he used to farm and how the country had changed and just about anything but his dead son or what had happened. When the old man fell asleep, I left. The boy never took his eyes off me. I kept waiting for a Saturday night special in the back all the way down the front walk to the car."

Jill blinked. She looked down at the seat, picked up the black-and-white photo of the house. "Why on earth would Riff send you here?"

Kirk sighed. "Who knows? To punish me? Endanger me? Test me? If he knew anything about the case, he must know how painful this would be. How potentially dangerous if Dieter's other son is still vengeful. I don't know, Jill." He shook his head slowly. "It's either a sick, twisted joke or a brilliantly conceived game of some kind."

He grabbed the door handle again. "But it's the only clue I've got to Meg."

He got out of the car, hurried up the front walk, avoiding discarded beer cans and piles of debris. He thought about hurrying up Sally's front walk earlier today and what that had wrought. He wondered if another fistfight awaited him behind this little paint-flaking door; God, he hoped not, he was tired. Physically and emotionally drained. It had been a long drive out here, and he'd been on edge the whole way. He was running on vapors, needed a rest badly.

If he could rest.

He rapped at the thin wood of the weather-scarred door, but before the third rap was even completed it flew back and an angry-looking black adolescent stood there scowling at him, dark skin framed against a darker interior. A familiar odor wafted toward Kirk: the odor of staleness and poverty and hot-plate meals and forgotten hope.

"The fuck you want?"

The voice was low and mean, honed with youthful arrogance and poverty venom. Muscles rippled beneath a tight, tie-dyed T-shirt, sleeves ripped off at the shoulders, exposing ebony skin so bright with sinew it made Kirk nostalgic with envy.

Kirk shifted warily on the crumbling porch, longing for the days when the flash of a shield would admit him anywhere. Not that it would have impressed this kid much. He knew exactly who Kirk was. He'd been waiting. Scratch any hope of a peaceful reunion. "I'd like to see your father, please. I'm a—"

"I know who you are, suckah. You got some big white balls comin' in this neighborhood, even if you is packed. My brother had friends here. Toros don't forget."

Toros. That would be the name of his gang. This young soldier was doubtless a member now, a daily reminder to the others of his martyred sibling. Christ, this could be suicidal, and Jill was alone in the car, those big cantaloupes straining at the yellow halter top.

For just a moment he actually considered retreat.

"Let the man in, Lamar."

The aged voice sounded familiar but weaker.

Lamar turned a thick, corded neck. "It's the white trash that killed Joey, Daddy."

"I know who it is, son, let the man in."

The adolescent glared defiantly at Kirk for a few heartbeats, then pulled back the door resentfully. He waited until Kirk was inside before spitting a wadded challenge at Kirk's shoe. The wad missed, splaying gelatinously across warped floorboards, but the challenge was right on target. Kirk ignored it and moved into the dark little room where Kirby Dieter sat gray-haired and bent before a three-legged canasta table dealing himself a hand of solitaire. The old man took a pull of Coors as Kirk came near, and a twisted, arthritic claw motioned to a chair opposite his own. "Ain't got no more beer, but sit for a spell anyhow. Lamar, finish up in back."

"You gonna sit with this trash, Daddy?"

"I'm goin' box yer ears, you don't listen your old man."

Lamar retreated into shadow, certainly from respect, not fear.

Kirk took a warped metal seat that complained rustily under his weight. He gazed into blue-glazed eyes, week-old stubble, a face carved from poverty, struggle, and a wisdom that was beyond poignant. "Hello, Mr. Dieter."

"Mr. Kirkland. Keeping well?" Gnarled talons plucked expertly at numbered pasteboard, placing kings, arranging jacks.

"Well enough. And you?"

Dieter snapped the cards into place before him with yellow-nailed fingers. "Well, I can't complain. When you ain't got nothin', it don't get broke."

Kirk let himself smile. His eyes swept the rumpled bed, torn wallpaper, precariously leaning dresser, silt-filmed windows.

"Blackjack your game, Mr. Kirkland?"

Kirk leaned back. "Beat the whiskers off you."

Dieter cackled, showed snaggled bridgework, slapped the table soundly. "Hot damn! Put your money down, sir!"

Kirk fished in his wallet. "Okay. But ones only, huh? I'm a little low today." He threw down a fifty-dollar bill.

Dieter nodded, fingering the fifty. "You'll spot me this first round?"

Kirk smiled. "Sure."

Dieter shuffled gleefully. "I'll just deal so's you don't succumb to temptation and peek." He manipulated the cards like a Vegas pro and dealt each of them two facedown.

Kirk scooped his up. He remarked casually: "Life treating you all right, then, Mr. Dieter?"

"Tolerable."

Kirk nodded. "Nothing unusual going on, no problems since our last conversation? No prowlers, things of that nature?"

The old man scratched bony chest under ragged plaid shirt. "The poor don't steal from the poor. But your friend's been here, if that's what you mean." He dealt himself another card.

Kirk looked past his cards. "What friend would that be, Mr. Dieter? Hit me."

Dieter dealt him a card. "Well now, I wouldn't rightly know, he ain't my friend. You standin'?"

Kirk looked at his hand. "Yeah."

Dieter laid down a jack and an ace. "Twenty-one!" He chuckled behind blind eyes, making the frail shoulders dance.

Kirk tossed him his cards. "Nineteen. What did he say, this friend of mine?"

Dieter shuffled. "Oh now, he didn't say a word. He mostly just creeped around the house a bit. Late at night, Lamar never heard him. Don't yet know how he got in. Clever fella. Moved like a cat. Had the funniest feelin' he knew I was lyin' there listenin.' Any idea who he is?"

Kirk watched the glazed eyes. "What makes you think he was a friend of mine?" he asked carefully.

Dieter held up the deck of cards. "Yer wonderin' how I do it." He motioned Kirk closer with his free hand. "Have a look here at the left-hand edge. See the cuts? No? Look closer . . ." He thrust the deck in Kirk's general direction. Kirk noted the tiny, almost indiscernible slits along one side.

"Numbers on the left side. Diamond's at the right corner, spades the left, queen halfway down, king top middle and so on. Ain't no way to beat me in a real game!" He grinned and showed his picket-fence teeth. Then the grin dissolved.

Dieter lowered the cards to the table, glazed eyes watching them. "You're older, Mr. Kirkland, older than last time. Hear it in your voice. Years ain't been kind?"

Kirk closed his cards together into a single fat seven of hearts. "Not very, Mr. Dieter."

The old man nodded knowingly. "That a shame. Life ain't long enough it should be burdensome to a man." He shuffled the cards absently. "Thought maybe you'd be back again afore now, maybe play a little poker. I'd let you win, sometimes."

Kirk smiled wanly. "I . . . didn't know what to say."

Dieter shrugged. "Just playin' cards with an old blind nigger's sayin' somethin'. Time you let it go anyhow. I did. Time you did. It was an accident."

Kirk swallowed, felt something move behind his eyes.

"I been checkin' on you. I got my ways. You ain't that kind of man, Mr. Kirkland. You an unhappy man, but you ain't that kind of man. You got no prejudices again niggers, and you sure ain't got none agin young boys, hopheads or no. The boy was stoned. He was always stoned. Probably thought he could fly. His mother was a beautiful woman, you believe that lookin' at me?"

"Yes, I do."

"Well, she was indeed a beautiful woman. And she loved the boy, and she taught him well. Only thing, the other boys taught him too, and you can't be there all the time, can you?"

"No, sir, you certainly can't."

"No, indeed. She died birthin' Lamar, you know. Wish she'd been around to teach him. He's full of the hate. We old folks, we accepted it best we could, but the young today . . . full of the hate, like a cancer. He's layin' for you, Lamar is."

"I know that."

"Only reason I'm not sorry you didn't come around again for cards, 'count of Lamar. He'll lose the hate. He's young. The old don't hate, they just grateful for what they got. It were an accident, Mr. Kirkland. Time you let it go."

Kirk said nothing.

Dieter grinned. "Wanna see a card trick?"

"Sure."

Dieter flipped the deck rapidly through his nimble fingers. He withdrew two cards, handed them to Kirk: a six of diamonds and a five of hearts. "What you think of that now?"

Kirk looked at the cards. "What am I supposed to think of it?"

Dieter shrugged, shuffled again. "Nothin' much 'cept I ain't got no idee what them cards is, and without 'em there's still fifty-two in this here deck."

Kirk studied the two cards in his hand, ran his

finger down the smooth, unserrated edges. "Someone put them in there."

Dieter nodded. "Two nights ago when he was creepin' around the house. What are they?"

"A six of diamonds and a five of hearts."

"Uh-huh. Hope that means somethin' to you 'cause I don't believe the message was for me."

Kirk turned the cards over, inspecting every inch of them. Just a couple of Bicycle playing cards.

"It's a kind of game," Kirk said at last, "like a treasure hunt."

"Uh-huh. What the treasure?"

Kirk put the cards in his shirt pocket. "Somebody's life, I suspect."

Dieter nodded. "I see. You best be on your way, then."

"I think so. Thank you, Mr. Dieter." He stood. "For everything."

"Thank you for the game, sir." Dieter held up the fifty-dollar bill. "Next time I'll clean out yer wallet!"

Kirk grinned. "Next time." He turned, then turned back. "May I shake your hand, sir?"

Dieter extended a claw.

Kirk took it firmly. "I'm sorry about your boy, Mr. Dieter."

The old man nodded. "I'm sorry it took you so long to tell me. We could have had us some good card games." He held onto the hand. "I think you got troubles way down . . . down deep beyond my son. Deeper even than this here card business with your friend. I hope you learn to see them someday."

Kirk swallowed thickly. A blind man wishing him the ability to see.

At the door, Dieter called to him. He waved the fifty in the air. "Ain't no Washington head, is it?"

Kirk shook his head. "No, it's not, sir."

Dieter grinned. "But I'll take it anyway 'cause I know it ain't no charity neither."

"It's not charity, Mr. Dieter. Good-bye, sir."

Lamar was waiting in the front yard.

He stepped out from behind the big oak about ten yards from the car, and there was just no way to avoid him. He shouldered in front of Kirk.

"It ain't that easy, whitey. You got to pay for my brother."

Kirk heard the "snik," and didn't have to see the shiny switchable in the gathering dark.

Lamar held it up for him anyway. "Go for that piece on your shoulder. I'll give you more a chance than you gave Joey."

Kirk was so full of sudden, untethered anger he had to consciously hold himself back.

"Listen to me, Lamar: I've driven a long way, and I've got a long way yet to go. I'm tired and I'm depressed and I'm sorry about your brother, but if it weren't for your old man in there I'd take that pig sticker and shove it so far up your ass you'd need a miner's helmet to find it. Now get the hell out of my way."

Kirk started past. Lamar shouldered in front again. "Fuck you, pig!"

Kirk started past again, and this time Lamar made his move with the knife.

It was fast, but Kirk had long before calculated for youth and speed and street-fighting technique, and when the knife came up and at him, he simply wasn't there anymore. Oh, he was enough there to get a scrape along the forearm—enough of a scrape to remind him of his age and his lack of practice—but the knife wasn't even that sharp and by the time Lamar had recovered for the next jab, Kirk was behind him, and then beside him, and then behind him again until Lamar was staggering around the front yard in a drunken little impotent dance that left him looking silly and feeling enraged. The rage made him reckless, as it was supposed to do, made him swing wilder and dance sillier, and no matter where he sent the knife, Kirk managed to be somewhere else. Until Lamar was gasping and cursing and, finally, crying and screaming: "Motherfucker! Motherfucker, stand still!"

He was finally obliged to haul off and throw the knife, and Kirk was not there for that one either—the knife clattered harmlessly across the sidewalk—and by the time Lamar made one last dizzy attempt to launch himself bodily at the flitting ex-cop, the adolescent was exhausted and crazy and a full-fledged target himself. Kirk feinted to one side, hooked a shoe around the boy's ankle, and sent him crashing heavily to the debris-strewn grass, where he didn't move for a time.

Kirk got into the car and slammed the door behind him and locked it.

When he looked down at his hands, they weren't even trembling.

Jill's mouth was hanging open, a look of awed stupefaction on her face. "Jesus, that was just incredible! I've never seen anything like that! Are you okay?"

Kirk turned to her in the seat, his face serene. It frightened him how great he felt.

She touched his shoulder admiringly. "That was some kind of oriental fighting, wasn't it? Incredible! Are you scared? You didn't look scared. What do you call that kind of fighting?"

He blinked reflectively at her. "Tai chi, I think. It's oriental. The art of fighting without fighting."

"You 'think'? Where'd you learn it, in the army?"

And now he wore a puzzled look. "I guess I must have."

Ten

They left the restaurant at 11:05, having said little or nothing through their meal after the incident with the wineglass.

Meg thought several times about breaking away at some point during the course of the meal, leaping up suddenly, and screaming, *"Kidnapping!"*—heading for the nearest exit. She thought about it. But she did nothing. It was Riff. He was just too powerful a presence, too all-consuming an entity. He'd be on her in a flash, like a spider on an insect, breaking her neck with a single sharp blow, then vanishing from the restaurant before anyone knew he'd even been there. Or maybe she would escape, tear herself away somehow, contact the authorities, find herself under police protection. And then, just when she thought herself safest, there would come that one brief moment when she was alone, maybe asleep, maybe in a bathroom somewhere—only to look up and find that she was not alone at all, that he had come, and her life was over.

He exuded that kind of power, perpetuated the

illusion he could fade through walls. It was his absolute cool, detached calm, his unwavering confidence as he'd sat there leisurely forking food into his mouth. You just knew he was in control of the situation, of any situation he was involved with. You just knew he would win. It was intimidating beyond anything she'd ever experienced.

So she'd sat there. And ate. And didn't even ask for permission to go to the rest room. Because she was afraid he'd say no and the flat edge of anger would be in his voice and he would use the anger on her later.

She'd been terrified, there in the silence between them. It had made her heart pound and her senses tingle and her mind crystal-bright alert.

And it had made her feel very much alive. . . .

They drove into darkness, heading in what she thought was a westerly direction. She had no idea what the next stop was or what it would bring. She only wished that her heart would stop pounding and that he would say something and that things could be like they had been before he slapped the glass from her mouth, like they had been when he was being handsome and charming. That was very much preferable to this . . . to how it had been with him at the lake.

She sat quietly and watched the high beams throw ghostly illumination across the rushing branches overhead.

It was very dark out; they were deep into rural hills, bouncing over a paved but unkept country road, miles from the nearest superhighway. The

noise of the car seemed preternaturally loud, a
thing of oil and smoke invading solitudinous nature.
When she looked up, past the side window, the
Milky Way shone brilliantly with crystal detail.

It took several glances askance at him for her to
realize he was inordinately preoccupied with the
rearview mirror.

She took a chance and broke the silence.

"Is someone following us?"

He didn't answer for a time. When he did, there
was no trace of anger or resentment about the incident in the restaurant; it was as though that were
long forgotten. "Well," he replied calmly, gray eyes
still flicking to the rectangle of glass, "someone's always following us somewhere, aren't they?" It was
rhetorical. Which was a good thing because she
had absolutely no answer for it.

Her eyes sought the side mirror at her elbow. She
might have seen a brief trace of glow against the
black, undulating hills behind them but maybe not.
It could have been a car or it could have been
imagination.

"Here's a little game you probably played in high
school."

He reached out and turned off the headlights
completely.

Meg gasped. Blackness engulfed them.

He didn't slow the car, didn't flinch in the least.

It was like hurtling down a bottomless well, rushing toward infinity, and Meg found herself gripping
the upholstery with white-knuckled fingers, fighting
down her terror. Then she relaxed a notch: the dim
outlines of trees materialized before her receding

retina, the pale ribbon of road, fences, rocks, the moon. You could see quite plainly after a moment. It was undoubtedly dangerous, but you could see well enough. And there was no opposing traffic.

There was something dreamlike about it, barreling into endless night unheedingly like this, something almost ethereal. And in the end, relaxing. And at the end of the end: fun.

But she sensed the fun was for herself alone; there was a method behind his madness.

The car slowed now. Then crept to a halt.

Riff sat quietly, watching the mirror.

Meg could hear crickets. Her own breath.

The interior trembled nervously under the obediently idling motor. Silence.

She glanced at the side mirror: blackness.

Riff shifted smoothly and pulled ahead a few yards, then eased the car carefully onto a weed-choked shoulder, kept rolling across a shallow gully, bounced up to a stretch of starlit meadow. He pulled the vehicle toward a camouflaging copse of trees, cut the engine, sat still.

"What is it?" she whispered tensely.

He said nothing, sat unmoving—listening?

After a time he looked up at the blanket of twinkling stars. "Incredible, aren't they?"

Against the preceding stillness his voice was startling. She looked. "Yes, they are."

He stared upward. "Times like this I really long for a cigarette."

"I know what you mean."

"Bad for the old lungs, though."

"Yes."

"And the heart."

She made an affirmative sound.

He sighed. "But oh, for that first morning drag, huh?" He grinned at her and she smiled back uneasily.

It was still as death in the car.

"Are you tired?" he inquired politely.

"Not very."

He nodded. "Good. Would you do something for me, then?"

"What is it?"

"Would you take off your clothes, please?"

She stared blankly for a moment. But then she couldn't meet his eyes anymore.

So this was it. Finally. Well. At least he said please.

She hesitated. She could ask why, but that was rather forgone, wasn't it? She could say no. That was pretty forgone too. She could struggle. Yeah, sure.

She couldn't scream, that was for sure.

She could submit peaceably and hope he wouldn't hurt her.

Yes. That was about what she could do.

She reached for buttons. "All right."

It didn't take long to undress.

And she didn't even bother, once she was naked, to fold her arms across her breasts. What was the point? She just placed her hands lightly at her sides and waited, moonlight streaming coldly across her, giving her skin a glowing, otherworldly cast. She looked down at herself briefly and saw that the moonlight and deep, accentuating shadows made her breasts look rather beautiful, actually.

When she finally looked over at him, he was nearly naked too. She swallowed and tried to will her heart quiet, a thankless task.

He finally lay his socks neatly atop the rest of his clothes, also stacked neatly on the seat between them, and reached up and pulled the little plastic plate off the ceiling light and unscrewed the tiny bulb there. He turned to her, eyes glittering. He winked. "Let's do it!"

He opened the door and got out.

Oh, dear God, not in the wet grass.

He came around and opened her door for her. She got out, accepting his hand.

He shut the door softly and stood facing the moon, still holding her hand. Night wind kissed her genitals and she shivered once violently, not really from coldness. It was, in fact, quite warm out. He turned with a fierce smile and looked down at her. "Ready?"

"I'm ready," she whispered.

He ran. Pulling her bewilderingly along.

They charged across the open meadow, hand in hand, barefoot, clothesless, mindless, wind screaming in their ears, wet grass slapping at their feet, hearts thundering in their throats, starlight opening a soft, lustrous path. And the smells . . .

Clover. And birch. And newly formed sap. And the sweet, musky pungence of deep humus.

If the running alone wasn't making her breathless and dizzy, the intoxicating odors were. The bracingly inconceivable freshness of it all.

And he *kept* running! Kept pulling her along at a speed, a pace she never dreamed herself capable of, legs flashing white and muscular, arms pumping rhythmically, breasts swaying heavily, nipples taut and tender. Head thrown back to catch great gulping lungfuls of the rich, clean, overpoweringly aromatic night.

Until the legs would no longer flash, the arms no longer churn, the stars no longer twinkle under the gelatinous smear of wind-stung tears, and the body sagged, and stumbled, and collapsed like a rag doll to the heaving bosom of the undulating earth. It seemed to take a long time, the falling; it seemed to come from very high up and very far away, and it didn't hurt in the least because his arm was there and the soft clover was there and she was too deliriously drained to care anyway. She fell in a great tangle of weighted limps and whipping, moonlit hair, and giddy, dreamlike abandon.

She lay on her back, panting and heaving like a dog, unable to get enough of the sweet, delicious air, the grateful swath of cooling breeze, unable to stop the roaring in her ears, the distant booming that seemed to come up from the core of the earth itself and rock the convulsive drum of her chest.

And not until the spinning trees began to right themselves, not until the stars stopped their spiraling dance and her breath became a pleasant, aching wheeze, did her thoughts coalesce enough to actually form concrete images . . .

. . . and the images that formed startled her.

The images that formed were of Peter.

And it startled her because she hadn't thought

about Peter in years, decades. Not clearly anyway. And just now she was remembering him very clearly indeed, and the memories were sharp and delineated and crystal in their clarity.

Because the night, that long-ago, far-flung night of her evaporating youth had been exactly a night like this. Right down to the seductive summer breezes, right down to the marvelous smells and the soft bed of earth.

Right down to the naked figure gasping softly beside her.

They were cousins, she and Peter, first cousins that had spent a lot of time together during grade school days. But by the time junior high rolled around, Peter and his mother, Meg's mother's sister, had moved to faraway Missouri and bought a farm and set up a life as distant and alien to Meg as anything she could image. Peter wrote to her occasionally, and sent her strange pictures of dairy cows and hay-bailing machines while Meg lost herself in cashmere sweaters and suburban kissing parties. It was an entirely new Peter Richards she saw three summers later on a visit to the farm, and a taller, broader, more muscular Peter that took her for a bumpy ride on the tractor and threw paw-paw balls at her and raced her down to the lake on a summer night as clear as this one but degrees more hot and humid.

Peter had thought nothing about skinny dipping in the old lake, it being the chief form of entertainment in a life not redolent with varied forms of entertainment. Meg had followed suit both because the cloud-obscured moon would hide her budding breasts and because it would have been more embarrassing to refuse than concede and besides, there were only the two of them and they'd be dry before they got back to the farmhouse.

They swam until exhausted from exertion and laughter and then sprawled on the muddy bank and watched the parade of impossibly bright stars and the strobic dance of fireflies and told ghost stories and laughed some more. Never particularly conscious of their nudity until Peter just as unparticularly got an erection and rolled over quite unabashedly to show it to her.

Why it didn't embarrass her she still would not know years later, maybe because they'd known each other for so long, maybe because they'd spent half the evening naked anyway. But she couldn't stop looking at it. And he didn't seem to mind, lying there with his arms folded behind his head, somewhat fascinated with it himself, explaining all about how it sometimes did that on the bus, or in the classroom or anywhere at all for no particular reason, no reason at all. And when it began to unlimber somewhat, she wanted to know all about that too and why, when he touched it, it grew firm again and would it be all right if she tried and that was okay by him too.

She tried several times before the moon rose high and unwinkingly above the clouds and showed everything in a soft, pure light. She touched and she marveled and she petted and squeezed and she made little noises come from Peter's throat and she quite luxuriated and gloried in her power at doing this, and when he came, twice, she washed her hands in the lake and came back and tried again. The last time he came it was in her mouth, and she was sorry it was the last time because she wanted very much for him to come some more somewhere else, even though she didn't dare ask and it was long past time to go back. And once there, back in the harsh glare of the cinnamon-smelling kitchen, she could not bear to look at him nor he her, and her nightmares were vivid later in the lumpy farmhouse bed and full of drowning lake water and thrashing snakes and she was secretly glad when her mother had to be at work and it was time to go back to Chicago.

Lying here now next to naked Riff, still gathering her ragged breath, finding her dazzled senses, she had—insanely improbable as it seemed—the distinct sensation that he knew all this. Knew all about her past, the lake, the stars, Peter's laughing eyes and twitching cock. Knew it, was amused by it, and had somehow recreated the exact experience here in this meadow twenty years later. It was impossible, of course. He might know everything about Kirk, he might know quite a lot about her, their marriage, but he couldn't possibly know that! She had never told anyone, not even her closest girlfriend. The memory of that night still sent thrills of embarrassment through her. Of shame. They were cousins! It was wrong. Innocent enough, perhaps, in the callow light of youth, but wrong. No. He couldn't possibly know about that. It was just coincidence. Yes, that's what it was. He was formidable in his knowledge, his expertise, but he couldn't read minds.

Could he?

The idea, silly as it was, had its effect on her; she felt herself flaming red from the tip of her dew-flecked toes to the top of her tight-nippled breasts.

What did he want, this strange, enigmatic, *terrifying* man? What did he want from them?

She started again as his deep voice broke the cathedral hush. "Nothing like it, is there? Sometimes I think I could just go on running and running like that all night, just tearing along wild and free like an animal until I run out of ground altogether and just fall off the earth. Can you smell that? We're in eastern Kansas."

Kansas. Already. So far from home. She must have missed the signs.

She turned her head toward him. His grinning profile was outlined softly in a moonlit corona: handsome, almost savage. "Do you do this often?" It sounded more flippant than she'd intended; she prayed he wouldn't take offense.

He didn't, apparently. "When I get the chance. It's harder and harder these days."

She turned her next question over in her mind, considering carefully. "What is it you do?"

He retained the smile. "I'm what you might call . . . a servant of the people."

She pressed, trying to even the odds. "You mean like a doctor, or a policeman?"

He chuckled softly and there might have been a sardonic edge to it. "Well, more like a policeman than a doctor, certainly."

"Do you . . ." Her voice trailed off as she felt his

hand press gently against her tummy, large and warm.

She held her breath.

He turned his head slowly toward her. His voice was hardly audible. "Be very, very quiet. When I say so, I want you to sit up with me as slowly and quietly as you can. Just sit up, don't move." His hand left her stomach and sought her open hand, which he gripped. "Are you ready?"

She didn't recognize her voice. "Yes!"

"One . . . two . . . now!"

They rose in tandem in the moonlight.

She sat cross-legged beside him, feeling a fleeting wave of dizziness that passed quickly.

"Do you see it?" he asked quietly.

She squinted at the darkened cyclorama of trees. See what?

"To your left, about ten o'clock."

She shifted her gaze and caught the deer.

It was a female, a doe, a large one. It stood absolutely still in the silent meadow, head erect, turned toward them, watching them, eyes and nose like a triangle of black coals. It must have come into the meadow after they'd run, unheedful of their quiet talk as they rested. Now it realized it shared the meadow with them. It was less than fifty yards away.

Meg was thrilled. "It's beautiful," she murmured.

"Yes." There was sadness in his voice. "Our noblest, stupidest animal."

She glanced at him.

"We keep running them over, but they keep right on mindlessly fucking."

Her gaze shifted back to the doe; Riff was just too unfathomable.

The animal's left ear twitched once nervously, but other than that it remained absolutely frozen against the night. Meg sat frozen as well, wondering in this test of wills who would break the spell first. Riff leaned toward her a fraction. "Want to have some fun?"

"What—?"

He grinned his infectious grin. "Let's go get her!"

Meg looked appalled. "Catch a deer? Are you crazy?"

"I didn't say anything about catching!"

And with that he was up and she was being jerked after him with a surprised yelp and they were thudding off across the meadow again against the night wind before she even had time to think. The doe waited longer than Meg would have guessed a wild animal like that would—as if it too were having difficulty believing these two naked, insane humans were galloping around loose—then it finally bolted for the woods.

But the woods behind it was simply too compacted with trees and brush, and the startled creature was forced to change direction, pounce about in an elegant, indecisive circle, then come bounding directly toward them in graceful leaps. Meg screamed in delighted fear as it flashed past—close enough almost to touch—then screamed again with laughter as Riff pulled her around and they charged off in this new direction.

They chased about in almost a complete circle around the little meadow before the doe bounded casually toward an opening and disappeared with a muffled crashing into the thicket. It hadn't been all that afraid, Meg thought giddily, trying to find her breath again. It had almost been playing with them, seeing what it was these silly two-legged creatures thought they were doing stumbling clumsily after a fleet young doe. But what was amazing, what was so wonderfully exhilarating, was that at one point during the course of the chase, Meg had actually felt a kind of kinship with the deer—a kinship with nature itself. She had, for the briefest moment, become the deer, known its fear, its haste, but also its wild abandon and majesty, its unalterable link with all that is raw and untamed and real. It was a breathtaking moment she knew she would never forget. And—God help her—despite her plight, it was fun!

They paused at the edge of the thicket, and Riff let go of her and let her lean against a big birch and hold her sides and laugh and find her breath again.

He was grinning at her, hands on his hips as he sucked in air. "You run like a wild animal," he remarked between gasps. "Beautifully!"

Meg let her head hang down a moment, then threw it back with a great throaty whoosh. "Oh, God, that was marvelous! I've never done anything like that! You should feel my heart!"

Then, realizing what she'd said, and fearful he might interpret it as an invitation, she backed away demurely a few steps into the brush.

But he wasn't even watching her anymore. He was standing to one side, taking that big thing in his hands and letting go with another one of his famous streams at the weeds and rocks. She had seen more urinating in the past few hours than in her entire life! He took another deep, cleansing breath and turned to watch her, again without an iota of modesty. He nodded at her. "Go on. You haven't pissed all night. I know you have to."

She turned away, fingering her wind-blown hair. "It's all right . . ."

He sent a forceful stream at a tree trunk, creating a deep, drumming sound. "Go on, for chrissake. Who's watching? We're in the woods. You just chased a full-grown deer around like a berserk rabbit. I guess you can take a piss in the woods like the rest of the animals."

She turned her back. "I really don't have to—"

"Oh, bull! You know you do!"

It was true. She'd had to go for some time now. But this way? She wasn't at all sure . . .

She turned back quickly as he stepped toward her, naked feet crunching on fallen leaves. He reached out and took her hand. "Come on! Just like the cavemen! Squat!"

"No, really—"

"Squat!"

She squatted on command, knees bending with a snap of cartilage, hand clinging to his for support.

"Wasn't so hard. Now, let her go."

She looked away. A length of grass or weed caressed her vulva. She bit her lip.

"Look at me, Meg."

She gave him her upturned face. He was smiling warmly, unthreateningly. "Now, pee. Go on."

Her mouth fell. She untensed, looking right into

his eyes, and opened her bladder in a sudden hot rush. He squeezed her hand and she felt herself flame, blood rushing upward from her loins to fill her throbbing temples. But not, to her amazement, from modesty.

She dropped her eyes and found herself gazing at him again, a final drop of moisture clinging to the dark purple knob of his cock.

Something seemed to break inside her, something that held barriers against dark and ancient stirrings. The odor of pine and her own urine rose to meet her nostrils, causing them to flare. She felt a light-headed tingling, a sudden oneness with the earth and the stars and the endless eternity of time itself.

She received another warm squeeze from the big hand. "Feels nice, doesn't it?"

She nodded.

"All through?"

"Yes."

And he pulled her upright.

She gazed back out at the moon-swept meadow, wondering about silly things like toilet paper and washing her hands when she saw the figure.

It stood at the far edge of the clearing, cloaked entirely in shadow. It seemed to be staring at them.

It took her a moment to realize the significance. *Go! You're free!*

She was already tensed, already set to burst onto the meadow, rush forward shouting, waving her hands. But she hesitated. Riff, behind her, must have seen it too by now, nothing escaped him. And he wasn't saying anything.

She stood with her back to him, eyes glued to the distant silhouette, heart suddenly in her throat.

"Who is it?" Her whisper like a cold blade entering flesh.

Riff didn't breathe.

The distant figure stood silently, unmoving. Staring?

She could almost make herself believe it was a scarecrow, except that there was no need of a scarecrow out here in the wilderness.

She stood quietly, unmoving, even as the doe had stood a moment before, making herself breathe through her nose because breathing through her mouth sounded thunderous. She swallowed coppery bile, eyes luminous, every sense attuned to the night, to the darkened statue across the meadow. Wondering what there was about it that terrified her.

"Riff . . . ?"

She turned to him now.

And found him not there.

"Riff!"

Her head jerked in every direction, a cold stone forming in her stomach.

She was alone in the woods.

She spun, pain lancing her neck, eyes lurching back to the distant figure. A little animal moan started unbidden in her throat. The figure was moving toward her now, out of the shadows. It was a man.

She could discern no details, but he didn't appeared to hold any weapon. He made no threatening gesture.

A farmer maybe? A cop? But that didn't look like a uniform. What was he doing out here in the middle of nowhere?

Never mind, run to him! This is your chance!

Maybe it was merely her own nakedness. Maybe her exhausted mind. But she couldn't shake the numbing apprehension; it repelled her backward from the figure like an opposing magnet.

"Riff!"

She continued back with sightless steps, letting the leafy shadows envelop her.

The figure loomed larger.

Her heel found a twig, ankle twisting, throwing her awkwardly to one side, rustling leaves and limbs loudly; she caught herself at the last second on a protruding branch. She didn't know if the noise or her image protruded into the meadow or not, whether she had been spotted or heard or either. She didn't know what the man wanted. She didn't know where Riff had gone.

She knew only that for the first time since her abduction, she wished very, very much he was still there.

She kept stepping backward clumsily as the figure moved toward her. It was halfway across the meadow now.

"Riff, goddamn it!"

If she did that again, the figure would hear her for sure.

Could it see her? Riff had appeared luminescent in the milky moonlight—she must appear that way too.

Something slapped her naked backside.

She yelped, spinning, saw only a long-branched bush. She stepped around it and continued moving backward, hands thrust out behind her in the darkness like a blind person. When she looked back to the meadow, the figure was gone.

She stopped, sucking in cool night air.

She stood absolutely silent and unmoving, eyes straining toward the clearing, which appeared as a flat, glowing swatch now in a sea of ink. Her breathing was so loud it must be carrying for miles. But she could do nothing to alter it, or the sudden violent trembling of her knees.

She was unequivocally—profoundly—vulnerable.

The idea sent spasms rocking up her spine.

She heard a distant whimpering, like a lost, terrified animal, realized it was coming from her.

Where the goddamn hell was Riff!

The silence was thunderous.

She remembered reading somewhere about a skin diver who had descending into nighttime waters, and how the surrounding blackness had seemed abruptly alive with sharks.

An overwhelming sensation of something creeping up behind seized her; her naked back and white buttocks were like a flag.

Very carefully, very slowly, Meg began to turn around, taking little mincing half steps, wincing when her shoeless feet struck a stick or pebble.

Eyes now averted from the flowing patch of meadow, she encountered only soundless ebony; she might have been spinning at the bottom of a well.

She screamed as something rushed past her ankle, went crashing off into the brush. Some woodland animal more terrified than she. But now she'd given her position away.

Her mind, locked in its own paralysis, kept screaming at her to do something. She could fashion no answers for it. She could not bear to remain in this spot now that she'd drawn attention to herself, but the thought of crashing along blindly through the dark underbrush was just as unimaginable.

Please, God, let me wake up from this.

She stood in a half-crouched posture, legs pressed together, arms drawn up to her chest, anus clenched, eyes jammed tight. Again the high, almost musical whine from her throat.

She felt herself dwindling, shrinking, falling away into a blackness as bottomless as death. She thought of a grain of sand on an endless black beach, a pale flower at the bottom of an unfathomable sea.

Knees giving way, back bent, she began to sink, thus immobilized, to the soft loam. Down, down . . .

Shrinking. Dissolving. Fading. I'll flicker once like a final, insistent heartbeat. Then wink out.

This is what insanity is like.

This is the mind at the bottom of the pit.

Her eyes flew open at a crunching sound.

She was hunkered awkwardly against a sapling, curved fetally into herself, chin down, arms grown into her knees, a pale lump in the unending nothingness. Another pale shape formed wraith-like before her, evolving and growing like iridescent fungus on the skin of night.

Moving toward her.

She opened her mouth to scream, hands pressed nonsensically between locked thighs.

If she sat very, very still . . .

But it had seen her.

It bobbed and billowed and coalesced and became Riff. "You okay, Meg?"

His voice was a rush of heart-swelling freedom. But she couldn't make her own work. "C-c-c—"

He bent, took hold of her shoulders. "Hey? It's okay. I took care of it."

She spastically clutched his wrist.

"It's all right now, easy."

He cupped her face and kissed her mouth lightly.

"Can you stand?"

She nodded like a marionette, grasping his other wrist, letting him guide her up. On her feet, she was more stable than she'd have thought.

She let him hold her and, after a moment, held him back.

"You're near shock. Let's get to the car."

Arm about her, he led her to the meadow and beyond.

"The man . . ."

He squeezed her arm reassuringly. "Don't worry, he can't hurt you now."

"Who was he?"

She could feel his smile in the darkness. "Our waiter."

Her brain was stuck in second. "Waiter?"

"At the restaurant, earlier tonight. The one who poisoned our drinks."

She wavered drunkenly. He held on. "P-
Poison . . . ?"

"Sh. It's all right. I broke his neck."

She remembered seeing the car, dark and hulking near the ribbon of road. She remembered moving toward it across the damp grass. Then a greater
darkness reached up and snatched it all away.

Eleven

He awoke to the crunching sound of gravel, and by then it was almost too late.

The Nova was already well into the shoulder, spewing rocks from radial tires, then dipping with a gut-jolting lunge and bouncing straight for a big maple. In the bright headlights its branches seemed to reach out to him in a last, leafy embrace.

Kirk threw his weight into the wheel and slammed the brakes—too hard, locking them. The car skidded wildly on the pebbled roadside (which is what saved them), missed the tree by impossible inches, and headed for a dark barrier of brambles and creepers. He remembered to pump the brakes from winter days on icy Chicago streets and, despite a vicious slashing from overhead branches across the windshield, and the deep knock of rocks somewhere across the undercarriage, he got control again and steered them shakily back into the proper lane.

Jill, when he looked, was white-faced and frog-eyed. "Jesus!" It was obvious she'd dozed off too.

He cleared his throat, gouged his eyes with trembling fingers. "Sorry."

"Kirk, I *said* I'd drive!"

"I'm *sorry!*"

Their voices were collective with recent terror, taut and shrill.

When his hammering heart had eased somewhat, he found his composure and looked over at her. "Are you all right?"

Her tone was sour with fear, hoarse with sleep. "I'm all right."

He rubbed his face fiercely, made a Halloween face at the windshield, trying to retain alertness.

She reached out a hand. "Try the radio . . ."

"I did, it's just static. We're in the boonies."

An irritating crackle confirmed this, and she switched it off again. She flopped back on the cushion with a weary sigh. "Where in the boonies?"

He stiff-armed the wheel, pretending to stretch, trying to contain his trembling in reality. "Almost to the Kansas-Missouri border. We're going to have to stop soon; even if we weren't low on gas, I can't do this much longer. Maybe when I was younger, but not now."

"Let me—"

"No. We need real rest, in a bed, some place we can shower and eat and get fresh again. It's too early to start pushing it yet. The time for that will come soon enough, and I want to be fresh when it does. Besides, unlike me, Riff has an unwilling passenger. He won't be able to rest properly as long as Meg is with him. I'm counting on that."

The near accident was making him abruptly cautious. These thoughts had not occurred to him until just now. Maybe they actually made sense.

Jill watched him a moment, then reached in the backseat, fishing about. She dredged up a plastic thermos they'd bought in a little town three hours back.

"It's empty," Kirk said, "I finished the last of the coffee before midnight. Sorry."

She tossed the thermos on the floor between her legs. "Don't apologize, you're the one that's driving."

A small white sign reading 56W flashed by them.

They had taken that highway and that direction after leaving Dieter's little shack because, placed side by side, the two playing cards read either that or 65 and Kirk couldn't find any 65 on the map. The westerly direction was a guess. But then, so was all of it. The clues were becoming more elliptical. They could mean anything, as Jill was so irritatingly quick to point out.

"Maybe it means fifty-six miles," she'd suggested back there when Kirk had first swung onto the new highway.

"Maybe," he'd grunted sullenly.

"Or maybe sixty-five miles. Or maybe sixty-five stoplights from Dieter's house. Does the number sixty-five have any special significance you can trace in your memory?" All of a sudden she'd become Sherlock Holmes. His frayed nerves had no patience for it.

"Yeah, it comes after sixty-four and before sixty-six."

"I'm just trying to help."

He'd thrown the cards in disgust at the seat between them, where they'd remained the rest of the night. "Look, I don't know what the goddamn cards mean, or if they mean anything at all. Half of me is straining to stop at the nearest pay phone and call the highway patrol and put out an all-points on this fruitcake, and the other half is scared to death of finding Meg in a ditch somewhere if I do. And while that shit's going through my mind, I'm searching every crevice of my memory for some clue, some half-forgotten recollection of who this guy is, where I might have met him and what that meeting might have to do with a five of diamonds and a six of hearts, where he might have been in my old batallion, how he knows all about me and I don't know jack shit about him, how he could be brazen enough to pull off kidnapping a man's wife without being completely insane or completely brilliant or both, how long he's going to let the chase go on before I either catch him or he lets me catch him or he kills my—"

"Okay, okay." She'd patted his arm. "I'm sorry. You're right, Route 56 west is probably the best clue, probably makes the most sense. Take it easy. We'll get the bastard."

She'd touched his fists where they were knotted bloodlessly on the wheel. He'd let them relax a notch, blew out pent-up breath. And kept on driving . . .

She sat across from him now and watched the weary profile, the heavy lids, the tightened jaw, the dark crop of sandy hair. It was, despite the puffy look of fatigue, a pleasant face. A little too roundish to be called truly rugged, at least rugged in the way

Riff's face was, but it wasn't an unhandsome face in some ways. And for a man in his early forties, it was holding up quite well, though the chin was beginning to double just slightly. The eyes were nice. Though there was anger behind them, and maybe fear. She'd noticed this even that first night, before the chase began. She'd looked in his eyes while dancing with him there in his living room, and seen the eyes of a man in a marriage that wasn't working, and a life that hung suspended. And because it was a nice face—a face she could have been attracted to if circumstances had been different—she wanted to ask him about it, pry him loose a little, get him to talk and, hopefully, to smile. He did smile, a little. But he didn't really talk.

He danced well, though.

His lids began to sag . . .

"Hey!"

His head jerked up, eyes bright. "Sorry."

She leaned over and gripped his shoulder, began massaging lightly. "Keep 'em wide and sparkly."

He nodded. "I need something to look at besides this goddamn monotonous road."

She kneaded deeper. "I could take my top off."

He looked over to find her yanking frustratedly at the burgeoning yellow halter with her free hand. There was just about enough material to cover her.

He looked back to the road, managed a smile. "Yeah, that would do it, I'm sure."

She sucked in a breath. "At least then I could breathe."

"Yeah, but could I?"

She worked her fingers into his neck, looked

back out at the road, a wan smile under fading lipstick. "They're just oversize sweat glands."

He chuckled derisively. "Tell that to a GI in a foxhole in the middle of a foreign land. With a perfumed letter and a photo of little Suzie in his hand."

She smiled. "Was that your girlfriend's name in Vietnam, Suzie?"

He leaned into the massage, savoring it. That edge crept back into his voice when he answered. "My girlfriend's name was Patty, and I slept with her every night right there inside my pup tent. I held onto her smooth little butt and oiled up her chamber and shoved it into her until she was full. And if anybody I didn't like walked by in the middle of the night, I squeezed her real tight and blew his fucking head off."

She watched him curiously. "Cute. Your language deteriorates markedly whenever you talk about Vietnam, did you know that?"

He shrugged. "I'm not surprised. The one word everyone in that little country understands, north or south, is fuck." He shook his head wryly. "There's a whole lot of ways and means to get yourself fucked in good old Vietnam. First it was their people that got it. Then it was their infantry. Then it was our infantry. Now it's just the people again."

He shook his head again, this time with bitterness behind it. "All those years we spent giving it to each other up the ass . . . and all we accomplished was killing some people and moving some people around and giving some people different homes. In the end, it's all the same, on the same tired-ass little planet we started with. Nobody gains, nobody really loses . . . we just change spots. Jesus, that feels good . . ."

She relaxed her hand. "Hey, it feels too good, you're going under again."

"No, come on, it's keeping me awake."

She started in again but rougher.

"Hey, leave some skin!"

"Talk. Tell me what you did in 'Nam."

" 'Sboring."

"No, it isn't, talk! Tell me about your real girlfriend."

He was silent for a time, and she thought she felt his neck muscles tighten again. "I didn't have one."

She barked a laugh. "Oh, come on! All that beautiful dark-eyed stuff running around over there and you never had one teensy-weensy little girlfriend? I'll bet you had them knocking down your tent flaps."

He had that faraway look again. "No, I let the other guys do that. . . ."

"Yeah? Never once tempted, eh? What about that foxhole in the foreign land and the perfumed photo? Didn't that ever get you to thinking?"

Kirk shook his head resolutely. "No, not me. I was too . . . busy. War going on, you know."

"Too busy for that? Come on, Kirk! What was her name? Tell me!"

He turned to her so fast his chin caught and pinned her hand. "Look, I never had any goddamn girlfriends, okay, so let's just drop it!"

He spat the words with a viciousness that froze her in place.

He stared at her for a moment, surprised himself at the outburst, then returned back to the road.

Jill pulled her hand away and folded her arms. "Sorry. I was just trying to keep you awake by talking."

"Let's just drop it." He knew he was being a prick but couldn't seem to stop it.

But she was hurt, wouldn't let it go. "I thought it might keep you awake. Or would you rather pile this piece of crap into another tree?"

He had another swipe at his face, digging at his reddened eyes. He seemed to be shaking slightly. Tiny beads of perspiration dotted his brow. One started down his cheek and he slapped it. "Christ, it's hot in here!"

She looked over at his glistening face. "It's not that hot. What's the matter with you?"

His tongue flicked out over chafed lips. "Nothing. It's just that we didn't treat those people too well over there. I don't like thinking about it, that's all."

"Those people didn't treat us so well either."

"I'm talking about the civilians, especially the women, the girls. Some of our boys could be pretty crude. You have no idea."

"Tell me about it."

"I'd rather not."

"Tell me, I can take it. It'll keep you awake."

He was silent.

"Come on, Kirk, tell m—"

He slammed on the brakes.

She flew into the dash with a yelp, head forward. Fortunately, he had insisted on seat belts. Even so, the shock was like a punch in the belly, and sent a volley of curse words spewing from her.

A wall of translucent gray dust was roiling past the car, sealing them off from the world. When she gathered her senses, she saw he was turned halfway around in the seat, staring back over his shoulder at something in the darkness behind them. "What the hell are you—"

But he was working the gears frantically now, grinding them shrilly, tromping the pedal, and rocketing backward with a neck-snapping jolt. "Are you crazy—!"

The car bounced backward for twenty yards and slowed to a halt. He was looking past her, ducking down to see out her side window. There was a vivid stripe of red on his face, now gone, now back again. She turned and saw the winking neon sign across the rolling hilltop, the low-slung row of fifties-style gravel-roofed bungalows beneath it. The sign read: LUCKY 6 MOTEL. Framed in a playing card design.

They sat in the gravel parking lot, just to the left of the tiny motel office.

Kirk held the .38 in his right hand, scanning the rows of cars parked before each of the little country-style units. There were a lot of cars, one, it seemed, for every white-trimmed door and number. Which seemed strange for a place this far off the beaten path.

Jill acknowledged the gun in his hand. "They aren't still here, surely."

Kirk hesitated, hand on the door handle. "If they

ever were here." He scanned the rows of vehicles. "All these cars, what's going on?"

He glanced at his watch: 12:48.

He holstered the weapon and turned to her. "Sit tight. I'm going to see what I can find out. Keep the doors locked. If you see anything the least out of place, lean on the horn. Most of all, *stay in the car!*"

He got out, slammed the door. He crunched up the winking red gravel to the little office, which appeared to be empty. Once at the door, however, he saw a little balding head and reading glasses seated behind the knotty pine desk within. The glasses looked up from an evening paper as Kirk entered with an overhead jingle.

"In under the wire!"

He was in his sixties or early seventies, with a permanent, calcium-deficient stoop that did not alter as he struggled to stand and face Kirk with a groan. He looked like the smiling, kindly old man in the lemonade commercials on TV.

"How's that?" Kirk asked.

"We got only the one unit left, you made it just under the wire! Hope you don't mind a single bed."

"Busy time of year?"

"Four-H convention over in Topeka. Can't get a room for forty miles square. Just the one night for you?" He began assembling paper and pen for Kirk to sign.

"Actually, I—my wife and I—were supposed to meet another couple here this evening. We got held up in Chicago. Could you tell me if there was a man named Walker registered here tonight?"

The elderly gentleman reached with a grunt to a

nearby metal filing box and began flipping through index cards. "Walker . . . Walker . . . nope. Wallace is close as she comes."

He looked up at Kirk, awaiting the next question patiently.

"I see." He grinned, he hoped disarmingly. "This buddy of mine, he's what you might call a practical joker. Be just like him to register under a phony name, punish me for showing up late. Maybe you remember him: a little shorter than me, stocky, narrow face, thin lips, razor-short haircut."

"Razor-short?"

"Like a marine."

The elderly gentleman nodded. "Kind of a pretty wife in tow?"

Kirk swallowed. "That's him."

The liver-spotted hands began to flick cards again. "Came in about six or so. Put him in cabin seven. Registered under . . . here it is: Kirkland."

Kirk tightened. "About six, huh?"

"Yessir, but he ain't there now. Checked out again around nine or so. Called to say he was leaving the key in the room. I'd prefer they didn't do that, hard to find where they leave 'em sometimes."

Kirk forced another chuckle. "That son of a gun! Didn't catch which way he headed, did you?"

"Sorry."

Kirk shook his head, grinning. "Just like that old s.o.b.! Probably went on up the road a ways just to give me a fit. Would you know the name of the next motel on 56 West?"

"Kind of a weird sense of humor this friend of yours has got."

Kirk nodded, grinning his ass off. "That's Walker, a real weirdo! How far would you say the next motel was?"

The old man shut the metal box, not in quite as helpful a mood now that it looked like he was losing a customer. "There's a Holiday Inn just over the Kansas border, but that's a couple of hours from here."

"I see. Well, we're pretty tired, the wife and I, maybe we'll just stay here the night. I'll light into that rascal in the morning!"

The old man brightened, shoved the pen and paper at Kirk. He probably hadn't had the complex completely filled in years.

"That cabin number seven he was in, is that still vacant?"

"No, I filled that just a while back, couple of young Future Farmers. Eight right next to it is open, though, if you don't mind the single bed, like I say."

"Eight will be fine." Kirk signed his name, home address, and license number.

"That'll be thirty-seven dollars in advance. Here's your key. Cabin's just to the north of the office there."

"Thank you."

"Have a good night's rest!"

Kirk shut the door behind them, flicked on the light as Jill fell gratefully across the lumpy little bed.

He turned to her resolutely. "Don't get too comfortable, we're not staying here."

She propped herself on her elbows. "Where, then?"

He jerked his head. "Next door."

"How?"

He walked to the bathroom, turned on the light. "I'm thinking on it."

He threw cold water on his face, toweled off.

She was in the same position when he came back, breasts thrust forward from the backward arch of her shoulders, eyes on him. "Well?"

He paced. He took off his neighbor's jacket and rechecked the chamber of the .38. He knew it was fine, but it gave him something concrete to do in a day increasingly lacking in tangible options.

Jill watched him. "Are you going to shoot the conventioneers?"

He looked up. "I'm tired enough to."

She sighed heavily, pushed up, stood before him. "How do I look?"

"You look fine, why?"

She turned toward the bathroom. "You're too kind, I look like shit."

She walked into the bathroom, flicked the light, stared at herself in the mirror. "Jesus. My kingdom for a good compact." She pulled a tube of lipstick from the tight white shorts, the tube she'd bought when they'd stopped to get the coffee thermos. She'd begged him to stop somewhere and let her buy at least a cheap blouse that would fit her, for chrissake, but he'd said she looked fine and didn't want to take the time. She applied the lipstick wearily now, touching it to her cheeks and blending it like rouge.

She returned to the bedroom and stood before him. She tugged the yellow halter down to just above her nipples. "How do I look now?"

"What are you doing?"

"Give me fifty bucks."

He burrowed for his wallet and handed her the money. "Answer me."

She plucked the fifty from his fingers and brushed past him. "Getting your room for you. Come on. And stay behind me."

She knocked on the door next to theirs.

The single, curtained window was illuminated with a bluish glow, and the raucous laughter of the television seeped beneath the molding. After a moment a youthful, sun-baked face appeared in a corona of flickering light. "Yes?"

"I'm sorry to disturb you," Jill began in a breathy voice, "but I have a tremendous favor to ask of you." She thrust her plunging cleavage at him, but she didn't need to: the adolescent's eyes were already filled with it. "My husband and I spent our honeymoon in this cabin five years ago tonight and, well, it would just mean the world to us if we could spend our anniversary here! The man in the office said it was taken, but I thought: gee, if you don't ask, you never know!"

"You want to switch rooms, that it, ma'am?" The accent was viscous with Midwestern drawl, resplendent with callow wonder. The hypnotized eyes remained unable to rise above the taut halter.

"It would really mean a lot to us." She dipped a hand into the front of the halter, deliberately snagging the material downward. Just when it seemed the swelling flesh might pop free, she withdrew the fifty. She handed it to the boy. "Really a lot."

"Uh, I'll have to check with my friend."

"You do that."

When he disappeared, Jill turned to the shadowy figure behind her, smiling demurely. "I guess two 38's are better than one!"

"You're good. You really are."

The boy reappeared almost immediately, eyes still ignoring her face. "He says it's all right with him."

Then he stepped back, eyes suddenly skyward, as Kirk moved into the porch light. "Great, we'll help with your luggage!"

Once inside the new cabin, they began to search everywhere.

"What is it we're looking for?" Jill inquired in a muffled voice, head under the bed, rump in the air.

Kirk called from the bathroom. "I haven't the slightest idea. Anything that looks askew. Anything that catches your eye." He ran his fingers lightly over the medicine chest mirror, opened the door, and looked inside at empty metal shelves.

"*What* eyes?" she called back, voice drugged with sleepiness.

Kirk leaned back against the sink, rubbed his face again, fighting the double vision, the mantle of exhaustion pressing in like a dead weight from all sides now. His eyes flicked to the ceiling, the shower stall, the toilet. Everything looked perfectly in order. "I know," he called, "we need coffee."

"We need sleep. You especially."

He ran cold water in the sink. "They might be close."

She came into the bathroom, leaned against the jamb, shoulders slumped, beat. "And you'd be in great shape to confront him."

He toweled his face, leaned forward stiffly on the lip of the sink, head bowed.

She was right. He knew she was right.

The urge to lie down, even for a few minutes, reached up to engulf him. "We've got to find the next clue," he insisted. "I know it's here."

She watched his drawn features in the mirror. "Then it will still be here in the morning. You said yourself he would be the one with the sleeping problems. Use it against him. Start fresh tomorrow while he's still groggy from watching Meg all night."

He turned to her, feeling himself caving in. "I can't wait that long."

"A couple of hours, then, at least. You've been under unbearable stress since early this morning. You can't keep going on vapors forever." She came to him and took his wrist, turning it toward her. "It's just after one. I'll call the desk and have them wake us at three. We can continue to search then. Okay?"

He shook his head automatically. "No, we've got to keep—"

Her exhaustion broke her. "Goddamn it, Kirk! He's got you following his orders like a puppy dog! I know you're concerned about Meg, but quit playing into his hands all the time! Stick to your own rules! Outwit him! It's all you've got! Know when to back off, get your second wind! You can't fight him half awake!"

Her insightfulness startled him.

He considered. But his mind was too fatigued for even that. He nodded at last, listlessly, and plodded for the bedroom. "All right. But only two hours."

He sat heavily on the edge of the mattress and pulled off his shoes with groaning effort.

As the first one hit the floor and rolled, Kirk hesitated, eyes lingering on the metallic grid of the heating vent on the floor against the headboard wall. He worked the other shoe off carefully, brows knitted, and set it down gently on the carpeted floor. He stood and padded to the foot-long rectangular vent, stooped down to get a better view of it.

"What's up?" Jill sounded behind him.

He got a finger between the metal shutters that directed air flow, pulled upward, bringing the trough-like cover with him. He bent lower and peered into an aluminum tunnel that quickly went to shadow.

"Turn on that night table lamp, will you?"

But even with the stronger light, the tunnel remained dark. Kirk put his hand inside, then his arm, thinking of rats and spiders, and fished about. Nothing to the right. But to the left his fingers brushed hard plastic. He strained at the shoulders and withdrew the palm-sized micro tape recorder.

Jill hurried over. "He's got the place bugged!"

Kirk shook his head. "No, this is for us."

He brought the recorder over to the bed and the light, sat down, and found the Play button. He pushed it.

For a moment nothing. Then:

(click)

"—ot your things? We won't be back."

"I've got them."

"Hungry?"

(pause) "Yes."

(pause) "Are you all right, Mrs. Kirkland?"

"Yes."

"You're sure? No broken bones, no abrasions?"

. "I'm all right."

"You're sure, I mean, you'd tell me if you were hurt in any way?"

"I'm perfectly all right, thank you."

(click)

Kirk rewound the tape with a shrill squeak and played it again. Then twice more.

Then he sat on the bed and stared at the tiny recorder in his hand. He felt suddenly very awake.

"What does it mean?" Jill asked softly, seated beside him now.

He shook his head slowly. "How did she sound to you, Jill?"

"She sounded . . . all right."

"Not coerced, like she was reading it or something?"

"No, I don't think she was reading it. It sounded too impromptu."

He nodded. "That's what I thought."

He stared at the machine a moment, then played the tape again.

"Is he trying to torture you?" Jill offered.

"Maybe. Or reassure me. She sounded genuinely unharmed. Almost . . . calm."

"Yes. Like she had the situation in hand."

"Or at least was relatively unfearful of him. Of course, she could have had a gun to her head, but she sounded pretty cool and collected, didn't she?"

"I'd say so."

He played the tape again.

"*—I mean, you'd tell me if you were hurt in any way?*"

"*I'm perfectly all right.*"

Kirk switched it off and set it on the bed beside him.

"Hear any clues in there?" he asked Jill.

She sighed. "I was listening for one, but frankly . . ."

"Yeah, me too. Maybe there's something there we don't hear or maybe we're just too punked out to get it."

Jill put a hand on his shoulder. "Anyway, we know they were here, we know Meg's unharmed."

"No, we don't. That recording could have been made this morning in Chicago. He could have been here at the motel alone when he left the recorder. She could be in a ditch somewhere."

She pressed his shoulder sharply. "Don't."

He grabbed up the recorder suddenly and turned to her. He took her arm and led her to the center of the room. "Let's imagine this is the most likely place for them to have stood when the recording was made. When I give the signal, you say: 'I'm perfectly all right.' Got it?"

"What for?"

"Just do it!"

He let the tape play past the brief recording, then he stopped it, hit the Record button, and held the machine at his side. He said: "You're sure, I mean, you'd tell me if you were hurt in any way?"

He pointed at Jill.

"I'm perfectly all right."

He nodded, reversed the tape, and played it from the beginning. After Meg's last words, there was a brief pause, click, and then Kirk's own voice:

"You're sure, I mean, you'd tell me if you were hurt in any way?"

"I'm perfectly all right."

He played the whole thing over again.

When he was through, Jill asked: "What are you listening for?"

"Ambient sound. This room has a sound peculiar to itself: the walls, ceiling, placement of furniture, all of them contribute to it. It's there, even when no one's talking. What they call white noise. Did it sound the same to you during both recordings?"

"I think so, yes."

"Me too. Which means they were here."

He seemed somewhat relieved.

He turned, placed the recorder on the night table, and lay back against the pillow. He stared at the ceiling, arms folded behind his head. "But which way from here . . . ?"

She sat beside him, patted his shoulder. "Why don't you take a quick shower? I'll leave the wake-up call at the desk. That way we'll be able to leave as soon as we get up."

Despite the fact that nothing was really different, there was a feeling that they were getting somewhere, that they had done things right up to now. He could hear it in Jill's voice. An excitement not there before. Almost prideful.

"Don't you want to shower too?" he asked.

"After you."

"All right. A shower might do me some good."

He padded to the bathroom and shut the door, peeling off clothing he was glad to be rid of. She was right: tomorrow they'd have to take time to stop and get some decent clothes. And a decent breakfast.

He was surprised, shocked, really, at how good the shower felt.

With the hot spray needling across his back, his shoulders, he felt some of the tension slip grudgingly away. Light-headed, he let the water pound him numb, until he and the driving water were one.

He was rising up and out of himself and into the night on a mindless cloud of drumming mist. He might sail clear past the moon if he deemed it so. Giddy, he actually had to cling momentarily to the shower handles for fear of fainting. The sensation was brief, but while it lasted it got him outside of his world of grief and anxiety and off to another plane.

And then he had another sensation. It lasted for only an instant, but it stayed with him indelibly; he imagined Meg was really dead, had been dead for years, and that he didn't care anymore because the

time for caring was long past, because now there
was no point in going on and on and he could,
thankfully, put all the anxiety and frustration and
black, cancerous turmoil behind him. He was sorry
she was dead, but he could no longer torture himself over it. He imagined himself Free.

And knew the price for freedom when he came
back, the water still drumming his skin.

He sagged against dripping tile, a mass of aching
muscle and guilt. His mind, he realized bleakly,
seeking some blind avenue of release, was turning
against him. The thought made his stomach roll
with nausea.

He turned off the shower and toweled with one
of the Lucky 6 imprinted towels, wrapping it
around his waist when he'd finished. The light-
headedness would not leave.

When he stepped into the bedroom, Jill was already asleep under the sheet, yellow halter lying
across a vinyl chair, sharp points of her nipples
tenting the thin motel sheet, rising and falling in
rhythm.

If his mind really was deserting him, he'd need
this woman all the more. Need her closer than
ever.

He turned off the light, threw the towel at the
chair, and climbed in on his side. He was lost in a
black oblivion before he could think anymore.

Twelve

Her eyes fluttered open on a room with which she was not familiar.

That it was a motel room was obvious from the requisite details: large double bed, benign, unaesthetic wall paintings, functional table unit, color TV with Free HBO card on top, heavily draped picture window, low, flock-sprayed ceiling, minimum hall with minimum closet, check-out rules posted on the front door. If she attempted to pick up the heavy, potbelly lamp next to her, she'd find it bolted to the night table. As was the TV bolted to the table unit. As were the wooden hangers without hooks.

Yes, a motel.

Meg heard a rustling from the direction of the bathroom and rolled over beneath a single sheet to find Riff poking his head out the bathroom door, face bearded white with shaving cream, grinning at her. "Be right with you!" And ducked inside again.

How had he known she'd awakened at that precise moment?

Instinct.

She looked down at herself, at the sheet drawn across her breasts. She peeked beneath and found herself nude. She'd been nude when she'd fainted in the woods—perhaps he just hadn't bothered to dress her again. Well, that's one reason he might have been willing to leave her unguarded. Though she wasn't sure it would have stopped her if she'd awakened without his knowing it. For some reason she smiled. The thought of herself running naked down the hall shouting for help struck her as remotely humorous.

She looked about the dimly lit room for some sign of her clothing. A bright band of light shone beneath the heavy curtain, the room itself was like soft twilight. There was no sign of clothes, so she presumed he'd hung them in the closet. Probably neatly. That was nice of him.

She pulled tangled hair from her forehead. She couldn't remember anything past the point when they had seen the man in the woods, standing there in the moon-swept meadow.

There was some vague recollection about being in the car again, the rocking movement of it, of Riff muttering something, of doors slamming . . . but it wasn't clear.

Her heart skipped a little beat. He had doubtless drugged her again; that's why she couldn't recall coming here. When, though? They hadn't drunk anything in the meadow. It must have been at the fancy restaurant earlier. Probably her water glass. Not her wineglass, that's for sure.

She felt an inward chill. She hated the fact of his

drugging her. It was a surreptitious defilement she could not control, that ugly part of him she feared and despised, a wedge of distrust between them. And a constant reminder of just how dangerous this all really was.

And something else. She had wanted to believe, for reasons that were probably as stupid as they were foolish, that they were somehow beyond all that. That they had reached some kind of mutual understanding, some unspoken truth whose roots lay in respect. An unorthodox respect, to be sure, but a respect of their own making, shared by them alone. The drugs debased that. Left her hollow and hurting and furious inside.

And the fact that she felt these things made her more furious still.

She should not be thinking these things. He was insane, dangerous. This was her life they were talking about. She should be concerning herself with escape, with Kirk.

Damn Kirk. Why didn't he show up? Damn him.

"Sleep well?"

He was bright and cheery and swathed in a motel towel, naked to the waist. He rubbed his face with a washcloth. He smelled sweetly of lotion. She decided she didn't like the smell.

"You shouldn't drug me." It came out before she could check it.

He stood over her a moment, dabbing his neck.

Then he sat down next to her on the bed. "You think not?"

"It makes me ill." It was a lie, it hadn't even caused a headache this time.

"Oh? It was just something very light, over-the-counter. You needed the sleep."

"I would have slept without it," she muttered petulantly. *This is ludicrous, my being petulant.*

"I thought you might have been frightened . . . the man in the woods."

She looked at him now. "Who was he?"

"I told you: our waiter. He won't bother us again."

"Our waiter."

"Tried to poison us with the wine. An old trick. Too chicken-shit to face me one on one. He knows my rep. Luckily I spotted him."

She looked unconvinced. "How did you do that?"

"He was CIA. I can spot those clowns ten miles off. Matter of fact, that was about the distance he'd been pacing. Didn't you notice the blue car?"

"I can't say I did."

He shrugged. "Well, you weren't trained. Feel like a bath?"

"Why would the CIA be interested in us?"

"We're interesting people. Of course, he could have been FBI. They've been after me for years. Or even the KGB." He snorted. "I love those little abbreviations, don't you?"

She watched him levelly. "Maybe he was the PTA."

His laugh was loud and heartfelt. "You're pretty good! No, he was CIA. Those guys have their own look, their own way of operating. You get a sixth sense about it after a while, know what I mean?"

"No, I don't."

She was buying none of this. He was lying as fast as he could talk. Either he had frightened the other man away with his nakedness, or the other man had simply gone away. There had been no killing. She had not been abducted by a killer. She had not been kissed by a killer.

"If he was only interested in you, then why did he try to poison me too?"

"You were in the way. To the CIA that makes you expendable. They're not what you'd call a discriminating bunch."

She folded her arms patiently. "And they'd just leave my corpse there in the restaurant for all the world to see?"

"Not in the restaurant. It's a slow-acting poison. I've used it myself. One of the triglicerides. We'd have gone under on the road. Fallen asleep at the wheel, get it?"

"Not really, Riff."

"How about that bath?"

She looked away loftily. "Thanks, I had one last night."

"How about another?"

She was about to answer when she saw it wasn't really a question. "Oh, I see. It's you who wants the bath."

He patted her knee once jovially. "It's a small car, I'd hate for your abductor to offend you."

If it was an attempt at levity, she wasn't in the mood. She was still angry about the drugs. "And you don't want to leave me alone that long, so we're taking a bath together, is that it?"

"If madam doesn't object. Then we'll get a good breakfast, some hot black coffee, how does that sound?"

"And if madam does object?"

He stood. "She won't, though, will she?"

She folded her arms. "I don't have a robe. May I at least have a towel?"

He bowed graciously. "Oh, but of course, Mam-'selle!"

He took off his towel and handed it to her.

She took it without looking, face sour. "Thanks."

He laughed and walked back to the bathroom, began running water.

She sat holding the damp towel, staring absently at the black screen of the motel TV. I'm tired of this now, I'm tired of this nutcase and his woodland fantasies. I want out of this now. I want my own bedroom and my own coffee, and my own life.

But the only way to that was to first get out of this bed, and then see whatever would eventually come, right?

After a moment she threw off the sheet and followed, towel wrapped around her. She knew she was angrier than the situation warranted, or at least angry at the wrong thing.

He was sitting naked on the lip of the tub, testing the steaming water with his hand. "Hope you like it hot!"

She came in and leaned against the sink, thinking of hitting him very hard in the back of the neck, knocking him into the tub. Running.

"Close the door, will you? Lets the heat out."

She closed the door.

He was getting in as she turned, presenting his hard buttocks to her, genitals swinging between the fork of his legs as he bent to the task. He gripped the sides and eased downward, ahhhing.

He pulled the curtain all the way back to see her better, and smiled. "Come on in, the water's fine."

"I'll just wait my turn here, thanks."

He laughed. "I'd feel ever so much more comfortable if you were in here and away from that door."

What's the matter, don't you trust me? She pushed away reluctantly from the sink and came to the edge of the tub. She had to look down to maneuver. His penis was a floating log. "You'll have to move over."

He drew up his legs.

She stepped in gingerly, holding onto the tile wall, one hand gripping the bodice of the towel. She stood for a moment feeling the rising heat.

"Oh, for God's sake, Meg, take off the towel, we've already seen each other!"

God knows that's the truth. She threw the towel over the toilet and sat down quick. The hot water made the top, unsubmerged part of her suddenly cold. She wrapped her arms around herself and stared at the wall beyond his head.

"Here, put your legs on either side. Go on, I'm not going to bite."

She did as she was told and felt immediately warmer.

"Great, huh?" he urged.

"Colossal. Almost enough room to get clean in."

He laughed his carefree laugh. "Make do in any situation, that's the army way. We did with considerably less than this in 'Nam."

Asshole. You were never in 'Nam.

He stretched out his legs, overlapping hers until his feet brushed her hips and his heels rested against the far lip. He scooched down in the water until his chest was covered with the steaming liquid, and closed his eyes. She sat with her back against the faucet, relaxing from the heat in spite of herself.

"Tell me about Kirk."

She watched his serene, narrow face; he looked asleep. Of all the times, the places, to mention Kirk. The gall of this jerk!

Her continued anger with him was beginning to annoy her. It was beginning to seem petty, not like her, but she couldn't seem to stop it. She felt betrayed because of the drugs. "What do you want to know?"

He shrugged and made gentle waves that warmed her thighs. "Is he a good husband?"

"Of course."

"Are you happy with him?"

She searched for and found the soap to give herself something to do. "Yes."

She caught his smile.

"No, you're not. Tell the truth."

She ran the tiny motel bar over her arms. "You're the expert on the Kirklands, you tell me."

"No, I'd rather hear it from you. Where did the marriage first go wrong?"

She washed the soap free with handfuls of water. Something about his presence made lying difficult. To him, to herself. She found herself confronting things she'd hitherto put off to the next day. Days that had become years.

"I don't know . . . it's been wrong a long time." Why was she talking to this idiot?

"Since he first started working with his brother, would you say?"

"I suppose."

"Since he got back from the 'Nam?"

She sat watching the little bubbles curled about her ankles.

"Megan?"

"I didn't know him then."

"That's right, I forgot. What is it, the sex?"

A great sadness welled inside her.

"Why are you doing this?" she asked plaintively.

He opened his eyes, and there was no mocking glint to them. "The questions? I hate to see people unhappy. And you're unhappy. I thought you might like to talk about it. You've nothing to lose with me: I was a stranger before, and I'll be a stranger afterward."

She seized impulsively on the hope. "Will there be an afterward?"

"There's always an afterward, Megan."

Something about his speaking her full name broke a dam in her. Tears came at last, and there were a lot of them. She covered her face, shuddering in the tub.

She heard the inward rush of water as he sat up. His big hands gripped her shoulders. "Hey . . ."

But she couldn't stop now.

He pulled her close, heedless of the roiling water slopping over the lip. "Hey, now, don't . . ."

She let herself be held, and she let her forehead sink to the cushion of his shoulder. And she let herself let it all out. It hurt worse than she'd have thought.

He let her run the course, holding her lightly but protectively, rubbing her naked back with palms cupped with warm water.

"Can't you just let me go? I'll never tell anyone. I swear it!"

But it sounded as unlikely to her as it must have to him. He had, of course, been anticipating this moment for some time now. He held her silently.

After a time she seemed to gather herself. In a barely audible voice she said: "Please don't kill my husband."

"He may well kill me," he answered in her ear.

She choked on another sob. "But it's so . . . *useless!*"

He sighed patiently, rubbed her back some more. "But unavoidably necessary."

She shook her head against the taut muscles of his pectorals, slowly at first, then faster and faster as if trying to rub the fact of him away with her forehead.

And then, to her astonishment, she was hitting him.

It was as if the crying had been merely a prelude to true hysteria. It seemed to take hold of her arms and back, and control them with a will of its own. She saw her flying fists, saw the red marks they were making on his chest and shoulders, heard the shrill chittering of her voice, but from somewhere up near the ceiling, as if she were gazing down from a balcony at a play.

She seemed to be screaming some word over and over again that echoed like the piercing cry of a gutted animal in the narrow, tiled confines, but she couldn't for the life of her discern what it was she was saying.

It might have been minutes or merely seconds before he slapped her, but he slapped her hard and that stopped it. Seemed to knock all that remained of it out of her, even the last few tears.

She sat looking straight into his eyes but not at him, mouth hanging open, brain spinning somewhere out beyond the small, steam-filled bathroom. He saw the look and his brows knitted with concern, gray eyes searching hers worriedly.

He pulled her close and kissed her hard on the mouth, mashing her lips.

He pulled back and looked again, and this time she was looking back at him somewhat.

He kissed her again, more tenderly this time, and moved his hand to her breast.

When he drew back this time, her eyes were closed, a drop of moisture clinging to her lower lip. He caressed her nipple and kissed her cheek gently. She said: oh, and her breathing began to change.

Meg let herself fall. Lost in warmth, she felt herself rushing away toward a grateful peace, the consequences of which were snatched away in the hot wind of her headlong flight for solace, escape.

He took away his lips, leaving her trembling and marooned. He brought the soap from the shelf, lathered her hands until they dripped. Eyes on the

serene, helpless face, he guided her hand to his organ, closed her fingers about it, began to work
them gently over the shaft, kissing her neck with
the softest, gentlest pecks.

Meg opened her eyes dizzily and gazed at him.

He smiled tenderly, kissed her forehead lightly,
stroking himself with her hand.

She looked down, mesmerized, saw the won-
drous transformation begin; already she could
barely contain him in her hand. Soon he was ballooning skyward, a fat garden hose, helmeted head
lifting torpidly on the brontosaur neck, flushing red,
and redder.

She gazed deliriously into his eyes, found them
filled with an almost heartbreaking trust, a fanning
need that she and she alone had put there, she
alone controlled. She felt a welling flame inside.

She had him! *She* had *him* now!

He let his own hand drop sleepily away, en-
trusting.

She looked down, the lather-slick column twitching once in her fist, beseeching. She had never
seen anything like it: an elegantly curved palm bole,
jutting imperiously above the milky sea, haughty
and sure but helpless beyond the magic of her caressing fingers ... fingers that pistoned smoothly,
confidently, and—to her surprise and thrill—
skillfully.

When she remembered to breathe again, it came
with a painful hitch, her eyes glitter-blurred with
tears, her teeth grinding. The fist a soapy blur.

He winced, groaned, returned the delicious pain
by pinching her nipple.

She squeezed harder, breath hissing between her teeth.

He pinched back, harder still.

Meg gasped, mouth a startled O, crying out silently, free hand fluttering at the steamy air like a wounded bird.

His groan echoed, guttural deep, face contorted. Close.

It was a race she was determined not to lose.

Lips drawn back on the edge of a scream, nipple on fire, she watched in grinning triumph her flying fingers pull him over the brink, the angry head beneath them pulse, turn deep violet, deeper, fountain.

Their cry, simultaneous and shrill against the ringing tile, ended in a strangled laugh, echoing with a fading melancholy.

She came back in his arms, head reeling.

A waft of cold air sent her back spasming.

He was carrying her, dripping, across the room, laying her gently across the motel sheets.

It actually took her a moment to realize she had climaxed in the tub, the steamy enclosure, hot water, excitement, all conspiring to achieve a momentary swoon.

It was her first climax in months, and even those before had been self-manipulated. No wonder she came so forcefully.

But that she came at all—with only his fingers at her nipple—amazed her. Just that single tactile sensation, no other part of her body touched.

Except that it wasn't exactly singular: she had

had her hand on him as well. That had been as exciting as the other.

She collapsed supine, body a sack in which bones had been collected. She had never felt so utterly drained.

Riff rolled her onto her stomach, her mouth pressing the mattress, nose mashed indignantly, uncaringly, hands pinned, buttocks high. He left her that way, the cool air reviving her by uncomforting degrees. It had been nicer at the edge of sleep. She wanted sleep now, and the warmth of his closeness. Self-recrimination—even repugnancy—would surely come later. Right now she wanted to revel in the afterglow of the long-awaited climax, in the dreamy tingle that held back reality.

And then he was back, taking her wrists roughly but not too roughly, wrapping something around them, cinching it, harder, getting a satisfying yelp from her, repeating it all with the other wrist, and hoisting her across the bed. Her head bobbed up languidly to see him securing the cords to the posts.

She was temporarily beyond fear, but not curiosity.

"What are you . . . ?"

She grunted as he yanked her down by the ankles, snapped cord around each of them and secured her spread-eagle to the footboard. Another tremor rocked her.

"I'm cold . . ."

He was moving about somewhere beyond her. "You won't be."

What was he doing back there, she wondered lazily, she wanted him here. Couldn't he see that it was all right now, that she was his whore? She wondered vaguely if he had somehow drugged her again. Wishful thinking, old girl, it's all you. The guilt will come later, in truckloads.

Would this be alarming if the steamy climax hadn't made her impervious to threat? If she could only get her gelatin brain out of second long enough to be afraid . . .

There was a burst of oriental music from somewhere, which he immediately turned down to a manageable volume. The sound moved to in front of her, and she heard him set something down on the night table, probably a radio or recorder. The music was foreign and twangy and, to her, rhythmless. But she smiled at the exotic—erotic—intent. Construed it as endearing.

The mattress gave behind her and he was there.

She strained her neck to see him, in vain. "Be careful . . ." Imagining that big thing deep inside her.

"You'll like this."

His wide hand was caressing her buttocks gently, warmly. The cheeks tingled beneath what must have been some kind of thin, very slick oil. She gasped a little as his finger entered her anus abruptly. She began a protest in her throat, but after a moment it was fine. Then pleasant. Then more.

She wanted him inside her, but not there.

Then the finger left her, replaced by cool air, and fear found her heart again.

"Wait a minute, you're not going to—"

But he already was.

She cried out, tightening under his weight, twisting involuntarily. The cord did its job.

"Wait, that hurts! I'm not—!"

She screamed once, her bowels ballooning as if pumped by air. Flashes of little girl enemas erupted like red explosions. It hurts, Mama!

And then he was past the worst and sliding in and in. And still in, for ever and ever, deep and deeper and how can there be any more, possibly any more, but there was. Like defecating, she thought, bug-eyed and helpless, like shitting in reverse.

—not that kind of girl.

"Christ!"

It was all she had breath for.

But it was better now.

He gripped her cheeks and withdrew, gently.

By the third thrust she was accustomed.

By the fifth she was nearly enjoying it.

Something about the impossibleness of the big cock up her ass; it was deliciously lewd, depraved. She wanted him squirting up there.

Somewhere down the line she was squeezing back for him, urging him on with chest-deep grunts, and somewhere after that exploding in a climax that left her shaking and frightened in its intensity.

He did not take it out of her.

The Sword of her Death remained impaled to her heart.

He bent his weight to her back and tongued her ear, big testes lolling in her crack. She closed her eyes at the warmth, let her breath run giddily from her. They melded liquidly, a throbbing unit. She squeezed hello and he pulsed back.

"Talk to me this time, sweet Meg." The softest whisper.

She opened her eyes as he began again.

"Talk to me . . ." So softly.

She felt the building return in spite of herself. "What . . . ?"

"Tell me how you like it."

"Yes."

"Tell me. Say: I like it, Johnny."

"Who?"

"Tell me!" faster

"I like it . . . Johnny."

"I like it this way, Johnny. I like you in my ass."

"Yes!"

faster

"Say it!"

"I like it this way, Johnny! I like you in my ass!"

"You like it too, Johnny."

"You . . . oh! . . ."

"Say it!"

She gasped ragged air. "You—you like it too, Johnny!"

"Fuck me, Johnny, fuck me good!"

"Yes! Please!"

"Tell me!"

"Fuck me, Johnny! F-fuck me good! Jesus!"

"Now, Johnny, *do it now*!"

faster faster

"Now, Johnny, do it, do it now! Oh fuck—I—!"

The climax slammed her, bowing her spine, leaving welts where the cords bit her wrists, souvenirs to marvel at in more lucid times.

She slid down the long slide to sleep, leaving the bedroom and all of it far back there somewhere.

"Never . . ." she mumbled at the damp sheet. Barely audible above the oriental twang.

He withdrew with a light plop, leaving the throbbing ghost of himself, dribbling semen on her inner thigh. Even that came in big glops. *This man has dripped cum and urine on me, and I'm falling asleep. . . .*

"What did you say?"

"Never . . ." she whispered, gone.

Not really knowing herself what she meant by it.

Thirteen

He awoke as he had awakened the previous morning, with the sound of singing birds, himself against the cushioned warmth of her buttocks. If he had dreamed, he could not remember.

This time his awakening was full with cognizance, and the awareness, in vivid detail, of where he was and all that had gone before. This was not his wife he held, whose bare backside he was prodding; this was a blond woman with large breasts whom he scarcely knew.

I have awakened two mornings naked with this woman, and I have not made love to her. There was an incongruous irony there somewhere.

Lying still so not to wake her, Kirk lifted the motel covers lightly, gazed down past his erection at the gentle curve of her spine, the rippled swell of rib cage, sudden dip of waist, abrupt cliff of pelvic bone, the flesh sheaving this latter, cool and unblemished as new porcelain, riding a thin, luxuriant layer of fat. The generous cheeks, though pinched now with gravity, belied a shapely fullness: she looked inviting from behind. Unusual. Women, he noted with nearly complete detachment, most women tended to be slight in the rear if generous in front, and vice versa. Jill was bountiful before and behind, wide, hourglass hips primed for child bearing, plump buttocks signaling the needed participant. Calendar girl figure. Scandinavian, probably. In this light—

Light . . .

He twisted away in alarm, eyes stabbing at the curtained window. The bright vertical bars at top and bottom showed clearly the sun's insistent attempts to enter, scalloped rays spreading toward him across ceiling and floor.

"Shit!"

He sat up too fast, with a twinge of pain in his lower back, grabbing his watch from the night table. It was bright enough in the room to read even with the heavy curtain pulled.

He swore again, erection fading, snapped the band to his wrist and shook the woman, harder, probably, than absolutely necessary. "Jill! It's after six!"

She awoke with a snort. "Wha—?"

"Come on! The sun's up, for chrissake! Goddamn desk clerk forgot to call us!"

He was out of bed and wrestling with his neighbor's pants, hopping about on one foot. The trousers were already too small, and he still had the partial erection. The zipper didn't want to go around it.

He looked up to find her watching him sleepily. "Don't cut it off."

He turned away, tucked himself in, and grabbed the sports shirt. "Get a move on! They're *hours* away by now!"

She let her head flop against the backboard. "Please. I need a shower."

The damn shirt wouldn't button. "There isn't time!"

"Kirk, slow down!"

He looked up from fumbling fingers, halted by her tone.

She was cranky from the unceremonious arousal. "You're spinning off in all directions again! You don't even know for sure which way to drive!"

"Fifty-six west, it's all we've got!"

She sat up, clutching the sheet halfheartedly. "All right. But another fifteen minutes isn't going to matter now. Let's get cleaned up, have something to eat. Take advantage of the sleep we did get. If you do catch him today, you'll be ready for him."

She was right again. He did feel better for the sleep, now that he was fully awake. And breakfast made sense. He'd already showered last night. Still, that pressing urge to make up time and distance lost between here and Meg—

He finished buttoning the shirt with steadied fingers, and this time the garment behaved. "Okay. You're right. You take your bath, I'll see where we can grab some breakfast." He had a phone call to make as well.

"Fine." She was mollified.

He sat back down on the bed and grabbed the receiver off the hook, looking up as she threw off the sheet and walked naked, sleepy-casual to the bathroom. She didn't hurry.

"Lucky Six Motel." It was the old man with the stooped back.

Kirk thought about chastising him about the wake-up call but decided not to waste the time; what's done is done. "This is Mr. Kirkland in room seven. Is there a place to eat on the premises?"

"No, sir, the sign states room and TV only."

Since there didn't appear to be a follow-up statement from the old gent, Kirk asked the obvious. "Where might my wife and I find some breakfast close by?"

"Copper Kettle diner about eight miles east, believe they're open for breakfast."

"Anything heading west?"

"Well, there's Dillon's Roadhouse four miles down, but I ain't sure about breakfast. Mostly a saloon."

"Anything after that?"

"You'd have to check the map, mister, sorry."

"All right, thanks. I'd like to make a call to Chicago, can I direct dial from here?"

"Long as it's collect."

"I'll use my GTE card. Thank you."

"Say, I recollect a Howard Johnson's down the pike if you can wait a spell."

"Thanks."

He hung up.

He could hear the sound of Jill's shower through the thin separation. He saw again the rounded curve of buttocks as she swiveled immodestly through the door.

He dialed the office.

"David Kirkland here."

"It's me. What's the news?"

"Kirk! For chrissake, I thought you were going to call last night!"

"We got in late, exhausted."

"Where?"

"Never mind."

"Jesus, will you drop this shit? Where are you? Have you seen Walker?"

"I've heard him. He left a little present for me at his motel. I'm here now."

"Present?"

"Tape recorder. Little tête-à-tête with Meg to let me know she's alive."

"How did she sound?"

"She sounded good, actually. What have you got?"

"A lot! We traced him down. Walker's a psycho, all right, but not a dangerous one."

"Explain."

Kirk could hear the rustling of papers on David's end, shuffling notes, dossiers. His brother began by quoting.

"Rifflin Walker, age thirty-eight, Caucasian male, five ten and a half. Born, Nathan Loren Walker, Watache, Wisconsin. Completed two years high school. Attended Pasedena Playhouse, California—kicked out. Drifted. Attempted employment with the Secret Service: rejected. Joined the Navy, 1967. Medical discharge from same 1972—prone to long crying jags. After Navy service lived briefly in New York City, tried to get work in off-Broadway shows.

Failed. Drifted. Arrested twice in '78 on shoplifting charges. Spent summer '78 at Men's Correctional Facility, Connecticut—did farm work there. Paroled in winter '79. Drifted. Arrested in '82 impersonating a clergyman! Got out of that one. Drifted. Get this—favorite movie: *West Side Story*! A guy in that film named Riff, wasn't there? Held small-time jobs as file clerk, grocery boy, etc. Arrested in '86 for teaching high school without a diploma . . ."

"He taught high school?"

"As a drama coach, it was bullshit. Spent one year farm labor, New Jersey Correctional Institution. Kept his nose clean there entertaining the cons with weekend variety shows, whatever the fuck that means. Out in '87. Drifted."

Kirk was silent.

"You there?"

"No homicides, no assaults, larceny . . ."

"Kirk, the guy's an actor, a pathological liar! He's never told the same story twice in his life! He's a wimp! He's probably staging this whole thing with Meg because he wants to write a book or something. Can't cut it as an actor, so he'll get the publicity elsewhere. Shake up Chicago's hero cop. Be a big shot. He'll pussy his way through this 'til we find him then make a bundle on it from *People* magazine."

"He's smart, David. He knows things about me even you don't."

"He got your war records! Your old police file. It's been done before. Hell, you can trace a guy back to kindergarten if you want to dig for it. We do it all the time. That doesn't make him brilliant, or dangerous. Use your head!"

He was becoming tired of people telling him that.

"I don't know . . ."

"Kirk, for god's sake tell us where you are! We can nail this pussy without a drop of blood, I guarantee it!"

"You guarantee it, David?"

"Ten to one he's too chickenshit to even pull a rod."

"Yeah, but it's that one I'm worried about."

"You're letting Meg suffer needlessly."

"She's still alive."

"Tell us where you are."

"Soon, maybe."

"Kirk, I'm asking you—"

"Gotta go. Thanks for the profile. I'll be in touch."

"You're making a big mistake—"

Kirk hung up.

He sat staring at the phone, hand still covering the receiver. His stomach gurgled.

"Is everything all right?"

She was standing in the bathroom doorway, draped in a towel. Her hair was combed and lustrous, nearly to her shoulders, the lambent epidermis of which shone like translucent marble. He thought absently: she must be naturally curly to keep her hair that nice without equipment.

"Kirk?"

"Yes. It was the office, just reporting in."

"Did they find anything on Riff?"

"A little. I'll tell you over breakfast. Almost ready?"

She came to the chair where the yellow halter lay. Her bosom swelled with a sigh. "God, here we go again."

"We'll stop for some decent clothing, I promise."

"That would be nice."

She bent and picked up his neighbor's wife's panties. "I hate to wear panties two days in a row." She tossed them on the chair, unknotted the towel in front, and dropped it on the bed.

He intended to look away, leave, but she was just so stunning. Her torso, nude, seemed smaller somehow, breasts full and heavy but jutting with firmness, right on her, proportionate despite their circumference.

The wispy patch below the dimple of navel, he noted, though darker, was true blond. Unlike Meg's russet tuft, this was spun of finer thread, airy and light, a cotton candy sheen teasing the eye from the pink envelope beneath. It gave the vulva a pout, a shelf to ride the sweeping juncture of inner thigh, jutting the cunt forward with confident promise.

All this assimilated in an instant, he was finally obliged to turn his head in deference to so much majesty, the images remaining in ghostly outline on the wall.

There was nowhere else to look, really, so he stood and moved away from the bed. "I'm going to see if I can find a paper."

Back to her, he reached for the door.

"Kirk?"

He turned.

"Be careful."

She wore only the shorts now, white and tight about her waist. It made her sexier still. She looked right at him.

"Be right back."

He walked into glaring sun, shielding his eyes with a flat palm.

It was a beautiful day, clear and crisp with only a breath of the coming heat against cloudless sky. He reeled at the lack of city smells and noise. He should always get up this early.

At the end of the courtyard he found a plastic-topped newspaper stand chained to a post. He shoved in coins and scanned the front page. The president was in Florida. Some movie star had died. He riffled through quickly, not sure what he was looking for, satisfied when he didn't find it.

Jill was brushing her hair again when he reentered the cabin. Deft strokes before the wall mirror, body angled and twisted in that way wholly intrinsic to her sex. He closed the door, watching her.

He sensed a warm, outside pressure on his chest, as though breathing was difficult but not unpleasant.

The rumpled bed seemed to stretch to unnatural boundaries between them, still personalized with their imprint. He caught her watching him in the mirror, absolutely sure their minds were attuned. She turned and held the brush before the yellow halter, pulling absently at embedded strands, tapered fingers caressing plastic tines. Her skin held that same translucent glow.

"All set?" he asked.

"I'm ready."

They didn't move for a moment.

And she not until he.

They held out for the Howard Johnson's, which was large and plastic and vapid after the humble country austerity.

By the time they arrived, Jill was famished and he piled eggs and sausage and pancakes before her, watching with amused satisfaction her devouring while he nursed coffee and nibbled toast. He did feel fresher, but the nervous tightness remained, taking appetite with it.

He kept looking at his watch.

"I'm eating as fast as I can."

He smiled wanly. "I know. Take it easy."

She forked pancake. "How did you sleep?"

He colored lightly; was this in reference to his morning hard-on? "All right."

"You tossed a lot."

"Did I?"

She nodded into the orange juice. "And talked."

"Really? What about?"

She shrugged. "Couldn't make much sense of it. You were perspiring, though, quite a bit. Was it a nightmare?"

She looked up from her food when he didn't answer.

"Kirk? What's the matter, you're pale as a ghost!"

He gulped coffee.

"What was the nightmare about? Was it Meg?"

He sighed, looking for the waitress. "No. It's a long story."

"Tell me."

"In the car."

"All right. Just give me another minute here."

"Don't choke," he said sincerely, "there's time." Though he didn't really feel this last.

Jill patted her mouth, and the waitress appeared right on schedule. "Anything else I can get you folks?"

"Just the check, thanks."

"Be right back!"

Jill sat back with a contented groan, hand pressing her tummy. "God, I didn't know I was so hungry! You've *got* to get me out of these shorts now!"

He smiled at the double entendre, and she caught it a second later.

"I know this is inappropriate under the circumstances," she began demurely, "but in some ways I'm really enjoying this. Forgive me, I know that's indelicate."

"I understand. It could be pleasant in another situation."

"Yes."

She toyed with the end of her spoon. "You know, I really expected you to make a pass at me there in the room this morning."

He tried to look innocent of the memory, despite the sudden shot of adrenaline. "Oh?"

"I mean, I was parading about pretty shamelessly."

"You weren't parading."

"I don't know what got into me. Pretty embarrassing, I guess."

"No. You're lovely."

"Maybe it had something to do with being prodded by that big thing two mornings in a row . . ."

He cleared his throat against a rising heat. "Well. Like you said: in another situation . . ."

"You said that."

"Right."

"Anyway," she went on, "I wouldn't have minded. The pass, I mean."

He didn't know what to say. "Thank you."

She smiled. "Don't thank me yet."

He could see she was as uncomfortable as he with this, but enjoying it too. It conjured memories of chocolate malt dates, fast cars, pimples— something he hadn't thought about forever. And there *was* a certain reckless raciness about it. Why shouldn't they make love? The impossibleness of the circumstances made it all the more plausible. Even romantic, in an angular sort of way. Desperate times made men do strange things. Like falling in love during a war—

His hand jumped involuntarily, knocking over his coffee in a great splash. He grabbed for it with trembling fingers.

"Hey, are you all right?"

Her brow was cleft with concern.

He righted the fallen cup into its saucer.

It seemed very loud, suddenly, in the restaurant.

"Kirk? Did I scare you off?"

He forced a grin. "Of course not. I really shouldn't drink coffee."

He couldn't seem to stop trembling. What the hell was this?

She stared at him.

He dabbed the beige splotch with his napkin, avoiding her eyes.

"I'm sorry," she apologized, "I was out of line."

"No, really! It's not you."

She caught the stabbing napkin, holding it. "What, then?"

He was searching for words that wouldn't come, images held in stubborn abeyance, when the waitress reappeared. "You folks have a good day, now!"

He picked up the check and fished for a tip, glad for the intervention.

Heading toward the door together, she grabbed his arm suddenly. "Oh, God, look!"

His hand was halfway into his jacket before he saw what she was heading so exuberantly for: a souvenir table stacked with T-shirts and summer shorts and other paraphernalia. All embroidered with a circular design proclaiming KANSAS! THE SUNFLOWER STATE!

"Oh, God, look, here's underwear too!"

"I'm not sure I like sunflowers on my underpants."

"Beggars can't be choosers. Grab 'em!"

She bought two blouses and a pair of shorts that fit, panties, a pair of clogs. He bought a couple of sports shirts, underwear, but had to make do with Foley's trousers and jacket. They found another section that sold toothpaste, brushes, and disposable razors.

She came back from the women's john grimacing, still clutching her package. "Wouldn't you know, they're cleaning the damn thing—I can't get in for fifteen minutes!"

He looked at his watch.

She caught his arm. "Skip it, come on."

In the car, underway, she checked in the rearview mirror, then unhooked the yellow halter.

She spilled free, alabaster bright in the open sun. He couldn't not look. Creased here and there from the suffocating halter, she jiggled expansively, happily, under the vibrating motor. Jill appeared oblivious, as if this momentary airing was a dutiful function performed for two plump, irrepressible children. She tore open the paper bag and slipped the new T-shirt over her head.

She worked the tight shorts off with a grunt, withdrew the new panties. She stepped into them, pulled upward, arching her pelvis at the roof like a belly dancer. She repeated this with the shorts, folded the soiled clothes in the bag, and tossed it in the back.

"Show's over."

She sighed in contentment.

She rolled her head toward him. "So? Any reaction from the peanut gallery?"

"Plenty, thanks."

"It'll be on my bill. Feel like talking now?"

The tightening again. "All right."

"About the spilled coffee?"

He couldn't stop from gripping the wheel, forced himself to relax before she caught it.

He glanced to his left. Endless rows of corn sweeping to the horizon. Lined with careful, time-honored precision by some sun-baked soul who probably never fired a gun in his life, never had anyone who hated him.

Something about it got to him—the unending fields of life-giving sustenance, the comforting isolation, the smell of earth, the knowledge that here was a guileless place where man's only intent was working hard to fulfill a productive end. The canopy of primitive blue stretching to the horizon.

Something loosened inside him.

Unexpectedly he felt the beginning sting of tears.

Get a hold of yourself, for chrissake!

But he needed to talk.

Now. To this woman.

Out here. Where the crows, and the corn, and the undulating phone wires asked nothing of him.

"Did you know Riff had been in prison?"

Jill raised an eyebrow ironically. "Nothing about Riff would surprise me!" She looked over at Kirk, who stared at the road, his eyes rigid, not speaking.

"Kirk?"

"Want to hear a story?"

She was rapt. "Tell me."

He searched inward, seeking the beginning. Wanting very much, for some reason, to get it right.

"Once upon a time in another world, I was a rookie cop. This was before I went into business with my brother David. I wasn't long out of the armed forces, and I felt being a cop was a job I was suited for, both temperamentally and because of my jungle training overseas: one kind of jungle is pretty much like another, that's what I figured. I turned out to be not far wrong.

"I was a beat cop for about six years. I did my job well, won some medals."

"Quite a few, according to your trophy case."

Kirk shrugged modestly. "I did okay. Before most beat cops were doing it, I was cruising in a black-and-white with Ken Brenan, my partner, an old vet. I was still pretty green as far as the precinct was concerned, but I was trying hard to get some grade and I had my war record, and Ken took me under his wing and helped. We worked well together and the others knew it, some were even jealous. I had my moments of stumbling, of course, moments of depression from the war. I'd done a lot of killing over there, too much. I wasn't always sure being a cop was such a hot idea. But Ken was there acting as buffer, covering for me when he shouldn't, talking me back up when the memories of 'Nam got me down.

"Anyway, I began to get pretty good. Then real good. It all just seemed to open up. Promotions started coming easy. Ken said I was a natural. Pretty soon even the others began to see that I was making my own breaks, taking my own chances. Deserving what I got. I fit in, was well liked.

"One night we got a call, a 918 over on Sycamore and Troost, somebody shooting up a tenement. Sounded like a typical Saturday night drunk, some welfare hothead making big noise for his wife. We'd seen it before. We pulled up at the curb and I ran up the front stoop, drawing my piece. I could hear the crackle of the box behind me as Ken called in to confirm, then went around to cover the back.

"Inside the tenement it was all dark hallways and

crying babies and piss smell. I was halfway up to the second floor when I heard the shot. Just one shot, sounded like a .22 pistol.

"The building got real quiet.

"I reached the top of the landing and started down this black tunnel, little white eyes peeking at me from behind thin yellow slits, whispering, children's shuffling. At the end of the corridor there was a room angled off by itself in a kind of alcove, several yards from the next closest one. It was from behind that I heard the noise. First a male voice, then a female.

" 'Talk to me,' he says, 'tell me you like it.'

" 'I like it,' she sobs, 'I like it, Johnny!'

"I could tell he was hurting her, hurting her bad, but I couldn't move there for a second outside in the hall, like my feet were magnetized. I just kept staring at that paint-peeling wooden door and listening, frozen to the spot.

" 'Talk to me,' he threatens, 'tell me how it feels!'

" 'I like it,' she cries, 'I like it in my ass . . .'

" 'Tell me,' he hisses.

" 'I like it, Johnny . . . you like it too!'

"That finally did it—she was suffering. I kicked the door in, squatted, aimed the piece."

Kirk paused, fingering away a rivulet of sweat about to find his eyes.

Jill was leaning toward him tensely. "Yes—?"

He wiped the hand on Foley's trousers, watching the road.

"She was on her stomach, arms and legs lashed to the bed, spread-eagle. She still had a wedding veil atop her head, the gown and flowers rumpled on the floor. She was looking right at me, the prettiest black woman I've ever seen, face contorted in pain, lips drawn back from these dazzling white teeth. He was on top of her, crushing her, a big white guy, his thing in her ass. He had a pistol pressed to her ear. He looked like a stepped-on frog when he saw me.

"For just a second nobody moved."

Jill waited. "Yes—?"

Kirk seemed almost in a trance. "Then she, the woman . . . she reached out for me . . . reached out for me . . ."

Jill watched him. He was there, but he wasn't there. "Kirk? What happened then?"

Kirk blinked.

Looked at her, swallowed. "The guy . . . then he, the guy, swung his piece toward me. I think I yelled, 'Don't!' Then we fired, both at once. His slug caught me in the right shoulder, slammed me against the door frame, spoiled my aim. When the smoke cleared, I heard screaming. He was staring down at her, pulling his own hair, screaming. I'd missed him completely, shot her face away.

"He just kept on screaming—terrible screams—so piercing in that little room. I think I covered my ears at one point. I got dizzy with the screaming and the blood. There was a lot of blood, like the walls—the side of his face—had been spray painted.

"I heard someone coming through the door behind me. Then . . . that's all I remember. Like I passed out or something."

Kirk looked over at her.

She was watching him, open-mouthed.

"I came to in the squad car. Ken was driving fast, all the windows down. He gave me this kind of half smile when he saw me coming around, patted my shoulder, asked me if I was all right. He said he'd found me up on the second level, unconscious. Not hurt, though, just out—exhausted. From overwork, he said."

"What about the couple in the—"

"He said there wasn't any couple. Just some kid at the end of the hall playing with his dad's .22 pistol. Nobody hurt. Routine. He said I needed rest, been pushing it too hard, he'd recommend a vacation to the captain. Not to worry, he'd cover for me."

"You mean, you dreamed all that about the shooting?"

"Apparently."

"Wow. Did you take the vacation?"

"Yeah. When my brother David got wind of it, he just hit the ceiling. 'You're getting out of that fucking suicide squad,' he said. Two weeks later I was working for him in the security business, making twice the money I had with the precinct. I missed the boys, but what the hell."

"Did you ever have the dream again?"

"Yes. Vacationing with Meg in San Diego. I had the dream twice there. And several times after that."

"The same dream exactly?"

"It didn't vary much. Then as the years went on, it seemed to trail off. I've only dreamed it occasionally over the past five years. And it began to get muddled."

"When was the last time you had it?"

"Yesterday morning. I hadn't dreamed it for years, then, wham, there it was again. Pretty vivid this time. I woke up in a sweat."

"Jesus. What do you suppose provoked it?"

"I don't know. I was thinking maybe it had something to do with whatever drug it was Riff spiked our drinks with. Maybe it made me hallucinate. Did you have any weird dreams that morning?"

"Not that I recall."

He shrugged. "Well, something caused it."

She watched the road a moment. "Have you— did you ever consider therapy, a counselor?"

"I was dating Meg when I had the dream the first time, back in a little Chicago flat with cracked ceilings. My life was chaotic, falling in love with her, trying to be a good cop at the same time, trying to make a success of civilian life. I guess I just pushed the dream aside, pretended it wasn't there, or thought it wasn't very important. I'm still not sure it's very important."

"Important enough to make you spill your coffee all over the table. You never told Meg about it?"

He shook his head. "I'd had some fatigue during the war, spent some time in the infirmary at Fort Dix. I figured the dream was just part of the same old bugaboo of war working on me, battle shock, the forty-yard stare and all that. A lot of fellas had combat fatigue, I didn't want to drag all that into my marriage. I wanted to be bigger than that, the right kind of man for Meg, a whole man, you know? I was young."

"So you never discussed Vietnam with your wife?"

"A little. Not much. I just didn't see the point. All those killings, it wasn't pleasant. Anyway, things were crazy enough just being a cop. Besides, everything was going great with us in the beginning, terrific. We were in love, had a . . . had a great sex life. At least . . ."

"At least, what?"

"At least until after the wedding."

"What happened after that?"

"Nothing. Meg was wonderful. I still loved her. I just . . . couldn't . . ."

"You stopped making love to her."

"Not all at once, but yes, pretty much. After a while, pretty much altogether." He nodded slowly, mind elsewhere. "Pretty much altogether . . ."

He dragged a sleeve across his forehead, coming back. "Christ, I shouldn't be talking about this."

"Why not? And then what, you met Susan?"

Kirk nodded.

"And fell in love with her?"

"No, not really. I mean, I didn't stop loving Meg, but Susan was . . . Susan was . . ."

"You could make love to Susan."

"Yes."

"Even with the dreams."

"Yes."

"Why?"

"I don't know. She isn't as pretty as Meg. I don't

know. I kept thinking it had something to do with the fact that we weren't married."

"You were tired of marriage, bored?"

"No, the funny thing is, I wasn't. I'm still not tired of Meg. I just . . . because of the sex, the lack of it, I'm just not sure I know her anymore. But I'm not tired of her."

"I see."

Jill was silent a moment.

"Could you make love to me?"

He looked over at her.

"It's just a hypothetical question," she assured him.

He looked back at the road. "Under other circumstances? Yes."

She lay her head against the seat rest, closed her eyes for a moment. "Well, then, remind me never to marry you."

He smiled.

"So what's the verdict, Doctor?" he asked.

"You mean the prognosis? I don't have one, I'm not a doctor. But my advice would be to see one immediately."

"A little late for that."

"You'll get her back."

"No. Not completely . . ."

She folded her arms, face impassive. "Don't be so skeptical. A good man is hard to find. I should know. Meg knows it too."

His smile was rueful. "But, as Mae West used to paraphrase: 'A hard man is good to find.'"

Jill made a wry face, then reached out and began

to knead his shoulder gently again. "Anyway, life goes on."

"Amen."

He smiled gratefully at the massage, feeling a growing lightness, an inner ease. Glad he'd talked to her.

"I've never told anyone about the dreams before," he confessed. "Not even Susan. You're the first."

Her face showed the flattery.

After a moment she squeezed his arm, took his hand from the wheel, kissed the back of it lightly. "Thank you."

He looked over at her, sighed, smiled ruefully.

"Don't thank me yet."

Fourteen

Meg and Riff swept past the Kansas-Colorado line in mid-afternoon, an event undistinguished but for the single, innocuous WELCOME TO COLORADO sign and its accompanying sparrow hawk. Certainly not by a noticeable change in the terrain. It remained flat, linear, and uninspiring—to Meg at least, a lunar landscape with wheat.

She shared little of her husband's newfound appreciation for farm and country: she was a city girl born and bred, though, contrarily, it was she who had talked most of some kind of outbound vacation among soot-free air and lofty balsams. Kirk, detached and ruminative, had been impossible to uproot.

She found herself—as they sped bullet-like toward the heart of their combined destinies—missing him suddenly.

Not in the way she would miss someone offering protection and solace, but in the ordinary, even prosaic way a woman misses her husband.

That they had not made love in months seemed

abruptly less important now since her recent de-
bauch with Riff. Probably because sex itself, once
gratified, seemed less important, or at least took on
a proper perspective.

Which was not to say she might not sleep with
Riff again.

You don't have to be sane, she was finding out, to
be a superb lover.

And she still hated Kirk somewhat.

It was difficult in one enlightened swoop to eradicate years of built-up resentment. She had—did—
blame him entirely for the ongoing dissolution of
their marriage, the gradual opaqueness between
them, built up like months of unchecked tartar. His
grinding secretiveness, unending brooding, self-
induced isolation, no matter to what degree she
reached out, and she had, often. Reached out until
it hurt. Until it was too late. Until she'd been
pushed into having the affair.

Who was she fooling? A one-night stand.

An act she'd instantly regretted. But been able to
erase. Unfortunately not so her anger with Kirk.

It was, in fact, something of a revelation—since
Riff—to discover just how humiliated and angry
she'd been by her husband's selfish indifference,
how much more debasing that was than her silly
fling, or even the worst kind of perversion she
might commit with Riff.

Indeed, her revelry with Riff she counted not at
all. It may have been a psyche-shattering experience to some, a wedge to strain the sturdiest marriage of the average woman; not Meg. To her it was
a cock up the ass. Membrane against membrane. A

physicality affecting the nowness of the moment, a fragment of time encompassing only itself, insulated from the universe, radiating nothing. And a better way than some of getting an orgasm. If the anus was the means, then let it serve. It satisfied.

She viewed all this not as immoral but as an immutable progression of ongoing circumstances, neither condoning nor regretting events not really in her dominion. Meg, at the first sign of illness, had been known to thrust impatient fingers down her throat and give the sickness to the toilet, flushing the problem with all the contrition of yesterday's gas bill.

She had, in her present situation, the convenient if ominous alibi of rape. Thus insular, she could afford to be philosophical, even look forward to the sex with some sense of propriety. It felt good when nothing else did.

Yet, just now, that prideful, lusting part of her temporarily sated, she seemed to be experiencing an exhilaratingly clearheaded view of things, and of Kirk.

Feeling again like a woman, she could discern him again as a man.

It made him attractive.

There was much to him beyond sexuality and husbandry that was worthwhile. Which, paradoxically, made him sexy.

She felt confident now in her ability to seduce him. For the first time.

And all because of Riff, his would-be executioner. Irony of ironies. Her troubles were just beginning.

Nor had the coupling with Riff diminished her fear of him.

She had never feared his penis, even when it was urinating on her. It became formidable only through its association with her, and then his balls were in her court. Without her heated entrapment, her power to transform it, his terrible saber was merely utilitarian, even silly.

But Riff, though inseparable from his sex, was not controlled by it. Even under different circumstances she would find no leverage there. He was too prideful of his bountiful gifts to be led by them, too centered on some larger sphere of order. Sexual prowess was something he'd conquered and put behind him early on; he sought more elusive affirmations. She could contain him to the extent that her helpless bucking supplied some necessary pieces, but she could never hope to become the puzzle; his parts were too varied for her hole, so to speak.

She would not be saved by fucking him.

Kirk alone could save her. Because Kirk gave Riff what Riff really needed. Whatever that was.

Kirk—she knew—would fill Riff's cup of need to brimming.

Yes . . . served up by his faithless wife.

Who now decided she was in love with him again.

The universe was not just.

She sat, now, in the windblown face of it, hair swept, chin high and resolute, eyes watching the highway, the future, unfolding. . . .

"Colorado looks just like Kansas."

"Eastern Colorado looks just like western Kansas," Riff corrected. "I was here for Secret Service training years ago," he grinned. "They've got a camp just a few miles from here. Disguise it as a farm, complete with missile silo! Think they're clever . . ." He looked out the window, his face unreadable. "It's flat, all right. Stays pretty much that way until Denver."

"And then?"

"Then mountains."

"Is that where we're headed?"

"Questions, questions."

"Sorry, I forgot; surprise me."

He grinned. "How're you feeling? Get enough lunch?"

"Not quite. Could we stop and get thirty or forty more of those delicious Big Macs?"

He chuckled. "Sorry about that. Necessity of the game; have to keep moving. We'll try to get some better grub tonight. You're all right otherwise?"

"My butt's a little sore."

"You flatter me, my dear."

She gave him a lidded smirk. "That's not exactly what I meant; I'm talking about the car seat."

"Best motel in Colorado tonight, I promise."

"Don't put yourself out."

"My pleasure."

"Why are you so concerned about my health?"

"You're probably going to need it; we might see a little action again tonight."

She looked at him flatly. "What does that mean?"

"It means we're in Billy Hallicur country, and Billy Halicur is one lean, mean sum bitch is what it means Ms. Megan Kirkland."

"Okay, I'll bite, who is he?"

"Billy Kick-in-the-Ass Hallicur is the A number onest. Nightcrawler that ever stalked tire-footed gook across a rice paddy on a moonless night is who Billy Hallicur is. Boy has a way with a knife in the dark, no doubt about it, yassah."

"A night what?"

"Nightcrawler. Didn't that war hero husband of yours ever tell you anything that happened over there in the 'Nam?"

"Not a whole lot, no."

"Well, that's funny, considering that he was the first Nightcrawler of the group. The first and the last and undeniably the best, don't let anyone ever tell you differently. There were about half a dozen of us in the beginning. We'd go out nights and knife gooks without orders, our own private little platoon, you might call it. And we got real good at it. A lean, mean killing machine is what we were. But Kirk, Kirk was the best of us." He shook his head and clicked his tongue in admiration. "Best all round goddamn soldier in this man's army. And probably the navy, air force, and marines to boot. You should have seen that sweet bastard in action, Meg . . . God-damn, it was enough to give you a hard-on!"

"I doubt it in my case. You sound like a redneck."

Riff shrugged undauntedly. "We all sounded like rednecks in the 'Nam. Hell, we didn't go over there to write poetry; we went to kill people. And we did it well. Some better than others."

"Like Kirk."

"Sergeant John Kirkland, 442 Combat Engineers. Motherfucker could slit your throat and steal your balls while you sat there finishing your cigarette. Walked like a goddamn cat. Over leaves! In the fucking jungle! Had what we used to call a natch'ral aptitude for it. Beautiful fucking thing to see, sweet Jesus, it was! Man was a friggin' shadow. See"—he molded air before him with his hands—"Kirk taught us that you didn't try to walk *through* the jungle. You couldn't beat it like that, make a noise everytime. You had to *become* the fucking jungle, that was the secret! Be at one with the trees and the vines and the mud and the other things that walked there. He was a killer of the mind first, the knife second." He gave his head another envying shake.

Meg watched him, fascinated by this lunacy.

"Of course, the other boys were good too, mind you. I think Ernie Little knew more about woodlore than any of us—part Cherokee, you know. But Kirk's the one who took hold of us. He's the one who learned quickest, sprinted ahead of the others. He was just a born soldier, that's all. How do you think he racked up all those stateside medals and citations with the force? By learning to be an animal. All that police work was just residue carried over from the jungle days when he was in his prime."

"He was in his prime then, was he?"

"Bet your sweet ass, Meggie, and you do have a sweet ass. Kirk was never in better shape than when in the 'Nam. As hot as you may think he was as a cop, it didn't come close to what he accomplished out there in the jungles. A couple of more like Kirk, and we'd have won us that war, pulled it right out from under Westmoreland's cold feet."

His tone went suddenly sullen.

"Then one day it all went to shit . . ."

She turned in the seat toward him, genuinely interested all at once. "What do you mean?"

Riff's face was like granite, cheek tensed into a bubble at the jawline.

"Oh, they got on to us; hell, I suppose it was only a matter of time before they did. Too many disgruntled sideliners flapping their yaps, and, to be truthful, our Nightcrawler fame had begun to spread. So in comes the old man one day and drags us off."

"Dragged you off to where?"

Riff waved at the air. "Oh, any goddamn where they wanted. The army, in its profound ignorance, figured if we were that good as a team, we'd be twice as valuable separately. Stupid assholes. What they didn't realize was, without Kirk leading, there were no Nightcrawlers. Even Dave Kirkland knew that."

"David? You knew Kirk's brother?"

He grinned. "He was right there with us, sweet thing, just a couple of ranks higher. Didn't Kirk tell you?"

Meg turned away angrily. "Neither one of them told me."

"Ah, yes, I forgot. You knew Dave first, didn't you? But you preferred little brother."

Megan turned to face him, but there wasn't a trace of sarcasm in Riff's eyes. They gazed thoughtfully at her, waiting her reaction.

She determined to give him none. She spoke coolly.

"So you're saying the army trained you to go out into the jungle alone and kill Viet Cong?"

"We were already trained, honey, trained by the best. They just rechanneled the action, so to speak, and made the choices. Oh, we were their pets! Ha! And we thought we were going to be court-marshaled!"

"What sort of choices?"

"Any choices they wanted. If Ho Chi Minh was contracted for, then Ho Chi Minh was dead. And believe me, he was a consideration. But the CIA had bigger plans for Ho, so that was dropped. Mostly it was political figures, a few Cong brass, people like that. They were just warming up, mostly in Saigon, which was a switch after working the jungle. But we adapted just as well to the back alleys. Oh, they had bigger fish in mind, bigger wars in mind. That's all Vietnam was, you know, a training ground for the big show. Half the time they had us studying maps of Red Square. Do you know how hard it is to get an *undoctored* map of Red Square? Fucking Ruskies keep altering them."

"You're telling me the CIA was in Vietnam?"

He gave her a patient look. "Dearest Megan, the CIA *was* fucking Vietnam! Where the hell did you spend the seventies, in a convent? *Some* of this shit must have leaked back to the states."

"This is really quite unbelievable, Riff," she replied calmly, gazing back out at the scenery.

He smiled. "Yep. Unbelievable. That was the whole idea. Logical, though. Oh, they already had the Green Berets, we weren't exactly a new concept. Of course, we made those guys look like Boy Scouts. Anyway, they broke us apart and that was the end of the fun. And the best damn team of undercover fighters since the ninjas. I've never gotten over it. I can assure you Kirk's never gotten over it."

"Well, he never mentioned it to me, Riff."

"Of course not, that was part of the code."

He was almost convincing, she was thinking. A complete loony tune, mad as a March hare . . . but almost convincing. He must have been an actor at some time in his life.

"Well, now, speak of the devil . . ."

He was looking past her out her side window, head bent, foot on the brake, slowing the car.

She followed his gaze across a sea of waving corn.

The car slowed further and came to rest against the shoulder.

"Why are we stopping? What's the matter?"

He nodded at her window. "See anything out there, Meg?"

She looked again. "Yes, a field of corn."

He nodded sagely. "Little early in the season for harvesting, wouldn't you say?"

She could see the big combine now, far off in the distance, a glint of red metal in the afternoon sun riding a yellow horizon.

"I really wouldn't know, Riff. Who cares?"

"Well," he began, unfastening his seat belt, "unless you don't care about a bullet in the back later tonight, or a knife through the larynx, I'd say you better care a great deal. And, unless I've missed my

guess, I'd say that's Billy Hallicur riding that combine."

Meg squinted. "How can you tell from here? You
can't see his face."

"I know how to drive a John Deere harvester
across a field of corn, which is more than that
sonofabitch knows. You ready?"

She turned to see him holding the big hunting
knife.

"What in the world are you doing?"

He grinned, eyes on the field. "I'm going to put
old Billy boy away before he does the same to me."

Meg was stupefied.

"But . . . now? Here in the open? What about the
police, the—"

"It's not the police you have to worry about,
honey. It's the home office. And they already know
we're here. Otherwise they wouldn't have Billy sta-
tioned out there on that machine posing—rather
badly—as a farmer, so he can nail us somewhere up
ahead."

She rolled her eyes. "This is ridiculous!"

He didn't flinch. "Don't bet on it. Didn't you see
that road construction sign back there? This highway no doubt makes a convenient detour onto an
unpaved country road that will take us right next to
that farmer's place. That's just the way the big boys
work."

She sighed. "Really? And if that's Billy What's-
his-name, then what did they do with the farmer?"

Riff tossed his head noncommittally. "Sent him
on a nice all expense-paid vacation, maybe. Told
him they had to run a radon check. Who knows?

They've got a million ways. Better slip your shoes on."

"I don't suppose you'd consider letting me stay in the car?"

He chortled. "You're a killer, Meg!"

No, she thought sourly as he hopped out and ran around to her side, you're the one that's supposed to be the killer.

He opened the door for her.

She was slipping on her left shoe. "This is a joke, Riff! The highway patrol will see the car!"

He was scanning the vacant horizon, bisected by the gray ribbon of highway. "Not many cops along this route."

He opened the trunk, pulled out a gallon plastic water jug. "But in case someone does stop, you can show them this; we'll say we overheated and went to the farmer's house for water."

He handed it to her.

It was heavy.

"Thanks a lot."

"Stick close to me now and keep your head down."

He guided her off the shoulder, across a narrow gully, and into the farmer's field. They were met immediately by a wall of barbed wire.

Riff showed her how to crawl under it. She was filthy with dirt and dust when they emerged inside the field.

"Now what?"

Riff bent, scooped up a handful of dust, and let it trickle through his fingers, watching which way the breeze blew it. It looked, to Meg, like a showy gesture, unconvincing.

"What's that for? In case he smells us coming?"

Riff, no longer apparently in the mood for sarcasm, dusted off his hands thoughtfully.

"He might see us; the corn will screen our approach, but this ground is pretty dry. We could leave a trail of dust if we're not careful. Take measured steps."

"Yessir."

She started off behind him, lugging the heavy plastic jug, immediately tripped and fell flat.

He turned around and gave her scornful look. "I can see you haven't had a lot of training in guerilla warfare."

She whacked dust from her thighs. "No, but it's right up there near the top of my list, just under corn husking."

"Hurry up, he's not going to be a sitting duck for us all day." He searched the cloudless sky as if for marauding planes. "The office has probably already spotted us and phoned him the information. Let's just hope Billy sticks to the old Nightcrawler code."

She struggled up, dragging the jug. "What, uh, code is that?"

"No guns."

They started down an earthen row, flanked on either side by six-foot columns of leafy corn stalks.

It was like walking in an English garden maze, green and yellow vegetation in every direction, except for the narrow portal behind them, which showed a small patch of highway and the front edge of the car parked beside it. Even that dwindled to insignificance in a few minutes.

The smell of earth, of green and growing things was heady, nearly overpowering, and struck something deep down inside her, something organic, rich, and almost cosmic.

Meg could see immediately that if they jogged over even a few rows in either direction, she would be completely lost in a labyrinth of corn.

So, naturally, that's the first thing he did.

"What are you doing? We're going to get lost!"

"Keep your voice down!" He turned to her. "And keep your *head* down, for chrissake! Haven't you ever stalked game before in your life? Christ!"

Meg lugged the plastic jug, the curved handle biting into her flesh, shoulder aching under the effort. She tried switching hands, but that helped only for a few seconds.

They moved past the rows of towering stalks, silent sentinels bending gently with the overhead wind.

Riff loped along like an Indian in the movies, back slightly bent, arms hung at his side, head cocked to one side as though listening for something. He was totally into it. Making a big show for my benefit, Meg thought. Jerk. He looks like an asshole.

She could hear a distant clanking noise.

"What is that?"

"The harvester. He's about eighty yards to our right, two o'clock."

"How can you tell?"

"I can tell."

"This goddamn jug is heavy!"

"Shh!"

He whipped around, finger to his pursed lips, eyes glaring at her. "Listen!"

She listened.

Heard nothing, aside from the constant clanking. "What?"

Riff hung his head, turned it from side to side like a dog observing a curiosity. He made a face.

"Shit. He's on to us."

She felt a little thrill in her stomach despite all the absurdity. "How can you tell?"

"He's stopped the machine."

Meg listened.

She didn't see how he could tell anything. It still sounded the same to her.

"Maybe he's taking a lunch break," she offered.

Riff was concentrating. "Maybe . . ."

She sighed heavily under the weight of the jug and finally set it down in the dirt.

"So what do we do now?"

Riff was listening, head cocked.

Meg looked about.

But there was nothing to see. Just the narrow corridor of towering corn stalks, twin walls of yellow and green leaves that seemed to recede in either direction forever.

A dun-colored starling lit atop one of the swaying stalks and plucked at something, darted off again. Meg caught Riff looking at it too, and knew he was thinking the same thing as she: if they could fly above the endless rows like a bird, they could see down into the maze. Spot the quarry.

"This way."

He was pointing at the green wall. He stepped through, pulling her along, green husks brushing their shoulders. He turned.

It was another corridor, another floor of dirt, another sky of blue.

Riff began walking along the row, head cocked, back bent, placing his steps carefully.

He stopped.

He turned. "This way."

He pushed through another wall, pulling her, leaves slapping her face. He turned again.

Another corridor. More corn.

He began walking.

It was a moment before she realized she'd forgotten the plastic jug. Well, to hell with it.

Riff stopped, cocked, listening.

"He's close."

Meg felt herself shudder once.

The clanking sound, closer-sounding a moment before, ceased altogether.

Riff listened.

Somewhere a crow cawed.

There was a far-off swishing sound. Probably a car passing on the highway.

Where was the highway? She wasn't sure anymore, they'd turned so often. Lost. In a farmer's field. It was almost funny.

She looked at Riff. And was struck with the sudden, utter certainty that he was lost too.

He doesn't know where the hell we are!

She turned to look down the endless corridor. Was it that way? She couldn't tell from the swishing sound; it seemed to come from all around them. Maybe it was the other way. That would be north. Right?

Right, Riff?

She turned back to him.

And found him gone.

"Riff?"

Not a sound, not a movement.

She was alone.

"Oh, Christ, not again!"

She spun in all directions.

"Riff? Shit! Come on!"

Alone! *Now's your chance!*

She started to run—

But which way?

The corridor looked the same at both ends, a greenish blur. The highway could be at either one or neither, they had turned around so much. Damn him, he did it on purpose, spun me around like that to confuse me!

It doesn't matter, it will come out somewhere.

Run!

She started again—

Froze as she saw a glint of red between waving shocks.

She crept forward, bent, peering between the leaves. The red expanded, became a shape. She pushed through into another corridor. And there was the big metal harvester.

Meg hesitated, eyes darting over the shiny machinery, the metal frame, the blades like riverboat paddles, the covered cab. Which was empty.

She stood staring at it, undecided. Would the

owner be back any second? Was he hiding somewhere behind it? Had Riff killed him already?

She spun, gasping, at a sound behind her. But
there was nothing. A bird or a rabbit or something.

She turned and faced the combine. The whole
hulking contraption looked like some titanic insect
that had landed out here in the middle of this rich
harvest, eaten itself to bursting, turned red, and
died.

"Hello?"

She regretted it immediately.

If Riff was really right about the CIA, they'd kill
her too. But Riff wasn't right, of course; Riff was a
lunatic. Right?

She crept closer to the big machine and climbed
up on the running board to peer into the cabin. Yes,
empty. An overturned coffee cup, a *Playboy* magazine, a panel of levers and dials, a vacant, jeans-
worn seat. A pipe.

Maybe she should get in and start the engine
and drive it out of here.

No. She didn't know how to start it or drive it,
and besides, then they really would know where
she was.

The best thing to do was find the highway.

She leapt down.

Okay, now which way?

She was trying to remember which way the harvester had been facing when seen from the highway: parallel to or at a right angle with the
highway?

She was suddenly very sorry she no longer had
the plastic water jug; she was terribly thirsty.

Think now. Don't go running blindly off. They had been headed west. The sun rises in the east, sets in the west. She looked up. The sun appeared directly overhead.

If only she could *see* something!

Never mind, just walk. Even a maze has an exit.

She took a step forward—cried out as something slammed into her with a grunt, driving the breath from her, knocking her to the earth with a shock. She rolled, settled, spat dirt, looked up in time to see a figure darting into the screen of corn stalks, disappearing. She could hear his crashing retreat. Riff? The farmer?

The crashing sounds faded.

Silence again.

She picked herself up shakily, listening, legs wobbling like rubber bands. Silence but for her own ragged breath. She began loping painfully down the narrow corridor of leaves and corn. Her ribs ached just under her left breast where she'd been struck by the man. She fingered lightly a swelling bruise there.

She'd have given fifty dollars gladly for a drink of water. Her mouth tasted of dust. How do people work out here all day in this sun?

Another thrashing sound.

She stumbled to a halt as the wall of corn twenty feet ahead of her burst open on her left, and another figure went flying past, arms pumping, legs flashing: Riff.

He disappeared, like the first figure, with a crashing of bent stalks and a fading thump of shoes on plowed soil.

Silence again.

Meg hesitated, blinking in the bright sun.

She thought she heard the swish of traffic again, but now it sounded like it was coming from her right.

Best to follow the sound. Otherwise she might wander around in this damn field all day.

She turned right and stepped through a screen of stalks. Into yet another corridor. Again the swishing sounds, still—it seemed—to her right. She cut over into one more row. Then she began loping down the corridor, wincing at the stitch in her side.

It still didn't seem like she was far enough to her right. Then again, she could be wrong about all of it, heading farther and farther away from the highway instead of closing in on it. All right, she'd cut over one more row.

She stepped through the screen of corn, turned left.

"Oh, there you are."

She spun. Riff was standing just behind her, wiping the big hunting knife with a flat green leaf. He was naked to the waist. There was a crumpled figure at his feet.

She stood staring at the two of them, hands clasped before her as if she were praying. The figure on the ground wore bib overalls, laced work boots. He was hatless, a shock of red hair catching the sun. She could not see his face from there.

"I might be wrong," Riff was saying, tossing the bloody leaf away. "It doesn't look like Billy Hallicur."

He shoved the body with his shoe, rolling it onto

its back. A pond of scarlet was gathering above the crotch. Riff bent, dipped a forefinger into the pool, began applying it to his naked chest in a serpent design.

This completed, he began his dance.

Meg crept forward as if pulled by invisible strings.

The face on the ground was white, impassive, younger than she'd have thought. Dead.

"Who is he?"

Riff stopped, kicking up a final puff of yellow dust.

He cocked his head above the tangled form, chest laboring like a bellows, the hair there matted red. He bent down, sliding his hand into a side pocket, then another. In a moment he withdrew an oxblood wallet. He flipped it open matter-of-factly, read.

"Thomas R. Gray, 1374 Northridge Road, Spalding, Colorado."

Riff scanned the tops of the stalks casually, as if he could see over them. "Are we that close to Spalding?" he asked nobody.

Meg took a step forward.

"H-he's just a farmer . . ."

Riff tossed the wallet on the dead man's stomach with a plop. "Don't kid yourself, he's CIA."

Meg stood over the corpse now, staring down as if mesmerized, face blank, pupils enlarged. ". . . just some poor dumb farmer . . ."

"Oh, the sunburn looks real, sure. Makeup. He's government, mark my word."

She whirled, fists above her head, shrieking at him like a crazed witch.

"He's a farmer, you stupid son of a bitch! He's a goddamn farmer! You just killed an innocent man! Can't you see that, you loony fucking creep!"

Face drained, spittle flecking her mouth, she stood there before him shaking apoplectically, her teeth actually chattering.

"Meg—"

"An innocent man! With a family! A wife, kids! An old hunting dog! Chickens! Cows! A fucking mortgage!"

"Meg, you're screaming. You're not used to this. I understand. In 'Nam, we—"

She screamed louder, shaking her head as a terrier shakes a rat, spittle flying to the sides. "There isn't any 'Nam, there isn't any 'Nam, there isn't any 'Nam! You were never in fucking Vietnam! You never knew my husband! You made it all up! In your head, Riff! It's all in your fucking head!"

He spanked the air in a calming gesture that was nearly comic. "You're hysterical, I understand. The sun—"

"It's not the fucking sun, Riff! It's you! It's *you*!"

He nodded patiently. "I didn't say it wasn't Billy Hallicur, I said it didn't *look* like him. Listen, those guys have plastic surgery all the time. Now that I think about it, it probably is Billy Hallicur. Or some other CIA plant. Don't worry about it . . ."

She gave him one final incredulous look and fell to her knees. Fingers tangled in her hair, she stared numbly at the sightless corpse. "You, and this sick little movie in your head! Oh Jesus, Jesus, I can't believe I—I don't believe I . . ."

Riff's face grew hard. "What? You don't believe what?"

Meg folded, sobbing into her hands, rocking to and fro.

"Don't believe you slept with me, with a killer? Is that it? Huh?"

Her body hitched with wracking sobs, rocking.

"Well, don't worry, Mrs. Kirkland, you won't be put through that again. That little episode served its purpose."

He jerked her abruptly to her feet, fingers digging into her shoulder. She hardly felt it.

He shook her hard. Again, until her head snapped back and she stopped the choking sobs.

She opened tear-filled eyes and regarded him.

His face seemed to soften, fingers relaxing slowly against her flesh. He looked into her blurred eyes, nodded resignedly, appraising her. "Maybe you're right."

She sniffed, wiped a finger under her dripping nose.

"Maybe I am crazy. After what they put us through in that hospital, I wouldn't doubt it. I wouldn't doubt it . . ." His voice trailed off, eyes wandering. "I wouldn't doubt it . . ."

A crow flapped noisily overhead.

Riff watched it lazily, chin in the air.

Then he was back. He patted her arm conciliatorily.

"I'm sorry. Truly. I know you're having a hard time understanding all this. It isn't easy."

He held her chin in his hand, wiped away a dust-streaked tear.

"But the game's almost over. I promise."

He brushed a stray curl from her eye.

"I'd like to at least stay friends until then. Can we do that?"

Meg stared listlessly at him, the top of her head baking under the bright sun.

Riff held out a peace-offering hand.

She dragged in a cleansing breath. Looked down at the hand. Took it.

He patted her arm again, put his around her shoulder, and she let herself be led down the plowed row toward the car.

Yes, she must find a way to kill him.

Fifteen

He awoke in the car, temple banging uncomfortably against the side window, jolting him.

He started, eyes wide, and sat up rigidly, fighting for comprehension.

Jill was smiling apologetically at him from behind the wheel. "Sorry about that; pothole. I tried to dodge it."

Memory rushed in. He fell back into the seat, rubbing his head absently. "Where are we?"

She consulted the map between them briefly. "Colorado. Just passed through a town called Spalding. Except I didn't see any town, just cornfields. Did you have a nice nap?" It wasn't sarcastic, it was concerned.

"How long was I out?"

"Couple of hours anyway."

He shook his head, lids closed. "My wife is in mortal danger and I'm asleep on the job."

"Don't be silly, you needed it or you wouldn't have gone out. Keep up the strength, that's what you've got to remember."

"Thanks, coach." But the guilt remained.

He glanced at his watch: getting on toward five.

He looked out over the vast, brooding flatness, the falling sun.

"Colorado looks just like Kansas."

"Only at the border. It'll change dramatically after Denver. Are you hungry? You didn't eat much of your cheeseburger."

"I'm okay. How 'bout you, tired of driving?"

"No, I'm fine."

He squeezed her arm. "I appreciate it."

She smiled. "I know you do."

She watched him a moment.

"You look worried," she said at length.

He ran a hand through his hair, sighed. "I am. I don't know where we're going, what we're supposed to look for."

She looked at the road. "I've been thinking about that. Feel like talking?"

"Can't dance."

"Okay. Here's some theories: maybe we've been going about this whole thing wrong, thinking about Riff in the wrong way, I mean."

"We did pretty well up to finding the tape recorder."

"That's not what I mean. I'm talking about him. His personality. Who he is."

"And?"

"Let's take a new tack. We've played the game by his rules anyway, let's explore those rules for a moment. He wants you to believe that the two of you were in the war together. Okay, let's stop dismissing that out of hand, pretend for the moment it's true."

"But it isn't—I'd remember him. I've remembered everybody, I told you their names."

Jill held up a cautionary hand.

"You're not thinking like Riff. Put reality on hold a moment. Look: what you want most is to rescue your wife, right? But if you insist on doing that alone—without squad cars and guns—then you're going to have to outwit him. Or at least satisfy him that you can play this game. Maybe the way to do that is to start thinking like him.

"Now so far, as you said, we've done well, going along, playing the game. But we're stuck for a clue as to the next location. Either we missed one back at the last motel—in which case it's too late—or there wasn't a clue to be had. Why don't we go on the second assumption? That would mean— assuming we're on the right road—that the clue is somewhere up ahead, en route. Some kind of visual thing like a sign or something. Okay?"

"I've sort of been counting on that, yeah."

"Right. Which means it's probably not a good idea for you to take any more naps."

He shifted uncomfortably. "You're filling me with confidence."

"No, I think we're all right so far. I've been watching and there hasn't been much more than corn and sky. Besides, I doubt he'd plant anything this early on. Probably he'll wait until tonight at the next rest stop."

Kirk was watching the roadside with tense antic- ipation. "Christ, I hope so."

"The point is, whatever the visual clue, it will have to be something you both would recognize as significant, some shared experience that trips a synapsis in your brain. Doesn't that reinforce the theory you've known each other before?"

He wasn't buying it. "I'm telling you I'd remember him. I never met the guy before night before last."

"How did he know about your war record, your police citations?"

"Because they're precisely that—*records*. On file. He looked them up."

"And old man Dieter?"

"That wouldn't be hard to trace."

"What about Susan?"

"Obviously he's been watching me very closely—or having me watched."

"The Silver Star he put in your trophy case."

"Got it at a pawnshop."

Jill made an impatient sound. "You keep throwing up a rational wall! Stick to that and we go nowhere. Assume he did know you from some time before, and the things he's doing begin to make sense. Then at least you've got revenge as a motive, not some abstract theory about hero worship."

Kirk was unswayed. "You're completely dismissing my brother's report; according to the files, Riff Walker was unsuccessful getting into *any* branch of the armed forces."

She sighed in exasperation. "It's just a police profile, Kirk, it isn't perfect."

"Jill," he began patiently, "you're insulting the department and my brother. If David says Riff Walker wasn't in the army, then he wasn't in the army."

"He could have changed his name, had plastic surgery . . ."

He laughed. "To what end? Why would he want to do all that? You've seen too many espionage thrillers!" He cushioned it. "Look, I know you're just trying to help, and I appreciate it, I do. But you're bending reality to fit your theories, ignoring the facts. Trained people are working on this, Jill."

"One trained person."

"David's the best. And my brother. Give him his due. Christ, I'm tying his hands as it is!"

She sat quietly behind the wheel, drumming her fingers pensively along the plastic rim of it.

That, and the thrum of the motor, seemed inordinately loud.

Finally he threw up his hands. "All right, I'll shut up and listen. Go on with your theories."

She sat up eagerly, shifted to a more comfortable position in the seat.

"Okay, let's take it from the top. You're sitting home one night with your wife, minding your own business. The doorbell rings and here's this guy you've never seen or heard of before, showing up like an old crony with war stories and good cheer. He's relaxed, confident, either telling the truth or a terrific actor. You ask him thinly disguised questions, checking on him: he gives them all back with an A plus.

"Everybody gets a little drunk and goes to bed. You wake up with your wife gone. There's a strange woman in your bed. Both you and the woman, not to mention the bed, are naked, the house stripped. Why would he do that?"

"To slow me down, humiliate me?"

"That would be the initial response, sure. But think about this: you just spent the whole night swapping war stories with this guy. That's all he talked about. Now, what was it you told me the Nightcrawlers used to do before going out on a hunt? Strip down half naked. Sometimes completely naked, right? You'd rid yourselves of all of society's trappings, make yourselves feel at one with the forest, like a jungle animal. That's how you beat the enemy. Right?"

"Go on."

"So, maybe he's not humiliating you before the chase. Maybe he's preparing you for it."

Kirk thought about it.

"Okay," she continued, "now think about this: if all the things I just described were to happen to any other individual in the world, what would be his first reaction?"

"To call the police. That's what I did."

"But you hung up. Why?"

"I thought better of it—the guy wasn't acting rationally, I thought he might hurt Meg if the cops came rushing in."

"Which is exactly what he wanted you to think, wanted you to do. *Knew* you would do."

"And how did he know that?"

"Maybe because he's played these kinds of games with you before. Like in Vietnam, for instance."

"That's stretching it, but go on."

"All right." She gathered breath. "There you are naked and defenseless in the house. Now, the first thing you have to do before you face the enemy is find food and clothing. The old combat rules, you told me yourself. Now Riff could have made you search for transportation too by slashing the tires on the car or fouling the motor or something. But he didn't. Why?"

"Tell me."

"Because he'd already proven his point. He wasn't trying to slow you down, he was trying to get you to think like an infantryman again. Trying to get you back into that survival mode. Trying to get you to *remember*."

"Remember what?"

"I'm getting to that. Now: how does a soldier track the enemy? By following footprints, broken branches, visual clues, right?"

"Not a whole lot of medicine chest mirrors in Vietnam jungles, Jill."

"Not a whole lot of lipstick either, but that's what he used to write the first clue with. It also happens to be the same color of the stuff you guys used to draw on your big hairy chests after one of your grisly night raids."

"We drew serpents, not birth dates. It was a lot of adolescent tough-guy histrionics. Sick shit."

"Maybe, but sick shit you were awfully good at. Let's move on: where did the first clue take us? To your illicit lover. That ring any bells?"

"Bells?"

"Connect in any way with your past, something you might have shared with Riff?"

"I've never had an illicit affair before."

She thought a moment.

"Okay. We'll skip that one. Maybe it was just another way to keep you on edge, shock you into that lean, mean survival spirit again. But it proved one thing: that you were capable of solving the first clue and discovering the second, the playing card in the photo album."

"You found that one."

"But I was there because of you."

He snorted. "You're stretching. Riff couldn't have predicted I'd bring you along."

"He might have, if he knew you as well as he claims. Combat soldiers get almost psychically close sometimes, you said so yourself."

"Proceed."

"Next destination, Dieter's house. How did it make you feel being there, Kirk?"

"At Dieter's? Humiliated."

"What else?"

"Well. Afraid. I wasn't sure I could take his kid."

"But you did, handily. And with a martial arts technique you thought you'd forgotten. I'm betting Riff taught it to you, or was there when it was being taught."

He groaned impatiently.

"Just *consider* it!"

"Go on."

"How else did the Dieter thing make you feel?"

"Humiliated, that's all."

"Are you sure?"

He thought. "I don't know. Yeah, I guess so. What are you searching for?"

"You tell me. If it's in there, you'll know it."

He slid down in the seat a bit, collar riding up.

"The boy ... the boy who fell in the abandoned building. I always felt responsible for him."

"Why? It was an accident."

He heaved a sigh. "I don't know ... because ... maybe if I'd been faster ..."

"You tried."

"Yeah. I don't know. I just always felt it was somehow my fault, like I'd killed him. Like he expected something from me I couldn't ... shit, I don't know."

"Anything like that ever happen to you before?"

He looked sharply at her. "Christ no! Don't you think I'd remember if it had?"

"Maybe not ... if you repressed it."

He studied her a moment.

Then looked away. "You're grasping at straws."

She shrugged. "Maybe. This is all theory, just killing time. Let's move on, or are you pissed off now?"

"Why should I be pissed off?"

"Okay. The next clue was in the motel. The tape recorder in the ventilation duct."

"Not really a clue."

"But it did require some initiative just to find it. Ever done anything like that before?"

"Raided heating vents? No."

"Anything similar?"

"No ..."

"What—? You started to say something."

He was rubbing his head again, lost in thought. "I'm trying to remember. It seems I did do some kind of duct work before ..."

"In the war?"

"No, all I did was jungle work in the war."

"Are you sure?"

"What do you mean, am I sure? Of course I'm sure."

"What about after the war, Kirk?"

"After . . . ?"

He looked all but dazed with reflection. Rubbing . . .

"What are you thinking about?"

He frowned, distracted. Shook his head.

"Nothing . . . probably nothing."

She watched him.

He shook his head again. "Forget it." He looked at her. "So, what's all this building to?"

"Just the theory that you might have known each other from before. And that Riff's trying to get you to remember when you did, by playing out this little treasure hunt, making you solve these combat-style riddles."

"Even if that was his intent, why be so elaborate about it? Why doesn't he just come out and tell me? Why the convoluted game?"

She looked at him thoughtfully, on the verge of something. "In the beginning we believed it was because he was trying to prove something, remember?—his masculinity or something—he's the best combat soldier, the best jungle tracker—the way to prove that to the world is by besting you. But what if it's not that at all? I mean, wouldn't he save himself a lot of trouble just by picking a fight with you? Yet he chose this other way, knowing the danger, the legal ramifications. He did it anyway."

"Right. Why?"

"He must hate you for something you did to him—some unpardonable sin ... only *you* can't remember what it was! And it's killing him! He wants you to remember! To relive something in your mind. Something you've pushed aside for years. The way you pushed aside that dream about killing the young bride in the tenement, the way you hid it from Meg. You hurt Riff badly and he wants his pound of flesh. Like Dieter's son—the one that challenged you on the front lawn because he thinks you killed his brother—that's the way Riff hates you.

"But," she continued animatedly, "revenge is meaningless if the offending party can't recall the event that's prompted it! That's why he's got you chasing all over the country, solving these little visual clues: he's trying to shake your memory, fill in that blank space you've chosen to forget."

"Again—why not just tell me?"

"He wants you to *feel* it. Experience the pain of it. Besides, where's the guarantee you'd believe him?"

"And once he does have me believing him?"

She was silent for a moment. "Then ... I suppose he'll extract his revenge."

He shook his head dubiously. "I don't know. You're asking me to believe there's a black hole somewhere in my past, something I just arbitrarily edited out of my mind years ago. Sorry. I can't relate."

"Kirk, you said yourself you tried to push things out of your mind to avoid telling Meg, like your Vietnam experiences, your dream about killing the young bride in the tenement. Why is this so hard to conceive of?"

He was silent, shaking his head slowly.

She glanced over at him, waiting. "Kirk, it's the only thing that makes sense!"

"I do not have a memory loss," he said measuredly. "I simply do not." His upper lip was peppered with sweat.

The finality of his last sentence hung in the windswept interior.

She took a hand from the wheel, placed it on his knee gently. "Kirk, how can you know that?" she ventured insistently. "You said you had some battle fatigue during the war. You were in a hospital for a while. Did the doctors mention anything about memory loss due to combat?"

He watched the road quietly.

"I don't remember much about the hospital stay, to tell you the truth. I had some shrapnel wounds, they had me on painkillers. It was all pretty hazy. I might have had some small memory loss, sure, but nothing as extensive as what you're suggesting."

He looked away from her, out his side window.

After a moment she squeezed the leg under her hand and patted it. "Look, it's just a theory. Don't be upset."

He looked down at her hand. "Pretty goddamn complicated theory—you must have worked hard at it."

She shrugged, smiled. "My mind tends to run on in an automobile. Why don't we just let it go for now? We should stop for gas soon, maybe we can grab some dinner. Okay?"

He was staring broodingly at the sage-littered hills.

"Okay, Kirk?"

"Whatever you say."

They hit Denver at dusk.

With no signs, no clues, nothing.

Kirk was visibly despondent.

They pulled in at a Denny's on the outskirts of town, and Jill parked the Nova. She set the brake and blew out a weary breath, shaking her head, loosening her hair.

"I could eat a horse. In fact, I could eat just about anything besides a cheeseburger."

Kirk unfastened his seat belt desultorily.

"Don't let it get you down," she said, appraising him, "we'll find the next clue. It's here in town somewhere, I'd bet on it. You'll feel better once you've eaten."

He sat morosely staring at the red and green Denny's sign. "I'm thinking about calling David."

"Why?"

"Telling him where we are, where we last heard from Riff."

Jill looked shocked. "Oh? May I ask why?"

"I'm not being fair to Meg. We're not getting anywhere. I'm exhausted. Meg's in danger. I can't bear thinking about that anymore. This was a mistake. I've had it."

"And what if you've been right all along and he does something drastic as soon as the cops show up?"

"They're fresh, organized, experts. David will get

us a SWAT team. They know how to handle these things. If it's not already too late, that is."

She settled back, folded her arms. "What happened to the expert tracker?"

He didn't meet her eyes. "That was a long time ago, Jill."

She reached out, slid her hand into his gently, rubbing the back of it with her thumb. "You are exhausted. From worry. And you're hungry. You barely ate today, your blood sugar's down."

His eyes looked listless, filmy. "I want this over with." He looked up at her. "Don't you?"

She looked away, down past her lap at the new shoes she'd bought at the souvenir shop. She pointed the toes. "Of course. It's just . . ."

"What?"

"I don't know, I can't help but feel we're getting close. They're here somewhere, in Denver. Can't you feel it?"

He looked out at the highway, the wave of winking city lights beyond. "I'm not sure what I feel anymore."

She squeezed his hand. "Tell you what: let's have dinner, a nice one with real meat and vegetables, a drink. Then get a room somewhere, a bath. If you're still set on calling David, do it then. How 'bout it?"

He rubbed his eyes, slapped his free hand on his knee resignedly. "All right. Maybe you're right."

After dinner—a big one of steak, green beans, mashed potatoes, garlic bread, coffee, apple pie—Kirk admitted he did feel better. He washed his face and hands in the lavatory, cleansing away the road film, combed his hair, and came back to the booth somewhat refreshed.

Jill had ordered the catfish and salad, a piece of carrot cake for dessert. She was finishing her coffee when he sat down again.

"Feeling better?"

"Better." Though dark circles still belied inward weariness. "What's the game plan?"

She gave a mischievous look, reached down on the plastic seat beside her, and produced a hefty Denver Yellow Pages, placing it on the table between them. "I stole this from the pay phone next to the rest rooms. Scoot around," she said, flipping pages, "and we'll have a look."

It was a semicircular booth, and Kirk edged over next to her as Jill found the Motels section.

He discerned her scheme immediately. "I'm supposed to look for the name of any motel that leaps out at me, right? What if Riff's decided to use a hotel this time? Or go up in the mountains, for that matter, and pitch a tent?"

"He hasn't so far. Anything look familiar yet?"

"I've never been to Denver before."

"That should help, actually; you won't be confusing Riff's clue with something you've already seen here."

But most of the motels were brand names, and none of the remaining generic titles provoked any response from Kirk.

They were through the list in a few pages.

"That's the last one."

"Sorry. Nothing rings a bell. Maybe the last clue

really was back at that motel in Missouri and we just missed it."

Jill closed the book, took a final swig from her cup. "These are mostly just names, words on paper. Only a few of the larger concerns actually printed their company logos. The Missouri motel—the Lucky 6—had a playing card for a logo. That's the kind of thing we're looking for."

"Shall we get back on the road and look, then?"

"My next suggestion!"

They covered the Denver outskirts twice, east and west. Then they drove downtown and covered the metropolitan area.

Kirk kept shaking his head.

Jill was beginning to yawn distractedly.

"You're tired," he offered, behind the wheel, "we should put an end to this tonight."

She covered her mouth self-consciously. "We still haven't seen the south side of town."

"Jill, it may not even be this town! We're both exhausted. I'm finding a place to stay the night and call David."

She sighed defeat. "Well, at least look for a place on the south side if you're going to quit."

He found a Travelodge half an hour later, pulled into the parking lot.

He cut the engine. "I'll check us in."

He paused, fingers on the handle, and looked back at her. "You think I'm doing the wrong thing, don't you?"

She lay against the seat, head back, eyes closed. "It isn't that . . . I just, it seems were so close, I hate to give up. We've done so well up to now. I guess I dislike the idea of a bunch of . . . strangers crashing in on us. The guns . . ."

"Jill, we've looked! Our eyes are red with neon! What else can we do without real clues?"

She shook her head, eyes still closed, arms limp. "I don't know."

He watched her profile, fair and glowing in the lot's dim lights. "It's funny, isn't it? I practically dragged you into this thing, and now you're the one that's cheerleading."

She rolled her head, looked up at him.

"I appreciate everything you've done, Jill. Really."

She watched him. "Do you?"

"Yes."

She looked into his eyes. "Do you, Kirk?" Her mouth said: kiss me.

He licked his lips once.

She reached up, cupped the back of his neck, drew him down.

He let himself be kissed but held back, making it mostly chaste.

When it was over, when he started to withdraw again, she caught his lapel, her fingers surprisingly strong. "What am I going to do with you?" she breathed. "I thought you could be more appreciative than that."

"Jill . . ."

She pressed a finger to his lips, lifted the WEL-COME TO KANSAS shirt with the other hand. In the soft sodium glow of distant lights, she was iridescent, nipples almost invisibly pale.

She eased his head down again.

He kissed the dilated expanse of her, mouth trembling, tongue lingering on the salty areolas, hearing her hiss. It would be so easy just to let go. More than easy . . . it would be escape . . .

She was already fumbling at his zipper, breath labored, face flushed. "Kirk . . ."

She shoved down the white shorts with a tearing sound, taking the panties with them, twisted up her knees, winced at the awkward position as she dragged the material down her legs, looped them over her heels, tossed them on the floor. She looked eagerly into his eyes. And her breath caught.

He was staring distantly out the window, his weight on her but not there anymore.

She let herself relax.

He sensed the change and looked down sheepishly. "I'm sorry."

"I understand."

"I can't, not with . . ."

"It's okay."

"I'm sorry."

"You said that. Want to get off me please?"

He pulled back, bracing himself against the dash while she adjusted the blouse. The air was suffocating with humiliation. He just stared at her, he couldn't say he was sorry again.

He watched as she fished for the panties and shorts, pulled them up smoothly, a blond curl dangling in her face. She folded it back with the flat of her palm, keeping her hand there against the side of her head a moment as if pressing back her virtue; sure it was in place, she brought the hand away.

Finished, she sat staring straight ahead a moment.

"Shall we get separate rooms, then?"

"No," he said, "I don't think that's necessary or even wise under the circumstances."

She didn't say anything for a time.

Then he heard her whispering, almost inaudibly. "Stupid . . . stupid . . ."

He didn't know what to say.

She pushed up in a moment. "Let's go, then, I'm bushed."

On the way to the room he wondered if he would regret it someday, or if regret were even part of his vocabulary anymore.

Sixteen

Meg lay in darkness, staring at darkness.

She lay exhausted and drained in flimsy underthings, the stress of the day, the big dinner, the hot bath that followed, all pressing down heavily on body and soul, leaving her weak, defenseless. Not that that mattered; he had made no attempt to touch her since they'd come to the motel. He'd simply stripped down, turned back the covers, switched off the light, and gone to bed. She'd followed suit a moment later, grateful for his indifference.

She loathed the sight of him now.

It was the second motel of the evening. As with the night before, they had entered Denver and sought one location for resting, bathing, unwinding. Then he had taken her to dinner at a nice place called the Hunter's Lodge—rustic, genteel, expensive—bought her prime rib, several drinks, then relocated them here at the Great Western. Meg assumed all this gadding about was to confound possible pursuers, Kirk included, probably. It seemed egregious to her, but Riff knew what he was doing, or acted like he did.

She had said very little to Riff since the incident in the cornfield. He didn't press, seemed to honor her desire for silence between them.

Repulsed now at the idea, she had nonetheless expected him to approach her sexually once in the bed. He had not, surprising her.

The longer she lay there against the cool sheets and thought about it, the more it began to seem that that first time he'd had sex with her would also be the last time. That it had, in fact, not been sex with him at all, but an act, a performance. To what end, she could not guess. Maybe it had been simply a test of her will, further proof of his dominance. She only knew that she felt used now. He had even hinted at that in the cornfield. He was through with her sexually.

Perhaps nearly through with her altogether.

There was a closing sense of finality about the room, about the entire atmosphere surrounding them. The end of this—if not at hand—was near. She could taste it.

And the biggest surprise of all—especially to him—was that she might even have been the catalyst.

He had killed a man.

Perhaps many men.

He would kill Kirk too. Then her.

He was insane.

Therefore, he must die first.

If she could do it. If.

The raspy sound of his snoring reached her ears.

She tensed involuntarily, having anticipated this moment all day. She felt the quickening knock of her heart.

It was time to move . . .

She allowed her head a deft, sideways move on the pillow. She could see his vague outline on the pillow beside her, but she could not tell if his eyes were open or not. His breathing was audible, regular. But that could be a trick. Knowing Riff, it probably was a trick. But she would never know for sure unless she tried. The time for prudent caution was behind her. It was try now or die later. She should have done this long ago.

Holding her breath, moving as quietly and carefully as possible, Meg turned her body on the giving mattress, and let her legs drop over the edge. She sat up rigidly, silently. Stayed that way for a while, facing the venetian blinds of the window, the hazy Denver night without. If he said something now, she was merely going for a drink of water. She had her mouth shaped for the words.

But he said nothing.

She listened for the soft burr of his breathing, found it, let herself loosen a notch. Next came standing.

The bed would give most when she attempted that. But she had been too undecided, earlier when she came to bed, to bring the weapon with her. She had thought about it, feeling the weight of it in her dress pocket as she folded the material over the back of the chair. But she had been afraid he would want to talk, or make love, and, in the process, find it. The thought had made her breathless with terror, locking her body in paralysis as she'd stood there in her underwear on the thin motel rug. He had caught her lack of movement, asked her what was wrong. She had shook her head, saying she'd wished merely that she had her nightie to wear to bed, the one in Chicago. He had grunted indifferently and lain back, switching off the light. Leaving her to stand there in the dark, listening to the slamming of her heart.

Meg took a deep breath. Now or never. And stood.

The bed groaned once, then was still.

Had he heard? Felt it?

There was no way to know. He was either asleep or playing with her. She'd find out soon enough.

She padded silently to the chair, turned, watched his dim outline a moment, and bent down to the dress.

The knife was not there.

A steel-gloved fist punched her chest.

When had he known? In the restaurant? The moment she'd slipped it from beside her plate when his head was turned, placed it on the seat beside her? Was it while he was leaving the tip, as she'd slid it silently into her pocket? Had he known even then? Playing out his cruel game with her the way he was playing it out with Kirk?

She stood shivering in her underwear, listening to the rise and fall of his breathing across the room.

She turned the dress over in her hands, checked the other pocket just to be sure. The steak knife was not there.

Trembling, sick in her soul, she lay the material

across the chair back again. She would have to make a break for it. Now. While he seemingly slept.

She pictured herself creeping to the door, placing her hand on the shiny knob, gently twisting the lock at its center, easing open the door, which would doubtless squeak loudly, tensing herself for the launch into the night—feeling his fingers clamping into her flesh, spinning her about, into his grinning face . . .

No. Running was impossible for her. She had known that all along. You probably couldn't even open the damn door without a key. She was done. Unless she contrived another way to kill him, she was done.

There was the phone. But he'd surely hear that. The bastard had ears like a hawk, that was the trouble.

She'd just have to bide her time a bit longer.

Though not, she felt sure, much longer at all.

She turned from the door.

Saw the glint on the rug beneath the chair legs.

She knelt eagerly and picked up the knife, its serrated edge gleaming dully under the feeble light from the blinds. It must have dropped out when she was in bed. A miracle he hadn't heard the thump.

Or had he?

She held it now by the thin wooden handle, fist abruptly slick with sweat. She tested the blade with a finger tentatively: it was sharp, and serrated, and long, and deadly. A good strong shove, and it would enter the tightest stomach, biting through muscle and tendon, bringing bright blood.

It felt—in Riff's presence—about as effective as a toothpick.

In the restaurant it had loomed large, a bright lance of steel against the soft tablecloth. Now it seemed unfairly flimsy, a weak extension of her trembling hand. It wouldn't cut butter.

She turned, walked carefully, slowly, back to the bed, one foot laid deliberately, precisely before the other. At the foot she hesitated: it's not too late to get rid of this thing, come back to bed, forget the whole hopeless business.

She lingered, weaving uncertainly, vaguely nauseated.

But she was dead anyway. Maybe better now than later. Out of the way, she might even somehow improve Kirk's chances.

Kirk.

Why had it taken this to make her realize how much she loved him? Dear God, what had been wrong with her? How could they have drifted so far apart? Is day-to-day survival so inane it takes courting death to make you see the obvious?

I love you, Kirk. I do this now because I love you. . . .

She moved silently to Riff's side of the bed, looked down at his lithe, angular shadow. It was dark, but she could see that the sheet was down. She had a sudden impulse to forget the stomach, the pulsing throat, and stab down at the great penis. To sever his pride and joy, the adoring icon he held in such lofty esteem that he even painted its likeness on his chest.

How would he look then?

Stick that up someone's ass!

But she dismissed it. That might not kill him.

And killing him is what it took.

She gathered herself, raised the blade . . .

And knew with utter certainty she could not do it.

One quick movement, one-tenth of a second, that's all it took. His life would be over, she would be free, Kirk would be safe. Life would be real again. And she could not do it. She could not do it.

She could not.

She stood there, shuddering spastically, knife fisted above her head, staring impotently at the dark, vulnerable length of him. The open, maddening invitation of him. The fist remained raised.

Words came before she knew it. "You're awake, aren't you, you bastard?"

Even in the gloom she could detect the curl of his smile.

With confident calm, eyes yet closed, he spoke in the darkness. "Those steak knives make a nasty wound. Jagged. Kirk and I used one in Saigon once, did I tell you? Suspected Cong insurgent parading as a minister of public works. We bugged his house—tape recorder in the air-conditioning duct. The knife was for a prowling houseboy. He bled a lot. But that's the CIA for you, they didn't want us taking weapons onto the premises, in case we got caught. Assholes. We never got caught. You going to use that thing or what?"

"You know I'm not."

"Shall you give it to me, then?"

"Maybe. Or maybe I'll cut off your fat prick first."

He grunted. "You won't have to. Kirk will do that when he finds out what we did in the other bed."

"He won't find out."

Riff said nothing.

"Will he? Riff?"

She was suddenly burning up.

"Riff? Oh Christ, what have you done?"

He reached out a hand.

"Give me the knife, and I'll tell you."

Seventeen

"No!"

He vaulted upright, throwing aside the sheet, face blanched, teeth bared, eyes starting grotesquely from his head. Body one rigid muscle.

Jill was beside him instantly, arm around him, hand cupping his sweat-bathed cheek. Holding him, holding him, until the straining tautness eased away.

"Hey . . . hey! It's okay! Kirk!"

His breath came so fast she was frightened he would hyperventilate, pass out. She vigorously rubbed his back.

But his eyes had lost that glazed look. He was focusing. Remembering. "It's all right . . . I'm all right."

His sweat-greasy hand sought hers.

She rubbed, patted. "The dream again?"

He nodded, sitting in the bed, pulling his legs up beneath him in a meditation pose, elbowing sweat from his brow. "Vivid."

She squeezed his neck muscles. "God, you're dripping! I'll get a towel!"

She was back in a moment, wiping him, patting. He was still shivering spasmodically. "It's okay," she soothed, "only a dream."

He closed his eyes a moment, reliving it. "Thirsty . . ."

"Here." She jumped up again and brought him back a motel glass of cold water. He took it gratefully, drained it. He turned and handed it back, managed a smile. "That's better, thanks."

"Can you talk about it?"

He shuddered, pulled the sheet up. "Same dream. Same tenement. Same couple on the bed, bride and groom. The screaming . . . screaming . . ."

"The man, you mean."

Kirk frowned abruptly.

He licked his lips, thoughtful. "No, it . . . it didn't sound like a man screaming this time . . ."

She tucked the sheet about his waist. "The woman, then?"

He shook his head slowly. "I don't think so . . ."

She studied him. "Want more water?"

"No, thanks."

Jill settled on the mattress beside him. "You mentioned before there was someone coming in the door behind you. Who?"

He stared into space for a time, then shook his head. "Can't get it, too fuzzy."

"Could that be where the screaming is coming from?"

He stared at nothing. Shrugged. "Could be. I'm not sure."

"What is it?"

He looked at her.

"You're thinking of something, Kirk, what is it?"

He gazed back at the motel walls, unblinking. "The walls . . ."

"What about them?"

"They were white this time . . . and soft."

"Soft?"

"Yeah, like clouds . . . like cotton."

"Cotton."

She could almost see the wheels turning in his head.

He turned to her abruptly, face bright. "Where's the phone book?"

"Right here." She jumped over him, fished the heavy book from the bottom shelf of the nightstand, flicking on the light as she handed him the bulky tome.

Kirk cracked it, flipped pages for the Motels section. Flipping, flipping, now tracing downward with an index finger. Stopping.

"We're in the wrong place."

Jill bent over, seeking the line of print above his finger:

COTTONWOOD MOTEL

She looked up at him.

He was nodding to himself, studying the black type on the yellow page. "That's the place. That's where they are . . . or were last." He seemed pleased with himself.

"It was in your dream?"

"The name of the tenement: the Cottonwood . . . no, no, wait, that's not it . . . club. Yes. The Cotton Club."

"A tenement named the Cotton Club?"

But he was up now, grabbing for his slacks. "That's the place! Get dressed! We're checking out!"

Jill tossed the book on the bed and did as she was told.

It was clear across town, an independent establishment, old, moderately priced. They had plenty of rooms at the Cottonwood.

The question was: which one?

Jill suggested seven because that was the number of the room at the Lucky 6 in Missouri, and because no other clues were available.

Kirk knew the minute they inserted the key in the door and pushed inside, this was it.

Jill went straight to the bathroom to check the mirror; he began to case the bedroom.

"Kirk, look!"

She came through the bathroom door holding up a tube of lipstick. "I found it behind the wastepaper basket! It looked like it had been deliberately placed there! Does it look like Meg's?"

He didn't even bother to examine it. "Could be. Doesn't matter, if there's a bigger clue."

He opened the heating duct and found it.

Jill hurried over to him. "A videotape?"

He sat down on the too-soft bed, holding the cassette in his hands, gazing at the Sony label. "Unless he's planted a VCR in the bathtub, we're going to have to go rent one."

She was at the phone book again. "Maybe there's an all-night place!"

He held the black plastic tape box lightly, turning it over in his hand, a queasy feeling growing in his stomach. This was it. There would be no more clues after this next one. They had done their job well, played by the rules. The payoff was coming, and coming soon. Whatever it was.

"Hello, Video Circus? You're open? Good. I was wondering, do you rent video recorders as well as tapes? Right. Uh, just a sec."

She put her hand over the mouthpiece, called to Kirk. "Only players, they don't record!"

"That's all we need."

"That will be fine. And you're open all night? Great. We'll be right over." She hung up. "We're in business!"

He was already reaching for his keys.

It was nearly dawn.

They stopped long enough at a 7-Eleven to get coffee before returning to the Cottonwood Motel. Kirk could not stop his hands from shaking as he set up the portable VCR.

When he had it plugged into the motel TV, he switched on the rented VCR, popped in the tape, sat back without pushing the Play button.

"What's the matter, Kirk?"

He sat staring at the snowy screen for a moment. "Nothing."

He leaned forward from the edge of the bed and depressed the button.

Another instant of snow, and then the show began.

Faint sound of twangy, oriental music.

The lighting was dim, but the picture quite clear for a home video camera. Riff must have used one of the later models with low-light capability. He was tying Kirk's naked wife to the motel bed with a length of cord.

Soon after that he was spreading some kind of oil over her buttocks.

Jill turned her head. "Oh, Christ, don't tell me . . ."

When she finally managed to look back, Riff was no longer lubricating her, he was in her.

Jill stood, reached for the Off switch. "Sick bastard—"

Kirk grabbed her wrist, painfully, and pulled her back to the bed. "We're watching for clues." His face was stone.

They couldn't hear Riff whispering to her, but they could hear Meg plainly enough.

". . . I like it that way, Johnny, yes! . . ."

Jill shook her head, turned away.

Kirk sat unmoving.

". . . I like it in my ass! . . ."

Jill groaned, watched the wall, arms folded.

". . . you like it too!"

Kirk swallowed once, motionless.

On the screen, Meg began her climax.

Jill jumped up and hit the button. "Enough is enough!"

She stood with her back to the snow-filled screen,

arms wrapped around her as from nonexisting chills; it was, in fact, quite warm in the little motel room.

Kirk sat watching the snow, eyes glistening with the bluish light.

"I'm sorry, Kirk. Truly. The guy is a fucking pervert!"

Kirk didn't move.

Jill rubbed her arms, turned, and switched off the TV, enveloping the room in blessed darkness.

After a moment she came and sat beside him, reaching out, then hesitating, drawing back her hand. "Kirk? Please. At least she's still alive."

"The Cotton Club . . ."

"What—?" And now she touched his arm.

"The Cotton Club. Riff was there. So was I. We weren't supposed to be—not ordinarily—but we were there that night . . ." His voice was singsong, emotionless. As if, knowing all along this was coming, it had been subconsciously rehearsed.

Jill was poised with anticipation; here it comes. She shivered once violently, felt like she was freezing. Or maybe it was because Kirk too was trembling again. The whole bed seemed to shake. And absurd as the notion was, it almost seemed there were other people there in the room with them.

"Vietnam : . . ?" she whispered.

The mattress moved under his nod.

"The club was supposed to be for officers and noncoms. I mean, there weren't any real rules, but the manager was very picky about the clientele. The grunts didn't usually get in. I had never been there before . . . not until that night . . . that night . . ."

If only he would stop shaking. She began to rub his back absently again.

"Riff was in Vietnam with you?"

She could see the black outline of him now.

"Yes. He was there. He was one of us. A Nightcrawler. One of the first. One of the best. Better than me maybe. Or . . . maybe not. But good. One of the best. Crazy. Reckless. He . . . liked it. The rest of us were just trying to stay alive, but Riff . . . Riff liked it. Crazy fuck. Good partner, though. Killed that houseboy with a damn steak knife, you believe that shit? Bastard sneaked up behind us while we were planting that recorder in the air duct. Riff got him, though. One thrust. Steak knife . . ."

She rubbed his neck, massaging. "Why did you go to the Cotton Club?"

She could feel him turning toward her in the darkness.

"Assignment. Cong infiltrator. My stick."

"Stick?"

"We drew match sticks for the tough jobs. The Cotton Club was well lit, lots of brass there to identify you. It was strictly covert. All the stuff we did for them was strictly covert. They weren't even really sure this mark was a Viet Cong, but by then they didn't much care. War was over anyway. They wanted this Cong dead. I got the stick."

She reached for his hand. "Tell me what happened, Kirk."

"She was enjoying it, wasn't she?"

"Who?"

"Meg."

Jill looked at darkness. "I . . . don't know."

"Sure. She was coming."

"Kirk, tell me about the Cotton Club."

He was silent for a time. Then he drew in a deep, shuddery breath. "Not all of it's clear. I do remember it was a solo job, like I said. Riff was on leave, he . . ."

"What? Tell me."

"He'd just gotten . . . married. Yeah, that's right. I remember now. He married this beautiful little . . . beautiful little Vietnamese girl. Hell, they were all beautiful really, that black hair, those eyes . . . but this one, what was her name? . . . Mi Ling . . . she was something else. Sweet. And stacked, for an Asian girl. Riff just flipped out for her. Never saw him like that. Confirmed bachelor. Going to marry this one, though, bring her back to the States. Sweet little thing, couldn't really blame him . . ."

"And you went to the Cotton Club to kill this infiltrator?"

"Night job. Most of them were. Ernie Little had the mark staked out. I went up the stairs posing as a customer. Chinese lanterns all over the place. Don't know what the hell that had to do with cotton. Oriental music piped all through the place, red carpets, lacquered chairs, fancy. Beautiful girls. Best in town. Some of them made a fortune. High-class ass. The mark was in room . . . in room seven. I waited until the hall was empty. Silencer on my automatic. Kicked in the door, came in blasting . . ."

"You shot him?"

"No."

Silence.

"Kirk?"

Silence.

"Kirk? Are you all right?"

"He was . . . fucking her ass . . ."

. . . I like it, johnny . . .

"Crushing the life out of her . . ."

. . . like it in my ass . . .

"Hurting her . . ."

. . . you like it too . . .

"I shot her . . ."

Jill gripped his arm. "By accident, Kirk."

"No."

"Honey, it was an accident."

"No." His voice was that of an automaton. "Orders."

She strained to see his features in the undulating darkness.

"Orders?"

"She was Cong. An infiltrator. Going to get us all killed. That's . . . that's why . . . that's why she married Riff . . . I shot her . . . Mi Ling . . . oh, sweet Jesus . . ."

Jill yelped as he leapt from the bed, pushing her aside roughly, sprinting for the bathroom. The lid was down, so he aimed it at the bathtub, got most of it in there.

She came up behind him with a warm face cloth, held him while he emptied again, then again. She wiped his mouth, ran water in the tub. His skin, when she touched it, was clammy and cool with sweat. She pulled down a towel and patted him dry, draped the terry cloth about his shoulders.

Kirk sagged against porcelain. Coughed.

At length he rolled to one side, sat down hard on his naked rump, back against the cool tub. She dabbed a line of mucus under his nose, combed back his hair with her fingers.

"God, I've been carrying that around for so long, so long . . ."

Jill sat down on the toilet seat. She nudged him with another glass of cold water.

Kirk gulped. "Thanks. Thank you."

"What happened then?"

He pressed the still cold glass to his forehead. "Then? Then I got out of there. Back home to mother. The geniuses from the Pentagon. Oh, I was good at what I did. I covered my ass. They made sure *of that! The bastards! The bastards!*"

"Kirk, shh! It's all right!"

She eased him back down, rubbing his neck.

"Bastards . . ."

"Easy!"

She patted his forehead again.

"Now, you're doing just fine. It's coming out, just the way it should. But you've got to get rid of all of it. Who was the man—with Riff's wife?"

Kirk shrugged, sneering. "I don't remember. Probably just some john, some dumb noncom. Nobody."

"And Riff never knew she was a . . . a prostitute?"

"No. I think some of the fellas had warned him maybe. You had to be on your guard against it. There were so many hookers over there, even girls from supposedly 'good' families. There was just so much poverty. But no, I don't think he ever knew. Poor bastard."

"You started by saying he was at the club, then you said he was on leave. Which is true?"

He blinked.

"I . . . did say that, didn't I?"

"Do you remember seeing him at the club that night?"

"I . . . I'm not sure."

"Could he have been the one behind you? Was Riff the person who came in the door? Were they his screams you heard?"

Kirk stared into space. Began nodding lazily. "Yes . . . that must have been it."

She brushed back stringy hair from his face. "Are you sure? It's important you remember it all."

Kirk licked his lips, looked up at her like a lost child. "I can't see it as clearly as the rest, but yes, it had to be him! I killed his wife and now he's going to kill mine. That's what this is all about. It makes perfect sense. Oh, God . . . Meg!"

Jill stood, retreated to the sink, began washing out the face cloth. "What happened afterward, Kirk? What happened when you reported back to your people?"

He was frowning, struggling inwardly. "I don't know."

"Come on, you were doing fine."

He shook his head helplessly. "It's all just a blank after that. I remember the hospital at Fort Dix. The R and R. The Ping-Pong. Movies. Music. The discharge, coming home . . ."

"But not the breakdown?"

He kept shaking his head. "I can't . . . I can't get that."

The water steaming now, she pressed the hot cloth to her face, gasped, kept it there, released it, looked at herself in the mirror. "Never mind. It will come."

She turned to see Kirk staring sullenly at the bathroom floor, arms wrapped around his legs. "Meg was enjoying it—it wasn't coercion . . ."

Jill put down the cloth and came back to him. "Try not to dwell on it, it's over."

He stared at the floor. "Who could blame her? She certainly wasn't getting any at home. Meg has a right to enjoy herself too . . . I certainly have been."

She reached over and ran hot water in the tub. "We're going to have a nice hot bath."

"I wonder if he'll kill her now that he knows I've seen the tape, now that her purpose is fulfilled."

Jill adjusted the flow, adding cold water to moderate it. "He doesn't know for sure. He doesn't even know we've gotten this far."

Kirk grinned mirthlessly. "He knows. You just don't know Riff. He has eyes and ears everywhere. You should have seen him track Charlie. He never made a mistake! Just when they thought they were safe, there he'd be like a bad penny."

"He won't hurt Meg, not until he's sure he's got you. And not even then, probably. It isn't her he's interested in."

"But that's the way he could hurt me most, by harming her."

"No. He knows Meg is an innocent party. It's you he wants to deal with."

"Let's hope you're right."

"I'm right. Come on, get in the tub. We'll get some breakfast and then start looking for them."

"Denver's not a small town."

"There can't be that many green Volvos here with Illinois plates."

He stepped into the steaming water, laid back. He had to admit it felt wonderful.

He was nearly light-headed, and not—he knew—just from the bath. A dragging weight had been lifted from his subconscious despite the agony of the purging. He did feel lighter. If only Meg was out of danger, he'd be almost jubilant. Even so, he felt more his old self than he had for years. When he did finally face Riff, it would be as a whole man, not a despondent paranoiac. And maybe that's even the way Riff wanted it—maybe it would be a fair fight. After all, he hadn't wanted to kill the girl; it had been orders. Even Riff knew that.

"He's really quite a genius."

She perched on the toilet lid. "Riff?"

"All those clever clues, those little visual catalysts planted along the way to make me remember, strike a chord. I had cut him—the event—completely from my memory . . . he brought it all back in a few short days. All that incredible research into my past, even my present. Old man Dieter. Susan. I thought Susan and I were insulated from the world—but not from Riff. He orchestrated it brilliantly, meticulously. No wonder David came up with an incomplete profile: Riff probably figured a way to doctor it. I wouldn't put it past him. And all to claim vengeance on a man who killed his wife almost twenty years ago. Why did he wait so long? What was he really doing all those years?"

Jill studied him a moment, looked away. "I think you're going to get the chance to ask him very soon."

The logical choice for breakfast was The Peak, a large, moderately priced establishment right next door to the Cottonwood.

It boasted rustic, polished brass and teakwood decor, wagon wheel chandeliers, real wood top tables—wonderfully scarred and beer-stained—lots of deer and mountain goat trophies, even a stuffed cougar with agate eyes leering at everybody from above the stone fireplace. Despite the feeling he'd just stepped into a taxidermist's shop, Kirk sensed a warmth and institutional realness about the place. It smelled of pine and good cooking.

They took a table near the large picture window on the east wall, and Jill gazed outward at a picture postcard view of Rocky Mountain National Park.

"It's beautiful," she murmured wistfully, watching a hawk scout a far-off fir-dotted rim.

Kirk followed her gaze. "Yes, like everything else on this sojourn, it would be truly enjoyable under any other circumstances."

Jill picked up her menu without looking at him. "Maybe we should try to make the most of what we've got." There was enough cryptic innuendo in her voice to make him look up quizzically.

But Jill was concerning herself with her menu now, so Kirk picked up one of his own. It had a red plastic cover showcasing a silver line drawing of an elk's head above two crossed Winchesters. It proclaimed: "Good Morning! Welcome to The Peak! Denver's Best Vittles!"

"I recommend the steak and eggs! Delicious!"

They looked up from their menus simultaneously to find Riff Walker sitting down between them.

Jill stared blankly, open-mouthed.

Kirk felt his right hand twitch automatically toward his jacket interior, but made no move.

Riff smiled disarmingly, plucked the menu from Jill's startled fingers, scanned it cursorily. "Think I'll just have the coffee. They make excellent coffee here."

He handed the menu back to Jill, eyes on Kirk.

"Congratulations. Once a Nightcrawler always a Nightcrawler, eh?"

Kirk didn't even put down his menu. "Where is she?"

Their waitress approached the table. "Howdy, folks! Coffee all 'round?"

Riff smiled at her, motioned randomly at the air. "The number three breakfast for my two friends here, just coffee for me, thanks." He winked at her.

The waitress, a pretty adolescent with long red hair and freckles, smiled back at him, poured the three of them coffee.

"Say, what time's your shift end?" Riff teased, tugging playfully once at her apron.

"Same time my boyfriend picks me up!" She smiled, showing perfect white teeth.

Riff placed both hands over his heart theatrically, made a pained face. "Shot down again!"

The waitress winked and sauntered off, sashaying a bit more, perhaps, than usual.

Riff watched her a moment with satisfaction, then turned to Jill. "You'll like the number three, real maple syrup on the pancakes!"

"My wife, Walker, where is she?" Voice level, calm. This was not the place, the time.

Riff sipped hot coffee. "She's fine. Safe. Sends her love. Mmmmmm," he smacked his lips. "Good coffee."

"The building's surrounded by police," Jill blurted.

Riff chuckled softly, not bothering to look at her, focusing instead on Kirk. "I honestly doubt it. How's the memory, old man? Any improvement?"

"Improving all the time, thanks to you."

"My pleasure. Anything for the greatest American combat soldier since Audie Murphy. You found the tape, I gather?"

"I found it."

Riff nodded in approval, sipping from his china cup. "Good. I trust there's no hard feelings, under the circumstances? My methods were chosen for effectiveness, not decorum. You needed a good psychic jolt. Nothing personal there, I assure you."

"Just tell me where she is, you can go your own way."

Riff replaced the cup with a clink, nodding rapidly, patting his mouth. "I intend to do that, I certainly do." He placed the napkin back in his lap carefully. Turned to Jill, smiled. Turned back to Kirk. "When I'm satisfied you've gained complete control of your senses."

Kirk lay a casual hand atop his table knife. "Your obstacle course was quite illuminating, thank you."

Riff brightened. "Then you do recall my beaming presence in good old Saigon town?"

"I remember you."

"And the Cotton Club, obviously—hence your current residence at the lovely motel next door."

"Yes, the club too."

"And what it was that occurred there?"

"I remember it all, Riff. Now please tell me where I can find Meg; you already have my word as a military man that you can go free without any interference from me whatsoever. We'll just forget this ever happened."

Riff beamed, reached out, and patted the other man's arm, the one above the table knife. He turned back to Jill. "And what about you? Do I have your word as well?"

"You slimy son of a bitch."

He looked back at Kirk with mock affrontery. "The lady doesn't seem to share your sense of propriety."

"Jill will do whatever I say."

Riff grinned. "Will she, now?" Turned to Jill. "Will you, now? Become fast friends over the last forty-eight hours, have we?"

She returned his wry smirk with a withering glare.

"Tell you what, Kirk, old man: you give me the details of what occurred on that fateful night so long ago and the lithesome Mrs. Kirkland is yours again. What do you say?"

Kirk watched him warily. "Details?"

"Everything that happened from the moment you stepped inside the Cotton Club. I want to hear you say it, I want the words to come from your mouth."

Kirk looked past him, out the window, at the majestic, snow-capped peaks. "What's the point, Riff? Everyone's endured enough. End it."

"From your mouth."

Kirk looked him straight in the eye. "I shot your wife. In the head. Killed her. All right?"

Riff watched him, face impassive.

"Orders, Riff. Orders. You were there. You were a Nightcrawler. You knew the rules."

Riff watched him silently.

Kirk swallowed. "If I thought it would make any difference, I'd say I'm sorry. I am sorry. It wrecked my life, certainly my marriage. I've been pushing Meg away subconsciously because of what I did to your wife, I realize that now. But I can't bring Mi Ling back, Riff. And I don't have it to do over again. It would be wonderful if we could edit the past, arrange it to suit our needs and desires. But we can't. The past is the past. And it's done. Killing Meg won't change that. She was no more a part of that than . . . than Jill here. I'll fight you, Riff, if that's what you want. A duel, or hand-to-hand like the old days, or whatever you want, whatever it is you need. I'll even trade my life for Meg's—you'll have your pound of flesh. But let Meg go, Riff. Let her go. It's the right thing to do. I think you know that."

Riff studied him a moment, then went back to his coffee, drained the cup.

"And afterward?"

"After what?"

"After you shot her. What happened then?"

"I went back to Base One."

"And?"

Kirk rubbed his knuckles absently. "I . . . don't remember. I suppose I had a nervous breakdown, that's what they told me. It wouldn't surprise me, considering . . ." He looked up at the other man. "Why don't you tell me? You were there."

Riff watched the lofty peaks. "I'd rather hear it from you, old man."

Kirk shook his head, a patina of sweat forming at his brow again. "I can't recall that part, I'm sorry. I remember spending some fatigue duty at Dix, coming home, joining the force, that's all. What more do you want from me, Riff?"

Riff stood.

"Do you know where the Gatlin Pass is?"

"No."

Riff tossed his napkin on the table. "Get a map, find it. Be there at noon. And think about your breakdown, Kirk. There'll be a written test later."

"Where's Meg?"

"Think about it. And bring hiking boots, a warm jacket." He turned to Jill, bowed low. "Good day, Miss Thorenson, it's always a pleasure to find fresh cantaloupes at breakfast!"

He turned back to Kirk, smiled, pointed a finger at him. "Tricky Dicky!"

And he was gone.

Jill grabbed Kirk by the arm, started up. "Aren't you going t—?"

Kirk turned to his coffee, pulling his arm back

with him. "It wouldn't do any good, Jill, he'd know we were tailing him. It would just stretch things out. Meg might be suffering somewhere, and it's better he gets back to her."

"You're just going to sit there!"

His fist slammed the table, rattling cups. "You think it's easy? I know him! I know what he'll do!"

People were watching.

He went back to his coffee calmly.

Jill sat back, hung her head. "I'm sorry, you're right, of course. It's just that the bastard's so smug." She looked over her shoulder at the way Riff had gone, saw the empty restaurant doors. "What's Tricky Dicky?"

"Nothing. Just a saying we had back in 'Nam. Sort of a cautionary catchword we used with each other before going out into the field."

Jill poured cream, stirred distractedly. "So what do we do now?"

"Finish our breakfast, go find a map, wait until twelve o'clock. It's all we can do."

She brought the liquid to her lips, peered at him over the rim. "We're near the end, aren't we?"

He was gazing outward past the glass, at the jagged peaks, steep escarpments. He had never been on a mountain before in his life. "Yes, I think we are."

Eighteen

Meg labored upright in the vinyl motel chair, bound fast, hand and foot.

Her head pounded mercilessly, her throat was raw from screaming. Much good that had done. Riff had chosen their dwelling well, far from the main building in an older wing, flanked by construction sand and cement blocks, adjacent to a highway continuously traversed by roaring, high-speed timber trucks. Every time one thundered by, it shook the cinder block walls. No wonder no one wanted to sleep way over here. The owner probably gave it away. Riff was nothing if not methodical.

After a few minutes she had given up on the screaming.

She had a new tack now. During one particularly zealous outburst of yelling, she had noticed the chair shuffling a few degrees to the left as she threw herself willfully into the shriek. She discovered that by heaving her weight violently to one side, she was able to actually move the four stubborn wooden legs half an inch or so across the thin motel carpet. Repeated lunges gained her a precious half foot.

It was exhausting work, and there was always the nagging fear she would stick and tip over, and that would be the end of it; but she was, however infinitesimally, moving.

She began in the direction of the door; it would doubtless be locked, but she might be able to bang on it with her head and attract attention.

But the closer she got, the louder the outside roar of the trucks seemed. She could pound away and yell until her head split open and not attract flies. She decided to detour to the phone beside the bed, a farther route but a safer bet.

It took her nearly twenty minutes.

Once there, her problems were only beginning. She couldn't reach the phone from her sitting position, which meant she would have to tilt the chair over, bang against the nightstand without tilting *it* over, wrestle the receiver off the hook with her mouth, and place it next to the phone without knocking it off the stand.

She accomplished all this with some success, although she nearly knocked herself unconscious on the phone itself when the tilted chair slammed her into it.

Meg maneuvered the phone around with her head, bit down on the hand grip, and laid the receiver carefully along the edge of the table, mouthpiece toward her.

Thank God for push-button dialing; without it, this whole thing would have been in vain.

A brief glance in the direction of the door, then she began to move her chin over the Desk button.

But then she froze.

What if the desk was busy, didn't answer right away—they usually didn't.

What if she succeeded in reaching them in time and they sent some incompetent flunky to her room that Riff intercepted on the way back?

Or what if Riff walked in on them just as she was being untied? It would all be over. Another death, and her the cause this time.

No, this was a job for a professional.

She stretched her chin toward the O button, pressed down, hoping she'd hit the right one, immediately twisting her head down toward the earpiece, straining to hear.

There was a *click*, then an officious monotone: "Operator 67, may I help you?"

Meg hesitated, an ugly thought forming.

What if the bastard was listening in somehow? It might sound absurd, but she wouldn't put it past him. What if she did put a call through to the police, only to have him follow up the call confessing the whole thing was a prank, don't bother to come. It would be just like him.

Probably she was overreacting—overwrought—but she couldn't shake the feeling that he was just around the corner somewhere, spying, gloating, waiting for her to make precisely this move.

She needed a friendly voice, someone she could count on.

"Operator, this is an emergency, I'm unable to dial. I want you to make a collect call to Kirkland

Security Industries, Chicago, Illinois, and ask for David Kirkland, please!"

"One moment."

Meg tugged in a ragged breath, glanced over at the door.

Waited.

"Would you know that area code, ma'am?"

"Uh . . . 341."

"One moment."

Shit. Hurry up!

She looked toward the door.

A truck roared by.

Her neck was beginning to ache badly from the twisted position of her shoulder. Her right leg was becoming numb from the cramp-inducing angle of her body. Tilted this way, all the blood was rushing to her head.

She heard a thump at the door and looked up with a gasp.

Nothing happened.

It must have been someone walking by. She should have called out, too late now.

"Your name, please?"

"Mrs. John Kirkland."

"One moment."

Come on!

It was getting harder to breathe, chest compressed against the edge of the table. She felt a growing light-headedness. Don't faint now, for God's sake!

"Kirkland Security, Bob Halliran speaking."

"I have a collect call for a David Kirkland from a Mrs. John Kirkland."

"I think Mr. Kirkland's gone to lunch, I'll check . . ."

Christ! This was a mistake! She should forget this and ask for local help!

She could hear office milieu from the earpiece, tacking typewriters, someone laughing.

A truck roared by.

"David Kirkland . . ."

"David!"

"I have a collect call from a Mrs. John Kirkland, will you accept the charges?"

"Meg! Are you all right?"

"Sir, will you accept the charges?"

"Yes, operator!"

"Go ahead, please, with your party."

"Meg, where are you!"

"In Denver!"

"Denver, Christ! Are you alone?"

"For the moment. He'll be back any second. Did Kirk—"

"He told us what happened—wouldn't bring us in. Went after you himself! Have you talked to him?"

"By himself? No, I—"

"Never mind that now. Are you at a pay phone?"

"I'm in a motel, David, tied to a chair."

"Jesus! The address?"

"It's the Travelodge motel on Route 42, just outside of town. There's a big Kmart nearby, that's all I remember."

"That's enough. Listen, have you called anyone else?"

"No, I thought—"

"You did the right thing! We've got people in Denver, I'll have someone there in five minutes. Whatever you do, don't call anyone else! Not even the manager, got that? This guy Walker is extremely dangerous. Let us handle it from here!"

"Whatever you say!"

"Do you remember Walker's license plate number?"

"No, I—"

"That's okay. I'm going to hang up now so I can make that call. Hang tight, sweetie, we'll have you home by this afternoon!"

"Hurry, David!"

But he'd already hung up.

She felt an overwhelming surge of relief that brought stinging tears to her eyes.

And an immediate corresponding surge of dread: Riff would see the phone off the hook, know she'd called someone, maybe kill her.

She twisted about painfully, trying to get her mouth around the hand grip again. Without the support of the hook, though, it was impossible to maneuver. It kept slipping out of her mouth.

Whining, she tried to wedge receiver against phone, against wall, anything to get some leverage. It kept slipping away, nearly dropping off the edge of the stand at one point. If it fell, she'd never get it back on. . . .

Finally she got the accordion cord in her mouth at the closest point to the receiver, jacked it up on one end, and trailed it across the top of the cradle. It slipped down three times, beeping loudly and impatiently, before she finally got it back in place. The ensuing silence was like a cool breeze.

Then began the arduous task of jerking the chair back to the spot he'd left her.

She was already too exhausted to move. Nevertheless, she got halfway there before the door came crashing open.

A figure leapt inside, squatted, holding arms stiffly outward. Silhouetted that way against the outside glare, it offered little detail; she didn't even see the gun for a moment. Then the light caught it as it began swiveling back and forth rapidly in a stiff arc, pointing at every corner of the motel room.

"Mrs. Kirkland?"

"Yes!"

"Detective Thomlin, are you alone?"

"Yes, he's gone!"

The gun sagged, the figure spun, kicked the door closed again. In a moment a sandy-haired young man in a tan suit and green tie was at her side, struggling with the ropes. Younger than she'd have thought. But here.

"Did he hurt you?"

"I'm all right. Please hurry!"

"One more second. There."

He left her to strip the cords away from her wrist, untie her ankles, while he went to the window, pressed against the wall, parted the curtain a fraction, and peered out, gun pointed at the ceiling. "Can you walk?"

"I think so, yes!"

"Shall we go, then?"

He jerked back the door, leaned out, looked both ways, signaled her. Meg ran to him.

"Stay behind me, it's the blue Corona at the side of the building. If you hear gunfire, keep running!"

"All right!"

Thomlin checked again. "Let's do it!"

They sprinted around the side of the unit, startling a white-frocked maid with a load of towels that Thomlin nearly shot. He flipped a wallet at her. "Denver Homicide! It's okay!"

The maid, a pudgy woman in her fifties, clung desperately to the towels, watched owl-eyed, chewing gum frozen in one corner of her mouth.

"I'm all right!" Meg tried to assure her, just before Thomlin shoved her inside.

He jumped in, holstered the gun, and they went peeling out of the parking lot.

Meg's head fell back with a sigh as they hit the highway. "Thank God!"

Thomlin drove very fast.

"Did he feed you, Mrs. Kirkland?"

"I'm fine, really."

The great, indomitable Riff Walker foiled at last.

"We can stop for something if you're hungry, but I need to get away from the vicinity as quickly as possible, you understand."

"Of course. Are you taking me to Denver headquarters?"

He glanced at her apologetically. "I'm afraid it's not quite over yet; we're holding a man answering Walker's description at Gorge Valley Road. We need you to confirm identification. Are you up to it?"

"Of course."

He smiled. "It won't take a moment, I promise. Then we'll get you back with your husband."

"Have you contacted Kirk?"

Thomlin shook his head. "He's being very stubborn about that. A real vigilante, your husband. But we'll have him pinned before nightfall, don't worry."

He glanced at her rope-burned wrists, made a disgusted face. "Bastard. Sure you're all right?"

"I'm fine, thanks."

The car shifted lanes and took a side road.

Ten minutes later, they were on yet another side road, a worse one, and well on their way into the mountains.

The car began to leave a plume of dust.

Douglas firs sprouted roadside, joined other conifers, grew taller, became immense. Still they drove.

"Did you just catch him?" Meg inquired.

Thomlin watched the road. "Right after you called Dave Kirkland."

They drove, the grade steepening.

The town evaporated behind them.

Meg looked out and saw a bighorn sheep watching them casually from a distant boulder. She nearly said something, but let it go.

The road became a one-lane trail that jounced the car roughly. Meg had to hold onto the paneling, teeth jarring.

After a time, the interior hazy with grit, the road leveled again, opened into a narrow meadow. A log cabin swung into view.

Thomlin braked the car fifty feet in front of it.

"Is this Gorge Valley Road?"

"This is it. Walker's in the cabin. All you have to do is nod, and we'll be on our way again."

Thomlin got out.

Meg sat looking at the rustic facade. There were no other cars in sight.

Thomlin opened the door for her.

"Where are the other cars?"

"Other side of the ridge, including Walker's. It's a better road but slower. Walker drive a green Volvo?"

"Yes."

Thomlin nodded, gesturing. "That's him, then. Let's get this unpleasantness over with and get you out of here, Mrs. Kirkland."

Meg stepped out. Thomlin took her arm, guided her toward the cabin.

It looked dark inside, one window shattered. The weathered door hung askew, half open. She could see no movement within. Then she could: a squirrel or something bolting outside into the weeds at their approach.

She dug in her heels. "Who are you?"

The grip tightened above her elbow. He was reaching inside his coat.

Meg screamed.

The sound was swallowed up and lost instantly. Not even the birds seemed to notice. He was dragging her now.

"Oh, Jesus, you're going to kill me!"

He jerked her along, jaw set. "Not before you're out of that dress, I'm not."

She stiffened, swung, but he'd anticipated it, blocked it with an elbow and punched the air out of her. She doubled, gasping, and he dragged her to the door by the waist.

He kicked it open with a shriek of hinges, a flapping chorus heading toward invisible rafters. The sunless interior reeked of mildew and dry rot.

Thomlin shoved her forcefully at the dim outline of a three-legged table, shouldering the door closed behind him. Meg bounced off the hard wood, came away with dirt-streaked arms, clinging strands of web. She backed into blackness, clenching fists to her chest protectively, a pencil ray of ceiling sun stabbing her eye. She tasted coppery bile, smelled the odor of her own death.

"There's a water barrel behind you. Roll it over in front of the door," he ordered flatly.

"Please . . . !"

"Now! Or I'll hit you again!"

Kirk will come, Kirk will come out of nowhere at the last minute and save me!

She turned, stomach flaring in pain, and searched the darkness.

"Move!"

She stumbled about frantically, knuckles scraping the edge of the barrel, reaping splinters. She got her arms around it, tried to lever forward. "It's heavy!"

"Roll it."

She thought her back would break. "I can't!" She sobbed, choking back tears and mucus; her own voice had sounded so wretched.

"Then die."

She grunted, tugging, reddish motes dancing sickeningly before her eyes.

This is how they will find me.

Straining miserably, every joint aflame, fighting a rising nausea, she finally got the heavy barrel to move awkwardly across the earthen floor. It nearly toppled on top of her twice before she maneuvered it against the door with a hollow boom. She crumpled against it, gasping, fingernails pressed into her heaving sides, pain whistling between her teeth.

Will it hurt when he shoots? Will it be my head?

"Now come over here and put your mouth on this."

She struggled up, holding the barrel lip for support.

Who are these people?

Will he bury me in the woods?

"Let's go, on your knees."

She stumbled toward him, legs buckling.

This is what you get for being a bad girl.

His fingers tangled in her hair, forced her down. She heard the clink of his buckle.

"Actually, she prefers it in the ass."

Meg started, gasping, head twisting about at the voice behind her. Thomlin held her fast, but she saw the outline of his gun coming up, pointing into the dark.

"Of course, she might not prefer that little stump of yours at all. How 'bout it, Meg?"

Riff. No question.

She jumped as the gun went off close to her head, a lightning streak of flame bathing the interior brilliant for one luminous second. She saw a predominate brown, the angular ghosts of wooden shapes, nothing human.

"Bad aim, Thomlin. Christ, has the CIA degenerated to putzes like—"

The pistol thundered again, answered by the angry whine of lead meeting steel pot.

Silence.

Echoes dying away within the tiny enclosure like fading ripples, cordite hanging pungently in the air. Meg could imagine the wispy smoke.

"Best tuck your pecker away and let the woman go, Thomlin. I don't think it's your day for a blowjob."

Meg cried out as the fingers tangling in her hair jerked her forward into a tightened, pulsing stomach. She could feel damp cloth beneath her cheek, smell fear. Thomlin was breathing rapidly, buckle scraping her chin. A hard finger thrust roughly at her temple—not a finger, his gun.

"Exit through the door, and I let the Kirkland woman go!" The voice was strangled with terror.

A ripple of laughter that seemed to come from everywhere. "I honestly doubt it. How about you, Meg?"

The fingers tightened in her hair. "I'll blow her fucking brains out, I swear it!"

Silence.

Thomlin twisted about in spastic jerks, as if responding to unheard sounds, unseen predators.

An eerie, otherworldly wail rose within the cabin, lifting the hairs on Meg's neck. Followed by an echoing, hand-cupped voice:

"Who knows what evil lurks in the hearts of men?"

Thomlin's pistol blasted twice more. Meg tried to

see, ears ringing, but the brilliance merely blinded
her this time.

Silence.

Followed by muted coughing, gagging.

Her heart froze.

"Ah . . . ah think ya got me, varmit! Ah think ya
done put out mah liver!" Copious coughing. "Yep
. . . ahm a-headin' fer the last roundup! It's good-
bye fer Yosemite Sam!" A theatrical thump.

Silence.

Except for the sawing of Thomlin's tortured
breath.

The fingers dug into her scalp. "Go move the
barrel!" he spat sibilantly.

Meg knelt, unmoving.

The fingers jerked painfully. "Do it!"

She cried out, struggled to her feet.

She turned, felt the bore of the automatic dig
into her back, shoving. Her fingers found the barrel; she braced against the heels of her hands and
pushed.

"Hurry, goddammit, or I'll blow a hole through
you!"

A scurrying sound.

The pistol barked twice more, deafeningly, throwing initiative into Meg's struggles. She finally got
the barrel clear of the frame.

Thomlin was behind her again, arm about her
neck, choking, gun muzzle pressed to her head.

"Make a move and I shoot her!" He seemed to be
saying it to the air.

He reached back, caught the edge of the door,
spearing light into the cabin. But it opened only a

few feet before being blocked by a pile of invisible
debris; the room remained dark. Thomlin began
backing the two of them through the frame awkwardly.

The glare outside was blinding.

Everything disappeared in a bright yellow haze.

Meg felt her heels stumble over the weathered
lintel, down a stone step, into weeds. The warm air,
sun on her back, was delicious.

There was a musical *twang* somewhere.

Thomlin shrieked as if stabbed. The muzzle left
her temple, the pressure relaxing at her arm. She
fell away to the earth.

Thomlin was still screaming.

Squinting up, she saw him doubled over, still
clutching the gun, digging at something wrapped
around his shin. His fingers were covered with red.

She jumped as strong hands got under her arms,
lifted her, and then she was staring up at Riff's
pleasantly smiling face. "Exactly where a rat be-
longs, wouldn't you say?"

Thomlin was dancing on one leg, still shrieking,
clawing, the big iron teeth of an ancient bear trap
bringing rivulets of bubbling blood that matted the
tan trousers to his left calf. His face was a rictus of
agony, beet red, sheeting sweat.

"Walker!" It was the shriek of the damned. "You
butcher!"

Riff was lighting a cigarette calmly, offering one
to Meg. "Sorry, you don't smoke, do you?"

"No."

He smiled, blew tufts at the air.

Thomlin dropped to one knee, the other leg trailing out awkwardly beside him, bent in a funny way. Hands quaking, shoulders heaving, he aimed the automatic at Riff, or approximated an aim, anyway. Meg clutched his arm. Riff gave her a patient look.

"Take it off or you're dead!" It came out through gritted teeth, sun-glinting flecks of spittle.

Riff held out the pack to the sobbing man. "Can't do that, old man. How about a smoke?"

"I mean it!"

Riff put away the pack. "I honestly doubt it. That's a Smith and Wesson, pardner, and you've got just the one bullet left."

"Which will go through your head!"

Riff grinned, puffed. Squinted up at the sun. "Weather man says it will get into the mid-eighties this afternoon." He shaded his eyes. "Looks like it might top even that." He turned to Meg, tucking in his shirt, cigarette dangling from his lips like a cowpoke. "I recollect seeing a steer down in Abilene some time back, got hisself tangled in barbed wire, couldn't get in out of the sun. Belly blew up to here when they found him." He shook his head, shivered histrionically. "Nasty way to die!"

Thomlin let the gun droop, face the color of rolled dough. "Oh, sweet Jesus . . ."

Riff winked at Meg, puffed smoke. After a moment he sauntered over to Thomlin. "Care for that cigarette now?"

Thomlin was trembling so badly, Riff had to light it for him. The leg was red now all the way down to his socks.

Riff clicked his lighter closed, hunkered down before the other man, shaking his head slowly.

"Yeah, them ol' bear traps is a bitch to pull apart. Durn near took my fingernails with it, and I had the key!"

Thomlin was on his rump now, rocking and groaning, teeth still bared painfully.

Riff just kept shaking his head sorrowfully. Then he looked up at the twisted face. "How's the wife and kids, Tom? Doing all right?"

Thomlin nodded, eyes glazed with pain. "All right . . ."

"Got plenty of coverage, I presume?"

Thomlin squinted at him, rose above the pain a moment.

"Christ, Tom, don't tell me you didn't take care of the loved ones!"

Thomlin hung his head. "C-company . . . too expensive . . . I was shopping around . . ."

Riff threw up his hands, twisted about, and gave Meg an exasperated look. "Damn it, Tom, I'd have given you more credit!"

"I was shopping, goddamn it!"

Riff heaved a sigh, shaking his head.

After a moment he reached into his jacket, withdrew a sheaf of papers. "Maybe we can still get you in at Beneficial . . ."

He pulled a ballpoint from his pocket, clicked the point, began scribbling on the top page, the pink one. He saw Thomlin watching him, and looked up. "It's a good policy? I'm fully bonded. Used to do this with Chatworth's people at the FBI."

"You . . . were with Chatworth?"

"Right after Hoover died. Sort of a loan-out.

Didn't care for it all that much, I prefer undercover work. Now, we should discuss what sort of coverage you think you'll need, Tom. Under the circumstances I'd say our family liability policy is your best bet. How old are the kids now?"

Meg, several yards away, sat down slowly in the warm grass, not really believing any of this. Either Riff was crazy or the other man was crazy or they both were. After a few minutes she didn't care; the sun was warm on her back, the wildflowers and Alpine violets intoxicating, the stately aspens somehow comforting. She felt herself grow languid as the men droned on and on.

A shuffle of papers brought her upright.

"Well, that ought to do it!" Riff was putting away his pen. "I'll predate this check and get it in the mail right away, but I don't think there'll be any trouble. No way to prove exactly when it is you died."

"I appreciate it." Thomlin looked sleepy. Shock? The two men shook hands.

Riff stood and walked back to Meg, glancing at his watch. "Best get going, we have a date in an hour."

She looked up dreamily. "Where's your car?"

"Over that hill. I came up the back way."

She walked with him through calf-high grass, minute, translucent baby grasshoppers scattering like chaff before them.

It was a beautiful day, the sky brilliantly blue.

"How did you—" she began.

"Passed you on the highway on the way back to

the motel—looked right in your face. Didn't see me, did you, Meg?"

"No."

"That's what you get for playing with telephones."

"How did you know—"

"The cabin? Hell, that place's been a hit man depository for twenty years! That and the old mine behind it."

"The CIA uses hit men?"

"Well, they've been known to, but he wasn't CIA."

"No?"

"Nah, Cosa Nostra all the way. Didn't you notice the suit?"

"The Mafia? But you said he was CIA in the cabin."

"Sure. That's what I wanted him to think I thought."

"But who hi—"

There was a loud report behind them. Then silence. Then the birds began again. Meg didn't turn around.

"Dumb shit," Riff muttered, "you don't need a key to open a bear trap."

"Who hired him, Riff?"

"Who? Dave Kirkland, who else?"

She felt a heated wedge of shock. "You're crazy! David's a security cop! Kirk's brother!"

"Well, that's brotherly love for you, hard to maintain these days."

"David Kirkland hired someone to have me killed? Is that what you're trying to tell me?"

"Bet your booties."

"Why, for God's sake?"

"Because you know me. Too well. And I might have told you what I know. Which is considerable, and very top secret. The CIA has a thing about that. Very precious that organization, very unforgiving. And a very hard job to walk away from—take it from one who knows."

"D-David's with the CIA?"

"No, Dave Kirkland's with the IIN. Independent Intelligence Network. What you might call a branch of the CIA. Except that they split off, that's why they're called Independent. Smaller, but a whole lot nastier."

"Wait a minute, wait a minute!" She held her head, watching the ground. "I'm confused! David owns Kirkland Security!"

"Which works for the INN. And the FBI, occasionally. He's also a member of Rotary and a former eagle scout."

"You know him?"

"I told you. Since 'Nam. He was our fearless leader!"

"Kirk never mentioned David being in Vietnam."

"He was, though. Kirk doesn't remember it, but he was. Kirk also thinks he didn't know me. I'd say our boy has a problem, wouldn't you?"

She looked at him levelly. "Exactly what kind of problem?"

"The clinical name is *amnesia nervosa*. Partially obscured memory. Certain incidents, in this case, that occurred in Vietnam."

"What incidents?"

"Sure you don't want that cigarette?"

"What incidents?"

He studied her a moment. "I guess I can tell you now, you've already done all the harm you're going to. For one thing, he shot a Vietnamese girl."

"Kirk?"

"Right between her big chocolate eyes."

"He never told—Oh . . ."

"He told you, all right—every time he refused to go to bed with you. Things kind of cooled off sudden-like after your marriage, right?"

She looked up sharply. "How could you know that?"

"It's my job, sweetie. The point is, old Kirkie seems to have this slight problem with sex and marriage. I'm not Freud, mind you, but I think it might have a little something to do with that newlywed he blew away twenty years ago, wouldn't you say?"

"Dear God, she was a bride?"

"Fresh from the altar. Of course, she was a whore too, but he didn't know that."

Meg swallowed thickly. "How . . . how do you know all this?"

"I was fucking her at the time."

She covered her face. "Oh, God . . ."

"She didn't suffer. Your husband was an expert shot."

Her stomach roiled, knotting.

"W-what happened afterward?"

Riff shrugged. "He completed orders, went back to Base One. Only once he got there, he apparently started thinking about what he'd done. He started acting strange, talking to himself. Then he just sort of fell apart. Went 'round the bend. Started tearing up the command post. Real bad P.R. for the CIA. So they strapped him down, called in their team of 'experts'—graduates of the Dachau school of medicine—and took a scrub brush to his brain, so to speak. Took out what they didn't want him to know, certain people, certain places, key events, little bothersome things like that. Problem is, you can't trust memories, keep cropping up again later at the most embarrassing moments. So they dispensed with plan A and proceeded directly to plan B, which was to kill him."

Meg was incredulous. "Why didn't they?"

He blew smoke at the sky. "Several reasons: for one he was Dave's baby brother and old Davie—creep that he is—wasn't about to allow that. Not back then, anyway. And Kirk was a war hero, not a man you could plan an 'accidental' death around with ease, too many people close to him asking too many probing questions. Also, I threatened to quit if they did. And they needed me badly. They'd already dumped far too much money and time into my hot little killer's body, including a whole network of covert activities stretching everywhere from Iran to stateside work. I was a walking catalog of very specialized knowledge and expertise. Invaluable. Of course, they'd have preferred to have had Kirk there working alongside me, but it was too late for that. So they let him come home."

"And David came with him?"

"Followed shortly. Set him up with the police force, chose his friends, kept a close eye on him. Made sure he wasn't saying the wrong thing at the wrong time. Even handpicked his wife . . ."

She spun, glaring.

"In a matter of speaking. Oh, they dissected you, sweetie! Your dossier stretches from here to Cleveland. Everything from that grade school picnic in St. Louis to that first blowjob in the back seat."

Meg staggered, buckled at the waist; he grabbed her shoulders, supporting her.

She clung to him weakly, head turned away. "I'm . . . I feel sick . . ."

"You're okay."

"I—I'm going to vomit . . ."

"Well, watch the Florsheims, they're new."

She retched once, but drily.

The ground was tipping.

"You need a nice stiff drink."

She tried to get her breath, clinging to his arm. "I don't know if you're crazy or not. . . . I don't know if this whole thing is even real anymore."

He was looking at his watch. "Like the man said: we're all just the dream of a sleeping giant under a tree somewhere in another universe. Would seeing your husband again help the matter any?"

Her grip tightened on his arm. "Kirk?"

"About forty minutes from here at a place called Gatlin Pass, ever hear of it?"

She bit her lip. "How do you know?"

"I had breakfast with them this morning while you were pouring out your life story to Thomlin."

"Them?"

"He brought Jill along for the ride. Old Kirkie always had good taste."

Meg dug nails into his chest, head thrown back supplicatingly. "You're going there to kill him!

Please! I know Kirk could never have hurt that young woman purposely! It was years ago! He doesn't even remember it! Riff, I'm begging you!"

He looked down at her with surprised delight. "Why, Mrs. Kirkland, you mean you actually acknowledge my veracity? Does this mean you believe me about the corn farmer too? And the waiter?" Riff grinned. " 'Cause they really were after us, Mrs. Kirkland, just ask your brother-in-law."

"Please!" Her hand slid caressingly down his abdomen. "I'll do anything you ask! Just don't hurt him!"

He caught her wrist, held it. "You're not giving your husband his due, Meg. He's a hell of a fighter when his back's to the wall." He fished for another cigarette. "Anyway, I'm the least of his problems right now."

"What do you mean?"

"Kirk was exposed to my brilliant mind too, remember? At your house. The CIA wants him dead a lot more than you. They were planning to get around to it one of these days anyhow. Kirk was starting to remember again. Too much of a security risk. Why do you think I wanted out of counter-intelligence? I kept losing all my friends!"

Meg paled. "But . . . we could warn him! I mean, I didn't tell David where Kirk is!"

He snorted. "They've known for days where he is."

She felt a wedge of dread. "But how——?"

He looked down at her, lifted an ironic brow.

She stepped back disbelievingly.

"Oh, God . . . not——?"

Riff grinned, blew smoke over her head. "Biggest knockers in the department!"

It was convenient that they'd finally reached the car because Meg needed very much to sit down.

He found her staring absently out the windshield as he slid in beside her.

"You and Jill are in this thing together?"

He looked astonished. "Oh, hell, no, I'm a defectee, remember? Jill joined the funhouse long after I made my exit. She's only one of about ten of them looking for me. She doesn't know I know it, though. She thinks she picked me up in a bar. But I can smell an agent a mile way, especially a woman. They have a special way of sitting on a bar stool."

Meg shook her head dizzily. "Bar stool. She told me you two were married . . . had a dude ranch in Wyoming . . ."

Riff chuckled. "The old dude ranch routine, eh? Boy, that's rookie stuff. Going to have to get Jill some new material. No, sweetie, Jill Thorenson and I never met until that night we came to see you and Kirkie. Bumped into her in a bar two hours before—a little too conveniently. She was pretty good. But I made her in a second. Had CIA written all over her titties."

"She was assigned to kill you?"

"Well, locate me anyway, then call in the heavy artillery."

"But she had you. Why didn't she report?"

He grinned, flipped his butt out the window. "Apparently she was enjoying my company. Know what I mean, Meg?"

She craned away, flaming.

He smiled, started the car.

They headed back down the bumpy mountain road.

Meg was thinking about grabbing the wheel, heading the car toward a precipice.

"Why did you bring her to our house that night, drug her? Why didn't you just get rid of her?"

"Oh, I planned to. Then I thought, no! She'll add to the game! She knows Kirk's background, she can help him track me—help him get you while he helps her get me. Teamwork! One team chases another team! Equitable arrangement, wouldn't you say?"

"Yes. If she doesn't decide to kill him first."

Riff nodded wryly.

"Now that she knows where I am, that's a real possibility."

Nineteen

They reached the Gatlin Pass sign at precisely noon.

Riff's green Volvo was parked roadside, windows rolled up, locked.

Kirk pulled the Nova to the shoulder and cut the engine. End of the line. There wasn't anywhere else to go anyway, the road ended here. He turned in the seat and gazed past Jill at the weathered sign.

"It looks like it goes straight up from here," she murmured ominously.

Kirk climbed out of the car, slammed the door.

He looked back at the dust-covered vehicle a moment before approaching the sign; he had the feeling he might not ever see it again. It had been a good car, a friend, in a way. It had brought him through much. It had brought him to his wife.

Jill came trudging up behind over loose stones as he stood squinting at the wooden sign. She wore the hiking boots, shorts, and jacket that Riff had suggested in the restaurant. Kirk was similarly appareled. They'd also purchased a light backpack, water bottles, foil-wrapped sandwiches, health bars. The man in the store said they'd need the health bars.

She stood blinking at the sign, then swept her eyes over the vast mountain range before them. "Gatlin Pass, sure, but which way?"

There appeared to be no trails.

"It doesn't look like a normal hiking area," Jill offered dubiously.

Kirk was scrutinizing the wind-beaten sign. "No, it wouldn't be; he'd want to stage the final act as far from the madding crowd as possible." He ran his fingers along the top edge of the splintered wood, studying the nicked and pockmarked grain.

"So which way?" she insisted.

He said: "Northeast," without hesitation.

"How the hell can you tell that?"

He fingered the edge of the wood. "Knife cut."

She leaned forward, squinting. "Kirk, there are cuts and scratches all over the damn thing."

"Not from a Whittier hunting knife, there aren't. And see how this cut is yellow, the others tan? It's fresh. Riff left it for us."

She made a skeptical face. "For you, maybe. How does one little nick tell you the direction?"

"Position on the board. Picture the sign as a map with the top edge as true north and you've got it."

She nodded at length. "Okay, but how did he know you'd look here?"

He started walking. "It's one of the tricks we used in the 'Nam. Let's go."

She hurried up behind him. "What did you do when there wasn't a convenient sign?"

"Trees, what else?"

"Of course, what else?"

There was no real path, except for the natural one of stone and shale cut by running water through the trees. To the right was pine and fir and, higher up, aspen forest: thick but not impenetrable. To the left a steep hill that eventually became sheer cliff, dropping away dizzily into a deep gulf and spectacular view. If they stuck to the left-hand edge, it should be fairly easy going; the grade was inclined, though not steeply yet. They were able to maintain a brisk rhythm. Even so, Jill could feel the pressure at her insteps, the tightening in her shins. Her breathing became labored after only a few minutes, pack straps cutting into her shoulders. The sun weighed heavily on her back.

"God, this is work!"

He turned to her, keeping a measured pace. "Try to find your rhythm. You'll be all right."

She was unmollified. "I thought you'd never done any mountain climbing before."

"Not cliff climbing, no, but you know, a forest by any other name . . ."

"I thought that only applied to roses."

"Whatever."

"What do we do if it gets steeper?"

"Find our second wind."

"Great."

Kirk stopped abruptly and moved to the edge of the faint path, shading his eyes at a jutting pine. He examined the bark carefully.

"Another knife mark?"

He made an affirmative sound.

"What are you looking at?"

He pulled one of the branches and held out a small brown object to her. "Piñon nut, seeds of the piñon pine. They're edible."

She caught it. "Well, we won't starve anyway. I thought you weren't a woodsman. Where'd you learn that?"

He gave her a blank look. "I don't remember."

"In 'Nam?"

"Why would North American conifers be the subject of training there?"

"It wouldn't unless they had other plans for you."

"Such as?"

"You tell me."

He shrugged. "I can't."

She started off again. "Just a theory. Shall we get at it?"

They huffed on for another twenty minutes until Jill's boot found a loose piece of shale and sent her crashing painfully onto her left knee. "Damn!"

He slid back to where she was and peeled off his backpack. He threw back flaps, worked zippers, and withdrew a white metal box with a red cross.

Jill sat on her rump, fingers pressed to the edges of the cut, gritting her teeth while he first poured cold water, then sprayed the area with Bactine, finally applied two large Band-aids.

"It's going to sting a bit when you walk where the skin stretches naturally, but I'm afraid you're going to live."

He put the things in the pack and craned his neck toward the distant summit, a dark line of firs perched arrogantly atop sharp, tumbled stone.

She read his thoughts. "How far up do you think he took her?"

He sighed, pulled on the pack. "No telling."

He started up, but she caught his arm. "Kirk . . ."

"What is it?"

She faltered, as if having difficulty choosing her words. "What would you say if I suggested a really crazy idea?"

"Depends on the idea."

Her hand tightened on his arm in an almost desperate gesture. "What would you say if I asked you to go back, climb back down the mountain, right now, this minute?"

He sat down again. "What are you talking about?"

"With me, right now! Just turn around and not look back. Go off somewhere, together, forget everything!"

He looked at her tightened fingers. "Don't you think we should talk about that after we find Meg?"

"There may not—it will be too late then."

"You don't know that, Jill."

"Yes, I do. Go with me, Kirk. Now. Away from this place. You like me, I know you do. I'd be good to you. I'd make you happy. We'd make each other happy. For a while at least."

"And after a while?"

"Then we'll deal with whatever comes next."

"And just leave Meg?"

"He won't hurt her. It's you he wants."

"Jill, you're talking nonsense."

"I know. It sounds like a bad Bette Davis movie, doesn't it? Kirk, do it anyway. There aren't many chances in life to do something purely nonsensical, completely selfish. I've never committed a totally selfish act in my life, not because I didn't want to, but because there was never a reason. Until now."

He gazed thoughtfully into her gray eyes.

Then he took her hand away gently.

"I can't walk away from this. You'd hate me if I did. I'd hate myself. Believe me, I know what years of unfinished business are like. We're so close now. So close to ending it."

She took back the hand, looked away, the softness gone from her eyes. "Closer than you think."

He watched her impotently for a moment. He was always turning her down, and never wanting to. He was beginning to wonder if maybe he'd reached that point in his life where he was past ever getting what he truly wanted, perhaps even knowing what it was. Funny thing was, it didn't seem so all-consumingly important now; the only thing that seemed important was finding Meg. He wasn't sure he knew himself all the reasons why.

"You've been a wonderful help to me thus far. Help me a little bit longer," he said gently.

She pulled on her pack. Her body posture had changed. "Look, skip it, huh? Just another of my crazy schemes. It wouldn't work anyway, you snore."

They got to their feet. He looked at her a moment, but she wouldn't meet his eyes. He turned and started up the vague trail again.

She followed in silence.

Riff sat on a lichen-encrusted boulder shading his eyes, gazing back down the path they'd just traversed. Meg lay collapsed on her back nearby, arms and legs flared, trying to get her breath.

"I need another drink."

He looked over at her briefly. "No, you don't."

"Please."

"You'll cramp."

"I'm used to it, I have bad periods. Give me the goddamn bottle."

He unhooked it from his belt and tossed it to her.

She drank deeply, wiped her mouth, and started to toss it back.

He waved her off. "Keep it."

"Yes?"

"I won't need it."

She lay back, pressing the bottle to her streaming forehead. "Macho man."

"Slows me down."

She threw an arm across her eyes, let her aching limbs go limp again. She was a mass of bruised tendons, screaming joints. Yet every time a squirrel or lizard made a sound, she jumped, eyes on the woods, fearful of another hit man.

Riff regarded this continuous distraction with distant amusement. "You can relax, it will be CIA the next time, and that won't be for a while."

"How do you know?"

"I know."

She sat up, following his unblinking gaze down the mountain. "Do you see them yet?"

He knew she meant Kirk and Jill. "No, but I can hear them. Or her, anyway."

Meg became intense. "You can? Where?"

"A ways. We've got time."

He was climbing off the rock.

Time for what?

He came toward her, dusting his hands. He looked very tall and dark in the bright Colorado sun.

Meg pulled her legs up unconsciously.

"You want to get your clothes off, please?"

Knotting.

"What for?"

"Please."

"You're going to humilate him before you kill him, is that it?"

"The clothes, please."

"Fuck you!"

He smiled, looked back down the trail again for a moment. When he turned back he wasn't smiling. "Meg, you know I can make you."

"Do it, then!"

He heaved his shoulders patiently, withdrew the big knife from nowhere.

She began unbuttoning the blouse tightly. "Bastard!"

Jill sat down so fast she seemed to crumple.

"*Whew!* Hey, I gotta rest!"

She was breathing rapidly, face pale. Kirk hurried back to her, unstrapping his pack.

"The air's rarefied this high up, I should have warned you. I've been preoccupied." He knelt beside her. "You need oxygen."

She sucked at the thin mountain air. "Got any in your medicine box?"

"Just sit still a moment, take deep breaths. You'll be all right."

"So you keep telling me."

He reached for his water, but she waved him off. "No, I'm swimming."

He looked at her scornfully. "I told you to take it easy with that stuff, you'll get sick."

"Sorry, master."

He grinned deferentially, moved a strand of blond hair out of her mouth. "You look like shit."

She lay back on the hard earth, too weary to scrape away the stone cutting into her back. "Does this mean you won't fuck me?"

He was looking at his watch. "We'd both pass out."

"What time is it?"

"Just past three."

"God. Where are they?"

"Impatient to get me killed now?"

She declined a reply.

"They're close."

She looked up at him expectantly from flat on her back. "How do you know?"

"That last tree cut was still oozing sap."

She shook her head. "Daniel Boone."

He nodded, watching the summit. "Amazing how much of it's coming back to me."

She propped herself on her elbows, appraising him. He was rubbing sunscreen energetically over his neck, his arms. "Look at you."

He paused in mid-motion, looked up. "What?"

"You're enjoying it."

"What the hell are you talking about?"

"It's true. You're not afraid anymore. We're almost there, almost to the point where you should be the most frightened of all, and you're steady as a rock. You're actually looking forward to this."

He went back to his rubbing. "You've got sun stroke."

She sat up all the way, studying him. "It's not Meg you're worrying about. It's whether or not you can beat him, whether or not you've still got it."

He ignored her.

"The truth is, you never even knew I was here."

"That's not true, Jill, you've been invaluable."

"Oh, I was fun in the clinches, but the fact is you wish now you'd never brought me, that you'd accomplished it all on your own. This manly thing you've got to prove. You're as crazy as he is."

He screwed the top back on the bottle. "Maybe. Maybe we were all crazy over there. I'll say one thing for Riff, he gave me back my senses."

"And took your life."

He looked out over the mountains. "Not much of a life. Not lately anyway. For me or Meg."

Neither of them spoke for a time.

Kirk got up and came over to her, reaching inside his jacket. He handed her the .38.

"What's this?"

"I want you to carry it."

"Why?"

"Because he might get me before I get him. The way to go after a man like Riff is not with a gun anyway."

"How, then, with a knife? Like a Nightcrawler?" She mouthed the word as if it were spoiled food.

"It's what he wants. If I play the game his way, even if I lose, he may let Meg go. If he doesn't . . . you've got the gun."

She accepted the weapon, weighed it in her hand, a resigned gesture.

"Yes, I've got the gun."

She turned away, stuck it in her belt.

Riff began to cord Meg's wrists.

"It takes a real brave man to take advantage of a woman when she's bound and helpless," she was telling him.

He ignored the remarks and lashed the other end of the cord to the wooden stakes he'd driven earlier. He'd also spread out the bedroll between them so at least she wouldn't have to lie naked against the dirt and rocks.

"Will you lie down please, Meg?"

"I hope he cuts your balls off."

"I'm sure he'll try; on your stomach, please."

She did as she was told.

He began to lash her ankles.

"That hurts!" It didn't really.

"I'll try to be more careful. Would you like some water? It's going to get hot."

"Go screw."

And she was immediately sorry she'd suggested that.

He lashed the last ankle in place and sat back a moment. "Last call for water."

"I'm not thirsty. And what if I had to pee?"

He began digging in his backpack.

In a moment she felt the warm oil over her back.

Her muscles bunched in anticipation.

"Don't get your bowels in an uproar, Meg, it's just sunscreen."

He massaged in the liquid, grinned. "Disappointed?"

"Up yours."

He spread the liquid over her arms, her back. "The sun's too far down to be a real concern. This is just a precaution."

He recapped the bottle, replaced it neatly in the pack. He sat back a moment and appraised his work. She did look inviting, her body glistening like polished wood in the afternoon sun. "Women are such beautiful, delicate creatures," he marveled sincerely.

"And you treat us so respectfully."

He looked down the trail expectantly. "You haven't been treated so very badly."

"No, it's been a real picnic, Riff." Her voice was muffled against the blanket.

He came around, sat next to her. "Come off the high horse, Meg. You enjoyed a good deal of it, I made sure of that."

"Like hell."

He lit a cigarette, blew blue smoke. "Megan, Megan, lie to me if you will, but don't lie to yourself. You've been aching to find another lover these past five years; you lacked courage, not inspiration. And as for being treated badly, you haven't exactly done an exemplary job with Kirk, have you?"

"Go to hell, you know nothing about it!"

He snorted. "I know everything about it, more than I care to know. I'm not saying it was easy for you—Kirk was depressed, hard to approach—but you should have reached out, Meg, you know you should have. He was a crippled man."

"I reached out, goddammit! I reached out till it hurt! He wasn't there! There was nothing to reach out to!"

He made a scoffing sound. "Nothing, huh? Is that nothing coming up the mountain now to save your life?"

She was silent a moment. "He's doing what is expected of him."

"Partly," Riff conceded, "but he could have called the cops, made it easier. He didn't because he was fearful for your life."

"Guilt."

"Why are you deriding him, Meg? You know you love him. You know you hate yourself for that one abandoned night—with his brother . . ."

Silence. Pain welling deep in her heart.

She was sobbing now. "You sonofabitch!"

He wiped away her tears with his hand. "Yes, ma'am. And my father was no jewel either. But you and Kirkie. I think you two really had something there in the beginning. How about it, Meg?"

She sniffed. Watched the horizon. Groaned. "Oh, hell, it doesn't make any difference anyway. You're going to kill him."

He looked back at the trail. "It always makes a difference, Meg."

He got up, began undressing.

"Remember what I said in the restaurant that night, the one with that comedian waiter that tried to poison us? I said I respected you. I meant that,

Meg. And I still do. I'm sorry for what I had to do to you. I'm not sure I would have done it at all if you hadn't met me halfway. You're a wonderful lover. And I won't forget. It's almost over now. I hope you'll come to learn why it was necessary. I may have used you, but it was reciprocal. And it's only ugly if you let it be."

He finished undressing in silence.

And after a time she realized he wasn't there anymore.

She twisted her head about.

"Riff?"

But for the birds, silence.

He stopped suddenly on the trail, stood still, listening.

Jill came up behind him. "What is it?"

He didn't speak.

"Kirk . . . ?"

She could almost imagine him sniffing the air.

She touched his arm. "Did you hear something?"

He turned to her as if acknowledging her presence again. "Crying."

Jill looked up the trail: rock, sky, a screen of trees. "Meg?"

He nodded grimly.

"Are you sure?"

"I've heard her crying." It sounded vaguely self-reproachful.

He was scanning the nearby trees, unstrapping his pack again. "I don't suppose you have any lipstick?"

"I didn't think I'd need it up here. Why?"

She gasped loudly as he withdrew the knife. The blade, a lethal wedge of reflective steel, nearly blinded her.

"Where did you get—"

Then she jumped reflexively as he snapped forward and flung it skyward.

There was a distant crash.

He eased back on his left leg, shaking his head. "Missed. I'm rusty. Out of shape for this . . ."

He started forward and she hastened to catch up. He even walks differently now, she was thinking: comfortably, confidently, almost lazily. Like a cat.

He's changed.

He was searching beneath a tall lodgepole pine, brushing aside the foliage with the toe of his boot. In a moment he bent forward, crouching. "No, I didn't miss."

He retrieved the knife, and the red-tailed squirrel it was embedded in.

Kirk stripped off his shirt, placed the animal on a rock, and, using the knife point as a brush, began to draw the serpent.

Jill watched for a time, fascinated, then turned her head away contemptuously.

"All just a terrible waste," she muttered at the mountains, "a silly, terrible waste . . ."

Kirk ignored her, eyes on the trail ahead.

It was nearly four when Kirk first saw her.

He grabbed Jill's arm firmly, holding her back. "What?"

He nodded through the trees.

"I don't see anything!"

"The whitish blur, two o'clock."

She strained. "I don't—"

He touched his fingers to her lips, leaned to her, sotto voce. "I don't want you to talk anymore. Signal with your hands. Step only where I step. Keep the gun in your belt unless something happens to me. If we get separated, stay on the trail and go back to the car. Got it?"

She nodded, heart thumping.

He stepped ahead of her.

She followed nervously—and, to her—clumsily. It was maddening: even over leaves his footfalls made no sound. Hers seemed thunderous, elephantine. If there was a dry twig in the forest, she found it. But Kirk never turned around, never gave a reproachful look. He moved forward rapidly, carefully in nearly a straight line. After twenty yards or so, Jill could see their goal too.

Meg was stretched out under the waning sun in a small clearing, spread-eagled between wooden stakes, lashed tightly as in the video. Her body glistened wetly. It was a good body, Jill couldn't help noticing, firm and lean and tighter than her own, muscular in a way she was not. Less voluptuous would be a nice way of putting it, but all Jill could see was the hard bubble of the other woman's buttocks, the slender legs; we always want what is not ours.

He was nudging her.

She turned to find him proffering a pocket knife, a Boy Scout-style instrument with a short blade, tortoise-shell handle. He still grasped the hunting knife in the other hand. "Take it. Cut her free."

Jill balked. "Alone?"

"Alone."

"What if he's waiting?"

"Let's hope he is. You have the gun."

She looked down at the knife in his hand. After a moment she accepted it reluctantly. "What will you do?"

"I'll be waiting right here."

Jill nodded, still wary. "All right."

He handed her his water bottle. "Give her one swallow only. Then come straight back."

She took the bottle.

She stepped toward the clearing, hesitated.

"I'll be right behind you with the knife."

She stepped out of the trees into sunlight.

Meg was no more than fifteen or so yards away. It looked like an open invitation. And felt all wrong.

She started forward, right hand resting over the pebbled grip of the .38, still tucked in her shorts; her other hand clutched the knife and bottle. She kept her eyes on the surrounding woods, not really expecting to see anything and not being disappointed. Yet he was there.

She kept wanting to turn about and make sure Kirk was still there, all right, but it didn't seem appropriate. If something was going to happen now, it would happen very fast; she would be alone with only the gun.

Meg appeared to be asleep as she approached. Or dead. She could detect no movement in the slender rib cage. How truly lovely she was; she might have been sunbathing out here amid the scenic mountains. Jill knelt by her shoulder.

"Meg? Can you hear me?"

Kirk's wife opened her eyes, squinted up into sunlight. Her brows knitted when she recognized the other woman. "Where's Kirk?"

"Waiting for us." She began to work at the nearest cord, sawing with the little knife. She wished she had the big one, but could appreciate why Kirk wanted to keep that. It was startling enough he didn't want to keep the gun. The cord parted after a moment, and Jill scooted over to the other wrist, eyes on the surrounding woods. Nothing moved.

Meg had turned her head on the blanket to follow the other woman, eyes on the police special tucked against her blouse. "That's Kirk's gun."

"Yes."

The other cord parted, and Meg labored to sit up stiffly, rubbing her wrists, unable to suppress a groan. Jill uncapped the water bottle and handed it to her. "One swallow."

Meg took it, eyes still on the gun, tilted it back. Cold and delicious. She splashed some on her face as Jill set to work on her ankles.

A cracking sound from the woods.

Both women looked up.

Nothing.

Jill's vision swept back to where Kirk stood, but against the dark shadows of the trees, the thick undergrowth, she could not see him. She busied herself with the cords again. Meg remained upright, rigid.

"Is Kirk all right?"

"Yes."

"Why do you have the gun?"

Another cord parted. Jill stood, moved to the last one, grabbing Meg's clothing lying nearby, tossing them to the slim, muscular figure. "Get dressed."

"I don't see Kirk . . ."

"He's there! Get dressed!"

She labored over the final cord, fingers stiffening with the effort, beginning to lock on her. She had to stop a moment, massage circulation back into them. Meg had the bra on, was slipping the dress over her head.

The cord parted with a *tung*! Jill threw down the knife and tossed Meg her shoes. Meg was slipping into the panties, hiking them up under the dress. She grabbed the shoes, pulled them on, tried to stand, fell back.

"Give me your hand!"

Jill pulled her to her feet, eyes sweeping the edge of the clearing expectantly. There was nothing. "Can you walk?"

"I'm all right, just give me a sec."

They stood there a moment, Meg balancing precariously, leaning heavily on the other woman. Meg's eyes kept wandering back to the revolver.

She took a few tentative steps, supported by Jill's hand, like a person learning to skate. Limping slightly, she was maneuvered this way back to the edge of the clearing. Jill kept swiveling her head around as though something was about to leap on them from behind. It seemed to take them forever with Meg's reluctant hopping. Jill kept having to fight back an urge to push her ahead.

"Where is he?"

Jill stood among the trees, gun drawn now, turning every which way. "He was right here! Kirk!"

She walked a few feet into the brush, calling, changed direction, walked some more, turned, called again, searching. "Kirk!"

She turned finally to Meg, who was watching her intently. "He was right here, dammit!"

"You shot him." Mouth pinched with fear, eyes accusing.

Jill regarded her a moment, then turned away dismissingly. "Don't be an idiot."

She moved about in the underbrush, stumbling, head jerking back and forth, .38 swinging this way and that. *"Kirk!"*

Silence.

Twenty

Kirk stood alone, swathed mostly in shadows, all save the top of his sandy head. That head was cocked just slightly now, listening.

His skin was pale from too many hours hiding from the sun in soft, comfortable easy chairs. His waist was disappointingly thick, muscle tone slack, coordination off. But his mind . . . his mind was sharper than it had been in years. Alert. Attuned. Ready.

The other man was in better shape.

But Kirk was ready.

He reached down, gathered a handful of dirt and leaves, and began smearing it across his pale shoulders, arms, his back, even around the outline of the serpent, right to the line where his jeans cut across his navel. Blend with your surroundings, basic army S.O.P.

He finished the job by smudging dirt across his cheeks, forehead, where it mingled with the dripping sweat and spread as smoothly as theatrical makeup.

He had heard a sound before. It was just after Jill had walked out into the bright sunlight to free his tethered wife. Jill hadn't heard it. Neither, probably, had Meg. But Kirk had. Kirk had been intended to hear it. It was for his ears alone.

There was nothing now. Just the birds, the leaves, the ambient forest noises.

But the sound had been Riff, no doubt about it. Kirk had heard it before. Long ago. In the jungle. Riff had a certain . . . gait.

Riff could move in utter silence when he wanted to, soft and supple as the wind, quiet and deadly as a bush master. But at certain times, in certain wars, you wanted to be heard, especially by your allies. And when you'd walked the jungles a million times with that ally, you got to know the sound of those movements as well as your own: subtle, distinctive, singular.

Riff was making those sounds now.

Purposely.

He wanted Kirk to know. Wanted Kirk to follow. The game was not over.

Merely narrowed.

Kirk turned silently and scanned the forest floor. Some leaves, not too many. He'd walked over worse terrain, far worse. The sun was up, the ground dry. There would be snakes, even some vipers. But he'd walked where a snake bite could kill you in thirty seconds. He'd walked through ankle-deep paddies chilly with morning frost, deadly with dung-smeared pungi sticks. He'd walked over land so seeded with Claymores that three of his buddies had been rent to geysering flotsam before his shell-shocked eyes. Compared to that, this would be a cake walk.

Of course, Riff had been on his side then.

That equalized the analogy somewhat.

He squeezed shut his right eye as a line of perspiration ran into it. The top of his head, just a small patch of it, was exposed to the harsh sun, baking down on it. But his position was too good to change. A little sun wouldn't kill him, though it was warming him up, giving him strange thoughts, thoughts of the past, the woods, the jungles in another part of the world. Never mind. As long as it didn't cook his brain, as long as it didn't interfere with his performance, slow his reaction time, let it shine. It felt good. And he didn't mind thinking about that other jungle. It was kind of nice. He could almost smell it. . . .

He reached down carefully and pulled off his boots silently. Then the socks.

He dug his toes into the soft earth. He couldn't repress the fierce smile playing at his lips. A familiar heat washed through him, upward from his groin. He was back. In many ways, in the best kind of ways, he was back.

"Feels pretty good, huh, old buddy?"

Kirk didn't jump, didn't twitch, didn't even alter the rhythm of his breathing. And he experienced a deep sense of self-satisfaction that his heart rate had increased only a fraction: the adrenaline staying in check for later use as intended; its time would come.

But neither did he answer. He wasn't a fool.

He rechecked his surroundings, even the canopy of trees above. He was well concealed, moderately well camouflaged, no metal parts glinting. It would have been better if his skin were darker, or smeared with burnt cork, but all in all he was relatively invisible. He nodded to himself confidently: chances were the other man hadn't actually seen him, at least not all of him; chances were he'd merely sensed him or, perhaps, caught the thinnest rustle of a displaced leaf. Kirk made a mental note to be even more careful. He cursed his lack of physical tone, then, as quickly, dismissed unproductive musings. We must focus. We must channel all our energy, all our thoughts, to the objective at hand: in this case, the death of Riff Walker.

We must maintain total control.

"Total control and complete concentration," Riff finished the axiom for him.

The voice seemed to come from everywhere at once, but that was the idea. Kirk froze, scanned the tangled woodland, eyes narrowed. Nothing.

Mind reading. One could almost interpret it as mind reading. Almost. It had unnerved Charlie, it had destroyed the enemy's confidence. But Kirk had an edge—he'd trained at the same school. He'd been a Nightcrawler too. It *seemed* like mind reading. But Riff Walker was merely human. Exceptional. But human.

And humans, no matter what their expertise, could be stopped.

Kirk cocked his head again, waited.

Nothing.

The sun beat down.

So hot. Just like the 'Nam.

The good old 'Nam.

Riff was smart enough to keep his taunting comments to a minimum, space them between vacillating locations: now to the left, now at ground level, now up above somewhere . . .

Oh, he was a master.

Kirk looked down at himself, pulled the serrated edge of the hunting knife half an inch from its belt sheath. It gleamed dully up at him, filled him with a tingling confidence. In the old days he could throw it forty feet and hit his target dead center. He could slip it out, put it in your belly, have it resheathed, under his shirt, and be on his way before you even noticed your own blood spreading across your shirt front. Speed. He'd had more than his share of it in the old days. The old days . . .

"But can you *still* fling it, that's the question, eh, old buddy?"

Mind reading, my ass; he'd been spotted.

Kirk leapt from cover like a flushed gazelle—no point in worrying about camouflage now—vaulted a bush, hit, rolled, purposefully throwing up clouds of dust.

He slid behind another tree, curled, drawing up his legs, knife drawn now, pressed to his naked chest, to the serpent's head, breath labored but controllable. He'd made a lot of dust. If Riff was behind him, he wouldn't know if Kirk had rolled left or right. If he was in front of Kirk, then Kirk was an open target.

Whatever the case, Kirk was inwardly gratified

he'd retained more agility than he'd previously thought. He wasn't quite the clumsy ape he'd been with Sue's husband in their kitchen. He'd be a foil for Riff Walker. An outclassed foil, maybe, but at least a foil. If he was going to end up with a knife in his belly at the end of the day, he'd at least like to return the gesture with a few cutting remarks of his own.

It would be an interesting fight.

He might even have a slim chance of winning.

He was just beginning to smile to himself when the shadow fell over him.

"We've got to get out of here."

But Meg was still watching her cynically. Every time Jill walked by her with the swiveling gun, Meg's eyes were glued to it. She stood to one side, rubbing her wrists, body tensed and bowed slightly, like a small animal ready to make a break.

"Why did Kirk give you the gun?"

Jill kept scouring the surrounding woods distractedly. "In case we got separated—like now."

"He left himself defenseless?"

"He has a knife."

"And he gave you the gun?" she queried skeptically.

Jill whirled. "Why don't you help me look for him instead of asking stupid questions? He did this for you!"

Meg eyed her levelly. "Let me have the gun."

"What for?"

"Why not?"

"Have you ever fired a gun?"

"Have you?"

"Yes."

"Where?"

Jill hesitated. Then brushed by her. "This is ridiculous, I'm going back to the car as Kirk suggested. Come or stay as you wish."

After a few yards Meg caught up with her.

"Why did you come along, Jill? What was the point?"

Jill walked briskly, eyes ahead, chin up, as though the other woman weren't there. "He asked me to help him."

"How could you help him?" She was struggling to keep up, her legs still shaky.

"I know Riff."

"Oh, right! You were married, weren't you? You must know him pretty damn well!"

Jill rolled her eyes. "What's the point of that now?"

"What'd he do, where does he work?"

"He never told me."

"You're lying."

"Okay, I'm lying."

"How about you, where do you work?"

"Chinese cookie factory."

"Yeah? Any good fortunes lately?"

"Life's a bitch, and then you die."

"What did you do with him?"

"Who?"

"Kirk?"

"In what sense, Meg, dear?"

"Where did you leave him?"

"He left me, sweetie. Us."

"You're lying."

"There I go again."

"Give me the gun."

"Get lost."

They were walking near the edge of the precipice, marching stiffly, rapidly, Jill facing forward,
Meg facing Jill, glaring at her, when the figure
came out of the forest.

He was bent, and winded, naked to the waist.
His upper torso was smeared with blood. More
blood dripped from a big knife blade, which he
held extended toward the ground as if from a broken arm. But when he saw them, the arm came up
reflexively, not broken at all.

Everyone stopped for a moment.

Meg opened her mouth first, but it was Jill who
found voice. "Where is he?" She held the gun leveled at him.

He glanced at the barrel. He was still breathing
hard. "I was going to ask you that."

She brought up the gun. "Don't play with me,
Riff, what did you do with him?"

Something about her voice. Meg glanced at her
briefly.

Riff turned to a big maple, tore away a leaf, and
began to wipe at sticky blade. "You're the one that's
been with him for the past forty-eight hours, Jill.
Why don't you tell us?" He gave the word *us* a
weight that suggested possible ulterior meaning.

Without hesitating, Jill raised the gun in both
hands and spread her legs slightly in a police offi-

cer's stance. The professionalism was not lost on Meg.

"I'm going to ask you once more, Riff."

He finished wiping the knife and threw away the leaf casually. He stood facing her, knife arm dangling loosely at his side. "I honestly don't know, Jill. Maybe he went home, got tired of all of us."

Meg stepped back out of the line of fire involuntarily.

The air became abruptly pregnant with the possibility of hurtling things.

There existed an unspoken acknowledgment among the three of Riff's prowess with a knife; probably his throw was like lightning, maybe even faster than she could pull the trigger—or at least, get out of the way having pulled it.

They stood that way for a time.

Riff smiled. "If you kill me, you'll never know where he is, is that what you're thinking?"

"Then he is—?"

"I didn't say that, Megan. Put away the weapon, Jill. If I don't get you, Meg will. I told her."

Meg gave her another searching look, could see by the other woman's expression that it was true. Which meant, probably, it was all true. And that so much else was lies.

The world was no longer sane.

Jill remained unmoving.

"Whom did you kill, then?"

He watched the barrel. "Guy named Limpert."

"Jim Limpert?"

"You know him?"

"I dated him."

"Sorry."

"Don't be. Prove it."

He nodded back over his shoulder. "His body's down trail about fifty yards, wedged between two trees and covered with half a pint of Grade A Riff Walker urine. Shall I take you there?"

"Not with the knife."

"Never go anywhere without it."

"Well, then."

They stood there.

A Colorado stand-off.

A fly droned obliviously somewhere.

It nearly covered the other sound, the sound of crackling leaves. Behind them.

Jill whirled, gun rigidly before her in both hands.

It brought the four men emerging from the woods up short a moment. They stood frozen in deep shadow, watching. Waiting. Then, abruptly they were running forward.

Too late. Jill remembered, whipped around to level at Riff again—found the clearing empty.

"Shit!"

David Kirkland and the three other men hurried up to the two women, all three drawing their service revolvers. Already David was motioning to two of the men with sweeping moves of his gun hand, directing them into the surrounding woods; the third man stayed at David's side; he, like the others, wore the same tan suit and wire-rim mirrored sunglasses. They looked like cool, efficient insects.

David holstered his piece and drew Meg into his arms. "Meg, thank Christ!" He held her, kissed her forehead. Meg, stiffening, let herself be held.

David looked into her eyes. "When we got to the motel you were gone! What happened, for God's sake?"

Meg regarded her mirrored image coolly. "You don't know, David?"

"We assumed Riff Walker had come back, spirited you away again." He looked askance at Jill, who still held the gun before her. "Is this a friend of yours, I hope?"

Jill held the gun levelly. "Who are these people, Meg?"

Meg worked herself free of David's embrace. "You mean you don't know?"

David's face was knitted with puzzlement. "What's going on, where's Kirk?"

Jill raised her revolver a fraction. The man beside David tightened. "Why don't you tell us? And start with some ID."

Frowning in irritation, David fished his shield from his coat, held it for Jill's scrutiny. "David Kirkland, Kirkland Security. This is Detective Olson, Chicago P.D., Officer Mike Tolin." He gave Jill a cursory once-over. "You're Walker's ex, right? The woman Kirk told us about."

After a moment she lowered the gun reluctantly. "Yes."

"Where's Kirk?"

"We don't know."

David pocketed the shield, turned to Meg again,

reaching for her with concerned arms. "Don't worry, honey, we'll find him."

Meg slapped his hands away, stepped back, face twisted with fear and anger. She was shaking all over. "Get away from me, you sonofabitch! You're CIA agents! All of you! You set me up!"

David hesitated, face aghast. "Meg, for God's sake, what're you talking about?"

"You're CIA, you bastard! You sent that—that Mafia goon to kill me!" She was backing toward a copse of trees, eyes still darting like a trapped animal's.

David took a step toward her, but hesitated when it was clear she was about to take flight.

He held up his hands, palms out, in a calming gesture. "Meg . . ."

"If it hadn't been for Riff, I'd be wedged in the corner of a filthy mountain shack right now, raped and gutted! He saved my life!"

David's hands flopped to his sides in patient amusement. "Riff Walker saved your life?" his voice coy with gentle sarcasm.

Meg kept backing, stomach muscles taut, breathing in short gasps.

David chewed his lip, considering the next move. It was obvious the poor woman was terrified. Pushing now would accomplish nothing. After a moment he shrugged. "All right, Meg, I suppose he could have saved your life—for the moment, at least. Until he got you together with your husband. Meg, don't you know the man's a homicidal maniac?"

"He killed a man to save my life!"

David nodded soothingly. "Easy, sweetheart. I know what you've gone through. But it's almost over, let's not lose our heads here at the end. Now think. Did you actually *see* him kill this man who accosted you?"

The memory of out-of-sight gunfire echoed in her brain.

Meg hesitated.

David waited patiently, hands folded before him. "How did he kill him, Meg? Did he shoot him?"

Her legs were trembling uncontrollably; she probably couldn't have run anyway. "He . . . shot himself."

David's expression was heartfelt concern mixed with barely concealed incredulity. He nearly smiled. "Shot himself? Meg."

"I . . . heard . . . it."

David coughed, gave his partner in the insect sunglasses a patronizing glance.

Jill started to say something to Meg, but David waved her silent. He turned to his brother's wife, still not attempting to approach. "Meg, I love you. I love Kirk. I'd do anything for him, I think you know that. But right now he's in very grave danger. I think you know that too, deep inside. I can't explain to you why a man like Riff Walker does all the crazy things he does, except perhaps to say that he's a pathological liar and a highly psychotic sociopath. I'm not even sure Riff himself knows why he does some of the things he does. But, sweetheart, one thing I do know: you must not, under any circumstances, trust him. For chrissake, Meg, he *abducted* you! Now, I know you've been under a terrific strain these past few days, but use your *head*!" He shouted the last word, hoping to shock her out of panic.

Meg was trembling all over now. "But the other man . . ."

David sighed in exasperation. Then said softly: "Look: Riff hired him, maybe, to help out if things got out of hand—which apparently they did. Maybe this guy double-crossed Riff. Maybe the whole thing was just a show to confuse you, torture you. Maybe Riff *did* kill him just for the fun of it! Who knows! Has he done anything successively in the past forty-eight hours that has made any kind of logical sense? I'm with the CIA?" And this time he did bark a single, harsh laugh. "Honey, the guy's a lunatic!"

Meg was sobbing.

She didn't even remember starting.

She only knew that she was exhausted. That these people might be right or might be wrong, but that for all she cared, they could kill her right now, because she just simply didn't have the strength to run anymore.

She was run-out.

"Megan . . ."

He came to her and held her and rubbed her back, and she let him, sobbing into his shoulder.

"David! Please! Please don't let anything happen to him! I love him so much! What I did with you—"

"We made a mistake, Meg! I'm to blame, not you! I promise I'll tell him the truth. We'll get it all out in the open when this is over with." Meg sobbed harder. David patted her back, gave her his handkerchief. "Don't worry. Riff Walker is good, but we're better. And we've got him outmanned. We'll get him. Now let us do our job, huh?" He kissed her forehead.

She pushed away, abruptly impatient with herself, and blew her nose. "I'm sorry. Go get him. Bring me back my husband, *please!*"

David nodded, motioned to the remaining detective. "Olson will take the two of you back to your car. You'll be perfectly safe with him until Riff Walker is apprehended. The area is surrounded, it's only a matter of time." He looked at Meg. "And don't worry about Kirk, he can take care of himself."

He reached over and squeezed Meg's arm once.

"I'd like to come with you ... if that's permissible," Jill said softly.

David regarded her a moment. "Do you know how to fire that weapon, ma'am?"

"Well ..."

"I think it best if you give it to Detective Olson and wait in the car with him. I know you're both concerned about Kirk. But there may be some gunplay, and we don't want any accidents—or hostages—at this stage of the game."

Jill nodded. "All right. Perhaps that's best."

She handed the gun to Olson.

David slapped the man on the shoulder. "Take care of them, Ben."

"I will."

David withdrew his own handgun, a .38 Colt, as

Jill drew Meg into her arms. He watched a moment as the two women, arms about each other, and the other detective descended across the precipice toward the valley floor.

Turning then, David Kirkland headed into the woods.

Twenty-one

Kirk quietly let the shadow fall over him. It only lasted a heartbeat, then was gone.

There was no need to hurry, no need to panic and lose control just at the moment he was in such complete command of it. Slow and easy and precise, that was the way; each carefully considered, carefully weighed microsecond at a time. He was at one with the jungle. At one with himself. He was a Nightcrawler.

The shadow didn't belong to Riff Walker anyway.

There was someone else in the woods.

Kirk shifted silently into a new position but couldn't quite get his baking head out of the driving sun. The air was getting thinner and he was feeling the exhaustion of the last few days . . . but with it a strange kind of alertness, an almost euphoric tingling in his limbs, his fingertips.

That sun. So warm.

A faint crackling to his left, two o'clock.

He still couldn't see for the screen of saplings, but whoever the enemy was, he wasn't in Riff

Walker's league. That wasn't one of Riff's purpose-
ful location-fix sounds; that was the clumsy movements of a lesser opponent.

An opponent nonetheless.

Caution was required. It could be anyone.

Even Charlie.

Another crackling, boots or rubber thongs on dry
leaves. Moving away now. Kirk stirred.

He pushed up in one silent movement, turned
his head, and surveyed his area, right hand clutching the worn hilt of the hunting knife. Too bad it
wasn't nightfall. He liked it better in the cloaking
shadows of the night, the gentle thrum of insects
covering your every move, the friendly moon guid-
ing you to the kill. Charlie was an easier target in
the night.

But this would do. This would do fine.

He stepped forward to get him.

He didn't have to step far.

A shadow detached itself from an oak about
twenty yards to his left, approximately ten o'clock.
It began to stalk toward a narrow clearing cautiously. Big mistake.

Rule number one: never walk in the open, even
if relatively small. It only takes an instant for the
enemy to spot you, another instant for him to pull
the trigger.

Of course, Kirk didn't have a trigger, and he
couldn't really discern, in the shadows, the enemy's
face, but none of that mattered. He had his knife.
And in combat—when in doubt—you strike first,
ask questions later. He would aim to cripple, not
kill.

Kirk unsheathed the knife again. Positioned himself.

Waited.

Three more strides and the figure would be forced to cross into the thin avenue of buttery sunlight; at that precise nanosecond he would be free of shadows, foliage, woodland obstructions: a clear target. At this range, from where Kirk stood, there existed but a narrow open corridor between the trees, a leafy passageway of no more than a few precious feet within which his knife could travel. A slight error in calculation, a fraction too far to the left or right, and the blade would embed itself in a twisted branch or solid trunk. It must be a perfect throw, perfectly timed.

In the old days it would have been a piece of cake.

But the old days were gone.

Kirk held his breath. Raised the blade-held weapon between thumb and index . . .

The figure stepped into sunlight.

Time to see if the old days were still with him.

Kirk drew back his throwing arm in one smooth motion, the serrated edge of the big knife catching the glinting sun for the smallest part of an instant. It was enough.

A shot rang out with a staccato crack that echoed with receding thumps through the leafy labyrinth of forest. The hunting knife shattered somewhere above the leather-wrapped hilt, raining shrapnel into Kirk's cheek, knocking him forward, off balance. Stunned, shocked, Kirk threw his own momentum into the force of the blow and slammed himself facedown onto the leaves.

He froze, cursing his stupidity, his plunging heart. Of course. It figured they would be a reconnaissance party of at least two; goddammit, he should have known!

He lay in the musty-smelling humus, feeling the thud of his heart against the earth, trying to discern where the shot had come from: probably behind him. He knew he was safe for the moment, invisible again against the camouflage of forest, but his position had been sighted. It would only be a matter of minutes. And he was weaponless.

His head seemed to buzz with the heat of the sun.

Think!

What would a Nightcrawler do?

The ground beneath him was cool. He wanted to press his throbbing forehead into it, to rest, sleep.

Two against one.

Weaponless.

Think!

A Nightcrawler is *never* weaponless; he has the vast resources of the forest all around him.

Something ran into his eyes. Sweat? Blood?

Kirk reached up carefully and touched his forehead, drew back fingers etched with red. Something was embedded up there. He twisted his head, reached up again, and lightly touched the steel knife shard jutting from his temple. It was pumping crimson. He hadn't even felt it.

He gritted his teeth and plucked it free: about an

inch long, jagged and sharp on one end, steel. Not a weapon. But a tool.

He twisted about silently and looked behind him. The boots. He needed the boots.

There was a rustling noise directly to his rear, thirty, forty yards off. The one who'd shot the knife out of his hand was coming for him. With bullets. He was heading in a direct line with the discarded boots.

Kirk searched about, selected a baseball-sized stone, and flung it expertly to his left about fifteen yards. Its crashing fall brought an immediate halt to the noise behind him, an indecisive halt; he had hoped for gunfire, but his enemy wasn't that gullible.

Kirk brought himself up to his knees, dripping blood across dirt-scoured thighs. He reached down for another handful of dirt, pressed it to his temple until the flow was stanched. He rose to his bare feet, peered carefully behind him, and waited.

Throw another stone?

No. The enemy'd be on to him then for sure; better to let him investigate the first one.

He waited.

In a moment the rustling sounded again, moving southeast toward the thrown stone. With any luck it would take the enemy away from the boots. Kirk had to have those goddamn boots back.

Another rustling sound behind him. The first target—the one he had aimed the knife at—was moving back to converge with his comrade on the thrown stone. They'd be there in less than a minute.

And when they found nothing, they'd come looking this way for him.

What to do?

If he made a dash, he'd probably reach the boots, but they'd hear him for sure. If he Indian-stalked it, he might evade them, but it would take longer, and for all he knew, the woods were filled with enemy scouts.

There wasn't time to muse over it. He elected to dash for them.

Not ten feet after he had begun his sprint, .38 slugs were whining overhead, making confetti explosions of the flora around him. He ducked, weaved, dodged behind trees, shrubs, gunfire rocking the quiet woodland, birds shrieking into the air in frenzied flight like windblown leaves. He could almost smell the acrid clouds of cordite.

The boots were gone.

He skidded to a halt, chest heaving, eyes darting everywhere around the big tree where he'd left the hiking boots. Gone.

They must have discovered them.

A slug ricocheted overhead, raining bark into his hair. Time to move.

He threw himself to the right, dived over a low shrub and rolled, spun, sprinted to his left to confuse them. Another explosion of gunfire, this time to his right, off target.

But they *couldn't* have discovered them! He'd been so careful!

He spun around a copse of trees, veered left again, zigzagged through a small sun-lanced meadow, rounded a big oak, fell flat. And there were the boots.

Idiot! You went to the wrong oak!

Gasping, Kirk yanked the laces frenziedly, fingers trembling, pulling the cotton cords through the leather eyeholes in quick, whipping movements, one eye on the screen of trees behind him. He had just yanked the last one free when dirt was kicked up beside his shoe, spraying his chest, followed by the distance-delayed report of the gun. Fisting the laces in one hand, Kirk sprinted ahead, ducked another bullet whistling past his ear, and flung himself over another hedge . . .

. . . into empty air.

The screen of bushes and trees growing out of the cliff's rim had hid it from view; he topped the edge of the hedge and—wide eyed with terror— kept right on falling.

Falling, falling . . . colliding at last with the steep face of the ravine, bouncing, somersaulting, arms and legs flung outward in clumsy surprise like a rag doll's. Hard shale smacked into his face, tore his forehead, bit into his knees. The world went over and over, cliff, sky, cliff, sky, cliff, sky . . .

Fetal roll!

It was what saved him.

He hadn't had time to see how deep the ravine was, how long he would fall, or what awaited him at the bottom, but the old army training came back in time to remind him to pull in his limbs, make a ball of himself, and just go with it.

He seemed to fall and roll an awfully long time. He was still rolling—in his mind—some time after he'd actually stopped. He opened his eyes to whirling vertigo, his equilibrium shot.

Somewhere a distant voice was shouting to *get up! move! get out of there, you dizzy bastard!* and by the time he realized the voice was in his own mind, bullets were already raining down, whining angrily off the stony creek bed.

Move!

I'm hurt!

No, that doesn't matter now! Move! Anywhere! Quickly!

Yessir . . . whatever you say, sir . . . right fucking away, sir!

He pushed up with a grunt, found himself in a shallow stream, and began limping off in tune to the ricocheting whines around him. It felt like someone was pushing down heavily on his shoulders, trying to drive his head into the happily burbling stream. It was a miracle he'd held on to the fistfuls of laces. If only the horizon would stop tilting. He wanted so much to vomit.

Magically the world began to right itself, the nausea eased, the bobbing stream stopped rushing up to slap him in the face.

A brief glance over his shoulder told him his pursuers numbered two, that they were firing on him from the top of the ravine, that he was probably too far away to be a viable target now, and that it would take them considerably more time to pick their way down the cliff face than it had taken him to fall down it.

Torn and bleeding, scored with dozens of livid abrasions, he had, nonetheless, broken nothing, and in all probability evaded them through the only plausible—albeit unintentional—escape plan available: falling off a cliff.

He found himself, despite his great pain, smiling as he ran. *The old s.o.b.'s got some zip in him yet! Mess with me, you yellow bastards, I'll smack your ass into next week!*

But they would follow.

That was a given. Charlie always did. Celebration was short-lived.

Staggering, stumbling, stream rocks cutting his naked feet, he began immediately to comb the rugged, foliage-thick shore with pain-slitted eyes, searching for what he needed.

Eighty yards downstream, he found it.

Growing out of the tangled bank was a forked two-year-old sapling—elm, just what he needed. Behind it was a mass of thorn-thick briars: dense and concealing. No one in his right mind would hide in there unless he had to. Perfect.

Kirk arrowed for it, dragging the broken length of steel blade from his jean pocket.

Working feverishly, head constantly snapping around to survey the empty streambed, he selected an oak branch of proper size and length, cut it down with the piece of broken knife, began whittling the end to a razor point. It took less than half a minute to make his arrow. He hesitated, wasting another precious half second: dove or pigeon feathers embedded in the butt end of the shaft would have made for smoother flight, but there wasn't time for that.

Testing the suppleness of the twin sapling

boughs, Kirk nodded satisfaction, got behind them so he was facing the stream, and uncurled the wadded mass of boot laces. These he tied end to end with a strong knot. He now had a string approximately four feet in length. Another fourteen seconds had elapsed. He could hear the first soldier tramping downstream toward him. His companion, if things ran to standard course, would race across the bluff above, descend farther downstream, and come for Kirk in the opposite direction, thus doubling their chances.

Cutting a second, shorter length of branch, Kirk fitted it between the sapling boughs and worked it down tight just above the fork.

Then he took one end of the tied-together boot laces and anchored it securely to the left sapling bough above the fork, left two feet of slack, and anchored the other end at the right sapling bough. His sling complete, he cut a notch in the blunt end of the sharpened stick, fitted it into the string, and rested the head of the arrow against the smaller branch wedged between the fork.

Then he waited, pressing himself back into his thorny cover of brambles, ripping his skin painfully but concealing himself completely.

Hitting the object wasn't the crux of the problem: Kirk had made dozens of sling arrow contraptions, arboreal and otherwise, and he could hit anything that moved. The trick was to do it silently and carefully so as not to tip off the enemy.

He had two things going for him: it was a fairly wide, fast-flowing stream and made a nice, loud gurgling noise. That should cover the rustle of the bending sapling branches. Also, the enemy would be walking into the sun, the glare, hopefully, distracting him from the jiggling motion of the leaves. Kirk wished he had an accompanying breeze to further camouflage movement, but you can't have everything.

At best it was a long shot, anyway.

If this Charlie was good, well-trained, not too exhausted, Kirk could probably kill him. If he was exceptional, he would shoot Kirk.

The answer was coming down the stream now, black Viet Cong pajamas stark against the white rocks, rubber-soled thongs crunching gravel, Russian Luger held before him. He walked confidently if cautiously: he knew Kirk was weaponless.

As before, in the woods, Kirk would have only a couple of precious seconds in which to draw back, aim, and launch his missile. It was all timing. It always was.

Now the enemy was in sight.

Now he approached the line of fire.

This was the tricky part.

Even blended as they were against the vegetation-thick bank, the leaves would still make some movement. Kirk had to draw back the sapling boughs before the enemy was close enough to detect it, but also have the strength to hold the arrow in place in case the enemy slowed or lingered. Too late and he'd give away his position; too soon and he'd grow exhausted holding the taut string. He smiled in his leafy bower of pain.

Isn't war fun? he thought.

* * *

Tolin had been a public servant most of his life.

He had fired at a lot of men, hit a lot of men, been fired back at as well. Three times wounded in the line of duty, he had been hospitalized in '74 with a shattered clavicle and almost resigned from service. But he'd come back. Not for the money. He liked the action.

He'd seen a lot in twenty years.

But he'd never seen anything like this.

His partner lay on the rocky streambed among the laughing rivulets and polished stones with an eighteen-inch length of oak branch sticking out of his left eye. There wasn't even very much blood. In all likelihood, the man hadn't even known what hit him. Tolin himself wasn't even sure how the shot had been effected. It was incredible. They'd thought the man they were pursuing was weapon-less.

But maybe not really so surprising.

Not in light of what David had told them about this guy Riff Walker. Walker could make a weapon out of any damn thing, just the tools at hand, and fire it with a precision that was as enviable as it was deadly. Walker was a master tracker, a superb woodsman, an accomplished survivor.

And this twisted thing in the water with the stick through its brain had to be the work of Riff Walker.

Who else would shoot a man through the eye and then piss on him like that?

A lucky shot.

Let's face it, he hadn't really been aiming for the eye. He had been aiming for the belly, a much bigger target. In fact, the enemy had, at the last instant, seen him, started to bring up his own weapon. Otherwise his head wouldn't have been turned that way. Otherwise Kirk wouldn't have gotten him through the eye.

As it was, nothing less than an eye shot would have killed him so swiftly; the enemy would have gotten off at least two rounds into the bramble bush. And Kirk would have been one dead combat soldier, one less Nightcrawler.

Lucky shot.

But that was part of the game too.

And what it had bought him was time, time to find a steep but navigable path up the bank, time to get his wind, gather his senses. Time to get far enough away from adversary number two to secure a new weapon. A more portable one.

He couldn't very well stop off at every convenient forked elm and expect the enemy to stroll obligingly in front of it. If he was going to compete with firepower, he was going to have to adapt to it.

This in mind, he set to cutting down another length of elm with the dependable piece of blade, and fashioning it into a strong, resilient bow. A bow he could carry.

It took some time.

There were a lot of things to consider when choosing bow stock, and although he'd gained a few precious minutes, the enraged partner of the first Cong would be along any minute, more determined than ever to weed out and destroy the Yankee interloper. So Kirk still had to work fast.

The worst part was the boot laces; flat and only

mildly flexible, they lacked the suppleness of jungle lianas, a much preferable but not immediately available commodity. Any good cable-producing epiphyte would do, but this section of forest seemed to be strangely lacking in that species of vegetation. And even if he'd had the time to cut a piece of workable vine, he certainly didn't have time to strip and thread it properly. So the man-made cotton laces would have to suffice.

He recut them to a suitable length, bound them between the arc of his newly fashioned bow, and tested it by twanging the string. It produced a low, pleasant *thrum* and Kirk nodded approvingly.

Next he chose his second arrow, and again the added time gave him the luxury of finding a straighter, more balanced length of branch. This he cut and sharpened accordingly, still wishing for the missing feathers that would give it true accuracy, eliminate wobble in flight, but consoling himself with the fact of his new mobility.

Already he could hear the enemy coming. Tramp, tramp, tramp. Christ, these two Cong were clumsy bastards! Wonder that they ever survived jungle warfare.

He was just nocking the string notch at the end of the newly completed arrow when he felt pressure across his left foot.

He had been standing still so long, had been so intent on his work and so intent on remaining silent to his enemy, he'd even concealed himself from the other enemies of the forest.

It was a male diamondback, a big one, six foot if it was an inch. It was crawling senuously across his naked foot, flat grayish head slightly raised, tongue flicking in and out, sending back pheremonal readings to its primitive but highly alert brain. It hadn't detected him yet because the foot it was traveling across was embedded in dirt and leaves. But Kirk's other foot was open and exposed. In another moment the heat-feeling pits on either side of the reptile's snout, lined with sensory cells, would detect the radiant heat of his exposed instep; the snake would stop, coil, and the resultant, hollow rattle would be a beacon for the advancing enemy. Kirk would either be shot or bit, depending on who acted first, enemy or snake.

The bite of a full-grown diamondback can kill a two hundred-pound man in an hour. Kirk wondered about this: diamondback rattlers aren't endemic to Southeast Asia. What was this one doing here in the 'Nam? Strange.

He reached down swiftly and plucked the snake from the earth.

Holding it behind its lethal head, Kirk allowed the muscular body to coil tightly about his wrist and forearm while he wielded the piece of shrapnel. A moment later, the viper's head fell to the ground.

Kirk discarded the writhing body quietly and picked up the head. He pried open the pink mouth and peered inside, careful to avoid the curved, hollow fangs. Someone had tried to tell him once that cobras were more deadly than rattlesnakes, but he had scoffed at the idea. The truth, of course, depends on how you like to take your death: from paralysis (cobras) or merely having your tissues turn to jelly (rattlers).

Holding the snake head in one hand, he withdrew a Scripto ink pen from his jeans pocket. Twisting the two casing halves of the pen apart, he withdrew the spring and plastic ink reservoir. He put the open end of the plastic reservoir tube to his mouth, squinted his eyes distastefully, and sucked out the bluish ink. Spitting out the remnants, he lopped off the metal nib with the piece of blade. He held the snake's left fang to the open end of the tube and, reaching back to the poison sac, began to milk the venom through the hollow tooth to a small opening near the tip where it drained into the now empty ink reservoir. He held a finger over the reservoir's other opened end. He repeated this procedure with the other fang until the snake was drained. It all seemed to go fairly satisfactorily considering he'd never done it before, merely watched his buddy Riff.

Discarding the head, he stoppered the now venom-filled tube and replaced it and the spring within the pen casing.

Now he began to file away at the tip of the pen, removing the steel head, and sharpening the remaining plastic tip to a near needle point.

This accomplished, he fitted the plastic "warhead" over the existing sharpened head of his arrow and fitted the whole thing to his bow.

It took the advancing enemy a full seven minutes to creep hesitantly within firing range.

He was very cautious now, wary of this enemy with the homemade arrows. He took his time, picking his way along.

Kirk crouched low in the dense foliage, supporting the base of the bow on his left knee. There were no jiggling branches to give him away this time.

At the proper moment, he drew back carefully, sighted expertly, let out his breath to steady the aim, and sent the plastic-tipped arrow into the Cong's larynx.

The spring within the plastic casing slammed nearly five ounces of pure diamondback venom into the left carotid artery in the neck.

It did not require an hour for the victim to die.

Leaping, screeching, tearing at his throat, the enemy was a convulsively frothing maniac by the time Kirk walked up to him. By the time Kirk had retrieved the man's pistol, the victim's face was black and his eyes rolled back white, swollen tongue protruding between his clenched teeth like a dark slab of liver. He didn't know Kirk was even there. Kirk sent a bullet into his brain.

He was just unzipping his fly to relieve himself on the enemy's corpse when he heard a sound behind him.

He spun with the revolver to find Lieutenant David Kirkland striding toward him in his dress khakis.

Kirk blinked.

Blinked again.

His head started swimming once more, and a fresh sheen of sweat descended into his eyes. He really felt as if he might faint just now, faint dead away like a silly schoolgirl. Wouldn't that be a kicker, swooning here in the line of duty, right in front of . . . in front of . . .

David held a pistol in his hand.

Kirk blinked, wavered unsteadily like a punched prize fighter. He was really quite tired now. Would it be all right, he wondered, if he went back to camp and caught some slack time? Maybe he should ask the lieutenant's permission.

"Hello, Kirk."

"Lieutenant."

David's eyes narrowed, troubled. He was staring at Kirk curiously. "What ya got there, little brother?"

Kirk looked down, wavering. "Dead Cong, sir."

David nodded. Slowly. Looked down at the dead man, then back up at Kirk. "Killed him yourself, did you?"

Kirk nodded. "Yessir."

David nodded.

Then slapped Kirk hard in the face.

Kirk staggered back, clutching his cheek.

He stood there wobbling for a while uncertainly, holding his cheek and staring dazedly at his brother. David didn't seem to be wearing khakis any longer. He was wearing a business suit. That was strange. You don't see that very often in the jungle. Now he was removing something from his belt: a white plastic bottle.

"How long since you had a drink, Kirk?"

Kirk stared back, confused.

David handed him the bottle and Kirk drank deeply, the water cool and sweet. He handed it back, and David poured some of the cool liquid over Kirk's head. It ran down into his eyes pleasantly. Kirk swallowed. "Since . . . this morning," he said at last. Something wasn't quite right, was it?

He was very close to something important. He'd have it in a moment. Just give me a moment.

He stared at David quietly, eyes focused now. "Jesus Christ . . . you were there, weren't you? In 'Nam." It was a sibilant whisper. "Weren't you, David?"

David looked at Kirk a moment, satisfied with the man's condition. He took a drink himself. Nodded. "I was there, Kirk."

Kirk rubbed his temple, forcing back the headache.

He kept shaking his head slowly in disbelief.

"Why? Why didn't you tell me? Why all the secrets? What the fuck is going on?"

David rebelted the bottle. "A lot. But it'll take a while to explain, and Riff Walker's still out there."

"Where's Meg?"

David held up a calming hand. "Safe. She's with Jill, back at the car."

Kirk shook his head. "Neither of them is safe as long as he's still alive. Have you seen him?"

"I was hoping you had."

Kirk rubbed his face briskly with both hands, shook his head hard, clearing the cobwebs. "I've got to get going."

He looked down at the dead Cong who wasn't a Cong anymore but someone in a tan business suit with broken, mirrored sunglasses. A Caucasian. Different but just as dead.

Before he could ask, David told him:

"Mike Tolin. We just hired him, you wouldn't remember him. His partner was Frank Leibman. Frank had a wife. No kids, thank God."

Kirk started to wobble again, and David gave him another drink.

"I'll cover for you, of course," his brother said flatly.

Kirk was still staring down at the corpse.

David frowned. "Are you going to go out on me, Kirk?"

Kirk's head snapped up brightly. He handed his gun to David. "Have you got a knife?"

"I'm not sure you're up to this."

"Yes, I am. Give me the knife."

"I don't have a knife, Kirk. Maybe I should do this on my own."

Kirk looked at him. "Is that what you want?"

David didn't have to answer. The answer was in his eyes. And the fear.

Kirk smiled. "It's me he wants, David. Go back to the car, let me handle this."

"You're not yourself."

"Just a little mild dehydration. I'm fine now." He nodded at the ground. "I can take care of myself."

"At least take a gun!"

Kirk shook his head. "It would just delay things. Riff wants this to be a one-on-one, no bullets, like in the old Nightcrawler days. Go back to the car, watch the women. I don't think this will take long."

"I can't let you do that, not all alone. Not weaponless. No, I'm sticking."

Kirk considered, knowing it was hopeless. "All right. Maybe the two of us can cover more ground. But not together. You take the south side of the mountain, I'll take the north. If you see him, fire the gun and I'll come."

"Won't that give away my position?"

"He'll already know your position."

David swallowed once nervously. "All right. But yell if you find him, Kirk. Don't try to take him alone."

"I'll yell."

"I mean it."

"Top of my lungs."

David stepped away, not liking at all the idea of being alone in the forest again. "Good luck."

"See you."

David nodded, looked the other man up and down one final time, then turned and headed into the converging trees.

Kirk waited until the other man's footfalls had receded into silence, then turned and faced the wilderness.

Twenty-two

Halfway to the car, Jill got sick.

She wavered on the rocky "trail," hand to her head, arm wrapped around her waist, head down.

Meg turned to her in alarm. "Jill? What's the matter?"

Jill faltered, grabbed the bough of an elm for support. She gave a throaty groan. "Sick . . ."

Meg took her arm, supporting her, put a palm to her forehead. "You don't have a fever," she offered with concern.

Jill moaned, rolled her eyes with nausea. "Burning up . . ."

Detective Olson moved in, pulling a plastic bottle from his belt. "How long since you've had water?"

Jill mumbled something unintelligible.

"Easy to get dehydrated out here in the sun."

Olson was a big bear of a man. He uncapped the bottle with clumsy, indelicate hands and held it to Jill's lips.

She took a tentative sip, winced, then grasped

the front of his shirt, pulling the material taut against his massive chest. She made a gagging sound. "Gonna throw up . . ."

Detective Olson tried to back away. "Not on me you're not!"

He stumbled back, losing his footing momentarily on a stone, arms wide. It was easy for Jill to reach down and pluck the revolver from under his belt.

She flicked off the safety, slammed the muzzle into the big man's temple, and darted her free hand under his coat, coming away with his service revolver. All of this before he could fully recover his drunken balance.

When he did, and gestured as if to lunge for her, she pressed harder with the muzzle and spat up to him, "Breathe funny, Olson, and you're dog meat!"

Olson obeyed.

She held his revolver by the butt, drew back, and arced it over the edge of the precipice. It fell soundlessly.

"Now talk."

"The fuck you doin', Thorenson?" He stood stiffly, both eyes jammed to the right side of his head, trying to see the barrel of the revolver planted there.

Jill pressed harder. "Don't give me a dancing lesson, asshole, I want the fucking facts! What's the plan?"

The broad shoulders bumped up against a big spruce, pine needles gouging Olson's ears as Jill pressed forward.

"You know the goddamn plan! Get Walker!"

She thumbed back the hammer, teeth clenched. "That was last week's plan, I need an update."

Olson winced at the wedge of steel against his head. "It's the same plan: eradicate Riff Walker. If you were better at your job, we wouldn't be here in the first place! Christ, Jill, get the piece out of my fucking face!"

Meg stood to one side, open-mouthed with astonishment. Something kept telling her to run, and something else kept telling her to stay just where she was.

"Talk to me, Olson, the truth this time!"

"It is the fucking truth!"

Jill kicked him in the nuts.

Olson bellowed, doubled, crumpled, holding his groin.

Before he bowed too tight, she stuck the muzzle under his chin, lifted. "Shall we try it again?"

Olson's face was pink with pain. He could hardly get his breath. "Christ, Jill . . ."

"What's on today's docket?"

He shook his head, tears running down his burnished cheeks, fingers digging pitifully at his genitals. From where she stood, Meg could see the back of this toupee coming up slightly. "Please, they'll kill me!"

"I'll kill you, asshole! Talk!"

The big man whimpered. "Eliminate . . . party . . ."

"Who, besides Walker?"

Olson sobbed.

"Talk!"

Olson choked. "J-John Kirkland."

Meg shivered convulsively once.

"Who else? Talk!"

Olson struggled for breath. "K-Kirkland's wife."

Meg closed her eyes.

Jill was nodding contemplatively, staring down balefully at the sobbing man.

After a moment she stuck a toe under his chin, lifting his tear-streaked face. "On your feet."

She stepped back to give the big man room as he struggled up, leaning heavily on the spruce. He was still holding his testicles when he finally found his rubbery legs.

"W-what are you going to do with me, Thorenson?"

Jill regarded him with disgust. "I ought to blow your nuts off, you goddamn ape, finish the job."

Olson implored, sobbing.

"Instead I'll just make sure you don't drive or walk anywhere." She aimed the gun at his right kneecap.

"Oh, God, Thorenson, *please*!"

"Sorry, Ben."

Meg started to say something, clamped her hands over her ears spontaneously.

Jill pulled the trigger.

thunk

Everybody stared at everybody else.

Jill pulled the trigger twice more *think-thunk* on two more empty chambers.

She stared stupidly at the revolver. "Oh, Christ, he took them out. Kirk took them out! He was on to me!"

It was all she had time to say before Olson lunged.

Olson had gone slightly to weight lately, despite condescending remarks from his superiors, and his testes still ached painfully; nevertheless, he was fast, particularly for a man his size.

Meg had never seen Jill Thorenson in action before, so the blond woman's agility was just as startling to her.

Even so, Jill's karate kick was only partially effective: the empty gun had caught her off guard, and Olson had been already toying with the idea of rushing her before anyone knew that. He came in hard, and Jill's kick, though somewhat successful, missed its mark (his groin again) and caromed off his left thigh just above the pelvic bone. It still hurt, and it unquestionably spoiled the thrust of Olson's rush, but not enough to prevent him from slamming into her left side, jarring her teeth, knocking her backward to the ground. Before she even hit it, she was screaming at Meg:

"Help me!"

There wasn't time for much else. Olson was spinning and lunging again, throwing up dust, growling like a huge, lumbering animal, murder in his little gray eyes.

Jill had landed hard on her rump, palms skidding in the dusty earth. She took the opportunity to gather twin fistfuls of the dry topsoil and hurtle both of them into Olson's enraged face as he fell on her. She caught him open-eyed and open-mouthed. And she began to roll instantly.

Coughing, spitting, partially blinded, Olson still

was able to find her right ankle and bring her slamming to the earth again. Jill felt pine needles and stones bite into the tender flesh of her bosom. Then she was being dragged backward unceremoniously, jeans tearing, flesh shredding. *Caught.* The word loomed large in her mind; this could be the end of it, she was already out of breath. Think fast, old girl.

Meg stood to one side impotently, eyes darting back and forth between them, legs bent for flight but paralyzed with indecision.

Olson had the blonde rolled over now, one hand at her slim, pretty throat. He loved the way her eyes bugged when he squeezed, the terror in her smug bitch's face. He savored the way her big tits strained against the torn fabric of her blouse. When he was through here, he'd have to get into that blouse, check things out.

Jill had about one second left in which her vocal cords would still be fully functional, and she took that second to scream again at Meg.

"Help me, you stupid bitch, you ever want to see your husband alive again!"

After that all she could do was gurgle and wheeze ineffectually.

Olson drove her into the dirt with both hands. Big hands. Strong hands, closing off and sealing her windpipe immediately.

But now something wasn't quite right: something was on the big man's broad, straining back, pulling, hurting, causing no end of annoyance. He swiveled his head slightly to take a look, and discovered the red-haired woman, the scared one. What the fuck did she think she was doing back there?

Meg hadn't the slightest idea herself.

She didn't even fully recall leaping upon the brawny back, wrapping her arms about the bull neck, pulling with all her strength: it had just seemed like a good idea at the time.

It wasn't. It was about as effective as a gnat attacking an elephant.

Olson reached around almost lazily with one of the huge hands, got it around her breast, and squeezed ... squeezed until Meg screamed and hollered and shrieked, and then kept right on squeezing, enjoying it immensely, copping a feel and hurting the enemy at the same time; it made him grin happily. And he was still doing it long after she had let go and was tearing at the crushing hand with her nails and snapping at it with her red mouth like a turtle.

When he finally got bored with this, Olson flung her casually against a tree. Nice titties. He hadn't had this much fun in weeks.

All of this had had its effect on Jill, though: a positive effect. With only one hand on her neck, he'd lost some of his devastating purchase, and a little air had trickled down her swollen throat to her lungs. It wasn't much, but it had brought her back from the brink long enough to open her eyes, retrieve her senses, and search about frantically, finally locating a fist-sized stone inches from her flailing fingers. When Olson brought his attention back to her with a triumphant, confident grin on his wide linebacker's face, Jill awarded it by smashing his nose with the rock.

Squashed flat, the ruddy probiscus disappeared into his face, cartilage and blood spewing out either side of the stone like an insect against a windshield. He didn't stop strangling Jill, but his heart wasn't in it anymore.

If he *had* stopped strangling her, he might have saved his two front incisors, which is the next thing she smashed with the rock. He repaid her by spitting one of them into her eye, blinding her temporarily with his blood. That didn't stop her from smashing out with the rock again, however.

This time Olson elected to reach out and check the blow by seizing her wrist. What she wanted him to do was try to take it away from her, which would require both hands on his part, thus freeing him from her throat. But Olson, only superficially a lummox, wasn't born yesterday; he kept right on throttling. Jill began to see the little pink spots again.

But now here came that other crazy woman, the one whose tit he'd wrung practically from her body. She was on his back again and this time she'd brought a stone of her own. And she was hammering away at the top of his head with it. Crazy fucking bitch. This time he'd tear both her tits off.

But he had to let go of the blond woman to do that, and the instant he did, she got her legs under him and pushed with all she had left at his chest. Combined with the weight of the woman on his back, Olson pitched backward, arms windmilling— and somehow ended up on his feet again.

He and Meg began to dance.

Round and round and round.

Hanging off his thick neck that way, bowing him backward, Meg made it impossible for him to get those big hands on her again. Olson lurched about in drunken spirals, the blood from his squashed nose filling his eyes and nasal passages, making breathing difficult. He was beginning to see a few pink spots of his own.

Which is when Jill began to kick his shins.

Bellowing like a bull, swinging those massive arms in all directions at once, Olson succeeded only in plowing them repeatedly into tree branches and brambles, scoring the knuckles, ripping the nails. Meg hung on dizzily like a rat terrier; if she let go now and flew off, she'd probably be killed anyway.

It took Jill a good three minutes of clawing and fumbling to finally get the big man's belt open, his suit pants and Jockey shorts down around his knees. After that it was only a matter of moments to get both her hands around his already throbbing nuts.

She led him, bellowing and frothing like a blind, dancing bear, straight into the biggest oak she could find. He hit it on the run, jolting Meg free, showering bark, lances of sweet oblivion concussing his frontal lobe.

Ben Olson slept for a while.

The two women lay among the weeds and leaves, trying to draw breath that just wouldn't come.

Meg was the first to find words.

She sat, chest pumping, every muscle shrieking, gazing dully at Jill. "Christ, you *are* CIA."

Jill propped herself against a tree, swallowed back dryness. "Right now, sweetie, that's the least of your problems. A man named David Kirkland and a man named Riff Walker are both trying to kill your husband."

She reached over and dragged the dropped revolver to her side.

Meg nodded breathlessly at it. "That thing's empty."

Jill concurred, tucking it into her jeans.

"But Kirkland and Walker don't know that."

She managed to stand by only falling once.

"Come on," she said to the other woman, "let's get going."

"Howdy, Dave! How's tricks!"

David froze in the middle of the forest, gun clutched tightly in front of him.

Shit!

He hadn't been away from Kirk five minutes!

This was precisely what he was afraid would happen! He should *never* have agreed to split up!

"You look good! Lost a little weight?"

The voice seemed to come from all around him.

He pivoted slowly, gun thrust outward, knowing it was hopeless. The woods appeared empty.

They weren't.

"Nice gun. Is that a new model?"

"Better come on out, Riff . . ."

"You think?"

"I mean it. You don't have a chance."

Riff didn't answer, his silence emphasizing the ludicrousness of David's last remark.

"The woods are surrounded," David added lamely. "I'll see you're treated fairly."

A throaty chuckle somewhere to the left.

David swung the gun around.

Or was it to the right?

"My men are in the area, Riff."

"Not anymore they're not. Pretty good, isn't he? Old boy's still got the knack, wouldn't you say? Well, once a Nightcrawler, always a Nightcrawler. Memory's a funny thing, huh, Dave? Can't always trust it. Then again, sometimes you can. Depending on whose memory you're trusting, and which memory they've got, if you get my drift. You get my drift, Davie boy? Or am I being too angular again? People have accused me of that."

David pointed the gun at the sky and fired two shots in quick succession.

"Is that a signal? Waste all your bullets that way, Davie, then what'll you do? Listen, don't worry about it, I've got a knife you can borrow. Ever fight a man with just a knife? No, paperwork's more your specialty, isn't it? Signing death sentences and such. Surprised to see you out in the field at all."

David took a step backward. And Riff Walker, naked to the waist, stepped out from behind a tree directly in front of him. He held a large hunting knife unthreateningly in his right hand. There was a red serpent drawn on his chest.

The two men stood approximately thirty feet apart.

Riff smiled winningly. "Allow me to take this moment to congratulate you on Ms. Thorenson. Nice choice. Terrific bazooms. Bright too. But I think she lacks the killer instinct, don't you? Oh, well, you can't have everything. How's the old firing arm, by the way?"

David leveled quickly and fired.

"Not so hot, huh? Too much time pushing a pencil; you ought to spend a few hours every week on the range, Dave, keeps you sharp." He smiled.

He might have just missed or Riff might have moved. It was hard to be sure with all this sweat in his eyes. He blinked rapidly and leveled again, supporting the weapon with both hands.

Riff Walker grinned.

The gun recoiled.

"Better. You need to check the sight on that Colt, though, little off on the windage there, I'd say. Care to try again? Or are you running low on the old ammo?"

A leaf fell past Riff's smiling face.

David was just pulling the hammer back again, eyes flicking upward in time to see another falling leaf. Riff got it—was just starting to move when Kirk crashed down on top of him.

David's inadvertent warning got Riff away from the full force of the fall, which would have broken his neck. As it was, he was slammed forward into the dirt, sent sprawling. But this off-center blow knocked his attacker askew too, and Kirk went reeling backward, arms pinwheeling.

Riff was up and on top of him in a heartbeat. Kirk got his hands around the knife arm, but he was the one on his back. Riff endeavored rapaciously that it should remain so.

For a time it did. Then they began to roll, locked red-faced and determined, the knife a glinting umbilical of death between them, as rock steady and unmoving as though welded there. Legs kicked, dust flew, David watched, mesmerized. They were rolling the wrong way.

Toward the edge of the bluff.

And, as if rehearsed, they froze at the edge of the escarpment, Riff still on top, pressing, pressing.

Little pebbles jumped away from them, toppled over the edge, fell away to forever. . . .

David leveled the gun again.

Until they began to roll again, the other way.

And dust covered everything, cloaking.

He lowered the gun, began circling, squinting, coughing at the dust. He found himself suddenly curious: beforehand he'd have bet on Riff flat-out, but Kirk was holding his own. It was an interesting fight.

They were rolling back toward the cliff, hair, faces, pink bodies covered with a layer of gray dust that clung in leprous clumps to sweaty patches.

Kirk's shoulders were against the lip of the bluff now, face twisted with exhaustion, arm giving by degrees as the big blade descended inexorably. Not in shape for this.

There was something in Riff's eyes . . . something he could almost read . . .

But now Kirk had gotten his knees up. He let the gleaming blade dimple his chest a fraction, let victory for his foe seem imminent, then lunged upward with the last of his strength—and flipped Riff Walker over his head. Over the edge.

And even then it all seemed too easy, even contrived. Couldn't Riff—stronger and in far better shape—if he'd really wanted to ...

Riff, falling, did not scream, the way they do in the movies.

And did not really fall—far.

The cliff formed a six-foot chin before curving under and vanishing beneath them. Riff clung to this as a child clings to its mother's apron. One hand found a length of root, the other clawed crumbling soil. The knife was airborne, flipflopping to distant pine tops two hundred scenic feet below, a winking daylight star.

It made Kirk sick to look down, but it probably made Riff sicker looking up.

Though it certainly didn't show in his face.

He looked, in fact, almost serene, relieved.

Kirk stood watching him. Had this been the true goal, the hoped-for outcome? A kind of suicide?

If he bent, reached out, maybe ...

"How's the memory, ace?" gasping, clinging.

"Good," Kirk gasped back.

"I don't think so."

Was the root breaking?

"No? How's that?"

"Pieces missing."

"I can reach you."

"Not yet." Riff blinked as sand slithered into his eyes. His gritted teeth were nearly luminous in the setting sun. The Vietnamese girls had liked that smile.

"You're slipping."

"So are you. Shitty memory."

"Best I can do. Take my hand."

"Tell me."

"I did."

"Again."

"Jesus, you're falling!"

"Tell me."

"I shot her!"

"Who?"

"Your wife!"

"Who?"

"The Vietnamese girl!"

"Who?"

"Your wife!"

"Who?"

"Mi Ling!"

"Who?"

"Your—"

like it that way, Johnny

" . . . wife . . ."

"Who?"

you like it too

"Mi . . . Ling . . ."

"Who?"

fall

Riff would fall

turning over and over

and die

like the boy

the boy on the catwalk

the screaming boy

screaming and screaming

like the other boy
the boy behind him
coming in the door behind him
the little Vietnamese boy
her boy
his wife's
Kirk's wife
Mi Ling
the boy's mother
screaming down at his bloody mother
"*No!*"
Riff smiled. I knew you could do it, pal!
The root broke.
Kirk lunged.
Caught naked forearm. Held.
Inches from his face. Gazing deep into his eyes. Deep. At the truth.

"You didn't have to fuck her, you bastard!" spitting words and saliva into the other man's constricted eyes.

"Everyone else was, pardner."

"But not *you!*"

"I had the knife ready, Kirk. I was waiting for her to . . . climax. I would have made it clean, painless. She would have died happy. You got there first."

"Liar!"

"Did it for you, pardner."

"Liar!"

"Guess you better drop me, then."

Kirk was aware of the presence at his back. Arm pulling from its socket, he looked back over his shoulder.

David was pointing his gun downward, past

Kirk's ear, at Riff's smiling face. "Let him go, Kirk. It will go down better all the way around."

Kirk looked down again to find Riff chuckling softly. "Yeah. Good idea. Write it off as a climbing accident that way. Only what about Kirk here?"

Kirk hesitated. He could feel tendons beginning to tear. All sensation was gone in the fingers that clutched Riff's hand.

"Let him go, Kirk. Trust me."

Riff was grinning up into Kirk's agonized face. "Sure, buddy, trust him! After all, he's your brother! Right? He never fucked your wife, did you, Dave, old chum? At least not your first wife! Oh, maybe just that one time when Meg didn't come home all night, but that hardly counts, does it, Kirkie?"

Kirk bit his lip, holding back a scream of pain.

When he opened his eyes again, Riff was gazing up at him with a look he'd never seen on the narrow face before. Was it—could it be—compassion? "Sorry, pal. This ain't been your day, has it?"

Kirk turned, looked at David. David gritted his teeth. "He's lying, Kirk. Let him go."

Kirk turned back to Riff.

Riff smiled again. "Tricky Dicky," he said.

Kirk began to haul him up.

The muzzle of David's Colt bit into the back of his neck.

"I said: Drop him, Kirk."

Kirk squeezed shut his eyes, the last of his strength gone. "You ordered it, David. You ordered me to kill Mi Ling."

"That's what the CIA trained you for, Kirk."

"My own wife . . ."

"She was Cong!"

"I loved her!"

David nodded patiently. "I made it up to you, made sure you got hospitalized—"

"*Brainwashed!*"

"I set you up on the force, even got you another wife. Who introduced you to Meg?"

Kirk grimaced. "Mighty thoughtful of you, David. I guess that gave you the right to have an affair with her." He pulled on Riff's arm.

David's face turned to stone. "You let me down, both of you. You couldn't help yourself, Kirk. You were always weak, but Riff . . . Riff is dangerous. Now *drop him!*"

"That'll do."

It came from behind them.

David turned his head to find Jill regarding him calmly with her gun. Meg Kirkland stood behind her. "Step away from there. Please."

David lowered the gun hesitantly, astonished. "Jill?"

"I mean it, David. Move."

"Oh? And what's this, Agent Thorenson?"

She shook her head. "You lied to me. You told me they'd go free once we caught Walker."

David sighed patiently. "I know how you feel, Jill, truly. I have exactly the same emotions about the matter, believe me. After all, he's my brother!"

Jill smirked. "I doubt seriously if you're capable of emotion, Kirkland."

"Jill, these orders didn't come from me."

"Maybe not, but these orders are coming from me. Now throw me your gun, please."

His look was one of vast patience, as though he were addressing a confused child. "And throw away twenty-five years of back-breaking work? Jill, think! This isn't just the end of your career we're talking about. Even if you get rid of me, they'll come after you. All of you."

"Maybe. Maybe we'll come after them. Throw me the gun."

"You're exhausted, hurt. This is a terrible mistake you're making."

"Throw me the gun."

He started to. Then hesitated.

A look came into his eyes. He smiled. "You're bluffing."

Meg froze. Don't show it in your face!

David watched them, eyes narrowed. "You would have fired by now. You wouldn't be asking for my gun."

Jill stepped forward, thumbed back the hammer, aimed directly at his chest. "I mean it, David . . ."

Nobody moved for a moment.

But David was still smiling. "Your piece is empty!"

Jill couldn't help it: she swallowed.

David sighed. "Your trouble, Jill, is that you just never could bring yourself to do what's necessary."

He turned and shot her in the head.

Gray eyes wide with shock and surprise, she catapulted backward into Meg, knocking them both to the ground. Meg screamed, grabbed the other woman, holding her against the earth, sobbing.

It all took less than three seconds, but, the gun averted from him, it was enough time for Kirk to haul his dangling charge up to safe ground again. They sat there, strengthless, perched at the cliff's edge while David swung the gun toward them again.

He stepped back a few cautious feet: even exhausted, Riff Walker could be a lightning-quick adversary.

But Walker was on his back, trying to get his breath. Kirk sat beside him, eyes lidded, trying to massage blood back into his right hand. Weaponless, beyond exhaustion, these two weren't about to try anything.

And there was nothing left to try anyway.

David motioned with the gun. "Up."

The two men on the ledge struggled upward, leaning on each other, finally standing wobbly-legged against the endless blue-green horizon. They regarded the agent with hooded eyes.

"You'll have to shoot us, slimeball," Riff muttered. "We're not jumping for any fucking CIA prick, right, Kirkie?"

Kirk nodded, too weary even to speak.

David raised the gun. He could hear Meg sobbing piteously behind him. He was wondering vaguely whether or not to fuck her one last time before killing her. Jill had been right about one thing. Whatever emotion he'd had had been washed away in a tide of blood and deceit years ago. "What's Tricky Dicky?"

He directed the question at either of them.

Riff fielded it, grinning triumphantly. "It's a kind of code. The Nightcrawlers used it in 'Nam in the presence of someone we didn't trust, assholes like you. It was a reference to Nixon; even before Watergate we didn't trust his slimy ass."

David nodded appreciatively. "Cute."

He thumbed back the hammer, aimed at Kirk's head. "I'm sorry, Kirk, truly."

Kirk stared at his brother.

David stared back. Did his throat move once? "You must know how much I didn't want this. What you can't know is how hard I worked to prevent it. They wanted you dead eons ago. You would have been but for me. I was there for you, Kirk."

Kirk nodded listlessly. "Not anymore, though."

David's gun didn't waver. "Don't sell me short. I went through the agonies of hell keeping you alive, sequestered, *safe*. Despite their demands! But I'm only a cog in a very complicated machine. It's so big, Kirk. Far bigger than we are by ourselves. Far more important than any one person. Riff knows that."

" 'Tis a far, far better thing I do.' " Riff smirked from the edge of the cliff.

David didn't even look at him. He looked at his brother. "You must know what I'm talking about, Kirk. You were a Nightcrawler."

"You never *knew* what it felt to be a Nightcrawler, asshole!" Riff spat at him.

David sighed, nearly showing emotion. "I'll make it fast and clean, Kirk. That's all I can do. After years of this torture, that's what it comes to. Whether you believe it or not, I say it again, I'm sorry." He hesitated a moment. Then shook his head. "Damn you. If you just hadn't started remembering . . ." He made a frustrated gesture with the gun. "If you goddamn just hadn't started remembering, we might have made it."

He aimed.

Kirk could hardly keep his head up. "Don't I even get a last request?"

"I won't harm Meg, you have my word."

Riff guffawed. "And we both know how good *that* is!"

Kirk ignored him. "No, that isn't it."

"What, then, hurry."

Kirk nodded to his left. "Shoot him first."

Riff barked a laugh. "And after all I did for you!" He sent his laughter to the clear blue sky.

Kirk sneered. "Bastard fucked my wives. Both of them. I want to see him die."

David smiled. "With pleasure."

He swiveled the gun toward the taller figure.

It only took an instant, but it was all Kirk needed. He thumbed the weapon from his jeans pocket and threw it in one continuous motion.

It caught David squarely between the eyes, stuck there half embedded, snapping his head backward. The agent's gun fired four times reflexively, all at the sky. Then he toppled backward to the hard Colorado earth, dead before he hit.

Incredulous, Riff Walker loped forward, bent over the fallen man. He pulled the glistening gold-leafed army medal free; it took some strength. One point of the Silver Star dripped dark red where it had impaled itself in David's skull.

Riff stared at Kirk. "Damn glad I left that thing in your trophy case, old buddy!"

Kirk walked over to David's body, pushed Riff aside, and sat down. He pulled David into his arms.

He looked up once mutely at Riff. Then buried his face in his brother's neck.

Kirk wept.

When he finally looked up, Meg was standing above him.

Without looking beyond her, he knew Riff was gone. Jill was dead. They were alone in the forest. Alone. Finally.

He'd imagined he'd have some trouble meeting her eyes. He did not. Nor she his.

After a time he said: "Are you all right?"

She licked her lips once. He'd also imagined her changed somehow. At last travel-worn. She was neither. She was exactly as she had been the last time he'd seen her. She was a lovely woman in her late thirties. She was his wife.

It might never have happened at all.

But it had.

"I'm all right." She cleared her throat once self-consciously, and something about that, the wholly feminine sound of it, was nearly endearing.

Her eyes lingered on him. "You?"

He didn't answer.

He didn't know.

It was a moment fraught with too many simultaneous emotions. A cranial assault. It seemed very necessary, he was thinking, to say something just right, and he hadn't the least idea what it was or if he should even be saying it.

You want to forgive her.

Yes. And to be forgiven.

But in light of so much, does such a word even hold meaning anymore?

Meaning is interpretation through conscious will. He had read it somewhere.

Meg lowered her eyes to the ground, bent, and picked up the Silver Star near Kirk's foot. Riff must have left it next to him before vanishing into the forest, silent as a panther.

She fingered the medal. "Was it yours?"

Kirk held out his hand, took it from her. "It belonged to Mi Ling. Riff must have found it among her things before they cleaned out her room. He put it in my trophy case."

Meg watched him. "How did she come by it?"

Kirk shrugged. "She told me it belonged to her dead husband." He grunted wryly. "Probably some crack shot lieutenant who got tired of being a hero, or maybe just some dogface private who didn't have the money to pay her for a trick. Maybe she stole it. Who knows? She was just a whore."

Kirk weighed the glinting medal in his hand a moment, then drew back his arm with an air of finality to aim it over the cliff.

Meg caught his wrist before he could. "No. It's all that's left of her."

She let go of his wrist.

Kirk looked into her eyes. Was there really anything left to say? Would there ever be anything to say again?

He put the medal away.

They stood looking at each other until they couldn't do that anymore, then turned and looked out toward the misting hills, the whole, vast Colorado splendor. It was growing cooler but still nice. A lovely sunset was beginning, pinking the western sky. They might have been on an afternoon picnic. "Journeys end in lovers meeting," she was thinking.

His profile, when she turned back to it, was almost achingly handsome. Or was that merely because she was seeing him anew? The old Kirk was gone, at least mostly gone. Certainly this wasn't the man she'd married. The question was: was that such a bad thing? The marriage had, for the most part, failed. But it had been a past built on untruths. Now the truth was out. What of the future? Everything from this moment forward was the result of a rebirth, negating, banishing, all that had gone before. Even the worst of it. The possibilities, if the participants were willing, were limitless. Weren't they?

Or was that just wishful thinking?

She nearly smiled. Riff had all but destroyed them; and in the process, liberated them.

Had that been part of his plan too?

"He never lied, did he?" she said.

Kirk looked at her.

"About the waiter who poisoned our drinks, about the farmer in the cornfield, about being CIA, any of it."

Kirk shook his head. "He never lied about anything."

Meg turned again, stared outward at nothing. "It's the rest of us who've lied."

In a moment she looked back at Jill's lifeless form. "Are they going to kill us too, Kirk?"

Kirk followed her gaze. "I don't think so. Not this time, anyway."

"How do you know?"

"Riff's gone."

She looked at him. "For good?"

He shrugged. "Who knows?" He nodded toward the bodies. "But someone will be here soon enough. They won't leave the woods looking like this. They'll cover their tracks, I'm sure of that. We should get out of here."

And now she couldn't meet his eyes. "Where? To what?"

He thought about it. It was time to say something. "To whatever's left."

He offered his hand.

She took it. A great weight, borne by hope, lifted from her heart. She bit back tears.

At the edge of the clearing she looked behind them once at the already darkening cyclorama of woods. Night would fall like a curtain out here. "I have the strangest feeling we'll see him again," she said.

Kirk grunted, guided her downward.

"Not if I see him first."

He put a steadying arm about her, and they traversed the remainder of the long mountain face to the trail, the car. And whatever roads and turns lay beyond.